Royally Crushed

Also by Niki Burnham

Sticky Fingers

Scary Beautiful

Goddess Games

And for more romantic stories:

Endless Summer

by Jennifer Echols

Love, Love, Love

by Deborah Reber

and Caroline Goode

Royally Crushed

NIKI BURNHAM

ROYALLY JACKED

SPIN CONTROL

DO-OVER

SIMON PULSE

NEW YORK LONDON TORONTO SYDNEY

SIMON PULSE

An imprint of Simon & Schuster Children's Publishing Division

1230 Avenue of the Americas, New York, NY 10020

This Simon Pulse paperback edition March 2011

For information about special discounts for bulk purchases, please contact Simon & Schuster Special Sales at 1-866-506-1949 or business@simonandschuster.com.

The Simon & Schuster Speakers Bureau can bring authors to your live event. For more information or to book an event contact the Simon & Schuster Speakers Bureau at 1-866-248-3049 or visit our website at www.simonspeakers.com.

Designed by Mike Rosamilia

The text of this book was set in Garamond 3.

Manufactured in the United States of America

4 6 8 10 9 7 5 3

Library of Congress Control Number 2011920045

ISBN 978-1-4424-0648-3

These books were previously published individually by Simon Pulse.

ROYALLY JACKED

For Lynda Sandoval,
the kind of friend who can peer-pressure
me into jumping off a bridge.
Thanks, because it was totally fun.

1

EXACTLY TWO WEEKS, ONE DAY, AND TEN HOURS AGO, my mother completely ruined my life. She announced over her usual dinner of Kraft macaroni and cheese (with tomatoes and broccoli bits mixed in—her attempt at being healthy), that she no longer wished to remain married to my dad.

She planned to move in with her new girlfriend, Gabrielle.

Yep. *Girlfriend.*

She went on and on about how it had nothing to do with me, and nothing to do with Dad, so we shouldn't feel the least bit bad about it. She'd simply come to realize that she wasn't the same person on the inside she'd been showing everyone on the outside. Yeah, right.

Needless to say, I have not yet told *my* girlfriends,

with whom I have a totally different relationship than my mother has with *her* girlfriend. Or partner. Whatever. I'm not exactly focused on how politically correct I am in describing my mom's bizarro crush. Especially since I can't describe Gabrielle to anyone yet. I can't even deal with telling them about the *divorce*, which—if I actually let myself think about it for more than ten seconds—is crushing in and of itself. I mean, I had no clue. None. Totally oblivious.

And what's worse, my friends will *freak*.

Then they'll treat me all nicey-nice, giving me those sad eyes that say, *We're soooo sorry*, when really they're thrilled to have something scandalous to gossip about while they're ignoring Mr. Davis's weekly lecture about how we're not keeping the lab area clean enough in Honors Chemistry. Or they'll be so horrified by my mother's newly found "lifestyle" that they'll slowly start ignoring me. In tenth grade—at least in Vienna, Virginia—this is the kiss of death. Even worse than not being one of the cool crowd. Which is the type of person I currently am. Not quite cool, that is.

So tonight I'm eating dinner at the table by myself, watching while my mom and dad stand in the kitchen and debate who's going to get the mahogany Henredon sleigh bed and who's getting the twenty-year-old brass bed I refused to have in my room (and that's going to need duct tape to hold it together if anyone decides to get a little action on it).

"Hey, Mom," I finally interrupt. "I know you want the Henredon, but when Gabrielle was here last week, she told me she thought the brass bed was wicked cool."

My mother shoots me the look of death. "Nice try, Valerie, but I don't believe Gabrielle's used the phrase 'wicked cool' in her life."

I deliberately roll my eyes. "She didn't say that exactly. Geez, Mom. I think she said it was . . ." I pretend to struggle for the right phrase, something that will convince her. Given Mom's behavior lately, I'm betting she'll do anything to make Gabrielle happy. "Shabby chic? Whatever that means. But it was obvious she really liked it."

I shrug, then look back down at the Thai stir-fry my father made for me before my mom showed up at the door with her SUV full of empty boxes and a list of the furniture she wanted to take to her and Gabrielle's new place.

If I'd had to bet which of my parents had coming-out-of-the-closet potential, I'd have put my money—not that I have much—on Dad. Let me state up front that he's no wuss. He drinks beer and watches shoot 'em up movies like a real guy. He goes to the gym every morning before work and has a smokin' set of biceps and pecs.

And according to my friends, he's kind of hot. For a dad, at least.

It's just that for one thing, his name is Martin, which sounds pretty gay. There's a guy at school named Martin who's a total flamer. Not that there's anything wrong with that—I have no problem with people being gay. Really I don't. I'm a live-and-let-live type. But Martin's a *friend*, he's not my *parent*. That's where I have the problem.

Aside from the name thing pegging Dad as potential gay material, he's the chief of protocol at the White House, which means he reminds the president and his staff of things like, "Don't invite the Indian ambassador to a hamburger cookout." Dad can also describe the proper depth to bow to the Japanese prime minister and the trick to eating spaghetti or the oversized hunks of lettuce they always serve at state dinners without making a mess of yourself. He knows how to tie a bow tie without a mirror and can tell you what kind of jacket is appropriate for a morning wedding.

Believe it or not, these are marketable skills.

Oh, and my dad is an awesome cook. Unlike Mom. I'm guessing Gabrielle's going to be cooking for them.

Playing casual, I flick my gaze toward my mom. "I'm just saying that if Gabrielle really likes the brass bed, maybe you could surprise her with it. That's all."

Getting that crap bed would serve them right for what they did to me and Dad. Especially if it fell apart under them.

Ick. I do *not* want to think about this.

My mother leans against the granite-topped island in our kitchen—designed entirely by Dad, appliances, cabinets, and all—and crosses her arms over her chest. She gives him the same cold stare I got when I was busted smoking a cigarette behind the high school last year. "I suppose, if the Henredon really means that much to you, I could take the brass bed."

My dad's mouth curls up on one side. "Sacrificing yourself for Gabrielle, Barbara?"

That's about as nasty as my dad ever gets. My mom just huffs out of the kitchen, yelling over her shoulder, "I'm taking the brass bed. And the Waterford table lamp."

"That was my mother's! Take the mandarin lamps from our room instead. You get two that way. Fair enough?"

She's already halfway upstairs. "Fine!"

"And don't forget to take all your self-help books. There are two boxes of them next to the bed."

My dad turns to me, his expression half sad, half angry with my mom. I think he wants to deck her. I guess she's butch enough to take it now.

I know, I know. *So* not politically correct. But she's the one who hacked off her long, wavy hair. Not that short hair's bad—it can be sexy. It's just that there's flirty, feminine short, and there's what-were-you-thinking short. No forty-five-year-old with a nice, conservative name like Barbara should wear her hair in a buzz cut. Especially when, at least until a couple weeks ago, she used to love going to the salon with me for a girls' afternoon out so we could get our hair and nails done and be pampered like movie stars.

It suddenly hits me that she probably isn't interested in doing those afternoons anymore. Now I'm getting depressed. And this isn't something mom's self-help books address. Not that I'd read them, even if they did. I have no desire to live my life according to Dr. Phil.

"I'm really sorry about all this, Valerie."

I shrug. I'm good at shrugging just right, so my parents think I really don't give a rip about anything. "It's not like it's your fault, Dad."

At least, I didn't think so. I mean, was Dad not giving Mom enough attention during their marriage? He was always surprising her with romantic gifts and flowers—and he's even taken her to the White House a few times for dinner—but was he being as protocol-minded with her in private as he was out in public?

I'm guessing not, since that's no excuse for getting an ugly haircut and moving in with a woman named Gabrielle who's ten years younger than you are. But I try not to think about my parents' sex life. Either them together or, as the circumstances are now, them individually. Eee-yuck.

"I don't think it's either of our faults. These things happen." He lowers his voice and adds, "But if you can save the Mottahedeh china from your mother like you did the sleigh bed, I'll make you whatever you want for dinner tomorrow night."

Whoa. I'm not really sure which china is the Mottahedeh, and I'm wondering why Dad thinks he's going to need *any* china—it's not like he's going to be throwing dinner parties like he and Mom used to anytime soon—as if! This whole begging-me-to-help-him thing is so not my father. Mom really must be knocking him for a loop.

"Even if I want Peking duck?" I ask.

Dad frowns. "You wouldn't like Peking duck."

"But it's hard to make, right?"

"No. Just time consuming." He squints at me for a moment. I think he's trying to ignore the sound of my mother going through the upstairs closets, rooting around for anything Gabrielle might like. I still say he should get a lawyer. Mom's going to run all over him. But he doesn't want a scandal. Wouldn't be proper, and Martin Winslow is all about proper.

Finally he says, "What if I take you out to dinner? Anywhere you choose."

Ni-i-i-ce. "How 'bout the Caucus Room?"

If you're not familiar with D.C., let me tell you that the Caucus Room is not cheap. It's the kind of place all the rich kids from school go with their parents so they can accidentally and on purpose bump into senators, Supreme Court justices, and the like, then brag about it the next day as if these people were their closest family friends and all hot to write them college recommendation letters. I have no idea if the food's any good—it might totally suck—but I've always wanted to find out. Just because.

"Haven't been there in a while," Dad says, tapping his fingers against the gray-and-silver-flecked granite. I can tell he thinks it's funny this is where I want to go. "But if that's where you'd like to dine, then why not? I'm certain I could get a reservation."

I am not believing my luck. I'd still take having my real mom back—the way she was before making her announcement, doctored Kraft dinners and all—over a dinner at the Caucus Room. But if my parents are going to get a divorce no matter what, as Mom informed me in no uncertain terms two weeks, one day, and ten and a half hours ago, and she's determined to spend the rest of her life shacked up with some peppy spandex-wearing blonde eating soyburgers and seaweed, I guess it's as good a consolation as any.

My dad picks up the phone and dials without having to look up the number. While he's waiting for the restaurant to answer, he asks, "You do know which is the Mottahedeh?"

"The flowery blue-and-silver stuff?" I guess.

"That's the Wedgwood. She can have that. The Mottahedeh has the tobacco leaf pattern in it. Lots of reds, blues, and greens."

I'm still not sure what he's talking about, but I tell him I'll encourage her to take the Wedgwood, if she wants china at all. Honestly, I think she's more focused on the bed thing.

He makes a reservation for Winslow, then grins at me as he hangs up the phone. The kind of odd grin that gives a girl a real scary feeling, like things are going to get even worse.

"This will work out well," Dad says as he helps himself to a plate of stir-fry. "A few things have come up I haven't told you about and we have a few decisions to make. Dinner out is as good a time to discuss them as any."

At the uncomfortable smile on his face, I'm wondering, what could possibly come up besides my dinner?

* * *

"They're going to make you choose," Jules tells me, in a been-there, done-that tone of voice. She's got her hands under her pits to keep warm, since we're huddled behind the Dumpster at Wendy's, where Jules works part-time. It's the only place we can safely sneak a cigarette without getting caught. Not that I'm a real smoker—it's an emergency-situation-only thing. I can't stand for my clothes and hair to reek. But I decided that telling my two closest friends, Julia Jackson, a.k.a. Jules, and Christie Toleski, that my parents have announced plans to divorce constitutes an emergency.

Of course, I left out the Gabrielle part. I'll figure out a way to explain her later. And just so they wouldn't think I was totally pathetic, I slipped in the fact Dad is taking me to the Caucus Room. It took me around two seconds to realize telling them about the dinner was a mistake, or at least, mentioning the part about Dad telling me we had some decisions to make.

Christie takes a long drag on her cigarette, which is only, like, the second or third she's ever smoked in her life. She's five-foot-nine and blond with decent-size boobs, plus she's totally smart and athletic, so she doesn't have many emergency situations. She'd be completely popular if she didn't hang out with me, Jules, and the rest of our gang. I'm sure she realizes it, since the snob kids invite her to their parties every so often, but we've been buds since before kindergarten, and I think she worries about being backstabbed by the cool crowd. We'd never do that to her.

"I don't know, Jules," Christie frowns. "Wouldn't both her parents sit her down to discuss it? You know, do the family meeting thing?"

Jules shakes her head. Her parents got divorced when we were in third grade, her mom remarried the next year, and then divorced the guy the summer before we started sixth grade. Her parents then remarried—each other, of all people—when we were in eighth grade. So Jules is kind of an expert on the marriage/divorce thing. "Not to be rude about it, Val, but what other decisions could your dad possibly mean? My guess is that he wants you to live with him, so he's going to take you out, tell you that you have a choice, then give you that look that says he really wants you to choose him."

As the last word leaves her mouth, her eyes suddenly bug out, and she starts to bounce, which makes me nervous. I hate when Jules gets bouncy. "Oooh, unless he's seeing someone! Do you think he's seeing someone? Maybe he's trying to hide it by saying you can live where you want, but he'll kinda pressure you to stay with your mom. Just so he can have time alone with his new girlfriend."

I roll my eyes at her. "There's no new girlfriend, Jules."

Not in Dad's case at least. But Jules sounds excited about this possibility, which pisses me off.

She'd better not tell anyone about the divorce. I consider this A-list-only information right now, and Jules and Christie are the only friends on my A list besides Natalie Monschroeder. Natalie got grounded yesterday for dropping out of Girl Scouts without telling her parents, which is why she couldn't make it to Wendy's. But since we all quit Scouts after fifth grade and her parents wouldn't let her, I figure she's dealing with her own problems right now and doesn't need to hear about my cruddy life.

Jules blows out a puff of smoke and gives me this poor-ignorant-you scowl. "There's almost always a girlfriend involved, Valerie. Otherwise why would they get divorced out of the blue like that?"

I try not to look right at her. If only she knew.

As a car engine revs nearby, Jules glances around the Dumpster to see if anyone is watching us as she talks. You can never be too careful, and none of us wants to get busted with cigarettes again. Our parents would assume we were secret chain smokers and would ground us for the rest of sophomore year.

"I can't see your mom having an affair," Christie says, which makes me cringe inside. "She's the total soccer mom. But you have to admit, your dad's always going to those upscale parties, and he gets to meet tons of famous people at the White House. Maybe one of them hit on him, and your mom thought—"

"Let's just say there's no girlfriend. Okay?"

"Fine," Jules says, but it's obvious she doesn't believe me. I don't want to clarify by pointing out that my mom is the one asking for the divorce, not my dad.

"So who are you going to choose?" Christie asks. "If that's what dinner is really about."

"I don't know." I hadn't thought about choosing. I know that sounds stupid beyond belief, given that my parents are now going to be living in two different houses, but it just didn't occur to me. I guess, in my gut, I kind of believed my mom would get over it and move back home. Decide it was a mistake and announce that she's not gay after all.

I'm getting way depressed now. Maybe I should have just told Christie and not Jules. Or kept my stupid mouth shut entirely.

"Your mom's going to get the house, right?" Jules asks. "The wife always gets the house. It's kind of a rule."

"Actually, she's getting an apartment and my dad's going to stay in the house." I really don't want to get into the details with Jules, so I grind what's left of my cigarette against the side of the Dumpster and I lie. "I think she wants to feel independent or something."

"Damn." Jules looks at her watch. "Gotta go. If I'm late coming off break, I'm gonna get fired."

She got in trouble Monday for not cleaning the Frosty machine the right way, so she promised the manager she'd redo it today. She's dying to get moved up to cash register so she doesn't smell like french fry grease at the end of every day.

"Listen, Val," she sniffs, "I'd normally tell you to stay with your mom, but if you're going to lose your bedroom and have to move into some tiny apartment—"

"But how could you not live with your mom?" Christie says in shock. Christie's been coming over to my house since preschool, so she knows my mom pretty well. At least, the way my mom used to be.

"I don't know," I admit. And it's true. I can't imagine not living with Mom. But I feel the same way about Dad. I don't want to not live with either of them.

Jules drops the butt of her cigarette into the snow, then pops two cinnamon Altoids into her mouth and passes the box to me before Christie steals one. "I gotta go. Call me tonight and tell me what happens. 'Kay, Val?"

"It's probably going to be late."

"First thing tomorrow then," she says, tucking the Altoids box back into the pocket of her black polyester Wendy's pants. "But call by nine. It's Saturday, so I'm on the lunch shift."

Once she's crossed the parking lot and ducked into the back door, Christie lets out a painful-sounding sigh. "Don't listen to her, Val. You know how she is."

"Yeah." I give her my *whatever* shrug.

"It'll be okay. And you know I'm here for you if you need me. Anytime, day or night. Just call me," she says, adjusting her hood so her hair is tucked inside.

It kills me how pretty Christie is without even trying. She had one zit—*one*—a couple months ago, and it was very nearly a cigarette-smoking emergency situation, she was so certain her boyfriend would dump her. As if. Over a *zit?* I wanted to smack her back to reality. First, over her lack of zittiness (is that a word?), and second over her boyfriend insecurity. He's totally into her. Still, she could do a lot better than Jeremy Astin, if you ask me. But Christie's way nice, and pretty much my best friend, so I don't want to hurt her feelings by telling her this. She loves Jeremy, even if he is a little too much into cross-country and runs in public wearing those icky nylon shorts, even when it's ice-cold outside.

I'm just about to say good-bye and walk back to school to get my junk out of my locker when I see a familiar green Toyota SUV in the drive-thru. It's my mom and, to my horror, Gabrielle is with her. Why I have no clue, since Gabrielle is a crusader-type vegetarian.

Before I can say something to Christie to keep her from seeing them, she grabs the sleeve of my coat. "I almost forgot to tell you, with Jules here and you telling us about the divorce and all, but Jeremy said that he and David were talking in the library yesterday and your name came up."

Since I have had a crush on David Anderson since, like, kindergarten, I actually look away from my mom and Gabrielle and pull Christie another step behind the Dumpster.

"Are you serious?" I ask, trying not to sound too excited, even though Christie knows I would just die to go out with him. "Who brought me up, David or Jeremy?"

"David did. He asked Jeremy if you were with anybody."

My heart does an instant flip-flop in my chest. You have to see David to know why. He's a total, one hundred percent hottie. Surfer-blond, with these fantabulous green eyes I can't even look into, they're so freakin' gorgeous. He could bump the sexiest man alive right off the cover of *People* and females everywhere would rejoice, I kid you not. And even though he's never asked me out, I think we'd be great together. I mean, we share a group of friends, we both have parents in politics, and we're hyper about our grades. "What did Jeremy say?"

"He played it cool. Said he didn't think so, but he knew a couple of other guys liked you."

"Wow. Good one." Jeremy just scored major points with this, as long as David didn't catch on to the bluff. Maybe Jeremy does deserve Christie after all. "Then what happened?"

"That was it. But Jeremy definitely got the impression he's interested. Like maybe we could all four go out sometime."

I think I am going to collapse. Right behind the Wendy's Dumpster, snow and old french fry muck and all.

Christie is grinning now, and I know she's excited she distracted me from the whacked situation with my parents. "Jeremy told me about it before saying anything to David because he wasn't sure how you felt. If you want, I bet he could hook you up. Seriously. Would that not be the *best*?"

"Well, yeah!" I force myself to chill, though. "But don't make me sound desperate or anything. And don't tell Jeremy that I'm *too* into David, if you haven't already. That'd kill it right off."

"Okay. I didn't say anything to Jeremy, I swear. I wanted to tell you first. "

This is why Christie is number one on my A-list, even if she is Miss Perfect. I guess I'm lucky she's going out with Jeremy, or David would be all over her. They could be Mr. and Miss Perfect.

Oh, damn. What if David's only interested in me because I'm Christie's friend? It wouldn't be the first time a guy asked me out because he thought it'd get Christie to notice him.

Of course, at exactly the moment this occurs to me, a familiar car horn blasts not twenty feet away, practically rendering me deaf.

"Val-er-ieee! Oh, Val-er-ieee!" My mother is pulling into the parking spot nearest to the Dumpster and has her window down. I see Gabrielle in the passenger seat popping the top off a salad and picking out the croutons. Guess they're not whole wheat or something.

I brace myself for Christie to ask who's in the car. Why, why, why me? I hate lying to my friends, and Christie, of all people, would be most likely to understand.

But I am not ready to deal with this. Not yet, not even with Christie. Maybe I can say Gabrielle's a neighbor. No, wait, Christie knows all my neighbors. Maybe someone from the Boosters? Or Mom's book club?

Geez, I despise lying. I don't think I can do it.

My mom sticks her head out the window and asks if we want a ride. Thank goodness, Christie says no, we're heading back to school. My mom waves and takes off, but I can tell she's curious. And so's Christie. Her mouth is hanging open, and she's watching the back of the SUV as it rolls out of the lot.

Book club. I'm going to say Gabrielle's from book club.

"Ohmigod." Christie looks like she's just swallowed her Altoids mint the wrong way. "What did your mom do to her hair?"

2

"DAD," I WHISPER, "WHAT'S A TIMBALE?"

I should never have asked him to bring me here. For one, I can't read half the menu. For two, he still hasn't said what decisions we need to make.

And for three, I'm still thinking about David Anderson. And the fact that it's Friday night, which means Jeremy probably won't see him again until Monday at school, since cross-country season is now over and Christmas break is only a week away. No more Saturday meets or practices where they can get together to discuss *moi*.

"It means that it was baked in a mold," Dad explains, and I can tell he's thrilled by his own knowledge of this useless information. I guess it *is* his job. "In most cases, the dish is cream based."

In other words, seafood timbale is probably going to be disgusting. "Oh," I say. "I'm not a fan of creamy."

Or molds. Only Jell-O should go in molds, and even that's iffy. But I don't want to upset Dad, since I did ask to come here and he's shelling out the big bucks.

"Me, either," he says. "But you might like the crab cakes."

I'm not a big seafood person, but since the rest of the menu's steak (I definitely don't like big hunks of meat), I decide to go with Dad and order the crab cakes to start and the poached snapper. It comes with mushrooms, which I do like.

Honestly, though, I could care less about the food. I want to know what this dinner is all about. It's not just a reward for saving the Mottahedeh from Mom, and we both know it. As soon as the waiter's gone, I look at Dad. I'm just too scared to ask. Thankfully, he brings it up first.

"Valerie, I told you last night we had some decisions to make."

He looks nervous and Martin Winslow rarely gets nervous about speaking. I mean, he's on the speed dial of not only the current president of the United States, but several former presidents, which means he's used to talking to anyone, anytime, about all kinds of strange topics. So I'm tempted to tell him to do whatever, that I don't want to be involved. Especially since my opinions don't seem to carry much weight. I mean, I thought I was being brilliant by suggesting my mom and dad have a cooling-off period before rushing into a divorce. The only way I know my mom even *heard* my opinion was that she later informed me she'd been "cooling off" for a decade.

"Well, now that your mother and I aren't living together any longer, we need to decide where you should live."

Before he's even finished speaking, I can feel tears coming up in my eyes. I try to play it off by taking a long sip of my Diet Coke. I hate that Jules was right about this.

At least she had the Dad-has-a-girlfriend thing wrong.

"Well, I'm not sure Mom wants me with her," I tell Dad. "Not *living* with her anyway." It's the first time I've said it aloud, but ever since she made her announcement, it's what I've been thinking.

Dad shakes his head, and I start feeling bad for him, too, since Mom definitely doesn't want to live with him. "No," he says, "she does want you to live with her. And so does Gabrielle."

I can tell he hardly wants to let Gabrielle's name pass his lips, but he's making an effort to be polite about it all. He takes a sip of his wine and adds, "I guess she and

Gabrielle have a two-bedroom apartment, and you'd have your own bathroom. So it's something to consider."

"But Gabrielle's going to try to tell me what to do, right?" I remember when Jules's stepfather—the guy her mom married in between being married to Jules's dad and remarrying Jules's dad—used to boss her around. One minute he acted like he was her new best buddy, but the next minute—as soon as Jules's mom wasn't around—he'd walk all over her. I remember thinking how glad I was I'd never have to deal with that. But now I guess Gabrielle's going to be my stepmom. Or something.

"I don't know Gabrielle well enough to speak for her," Dad says, his tone making it clear he has no interest in knowing Gabrielle. "But I know your mom will do her best to make you happy, no matter what problems she and I might have. She loves you as much as she ever has."

I think about this for a minute while I fish a roll out of the bread basket. "Do *you* want me to live with Mom?"

"I want you to do whatever you want. But your mother and I have talked about it, and whatever you decide now, we want you to know you can change your mind. We're not going to fight about custody. We agree that you'll be fine with either of us for the next two and a half years, before you go to college, and that you're mature enough to make your own decision."

Wow. I just stare at Dad. I totally expected him to ask my opinion, just to make me feel like I had a say, then do whatever the hell he and Mom wanted to do.

My dad gives me a look, though, that clues me in to the fact things aren't so simple.

"What's the catch?"

"Well, if you move in with your mother, you'll switch schools. Her apartment's closer to Lake Braddock. I'm sure you could finish out the year here, but then—"

"Forget it. I hate Lake Braddock." No way do I want to graduate from there. And how could I leave Christie, Jules, and Natalie? Let alone David. Not that I have David to leave—yet. But I never will if I transfer. "Besides, if I stay with you, I can see Mom whenever. I mean, she'll only be a few miles away."

I think this will be okay. I'll have my friends. I won't have to let anyone know what's up with Mom, at least not right away, since I know I'm going to cave and cry if I tell them now. I have to get a grip on this whole thing first.

And Dad won't be so lonely if I'm home. Mom has Gabrielle, but he doesn't have anyone. Well, except me. "I'm staying with you, Dad, definitely." This wasn't nearly as painful as I thought it'd be. "If that's all right, I mean. I kind of like my room, so keeping it would be a plus. And this way I can stay at Vienna West."

Dad twists in his chair, and that's when I notice he hasn't even touched his roll. "That's the other part of the catch, Valerie. But in a way, I think it's good news."

I flip my hand in the air over the table in a get-on-with-it way.

He leans forward and keeps his voice so quiet I can hardly hear him. "I'm about to be transferred."

"Transferred? To where?" As far as I know, there's only one White House, and that's his thing. He's been there since I was five, which means he's on his third president.

"Well, you know President Carew is quite conservative."

"Oh, yeah." He's, like, the hero of the right-wing Republicans. Conservative think tanks pretty much got him elected. The guy's very pro-gun lobby, anti-abortion, and totally against legislation that allows gays to marry or to adopt kids.

My dad is a registered Democrat, on the other hand. He's voted that way every election since he was eligible. Even though he's occasionally called on to help fix whatever media-catastrophe-of-the-moment there is at the White House, I've never once heard him utter a single word criticizing Republican presidents for their mistakes. Or cheering on the Democrats, come to think of it.

The way I figure, who cares who's in the Oval Office or what they do in their personal lives if the economy is good, health care is improving, and everyone's employed?

But Dad never talks about his political beliefs to anyone. I only know where he stands because I pestered him about it once for a solid week and he finally told me. He also told me it was his job not to have a political opinion, or even a personal opinion of the men he's worked for—some of whom I think drove him insane—so I need to keep the information to myself. Especially the fact he's never voted for a Republican in his life—including the Republicans who've employed him.

"Well, President Carew is up for reelection next year, and his staff will come under a great deal of scrutiny. With your mother and I divorcing, and given the unusual circumstances—"

"You're getting fired because Mom's a lesbian?" I try hard to keep my voice down, but a man at the next table glances our way. I can't help it though. This is just *so* wrong.

"No, Valerie." He reaches across the table and puts his hand over mine, probably as much to shut me up as to comfort me. "No. I felt, with the election coming, that I needed to tell President Carew what was happening. We both decided it would be best for the administration if I took a job elsewhere. I don't want this to become a political issue any more than he does. Could you imagine if the host threw it out for discussion on *Meet the Press*?"

I start feeling sick to my stomach, because I know stuff like that happens all the time.

I hate how D.C. works sometimes.

"The president was very understanding, and he found me another position. A great opportunity, actually." He lets go of my hand, and I can see he's actually excited he's getting canned. "Do you know where Schwerinborg is?"

I do, but only because we did Europe in World History and Geography last year. We had a quiz where we had to fill in all the names of the countries on a map of Europe, and I aced it. Schwerinborg was one of those dinky countries like Andorra, Lichtenstein, and San Marino, where you couldn't write the country name on the actual country. You had to fill it in on a line that pointed to the country.

Most of the class missed it. They either had no clue, or they wrote in "Smorgasbord." We all laughed about that forever, because it totally pissed off the teacher. She thought they were being smart-asses.

"It's very small, and it's in the Alps, between Germany and Switzerland," Dad explains, trying to get me jazzed about this. "They have a lot of skiing, and it's quite beautiful. I'll be chief of protocol to the royal family. I've been offered a two-bedroom apartment in the palace. The palace itself looks a lot like the Louvre—remember when we went there a couple of years ago on vacation?"

I remember the Louvre. I adore art, so spending the afternoon there was the highlight of the trip for me. Warning: The *Mona Lisa* is underwhelming, but if you ignore that, there's a lot of other good stuff in there. And the building itself is really pretty.

The waiter brings our crab cakes, and they're surprisingly good. "So, let me get this straight," I say between bites. "You're not even going to live in Virginia anymore? You're moving to *Schwerinborg*? And you'll be living in the palace?"

"Yes. Of course, I plan to come back after the next election. Either this president will be out of the White House and a Democrat will be in, so the circumstances of the divorce won't be an issue, or President Carew will bring me back. I have his word, and he isn't a man to go back on his promises." My dad gets a self-satisfied smile on his face. "I'm very good at what I do. Whoever's in the White House will want me there."

"I know."

"But in the meantime, I'd love to have you with me in Schwerinborg. I think it would be a real adventure to get to see more of Europe before you go to college."

"Not that I'm saying yes, because I'm not . . . but where would I go to school? What's involved here?" I mean, is there a Schwerinborg High? Do I have to learn German?

That I *cannot* do. French is my thing. I've had straight As in it since seventh grade. I think I might even get the French award this year, and that would rock on my college applications since those awards usually go to seniors and the occasional junior, and I'm only a sophomore.

"There's a private American high school near the palace. Prince Manfred and Princess Claudia send their son there to help improve his English. Most of the foreign diplomats' kids attend, as well. The program is impressive. The teachers are primarily Americans, and classes are conducted in English."

My crab cake isn't tasting so good anymore. Going to school at Lake Braddock versus attending some high school with a bunch of foreigners who'll be able to talk about me in German behind my back?

"I'm not getting much of a choice here," I point out, as if this isn't obvious to him. "Either way, I don't get to stay at my school. That's totally unfair."

"I'm sorry, but it's the best I can do. If you decide on Lake Braddock, you'll still see your friends after school."

"No, I won't. None of us have cars." Driver's ed isn't until next semester, and I'm one of the last of my friends to turn sixteen.

"I think your mother will make the effort."

Now I really think I'm going to cry. There's no way I

can avoid telling everyone about Mom if I live with her. I mean, what do I say about Gabrielle if she comes to pick me up at school? I lucked out that Christie didn't catch on this afternoon. Jules and Natalie would have immediately, and I can't handle their oh-poor-you-but-I'm-so-glad-it's-not-me sympathy right now.

As much as I love Mom, I really, really don't want to live with Gabrielle. I just know she's going to boss me around and make me eat organic greens and quinoa all the time. Besides, it would just feel weird. How would I handle being around Mom with anyone besides Dad, let alone a new *girlfriend*? I'm as laid back as the next person, but I get uncomfortable around Christie and Jeremy when they start playing tonsil hockey near me.

Then it occurs to me that David Anderson's dad is a big deal conservative lobbyist. David idolizes the man, partially because he was a big college track star, partially because he's always on the *Today* show or *Good Morning America* yammering away about family values. If the president is willing to ship Dad off to Schwerinborg over all this, what's David going to think about me when he hears?

I bet kids who go to high school in Nebraska or California or Minnesota and other *normal* places don't have to deal with this kind of political stuff messing up their relationships.

I swipe a tear off my cheek, because I do *not* want my

dad to see me cry. I am not one of those wussy girly-girls who cries to get things my way. Girls like that piss me off.

"Hey, it's going to be okay." I can hear the guilt in Dad's voice, which makes me feel even worse. "I'll come visit you as often as I can. And if you want, you can come to Schwerinborg during spring break. I have more than enough frequent flyer miles to cover the ticket. We'll go skiing together. Maybe we can go to Interlaken—"

"No, Dad," I interrupt. I'm finally realizing that I'm never, ever going to date David. Because as ticked as I am at my mother right now for ruining my life, I love her, and I can't be someone I'm not just to go out with David Anderson. If he's even interested in me. I mean, come on. One conversation with Jeremy about who I might be dating could mean anything. Right?

"No, what?" A serious pair of wrinkles forms in the space between his eyes as he looks at me. "You wouldn't even visit?"

"No, as in I'm coming with you. I'll move to Schwerinborg. Why the hell not?"

"Don't say hell, Valerie," comes his automatic response. Then he tilts his head at me, and I can tell he's trying very hard not to smile. "Really, though? That's what you want?"

"Yep." I grin, even though I don't really feel like smiling. "That's what I want."

Maybe I'll get lucky and someone there will be as godlike as David. And they won't care how my mom lives her life.

"I don't get it. Why not just suck it up and go to Lake Braddock?" Natalie hisses on Monday morning as our history teacher, Mrs. Bennett, turns her back to start a video on the battles of Gettysburg and Manassas. We've been doing the Civil War in United States and Virginia History for the last three weeks, and frankly, I'm sick of all the blood and gore. At least it'll be over after tomorrow.

On the downside, this Friday is the end of our second quarter, a.k.a. major exam time, and the next day I'm off to Schwerinborg. Just like that. Dad says it'll be easiest for me to switch schools between quarters, even though I thought I'd have a *little* more time. Like at least until after Christmas.

This is the one thing I hate about going to Vienna West. We finish each quarter before every other school in the district because our school's used for summer camps and they need us to be out of here earlier in the spring. If we were a normal school, we'd finish second quarter in January and I'd have another month to figure things out. But I don't. Which is what has Natalie so ticked off today.

Ticked off at me, that is. Not the Civil War or our exam schedule.

I ignore Natalie's question, but as soon as the video starts and the room gets dead quiet, a wadded piece of paper comes flying from my right and goes skittering over my desk. I catch it as it goes off the other side, barely keeping it from landing by David Anderson's feet, since he sits in the row next to mine, one seat back. Natalie is a terrible note passer.

I glance at Mrs. Bennett to see if she's noticed, since of course everyone else in the room has, and a few people start snickering. Luckily Mrs. Bennett is focused on grading our quizzes from Friday, and is looking down at her desk, punching numbers on her calculator. Good thing, because if Natalie gets caught with a note in class, especially when she's already grounded, her parents are going to hit the roof.

I frown at Natalie, since I've warned her to lay off the note passing unless it's urgent, then slowly open up the paper, trying to keep the crinkling to a minimum.

Did you at least argue? Ask your mom to maybe get an apartment here in Vienna instead?

Lake Braddock might suck, but it's got to be better than Smorgasbord. I would NEVER move there, just because my parents said so!

ESPECIALLY if David Anderson liked me. What kind of crack are you SMOKING?!?!

I fold up the note and stuff it in my pocket, fast. Natalie glares at me, but no way do I want to get caught with this. Not with David right across the aisle from me. With my luck Mrs. Bennett will catch us and read it out loud to the class. She's done it before.

I take a new sheet of paper from my notebook, uncap a pen, and scribble.

Like you would NEVER stay in Girl Scouts, just because your parents said so?

I know this is a low blow, so below that I add,

(You know what I mean.) I tried, no luck. It won't be so bad, except for missing you guys like crazy. I get to live in a palace and go skiing. And Dad says it won't be long. I'll probably be back for the second half of junior year. That's only a year away.

I know a year is a wicked long time. But since that's two months after elections, and Dad said he'd be able to come back to the White House by then, I figure this is a safe bet. I fold the note—a lot more carefully than Natalie did—and when I'm sure Mrs. Bennett isn't looking, I slide it across the aisle with my foot.

A few minutes later, right when a Confederate cannon goes kerblam and half the class jolts awake, the paper comes flying back onto my desk, hitting me in the hand while I'm taking notes. I almost scream. I'm going to have to talk to Natalie about throwing notes across the aisle during the scary parts.

But what about HIM?!

Him meaning David Anderson, and not Dad, I assume. I look over at Natalie and mouth, "Later!"

She flattens her hands against her cheeks and makes an Edvard Munch–like scream face at me, but I glare at her until she turns back to the video and starts taking notes, since all this stuff will be on the exam and we only have a few days to go.

I start writing too, but I cannot wrap my brain around the logistics of Pickett's Charge or remember whether General Longstreet was on the Union or Confederate side. Not with Natalie, Jules, and especially Christie so upset. They all cried when I finally told them last night, over Spicy Chicken Fillet Sandwiches and Frostys from the freshly cleaned machine at Wendy's—once Natalie's parents finally agreed she could come out for an hour.

It's nice to know that my buds will miss me, but I feel

guilty, too. They think I'm rejecting them, and just don't get why I'd move to Schwerinborg, even if staying means I have to go to Lake Braddock and I'd hardly ever see them.

And of course, I can't tell them the whole truth. They don't buy my story about Dad being lonely and me wanting to keep him company either. I think it's because they all secretly believe Jules's girlfriend theory. Like a girlfriend would follow him to Schwerinborg. I wouldn't go if the situation here was even remotely tolerable, and I'm his *daughter*.

I can tell that in their minds I'm going to be gone forever, even though I told them over and over that I am not going to live in freakin' Schwerinborg the rest of my life. I'd much rather be in Virginia with all my friends, chilling out in Christie's basement watching movies or making fun of the idiots who go on reality TV shows.

I let out a little sigh, then realize it was loud enough for Mrs. Bennett to hear. She's glaring at me, so I yank myself into something resembling good posture and begin watching the video for real.

They keep showing maps of the battlefield and reenactments of young soldiers running across fields and up hills, fighting for their lives. There's a voiceover, reading letters sent back home by the soldiers. Apparently, as the men were listening to the cannons and guns firing around them and to the agonized cries of their dying friends (which sound totally fake on the video), they weren't thinking about politics or slavery or any of that stuff. They were thinking of home and the mothers and wives and girlfriends they left behind.

I wonder if David will think of me when I'm gone.

I glance over my shoulder. David's totally focused on the video, which doesn't surprise me, because he's got the highest grade in the whole class. Well, except for me, though if I keep allowing the whole Schwerinborg situation to distract me, he may beat me on the exam.

But even just sitting there, staring at the video with the overhead lights off, the guy is totally hot. He's got one elbow on the desk, his fingers forked through his hair, propping up his head. He's taking notes with his other hand, and for a moment, I wonder what it'd be like to sit in the dark and have his fingers interlaced with mine. He has such long, strong fingers.

Is it possible for a guy to have sexy hands?

I'm guessing he's heard my Schwerinborg news. He must have. Christie would have called Jeremy on her cell after we left Wendy's last night, since she was upset and she always cries to Jeremy when she's upset, and Jules told me that David and Jeremy sit together in English during first period.

I start to turn back around so I can figure out the whys

and wherefores of Pickett's Charge, but then my eyes catch David's, and I realize he's been watching me stare at him.

Oh, *crap*.

I shift in my chair as subtly as possible, making like I was looking out the window at the quad, where the band geeks are all lined up to practice marching, but we both know I wasn't.

Then he gives me this long, slow wink.

Oh. My. God.

3

IN A PANIC, I TURN BACK TO THE VIDEO.

Oh. My. God. Ohmigod. I am so busted. What the hell did that *wink* mean?

That I'm a total idiot and he knows it?

Or that he's interested?

No. No way, no how, no matter what Christie says. I haven't had a boyfriend since seventh grade, when Jason Barrows kissed me on a dare and everyone went around afterward saying we were boyfriend and girlfriend, which doesn't really count as having a boyfriend, since he wasn't. My boyfriend, that is. Even though everyone told me he had a thing for me because I'm a redhead. I mean, ick.

The bell rings, and Mrs. Bennett gets up to stop the

video while everyone rushes to grab their stuff and get out of class before she can give us a new assignment. It's not as if we don't have enough to worry about with exams starting Wednesday. When I lean over to grab my backpack, I see that David is *still* looking at me.

Natalie grabs my arm. "We have got to talk. Now."

But as Natalie yanks me out the door, David shoots me this wicked grin that says, *I know exactly who you're going to talk about, too.*

I bet he saw the note Natalie passed me. Bet he read it over my shoulder. Even if Gabrielle's presence wasn't forcing me to already, now I *have* to go to Schwerinborg.

"Wait a minute," I tell Natalie as soon as we're out in the hall. "I think I left my notebook."

I elbow my way back inside as the last few people rush out the door, only to see that Mrs. Bennett has my notebook in her hand. Great.

"Forget this?"

I nod and take it, and she makes some comment about how I can't afford to lose it seeing as I need to ace the next exam if I want to turn my A into an A+ for the term. Then she blows by me on her way to the teachers' lounge, since this is her break period.

She must've seen Natalie pass that note, or at least she suspects. Otherwise she'd never be on my back about my grade. I mean, really. I bet *she* didn't have as high a grade when she was a sophomore. Sometimes you just know you've got more book smarts than one of your teachers.

I drop my backpack on top of the nearest desk and unzip it to shove my notebook inside while I try to figure out what to say to Natalie. I don't want to argue about this with her anymore, but I just know she's going to be all over me about moving once I go back into the hall.

"Hey, Val."

I look up, and there's David. Like, right there. Either he never left the room, or he followed me back in. How could I not have seen him? Usually I can tell whenever he's within a hundred-yard radius. After all these years of having an insane crush on him, I've developed a finely tuned David radar.

"Um, hey." This is about all I can manage, which makes me sound like a total dork. I mean, we've known each other forever, and we're kind of friends, so what's my problem? "What's up?"

He sits on top of the desk next to my backpack. I think I'm going to keel over, right here in room 104. David's butt is actually touching my backpack. Since I'm busy trying to unstick the zipper, I can't help but see the fabulous way his Levi's curve around his rear. And if I pull the backpack zipper all the way around, I could touch him. If I wanted.

Once last month I saw Christie and Jeremy waiting for

a ride after Christie finished volleyball practice, and she had her arms around his waist with her index fingers hooked in the back pockets of his jeans while he kissed her. At the time I thought it was kind of weird, but now I'm thinking I'd like to have my fingers hooked in David's pockets. Oh, yeah. I can definitely see how that would be fun.

He scoots on the desk, and I realize I'm staring at him. Again. I make myself focus on his eyes and try not to turn red. Of course, since I'm about as fair skinned as a human being can be, that's pretty much impossible.

And did I mention that his eyes are phenomenal?

"I, uh, I heard you're moving to, um . . ."

"To Schwerinborg."

He smiles, but only on one side of his mouth. Could he be any more delicious? "Yeah. Of all places. Can't believe you're going to Smorgasbord. Who'da thought?"

I need a ventilator. Not only has David heard my news, he wants to *talk* about it?

"I'll miss you, Winslow. I know we don't hang out as much as when we were kids or anything, but I've always thought you're one of the few truly cool people in this place. Plus, you're the only person who can outscore me in history. What'll I do without you here to challenge me?"

My mouth can't form a reply, since I'm thinking, *Me, cool?* Me, with my whacked red hair and freak show green eyes, when he is a complete and total sex god who can go out with anyone in the entire universe? Or at least with anyone in the entire school—which is still a hell of a lot of people, seeing as there are twenty-five hundred students at West Vienna High.

He stands up, and his gorgeous butt is no longer in contact with my backpack. "Will you have e-mail there?"

"I think so."

He fishes a piece of paper out of his notebook and scribbles down his e-mail address. "In case I forget later, with exams and all. Let me know what's up with you over there, okay?"

"Yeah, I will."

As I slide the piece of paper into my jeans pocket, he says, "I'd really like to keep in touch. I've been thinking lately that we should hang out more. It'd still be cool to chat, even if it's long distance now."

"That'd be cool." Cool. Understatement of the year.

He smiles back, then he leans over and gives me a lightning-quick kiss on the cheek before walking out the door.

I cannot move.

A few seconds later Natalie comes back in, but I don't even see her. I hear her first.

"Come *on*, Valerie. What is with you?"

David. David is what's with me.

* * *

Given the way this afternoon deteriorated on its way to evening, I should be really, really fried right now.

It's seven p.m., and my dad *just* got home from work, which means I had to settle for chewy reheated pizza, even though he promised me yesterday he'd get home in time to make his divinely inspired chicken marsala. Why scientists can't come up with microwave technology that makes a zapped pizza taste as good as one right out of the oven is beyond me, but that's actually not the main reason I should be upset right now.

I glance across the kitchen toward Dad, who's tuned in to CNN and shaking his head at some berserker pundit who's ranting about the Democrats (of course) and how if they'd just been a little nicer to the Republicans, and supported them and their last proposed tax cut and a million other issues, maybe people would have voted differently in the last election and President Carew wouldn't be in the White House. According to this jerk, Democrats like my mom (and secretly, my dad) aren't nice people, and that's why they aren't in the White House.

I hate listening to this stuff, because a) I really don't care about politics unless they directly affect me, which is practically never; and b) I know it's upsetting to Dad, who tries so hard to like everybody and be tolerant and play fair. That's how he manages to keep his job no matter who's in office.

And the icing on tonight's cake? My mother—the main reason Dad has to leave the job he loves—is on her way over. She's going to be taking care of the house while we're in Schwerinborg, and Dad has a few things he wants to go over with her. I just know they're going to get into it. Okay, not flinging dishes or anything, like divorcing couples always seem to on those Lifetime made-for-television movies, but still.

I'm not *really* upset by any of this, though. Pizza, loud-mouthed politicians, even Mom can't faze me tonight.

I mean, David Anderson *kissed me.*

Not a genuine, pressed-up-against-my-locker-between-classes-clawing-each-other's-clothes kiss, the way I've always dreamed he'd kiss me. But it was definitely premeditated—I mean, he was waiting for me to come get my notebook, or at least watching for an opportunity to get me alone—which makes me think maybe Christie was right. Maybe he really does like me.

After all these years of secret lust, scribbling *Valerie Anderson* and *Valerie Winslow Anderson* and the totally old-school *Mrs. David Anderson* in the blank pages of my diary (because who has time to actually write real stuff in a diary?) before shredding the pages into the trash, mortified with my juvenile behavior—is it possible he feels the same way?

The sound of my dad snorting at the television brings me back to the real world. This man is taking me to Schwerinborg in five days. If I go, I might never find out what David's really thinking. What am I going to DO?!?

Dad did say I could change my mind. So maybe I should. Or not. Oh, damn, damn, and triple damn.

I mean, it isn't like David hasn't had years and years to kiss me before now. Or at least give me his e-mail address, if he wanted to talk or get to know me as a better-than-casual friend.

But does any of that matter if he's interested *now*?

Then I realize why Dad is being so uncharacteristically vocal with the television. David's father is on and he's spewing his lobbyist crap.

What an unfortunate little coincidence.

I scoot to the edge of my chair for a better look. Mr. Anderson's head is neatly framed in a little box that says *Washington* under it. There's also a sharply dressed man in a box marked *Boston* and a prudish woman with square glasses above *San Francisco*. And they're all saying that Carew was elected because people believe in his values, and that he has an excellent chance of being reelected. David's dad loudest of all. Okay. *Now* I'm upset.

I let my head thunk against the table. This is too much

for one day. Why, why, why does David have to think every word out of his dad's mouth is gospel? And why do I have to hear all about Carew's value system via CNN, when those values are now ruining my entire freakin' life?

"Valerie?" Dad clicks off the set. "You all right?"

I lift my head off the table. "Oh, peachy."

Dad raises an eyebrow. "Is it CNN, or the fact your mother's on her way over?"

I try not to laugh. How many problems can I accumulate in one day? On top of the fact that I have a ton of geometry formulas to memorize before this week's exam. Geometry is—thankfully and surprisingly—much easier for me than algebra was last year (algebra was created by Satan, I'm convinced), but it's still no cakewalk. I'd rather take ten Friday quizzes from Mrs. Bennett than one end-of-quarter geometry exam.

And we won't even discuss the paper I have due in English on *Billy Budd*. My theory is that if Herman Melville wanted anyone to actually read it, he'd have called it *Killing a Sailor* or *Hang the Dude* or something equally attention grabbing.

"Look," Dad says, "your mother and I have our problems, but we're working them out. We don't hate each other, and we're not going to fight over furniture or place settings tonight."

Good, I'm thinking, because what's the point in having all the nice furniture if we're going to Schwerinborg, anyway?

"How about we ask her to stay for a movie?" Dad crosses the kitchen and rubs my shoulder. "I'll let you choose. What's that movie you wanted to see with the medieval knight?"

"*A Knight's Tale*?"

"Sure. It sounded interesting."

"Mom won't like it." She's into the indie film scene—the stuff that plays at Sundance and maybe a couple of art-fart theaters around your major metropolitan areas, if the producers are lucky. Not anything with drool-licious men like Heath Ledger wearing chain mail, may he rest in peace.

"What we watch isn't the issue," Dad says just as the doorbell rings. "Your mom wants to spend as much time as possible with you before we leave, and watching a movie together would make for a nice evening."

"What about you, though?" I drop my voice to a whisper and follow him to the door. "I mean, if it bugs you being around Mom, I can go watch a movie at her place." Even if it has one of those go-nowhere plots I don't quite get.

"Look, Valerie," Dad doesn't even bother to lower his voice, and I know for a fact you can hear what's said in the front hall from the front porch even when the door is closed. "Go wherever *you're* most comfortable. I've known your mother for nearly twenty years. I'm not happy about the divorce, but she's still the best friend I've ever had. We can handle seeing a movie together."

If it was me whose wife was leaving me for another woman, I'd sure feel uncomfortable having her over for movies and popcorn. Too much like a date, even if your daughter is there and everything is ostensibly for the sake of the kid. But I guess Dad's a better person than I am.

"Okay." I shrug as he flips the deadbolt on the front door. "Just checking."

This could be fun. I mean, if the two of them are nicey-nice, it might feel like it used to, before Mom upended everything. I could use a dose of that kind of normalcy, even if it's only for tonight and I know it's not for real.

I smile at Mom, but I can tell from her face—as she and Dad walk through the house and discuss which plants need watering, how the alarm system works, and who to call when the sprinkler system needs to be turned on in the spring, since these are always tasks that fell to Dad—that she's still surprised I decided to go to Schwerinborg with Dad instead of staying with her. She keeps glancing at me to see if I'm cool.

When we go into the family room for the movie, I work up the guts to ask Mom where Gabrielle is. If that blond mom stealer is going to show up and plop on the sofa next to me while Heath Ledger is midtournament, I need advance notice.

Mom says Gabrielle's out for the evening though. Get this: at a Weight Watchers meeting.

Shock must be as apparent on my face as it is on Dad's, because my mother instantly looks from me, to my dad, and back to me before saying, "And what's wrong with that?"

"Nothing wrong with it. Just . . . interesting." Dad hustles to start the movie simply to escape the issue, I'm sure, so Mom turns to me.

"Valerie?"

I can't help but snort out loud. I'm not as polite as Dad. "Interesting 'cause she's built like a runway model. Total rail. She lives on vegetables and soy and stuff, right?"

"She used to be eighty pounds heavier," Mom explains, using her I-wish-you-would-give-Gabrielle-a-break voice. "She was quite unhealthy. Borderline diabetic even. Her doctor sent her to Weight Watchers, and that prompted her to look into yoga and healthy living, and that's how she became a vegan. Now that she's lost the weight, she's a lifetime member. Going to meetings every so often keeps her focused on living a clean, healthy life. I really admire her for it."

This from the woman who believes chicken nuggets

and SpaghettiOs to be food groups in their own right? What she has with Gabrielle *must* be love.

I don't say anything, so Mom shoots a pointed look toward the kitchen, where the empty pizza box is sitting on the counter. "You could probably learn from her, Valerie. How many times have you eaten fast food in the last week?"

Oh, *please*. I hold up the popcorn I made for the movie. "Microwave light. Can't be that bad."

She ignores me and looks at Dad, who's now sitting in the chair as far from her as possible, remote in hand. "You're going to watch what she eats while you're over there in Europe, aren't you, Martin?"

"Mom!" I mean, it's not like *she's* a vegan or a size four. And if she gets on Dad's case again, I'll remind her of her own little trip to Wendy's last week. Gabrielle might've had a salad, but I saw that Biggie Value Meal bag in Mom's lap.

Thankfully the movie starts, allowing me to enjoy a little eye candy in the form of Heath Ledger. I think I'll pretend he's David. A nonpolitical, totally-into-me David.

"I think David Anderson looks a lot like Heath Ledger. Remember him from when we watched *The Dark Knight* at Natalie's?"

It's ten thirty and I should be asleep, since tomorrow's

a school day, but I can't settle. I have David on the brain. And Jules keeps her cell phone, with the ringer turned on low, on her nightstand, so we can chat in the middle of the night without her parents realizing she's awake either.

"Well, the hair, for sure," Jules says. "But not his eyes. David's are much nicer. More open, and green instead of brown. Heath's were brown, right? And David has a slimmer nose." She giggles, which is disturbing because Jules hardly ever giggles. "I can't *believe* he kissed you—or that you waited until lunch to tell me about it. I told Natalie that now you can't go to Schwerinborg. You can't know how totally stoked I am over this."

"On the cheek," I remind her. "And I'm going. I have to."

Jules gets really quiet, I guess because I told her the other night at Wendy's that I didn't *have* to go, that my parents were totally cool and gave me a choice. So I say, "Come on. Between this thing with David and you guys ragging on me, you're making me feel like shit on a sidewalk. This isn't an easy decision for me." They don't have half a clue how hard it really is.

"But you've loved David forever. And you're leaving *us*," Jules whines. "What the hell is going on with you? Something you're not telling me."

I roll over in bed so I'm facing my wall. I photocopied

David's yearbook picture last spring and stuck it to a tiny spot near my head where I can hide it with my bed pillows, so Mom and Dad won't know how totally obsessed I am. And so David's the last guy I see before I go to bed at night. Pathetic. I know.

I use my fingernail to lift the tape at the edge of the photo, and pull it off the wall so David's stamp-sized face is flirting with me from my fingertip. "You've seen *A Knight's Tale*, right, Jules?"

"Yeah."

"Well, at the end of the movie, who's Heath with? The snotty princess. I didn't like her at all. She was totally manipulative and he didn't even see it. He should have gone for the girl who made his armor instead. I mean, she saved his life with that armor, she was able to hang with his friends without dissing them like the princess did, and she was kind of cute. But he hardly even noticed her."

"And this has to do with Schwerinborg how?"

Jules can be annoying when she wants to be. I squash up the photocopied picture and toss it into the trash. "Duh. I'm the Armor Girl."

Jules groans, even though it sounds muffled by her sheets. "Get over it, Winslow. You're so not an Armor Girl."

"Yes, I am. Think. In the movie, Heath doesn't really know the Armor Girl—not the way she is on the inside.

He likes having her around, she pushes him to be a better person, but he doesn't really care about knowing her. He's all caught up in the Shallow Princess because she's gorgissimo, despite the fact that her incredibly stupid, completely selfish prove-your-love-to-me-by-losing-the-tournament demands nearly get him killed."

I flip onto my back and stare at the ceiling. "This is what *all* hot guys do, Jules. They take practical Armor Girls for granted, and to the world at large, this is okay. Everyone cheers when hot guy runs off with idiot Shallow Princess at the end, and the movie does a hundred million at the box office. Armor Girl gets a kiss on the cheek and a scribbled e-mail address."

"That's bull. Besides, how do you know you're not David's princess?"

Hello? How long has Jules known me? I'm not bad-looking, but certainly no princess. I'm a passable Armor Girl. And David knows me about as well as Heath knew the Armor Girl.

And even if David *did* get to know me, he'd always be able to ditch me for some princess. A Republican princess with a nice C cup, hair blonder than his, and a perfect smile. Certainly someone whose mother didn't have a midlife crisis involving a trip out of the proverbial closet.

"Well, let's see. I'm not a cheerleader, and I mock those

who are. I don't have naturally bouncy hair and don't buy every single article of clothing from the designer of the month. And I would *never* tell a guy to lose a game to prove he's in love with me."

"But that doesn't mean—"

"Look, Jules, I'm dying that he kissed me. But I have to be honest with myself here. He's had his chances. And he's dated Shallow Princesses for as long as I can remember."

"Well, I think it's wrong that you're not giving him another chance. You're as bad as the Shallow Princess in the movie, you just can't see it. You're moving to Schwerinborg to test his love."

"Yeah, sure. And my parents agreed to get divorced just so I could test my theory."

She's quiet. I can tell she's mad, but I can't figure out why. I mean, it's not her who's the loser Armor Girl in this scenario. And I feel like I'm having a moment of great personal growth here—being able to have David kiss me and still walk away, knowing it's the best thing. Maybe this means there's someone better out there for me. Maybe even in Schwerinborg.

Someone who'd consider me a not-shallow princess.

You'd think Jules would see that.

"Look," Jules finally says. "I don't think you should make major life decisions based on Heath Ledger movies."

"The decision's already made. I was just using the movie to illustrate the point so you, Christie, and Natalie would understand."

"Well, if you want to analyze your life in terms of a Heath Ledger movie, try *The Four Feathers*. Especially the beginning."

I hear my dad coming down the hall, so I tell her I'll check it out, since I haven't seen that one yet, and that I'll see her tomorrow, but not to be mad.

After my dad sticks his head in my door to make sure I'm asleep, and I'm alone again in the dark and quiet, I decide I should be thankful Jules didn't nail me with *10 Things I Hate About You*. Then the movie trailer for *The Four Feathers* comes back to me. Duh. Thanks, Jules.

The Four Feathers is the one where all Heath's friends accuse him of betrayal for not sticking with the group when things get rough, and not even bothering to give them a good explanation.

Which, in a way, is even worse than *10 Things I Hate About You*. It's group hate.

4

I THOUGHT, FOR A BRIEF THREE WEEKS, THAT MY mother ruined my life. I was sadly, sadly mistaken. I have done it quite by myself.

Northern Virginia is sunny and filled with places to hang out. Parks. Malls. Even fast-food joints like Jules's Wendy's, though clearly that's just where losers like me tend to congregate.

Schwerinborg, on the other hand, is prison gray. Everywhere. The sky, the apartment buildings and cathedrals, even the mountains are gray. Okay, I assume that it's mostly gray because it's December and foggy. But still. I'm not seeing teenagers. *Anywhere.*

"Valerie," my dad whispers. He doesn't have to elaborate.

His warning tone, combined with a disturbing divot forming between his eyes, is enough.

I yank my fingers out of my mouth, but reluctantly. I can't help it—whatever that bizarre party mix was they gave us on the Lufthansa flight from Munich to Freital, the capital (and frankly, I think the only real city) of Schwerinborg, is now permanently lodged between my gum and molar, and it hurts. But I suppose trying to pick it out while seated next to my dad, in a *limo*, no less, is a major faux pas.

Wonder what the German term is for *faux pas*?

Folkschen paschken?

This whole German thing has me in knots. In the Munich airport, where we switched planes, all the signs were in English, French, and German.

Here, it's all German, all the time. I can't figure out a thing, although *ausfahrt* is apparently the word for "exit," since I see it on every ramp.

I probably shouldn't think too hard about that one, or I'll be grossed out. Don't want to spew chunks in the back of the limo, which was pretty nifty of Prince Manfred, my dad's new boss and the ruler of this dinky little country, to send to the airport for us. Definitely a step above working for President Carew. When he sent a car for my dad, it was only a Buick.

Though I'm still wondering if, while this is great for Dad, I've screwed myself royally by coming here. At least they speak English at Lake Braddock. Plus Jules and Natalie stopped speaking to me—in any language—from Tuesday to Friday, though they did show up at the house on Saturday, a couple hours before Dad and I left for the airport, so they could say good-bye.

They didn't apologize for ignoring me all week though. Even if they are pissed off, that's no excuse. I mean, we've been friends for *years*. You'd think they'd want to spend as much time as possible together during my last few days, but no.

Christie was better, but not much. She kept talking to me all week at least, but never in front of Jules or Natalie, and she kept giving me these weepy looks that made me want to smack her beautiful, unblemished face. I understood though. Jules and Natalie were going hard core on her, trying to get her to pressure me into staying. I'd probably have caved to the Jules-Natalie assault machine if I'd been in Christie's shoes.

I almost caved myself, right before Dad and I left for the airport, when it was just me and Christie alone in my room for the last time. We were talking about all the stuff I'm going to miss next semester—like track season, driver's ed, and the art class trip up to New York to tour the museums—and I started to get emotional. Then Christie asked me where Mom was, and how come she wasn't there to say good-bye.

I used the book club excuse I'd concocted at Wendy's, but I came just-this-close to telling Christie everything. Only the thought that Christie would probably tell Jeremy (and therefore, through the grapevine, David, Jules, and Natalie) the real scoop about my parents' divorce forced me to zip my lip.

The limo takes a sharp turn, past one of the signs saying *ausfahrt*, of course. At the top of the ramp, we turn twice more, then head into a downtown area. The streets are much, much narrower than in D.C., and most of them are made of cobblestone, which is pretty neat. We pass through a congested square with a statue in the center, and I'm trying to figure out who's riding the sculpted horse (I'm guessing it's not Napoleon), when atop a slight hill, I see a true *edifice*. I love that word but never get to use it. This place justifies it.

I grab my dad's arm and ask if it's the palace. I get to see a lot of awesome buildings, living near D.C., but this rocks them all.

"It is." Dad's happy I'm excited about something for the first time in at least a week. "Think you can stand living there?"

I squint up as the limo driver pulls onto a side road and noses the car uphill, toward the building. Now that we're closer, I can see that it's definitely Louvre-like. It's constructed of gray stone, and looks a bit like D.C.'s nicer office buildings, but with columns and detailed trim under the eaves. The windows are all beyond tall, and hung with what I'm guessing are very expensive curtains. There are carvings of goddesses on the exterior, in between each of the windows.

No kidding. *Goddesses.*

I cannot imagine *living* in a place like this.

"If the inside's as pretty as the outside, I think I'll make do," I tell Dad. As long as I don't drop a Diet Coke on a fancy silk chair or one of the antique rugs or anything. And so much for eating sushi, if they even have it in Schwerinborg. I tend to spray soy sauce everywhere when I eat. You'd think Dad would be able to teach me the trick to that though.

I'm just about to ask him, but thank God, we pass a McDonald's, and it's walking distance from the palace! Happy, happy, joy, joy. At least if I need a fry fix, I'm covered.

Four hours later, after getting a tour of the palace, filling out paperwork, and making a two-minute exploration of our apartment—and two minutes is all it needs, since apparently a palace "apartment" is pretty much like a hotel suite, meaning a couple of rooms off a second-floor hallway—Dad is kind enough to give me the McChicken I've been craving. Between sips of Diet Coke—excuse me, Coke *Light*—I gently point out that, contrary to exterior appearances, our new place isn't exactly the Ritz.

The furnishings in our apartment are somewhat . . . spare. Not spare in a Calvin Klein, black-and-gray, ultra-modern way, but spare as in basic. In sharp contrast to the heavy tapestries and floor-to-ceiling mirrors that are in the main hallways and public areas of the palace, our apartment boasts two sofas worthy of a dilapidated motel. Across from the sofas, there's a TV—with cable, thankfully—set on top of a rickety black melamine stand.

Dad's room has a double bed, a dresser, and a small bathroom. My bedroom, on the opposite side of what I'll call the living room, is painted an uninspired brown. I have to wonder who decorated the place. I mean, who sleeps in a brown room? It has a twin bed, an armoire that my dad calls a *schrunk*, and a minuscule bathroom. The shower is beyond small, so I have no clue how I'm going to shave my legs. And there's not even a countertop where I can put my stuff. Just a pedestal sink.

I do not want to keep my face wash on the back of the toilet. I mean, *really*. I tell Dad that *schrunk* should be the German word for "bathroom," not for "armoire," because honestly, the armoire thingie is about the same size as the bathroom.

What's worse, the electrical outlets are all weird, and Dad says I'm going to have to buy a new hair dryer, since mine won't work here. I forgot about that from our trip to France last year. I hadn't bothered to do my hair then, since I knew I wouldn't meet any cute French guys with my parents two inches off my elbow the entire time.

Unfortunately we can't go shopping for a couple days, because Dad says he has to acquaint himself with his new job and his new boss. Bummer, because that means I won't be able to commence my David Anderson look-alike hunt anytime soon. It's pretty much the only thing I have to do in this country until school starts, so I figure I should take the time to make sure my hair isn't completely ugly.

And that's the whole apartment, other than the eat-in kitchen—complete with a Formica-topped table and four terribly tacky chairs—where I'm rapidly discovering that Schwerinborg's version of a McChicken comes with a sauce that smells vaguely of onions.

At least the fries are good. Dad scored some ketchup to go with them, which is a relief. We had trouble with that in France. They eat 'em with mayo, for some bizarre reason. But the French can be excused their quirks because they speak such a kickin' language.

"Valerie? Thanks." Dad sets down his Big Mac and gives me a smile like I haven't seen on him in a long, long time.

"For what?"

"For coming. I know this isn't like home, and the adjustment isn't going to be easy, but having you here with me means more than you'll ever know."

I take another bite of my McChicken. I'm actually having fun sitting here with Dad, just the two of us, but I don't want to *talk* about it. I get uncomfortable when Dad gets all mushy on me, because he never used to. It's like an alien infiltrated his brain the day Mom decided to go gay. Or, I should say, *the day she made her emotional breakthrough and realized her true self.*

Someday I really will be able to think about my mom in politically correct terms. And when I do, I'll mean it. Just not today.

"You know, Valerie, change is hard on everyone. Even an old geezer like me," he jokes. He's older, yeah, but no geezer, and he knows it. I saw at least three different women checking him out during our tour of the palace this afternoon. "This experience is what we make it. I think this could turn out to be a wonderful thing for both of us."

"Just as long as you take me skiing. Soon," I tease him.

He's *got* to lighten up. "When does school start here, anyway? They're out for Christmas now, right?"

"They finished their second quarter same day you did. You don't start—officially—for two weeks. But I'm afraid there are some placement exams you'll need to take. Just so you're in the right classes."

I drop my McChicken back onto its wrapper. "Hey. You didn't tell me that!"

"It's not a big deal, Valerie. The exams aren't the be-all and end-all of your placement. The school will also be looking at your transcripts and talking to you about which textbooks you were using and how much material your teachers in Virginia covered. And I know your school guidance counselor wrote up a report on how well you were doing in all your classes."

I steal a couple of his fries. I figure he owes me, since any exam is a big deal, as far as I'm concerned. "When do I take these?"

"You'll take two this week, and two next. So if we go skiing, it'll just be a quick day trip. I think it's wise for you to be well rested. Don't you?"

He grabs some of my fries, just to get back at me. I find it hysterical he does this with me, since he's so hoity-toity in public. I'm just waiting for the day he forgets who he's with and mooches off the First Lady's plate.

He pops a fry into his mouth and says, "You're not going to bail on me because of a few exams, are you?"

"No, not yet," I tell him, though he's got to know that I'm only half serious.

"Well, if it helps, I do have another surprise for you."

"Only if it's better than Mickey D's."

'Cause that's about the biggest surprise of my day so far, and on the grand scale of things, getting a meal that's sure to make my butt expand isn't exactly memorable. And it better not be one of those Chicken Soup books that's supposed to cure my messed-up teenage soul. Like some bizarro introvert writer spewing platitudes can fix *my* life. Hah.

"I think so." Dad wads up the burger wrappers and tosses them into the trash can beneath the kitchen sink. "What if I told you that Prince Manfred has arranged to have a computer, complete with Internet access, set up for us in about an hour?"

"Really? Then I say, 'Bring it on, Manny!'" Contact with the outside world? Wha-hoo!

"Valerie—" My dad's warned me for days that I have to be on my "public" behavior at all times at the palace.

"Oh, *come on*. You know I won't refer to him that way to anyone but you. I'm not a complete idiot." Good thing I'm an only child. I think I'm pretty normal, but if my dad had another kid to compare me to, especially one with his meticulous personality, I'd be in trouble.

"Just to be sure, you won't be here when the tech guys arrive."

"You're sending me *out*? Alone?" That's what he thinks.

"Just to the library. There's a small one here in the palace, and it's very easy to find. I have a list of what's covered on each of the placement exams, and Prince Manfred was kind enough to have your teachers send over copies of the textbooks you'll be using." Dad opens up one of the cabinets built into the wall of our living room and yanks out a stack of books. Same geometry text I had in Vienna, I notice. Same French book too. The rest are totally unfamiliar, but at least they're in English.

Dad sets them on the table in front of me, then drops the list on top. "Take an hour or two to look it all over, and you'll be set."

I am not believing this. I just got off what has to be the longest plane flight ever, and he wants me to cram? I cross my arms over my chest. "I thought you said I wouldn't have to study."

"It's not as bad as it looks. You just finished studying for your second-quarter exams last week, so you should be in good shape. Now quit making faces and remember that it's not going to be graded. It's just to get a general idea of what you've been taught."

"Dad—"

"When you get back, the computer will be ready. And I'll see if I can get the fridge stocked in the meantime. All right?"

He can always bribe me with food. It's pathetic. You'd think after my McChicken, this wouldn't work. But it does. *Stock the fridge* in Martin Winslow language generally means he's going to have something tasty for me while I veg out on the couch later.

I grab the list and look it over. Most of it isn't too bad, but I'm going to have to remind myself how to diagram a sentence. We did that last year and I promptly forgot how. The way I figure, I can *write* a competent sentence, so why the hell would I need to diagram one? I bet Shakespeare never diagrammed a sentence, and he turned out just fine.

Dad gives me directions to the library, puts the textbooks, a blank notebook (like I'm supposed to take notes?), and a pencil in my hands, then shoves me out the door.

Thankfully, the library's not as gray and boring as everything else. There's a lot of light from the windows, which overlook the whole city, and the oriental rugs are all a bright, cheery red. And unlike our apartment (which you'd think would be nicer, being in a palace and all), there's not a square inch of Formica to be seen. Just some comfy-plus armchairs, two long tables I'm certain are antiques, a fireplace, and walls and walls of books. Old, expensive-looking books on polished, dark shelves.

I think I'm in heaven. I love libraries, and this has to be one of the best on the cozy scale.

I settle down in the chair closest to the fireplace, since someone on the staff—which I'm discovering is huge and mostly invisible—has built a fire and left a neatly stacked pile of logs to the side of the marble hearth. Of course, this means I spend a full fifteen minutes staring at the fire and not opening the geometry book.

I finally give up and open my notebook, figuring that if I scribble out a few formulas, Dad will feel like he's being a good parent and I'm being a good kid. But instead of writing anything geometry related, I start sketching.

I have no idea what I want to do careerwise, though I can guarantee it won't involve algebra or geometry. But if newsrooms are still using artists to sketch court scenes ten years from now—you know, those penciled pictures they flash on Court TV or MSNBC when there aren't any cameras allowed in the courtroom—I'd love to do that for a living. I started back in sixth or seventh grade by sketching my teachers when I got bored in class. I'm awesome at faces and at showing emotions, and I draw fast. Obviously, I'm bored a lot.

Within a few minutes, I have a killer drawing. It's me, Jules, Natalie, and Christie. Just our faces, all in a row, grinning at each other. I'm just about to pencil in David's face when a voice behind me scares the bejesus out of me.

And I don't understand a freaking word other than *Valerie*.

"I'm sorry," I mumble once I've righted myself in the chair. I tend to sit sideways in armchairs, which gives Dad a near stroke when we're in public. "*Sprechen Sie Englisch?*"

This is the only sentence I know in German. Yes, it's pitiful.

Even worse than my attempt at German, I think I am going to have a stroke myself, right here in the palace library, now that I can see the guy. He's standing about five feet behind me, near one of the long library tables. The face attached to the German-speaking voice is mesmerizing. Not necessarily handsome—well, at least not in a David Anderson look-alike way—but he's definitely not bad. And he's *my age*.

"I apologize." He sticks out his hand, and it's even sexier than David's. Be still my heart! "I forgot you don't speak German. I'm Georg."

He says it like "*Gay*-org." Not the world's most attractive name. Not by a long shot. And the less I have to hear about anything gay right now, the better. Yes, I'm just that shallow. But his accent is one hundred percent to die for. I can ignore the name to hear that accent again. Yum.

And suddenly I get self-conscious about the fact I'm in my Adidas track pants and a T-shirt, with my hair in a ponytail.

I shake his hand and smile. "I'm Valerie Winslow. But it sounds like you already knew that."

"I hope you don't mind my intrusion. I saw you sitting in here, and thought I'd introduce myself."

"It's no intrusion," I say. Like I wanted to be sitting here studying geometry? But I can't say that, because this guy sounds almost as formal and polite as my dad. I've never met a teenager as stiff as this one.

"My father told me you were moving in." He leans forward, putting his elbows on the back of the armchair next to mine. "It'll be nice to have another high schooler around here. I hate being the only nonadult in this place."

"You live here?" I hadn't thought about it, but I guess if my dad and I get an apartment here, it only makes sense that some of the other staff get them too. "Do your parents work here?"

"They sure do." A slow, totally hot smile spreads across his face. I *so* want to draw it. It's just that fascinating and different.

It's like I can actually *see* him letting down his guard,

and I get that feeling of relief that comes from knowing the other person you're talking to has decided you're cool.

Okay, he's not David Anderson. But he's growing on me. Definitely.

"Cool." I wave for him to sit down. "You like it here?"

He walks around and takes a seat. He doesn't flop like most guys would. Even though he looks completely relaxed, he sits properly, without putting his feet on the chair or anything, unlike me. Dad would love this guy. Which also makes me think maybe Dad's right and I'm going to have to spruce up my etiquette skills before anyone else here sees me.

I'm also guessing now that Georg's maybe a year or so older than me. Don't know why, there's just something about him. Confidence, maybe? And his English is fantastic. Better than my French, and I really work hard at it. "I like it well enough, but it's my home country, so I'm biased. What do you think so far?"

I shrug, but not the leave-me-alone-already shrug I give my parents. This one's more polite. "I've only been here since ten a.m. Not much time to get a real impression."

"That's diplomatic. You can be honest."

I know I just met this guy, but his smile gives me the feeling he's for real. I think this about very, very few people, so I decide to tell the truth. "Well, Schwerinborg is pretty gray. And kind of boring. But I'm willing to give it time." I say this in a jokey-jokey voice, 'cause I don't want to offend him or anything. For all I know, he loves living here.

"It's not this gray all the time. I promise." I can tell from the look in his eyes he's trying to gauge my reaction to what he's saying. I must still be doing all right, because he isn't as formal as when he first walked in and said hello. "It's not going to be like living in the States, though. You're not going to be able to hang out at a mall. Or make fun of the contestants in the Miss Teen USA pageant."

"That's okay. I can't handle pageants, even as a form of amusement, and I'm definitely not the mall type. And if I get really homesick, I can always go to McDonald's."

He grins. "True. I hardly ever get to eat there, but I could nosh on fries all day."

I can't help but laugh. "Did you just say 'nosh'?" It sounds so bizarre, coming out in that accent.

One of his dark eyebrows arches up. "That's not right?"

"It's right. I just wouldn't think it'd be a word you'd use. Your English is amazing."

"I've had to take it since kindergarten. If it's no good now, I'm in trouble." He gestures toward my notebook. "But I could never draw like that. No matter how many classes I had."

Oh, geez. I still have my sketch on my lap. I'm always

careful in class not to let anyone see what I'm doing. Not so much because my teachers will get their panties in a twist about it, but because I don't want my friends telling me I made them look fat or made their lips too big or whatever.

"It's no big deal, really. I'm supposed to be studying—"

"You're very talented." He shifts a little closer on his chair and leans forward for a better look. "Are those friends of yours?"

I nod. I'd shut my notebook, but that seems like it'd be rude at this point.

"Do you draw all your friends?"

"I suppose so. Not intentionally, or anything. My pencil just starts going with whatever's on my mind. So at some point, all my friends and family get sketched."

"I bet they're flattered."

I shake my head. "Are you kidding? They think I make them look awful."

He runs a finger across the top of my notebook, just above Natalie's head, then taps the paper. "If that's awful, then your friends must all look like supermodels. If you ever drew me, I certainly wouldn't complain. I'm sure you'd do a great job."

Is Georg flirting with me? Whoa. Guys do *not* flirt with me. Especially not guys with accents. I mean, that David kiss last week is about the only flirting I've had in my whole freakin' *life*. And it took me *years* to get to that point with David.

"Are you asking?" I say, because even though I'm not sure what he's thinking, I can't help flirting back.

He leans back in the chair and gives me a shrug I take to mean *Why not*?

"Well, grab a book and read," I say. "Or do whatever it is you do when you usually come in here and I'll draw you." I give him a smile I'm sure he thinks is beyond dopey. I have to cover the fact that my hand is shaky.

"All right. I usually come here just to sit in front of the fire. You know, to get away from my parents for a while. But I can find a book. Or we can talk, if you can draw and talk at the same time."

"Um, I can't draw as well if you're watching me back. I have a thing about that." That's a lie, because I usually can. I've listened to my chemistry teacher drone on and on about neutrons and protons and atomic numbers, yet still manage to sketch him standing behind his monster desk and then ace the exam the next day. But Georg is throwing me off. "It might be better if you read."

I start to draw, and I'm about halfway done when he suddenly looks at his watch and says something under his breath in German.

"Have to go?" Maybe I took too long. Or maybe he only

asked me to draw him so he'd have someone to talk to, and me not talking is boring him out of his skull.

"My parents expect me to have dinner with them and I'm late." He looks unhappy about leaving, which makes me feel better. I mean, it's nice when an intriguing guy wants to stay and sit with you. People who look like Christie never appreciate it, because it happens to them all the time. But me, I appreciate it.

"Sorry," I say. "Didn't mean to—"

"If you'd like, I can come at the same time tomorrow. I need something to do. Before my parents find something for me to do. I don't think it's occurred to them that I'm on break yet."

"I hear you. I'm sure I'll be here. My dad's making me study for some exams I have to take before I start school."

He stands up, and I realize that Georg's pretty tall. Probably six feet. I sooo love tall. "I can help you if you need to know anything," he offers. "You'll be in year ten, right?"

"If that's what you call tenth grade."

He grins. "I'm in year eleven, so I had all your teachers last year. Just ask if you have any questions, and I'll give you the dish." When he says "dish," he hesitates, like he's not quite sure that's the right word to use.

I let it slide. "Thanks. That'd be cool."

I look down at the picture in my lap once he's gone. I'll

have no problem finishing it in my room tonight. Georg has a face that's great to draw—really high cheekbones, blue eyes, and fair skin. And he's got this dark, dark hair with just the slightest curl to it. There's a lot I can do with shading when I sketch someone like him. Lots of contrast to play around with.

I pile up all the textbooks, still unopened, and drag myself out of the comfy chair and back toward the so-called apartment. I might not have gotten any studying done, but I feel a lot better. Georg's absolutely delicious, even if he is David's polar opposite, lookswise, and he has a grown-up edge to him that makes me suspect he'd look down on me if he knew the real me—the me who stands behind Wendy's with my buds and sneaks cigarettes, or who stands in the corner at school dances and mocks the cheerleaders with their supertight, belly button–baring tops and over-processed hair. (Okay, I mostly do this because no one ever asks me to dance, so I have nothing else to do. I'll admit it.)

Or the me with a lesbian mother and a father who, while totally straight, knows the proper way to serve beluga caviar and which style wineglass to use for a cabernet versus a white zinfandel.

But I'm happy anyway, because I can tell Georg's going to be a lot more interesting to hang out with than David ever was.

Georg likes my sketches. And he actually *talks* to me, unlike David.

Okay, I take that back. David does talk to me. But it's not like he sets a time and a place when he says, "See you tomorrow." There's a difference.

I can't wait to see if my computer's hooked up so I can tell Christie I won't be totally friendless in Schwerinborg.

Or not.

I'll have to think about it first.

5

To: ChristieT@viennawest.edu

From: Val@realmail.sg.com

Subject: Official Schwerinborg Palace E-mail (HA!)

Hey, Christie!

Told you it wasn't like you'd never talk to me again. Less than 24 hours and here I am in your face already.

So here's the latest: I really am living in a palace. Not the fairy-tale kind with turrets—this one's more like a big mansion. There are lots of paintings of old men on the walls in the main part of the palace, and each and every one of these guys looks constipated. You'd think they'd get more fiber. Or, assuming they didn't have Metamucil handy, that the artists wouldn't immortalize them in oils looking so pained (and no saying that I make *you* look constipated, okay? I so *don't*.).

What really rots, though, is that my room feels like it's in Antarctica instead of Schwerinborg. You'd think that royalty could afford heat, but Dad tells me that European palaces constructed in the 1700s have their limitations.

The government offices—in a different part of the palace, next to where Prince Manfred lives—were done over a few years ago and are all beautiful and modern on the inside. Those rooms have heat. Of course.

That's it for now—I want to make sure this gets through before I type any more. If it does, you HAVE to tell me how things went last night at David's Christmas party. Did David actually get booze like Jeremy said he would? Did you drink anything? I just know I'd chicken out. I mean, how'd you get back in your house? My parents would smell alcohol on my breath from a mile away.

And—most important—any south-of-the-border action with Jeremy?

Needless to say, I have not met a single David Anderson look-alike yet, so your dreams of someday double dating with me and the real David are safe. If I have to judge by the looks of the guys who carried our luggage up to our rooms, I'm not expecting Schwerinborg to be Hottie Heaven. But I'll let you know if anything develops.

Val

After firing off my e-mail to Christie, I send slightly blander e-mails to Jules and Natalie, just so they won't feel unloved. I'm exhausted, but I just know that if Christie gets an e-mail tonight and Jules and Natalie don't get any until tomorrow, they'll get all whiny and overanalyze the whole thing, decide I've turned into a total bitch, and then they'll refuse to e-mail me back out of spite.

Of course, it won't even occur to them that they've ignored me for, like, the last *week*.

Sometimes girls suck. Guys would never be this way.

I probably should have told Christie about Georg, but—since, even though I adore her, Christie is a typical girly-girl too and overanalyzes everything—I'm afraid it'll make her think I'm not interested in David. And I still want to hear how, or *if*, David says anything to Jeremy about me being gone, before I say anything about Georg.

Plus, I figure I should wait and see if my first impression of Georg holds up before I announce that I've found a potential friend—maybe even a boyfriend—over here. Telling anyone would be making my expectations official, and I'm not there yet.

I curl up in bed, hug my pillow (a rather flat and hard thing—I may have to add *fluffy pillow* to *hair dryer* on the shopping list), and try to go to sleep. You'd think, given the fact that I've been up for a bazillion hours trying to regulate my body to European time, that I'd crash hard. But I can't. I'm obsessing over David.

I pull my pillow closer and wonder what it'd be like if it were David cuddling with me instead. Would his blond hair feel as soft as it looks when I'm sitting behind him at a football game? Would he hold me tight, with his body fitting right against mine, and tell me that he's loved me from afar for years and been too scared to say so?

I know it's impossible, but late at night, when I'm alone in bed, I can't help but pretend.

As my mind drifts, I find myself wondering what might have happened if I could have gone to David's Christmas party, and if my mom was her old self and I didn't have to give a rat's ass about David's dad and his beliefs. Would David and I have ended up making out in some bedroom or on the back porch, like Jeremy and Christie always do?

Of course, I've never seen south-of-the-border action, like I suspect Christie and Jeremy might have if they got enough privacy after the party ended last night. I haven't even seen *north*-of-the-border action. Christie suspects this, but I haven't told her for sure. Even though the A-listers know I've never had a serious boyfriend, I've tried to be real mysterious about what happens on family vacations or who I might've met when I had to go to summer camp during junior high. I don't want them to think I'm a total loser.

And besides, they're not going to tell me about *their* action if they think I won't get what they're talking about. But how can I get it—or get any, really—if they won't tell me anything? How else am I going to figure it all out so I don't make a complete and total fool of myself when a guy really does get interested?

I fold my pillow in half so it's almost like my pillow at home and close my eyes. But the second I get comfortable, there's a light knock on my door and I hear Dad whisper, "Val? You still awake?"

I take a deep breath and debate turning up the music playing on my clock radio. Finally I just click it off and answer, "Yeah. What's up, Dad?"

He opens the door, and enough light comes in from the living room to make me squint when I look in his direction. I think he's holding my notebook, but it's hard to tell. "Valerie, I'm sorry to wake you up. I hope you don't think this is an invasion of your privacy, but I needed a piece of paper, and—"

He reaches for the light switch, but I wave for him to quit. "Hey! No lights!"

He hesitates, then leans against the door frame. "Did you draw this picture?"

"If it's in that notebook, then yeah, probably. Hold it out in the light and I'll tell you for sure."

He takes a step back into the living room and holds up the notebook, which is open to the page with my half-finished picture of Georg.

"Yeah," I say. "His name's Georg. He came into the library after I went down there to study. He introduced himself and we talked for a while."

"Did he see you drawing this?"

I push myself up on my elbows and shrug. "It was his idea. Why? What's the big deal?"

"What do you know about this young man?"

I can't believe he woke me up for this. Or almost woke me up, at least.

"Geez, Dad, chill. There's nothing to get in a twist about. His parents work here in the palace, so he lives here, like us. We were just hanging out in the library, that's all. I promise. I sat up straight and acted like a good girl and everything."

Dad sucks in a deep breath, and even in the half light streaming in from the living room, I can see his nostrils going in, then out. "Did Georg tell you what his parents do?"

"Does it matter?"

Dad takes a step into my room. "Yes. Because Georg is

Prince Georg, Valerie. Prince Manfred is Georg's father. You didn't know that?"

Um, no, I didn't know that, so I just stare at my dad. I mean, the idea never even occurred to me. For one, that there were *any* kids in the palace, let alone that Prince Manfred might have a son my age—though now that I think about it, Dad did say Manfred had a kid who goes to the American school. Anyway, for two, even if I *had* known, who'd believe a prince would wander into the library and just start talking to me? Or that he'd know my name even before he came in?

I mean, *come on*.

Georg cannot be a prince. Wrong, wrong, wrong. He would have said something, wouldn't he? Especially since, if it *is* true, and he really *is* a prince, then by definition, he is the Coolest Guy in School. Numero uno, supersnob, and guaranteed prom king. And way, way too popular to have been hanging out in the library on the wrong side of the palace with Yours Truly. A guy like that would have made it crystal clear within two seconds of introducing himself that he was in his league, and I was in mine, even if we were now living under the same roof.

Oh, man. I bet he knows William and Harry. *That* William and Harry. He probably hangs with them on his family vacations and they ride horses or play polo or whatever snooty sport rich people play. 'Cause if Georg's a prince, that means he has more money than I could ever hope to count. He goes to all the best parties. He's probably even been to all-night beach parties with ultralean, ultrasexy European supermodels.

I have not been to an all-night party of any kind. Ever. And neither have my boring, just-cool-enough-not-to-get-picked-on friends.

What I *have* done is make a total ass of myself, acting so high and mighty sitting in *his* library. Telling him his country is *gray* and *boring*, while I live in a tiny little part of his father's palace where I eat McChicken on a Formica table and sit on a chair with unbalanced legs.

My dad is going to kill me if he finds out what I said.

At least I didn't tell Georg that most of my friends don't know the difference between Schwerinborg and a smorgasbord. As if I didn't make a big enough idiot of myself to start with.

"You didn't know, did you?" my dad asks again, though he can tell what the answer is from my face, so I don't even bother with the Valerie Shrug.

"I'm glad you met someone your age," he adds in his I'm-your-dad-and-I-love-you voice, which means a *but* is sure to follow. And it did. "But you need to be careful with Georg.

Remember when you were seated at the White House picnic last year with the Carew boys? Same thing applies here."

I roll my eyes. Dad lectured me in the car the whole way to that picnic. I wasn't to talk to the Carew twins—two megaspoiled freshmen who think they're God's gift—about anything personal. As if I would. I can't stand the Carews. Not because of politics, either. They're just revolting as people.

And Dad's lecture didn't matter anyway, because the Carews had no intention of talking to me. In fact, they made a point of ignoring me so I'd *know* I was being ignored. Jerks.

"Dad"—I look him in the eye to make sure he knows he's being ridiculous—"I'm not going to give Georg your credit card number or tell him you smoked pot in college or anything."

"Not only is that not funny, you know it's not true." He turns on the light, but since I'm totally awake now, I don't argue this time. I yank my feet up closer to my body so he can sit on the edge of my bed. When he does, he grabs one of my feet through the covers and wiggles it around, just like he did when I was a kid and I told him there was a dragon in my bed and he had to catch it before it ate my foot.

"Val, it's not that I think you're spilling your guts to a stranger. I know you're good about keeping our family matters private, but I just thought I'd give you a word of warning. That's all. We're new here and Georg's father is my boss. So let's keep our ears and eyes open and learn our way around, all right?"

I nod. I'm a listen-first-speak-second kind of person, anyway.

"Georg's an okay guy though, isn't he?" I ask a few minutes later, after Dad pesters me about whether I got any studying done. Maybe Dad knows something about Georg. He hears all the gossip about politicians, celebrities, and their kids, and he usually even knows which rumors are true.

"As far as I know, Prince Georg's fine. He's supposed to be quite intelligent, and he's never gotten into any kind of trouble that would embarrass his family . . . like smoking cigarettes. Or pot." He says this with a funny look that makes me wonder if he's joking, or if he's really thinking I might be taking the occasional drag at parties since I made the wisecrack about him doing it.

"Well, that's good," I say, not willing to give an inch. I've *never* smoked that stuff and Dad should know it. My grades are too important to me. Besides, I got in enough trouble just getting caught with cigarettes last year. Getting busted with a joint would be something else entirely, especially if I got arrested. Thanks but no thanks.

"I'll leave you alone then," he says, giving my foot one

last squeeze before walking to the door. I burrow back under the covers, but just before he shuts off the light, he turns around. "Valerie?"

"Yeah?"

"You have a lot of talent. I wish you'd shown me your drawings yourself."

"They're okay," I say, but secretly I'm glad he likes them. Dad has taste, and he doesn't give compliments easily.

"Have you ever shown them to your mother?"

"No."

"Oh." He stares at the sketch of Georg, and I realize he thinks this is a real bonding moment. He knows something about me that Mom doesn't.

Then, of course, he ruins it by going and suggesting art lessons.

"Dad—" I shoot him my best warning stare before he gets going about all the access I'll have to great teachers here in Schwerinborg. He should remember that piano lessons killed any and all interest I had in the piano. There's no way I'd do that to my sketches. Even if I never do end up making a career of it, what would I do to get through AP English every day?

"Okay. Just a suggestion." Then his eyes get a mischievous look. "But I bet Georg would be really impressed if you got his chin just right. Art lessons would help."

He walks off before I can hit him in the head with the nearest baseball-sized object, which happens to be my alarm clock. Lucky for him.

He is so not funny.

I'm in the middle of looking over the formula for determining molar volume—which means I'm mostly thinking about how much I hate chemistry—when I finally hear what I've been listening for. Someone at the door to the library.

Refusing to look anxious, I keep right on scribbling down the formula.

I do *not* want Georg to know I've been thinking about him for, oh, the last fifteen hours straight. I bet he gets a lot of that. Like, from every single female in school.

I still can't figure out why he even bothered to say hello to me, let alone ask if he could hang with me in the library again today.

"Fräulein Winslow?"

I jump about a mile. The guy standing behind me is definitely not who I was expecting. He's about fifty years too old to be Georg, and his voice sounds like he's been chain-smoking since he was seven. I wouldn't want my voice to sound like that even if I was a hundred. I make a mental note to limit my emergency smoking to once a year, if that.

"I hope I did not disturb you." The man smiles. He's got gray hair and a potbelly that sticks straight out. He looks more pregnant than fat. But he's wearing a nice suit and he's smiling, so I figure he's okay, even if he did call me a Fräulein and has such a thick accent I can barely understand him. Plus, this section of the palace isn't exactly open to the world. There's a metal detector and a fleet of security guards to get through first.

"No. May I help you?" I ask. Dad would like that I'm being all formal and polite.

"My name is Karl Oberfeld," he says, "but you may call me Karl. Your father mentioned that you are spending today in study, so I thought I might bring you some refreshment—a Coke and some pretzels, perhaps?"

I sit up straighter. "Um, sure. But you don't have to. I mean, I can get my own from my apartment." It still feels weird referring to a group of rooms with motel decor as an *apartment*, but Dad assures me that's what it is.

"It would be my pleasure to bring you a snack from the kitchen." I can tell from his expression that he thinks it's odd that I want to get my food myself, so I tell him okay, I'll take a Coke and pretzels, but to make it a Diet Coke.

Of course, when he walks away, I realize I should have said Coke Light. I sound like such an American. It's kind of embarrassing.

So a few minutes later, when I hear footsteps again, I turn around expecting Karl. Of course, *now* it's Georg. And of course, I'm looking desperate, since the very mention of Diet Coke has made me thirsty.

"How's the studying going?" Georg asks. I just wave at my books with a you-know-how-it-goes flip of my hand. He takes the chair next to me, but seems a little hesitant, as if he's afraid he's interrupting. I have to wonder: Why does everyone always seem to feel uncomfortable here? Like they're *bothering* you just by wanting to talk. Is this a palace thing?

"You don't have to memorize all those for the exams"—he jerks his head toward the formulas scribbled on my notebook page—"they give them to you. They just want to see if you've learned to apply them."

I can't help but groan in total disgust. "You're kidding, right? I've been trying to pound these into my brain all over again."

"You're better off not studying at all, I think." He leans forward as he says this, and there's a cute little twinkle in his eyes, like I'm amusing him. "Though I'm sure my parents would make me study too."

I laugh. He might be a prince, but he's cool. I hadn't thought about it, but I suppose it wouldn't look good for Prince Manfred and Princess Claudia if their only son flunked out of school. It'd probably be all over the *National Enquirer*. Or the *Schwerinborg Enquirer*, if there's such a thing. So much for Georg living a total life of luxury.

"I don't know what it is," I say, "but as soon as I finish an exam, all the formulas I have to memorize for it go right out of my head. I figure that if I get a job in a lab someday, no one's going to care if I open up a book and look up a freaking formula. Besides, since I'd be using them every day, and I wouldn't have to worry about learning stuff for five or six other classes at the same time, I'd memorize them whether I wanted to or not."

"Exactly!" He's giving me that slow, sexy smile again, and it's like we have this scary-weird-cool connection. Then he adds, "Not that I want to be a scientist. I think it'd be about the most boring job in the world. Or, at least, it would be for me," he says, covering, and I can tell he's worried that I'm secretly dreaming of becoming a rocket scientist and he might have offended me. "Is it something you think you'd find interesting?"

"No way!" I laugh again, even though all this giggling is probably making me sound like one of those bimbettes from Christie's favorite TV show. Eeww. I compensate by telling him, "My science grades have always been really good, all As, but there are things I'd rather do with my life."

"Like what?"

I hesitate. Telling him I want to sketch for a living would make me look like I'm too stupid to do anything *real*. Like be a lawyer or an architect or run my own business or something, which is what my parents want and expect. But I just can't get myself psyched up for anything like that. Not yet.

"I'm still thinking about it," I finally say. "Most of my friends' older brothers and sisters seem like they change their minds once they get to college, so I'm trying not to get too focused on any one thing until then."

"So what will you major in?"

"Nothing that has to do with science, that's for sure," I joke. "But I've got two more years to figure it out. You're a junior, though. So what about you?"

Of course, as soon as the question is out of my mouth, I think, *Duh, Valerie!* The dude's got his future all mapped out. He's going to rule a country! He's going to major in economics or political science or something like that, and then he'll work in some government job until his father kicks off.

I am amazed by how stupid I can be sometimes.

Thankfully I am saved by my dear buddy Karl. Apparently Georg saw Karl in the hall and told the old guy what he wanted too, 'cause Karl has a Coke Light for me, a Coke for Georg, and a mondo-sized bowl of pretzels. He also has a few cut-up sandwiches on a tray, which make my tummy start to rumble the minute I see them.

I can get used to service like this.

Karl gives Georg a little bow, then leaves the room. A *bow*. Georg must think, judging from my idiotic question, that I'm a disrespectful smart-ass.

"If I could be anything at all," Georg says, handing me a sandwich on a little plate, "I think I'd be a professional soccer player."

"Really? Do you play a lot?" It occurs to me that it's probably rude to ask, since I'm guessing most Schwerinborgians (if that's what they're called—I'll have to check with Dad—maybe it's *Schwerinborgers* or just *the Borg*, like on *Star Trek*) would automatically know this kind of trivia about their prince. But since this is the way I talk with my friends, and Georg's never actually come out and *told* me he's a prince—and doesn't seem to want me to know, judging from the way he was uncomfortable with Karl bowing to him in front of me—I decide to just be my laid-back, friendly self, and so what if he thinks I'm rude.

Although my laid-back, friendly self was also of the opinion that someone with Georg's background would dream of a sport that involves horses and where he has to wear jodhpurs. Not *soccer*.

"I play indoor soccer all year. And at school I made

varsity on the outdoor team my freshman year." He says it without bragging, simply as a statement of fact. "I had to work pretty hard to do it, though. I was certain I'd get busted back to the JV team after every single game."

"But you weren't, were you?"

He shakes his head between sips of Coke, and his cheeks get pink. It's totally cute.

"Next year, when I'm a senior, I hope I'm the captain. I'd really like to play pro for a year or two before I go to college." He glances up at the fireplace, where there's an oil painting showing a woman who's probably one of his ancestors. She's wearing a high collar and looks just as constipated as all the old guys whose portraits are hanging in the halls. For a minute, I wonder if Georg will ever sit for one and if the artist will be obliged to make him look just as cramped.

He looks away from the picture at the same time I do, then takes another long swig of his Coke. "There's no way my parents will allow it. They want me to go straight through school."

"Mine too," I reply as soon as I swallow my bite of sandwich. I don't know what magic Karl has worked on these things—they're filled with your basic deli turkey, cucumbers, and a sauce I don't recognize—because they're phenomenal. "I never thought of doing anything else, though.

But maybe if I was good at something like soccer, I would."

He doesn't say anything, so I wonder for a minute if he's kind of depressed about the soccer thing. Maybe if I apologize for calling Schwerinborg gray and boring yesterday, it'll remind him of how much he likes living here and cheer him up a little.

But then he'd know I know he's the prince.

I may have to ask Dad about how to handle this point of etiquette, though I don't want to let on to Dad that I get along with Georg so well. Dad will get all jumpy about it, and I don't want to get Georg in trouble either. I get the feeling he hasn't told anyone about his soccer dream. Or at least not his parents, and I don't want Dad to let on to them. Parents talk, as Jules, Natalie, Christie, and I discovered after Jules's mom saw us hanging out with a group of high school boys at the 7-Eleven during our lunch hour when we were all in eighth grade. I didn't get to go to that 7-Eleven again for almost a year, my parents were so sure that I was going to hook up with some older guy who might, in Dad's words, "take advantage of my youth." Right. We never even found out those guys' names.

"So what do you do for fun around here?" I ask. "Besides hang out in the library, I mean."

He gives me a smile that makes my stomach freeze. It's bizzaro—he's not *that* good-looking. At least not classically, every-girl-would-die good-looking. There's an edge to him that takes him out of total hottie contention. Still . . .

Maybe I'm just lonely is all.

"I don't, usually," he says, grabbing another of Karl's sandwiches. "I play soccer, I go to the movies. Stuff like that. But it's vacation time now and my parents both have schedules they couldn't rearrange, so we couldn't go anywhere this year."

"You wouldn't rather hang with your friends?"

One of his eyebrows shoots up. "Who says you're not a friend?"

6

"THANKS." I TRY NOT TO LOOK TAKEN OFF GUARD, but it's kind of cool, being called a friend by a freakin' *prince*. Especially since I can tell he actually means it. At least, I hope he does, because otherwise, I'm pretty much friendless here. It's a pretty safe assumption that if Georg decides he doesn't like me, I'm basically screwed at school. No one's going to want to be buddy-buddy with the girl the prince says is a total reject. And I wouldn't blame them either. *I'd* even ignore me.

"I would guess you have other friends besides me, though," I tell him, mostly to cover my own stupid smiley face reaction to what he said. I don't want Georg to think I'm desperate, because I'm not. Being an only child makes me tough that way, or so I tell myself. "Unless you're, like, a known ax murderer or something, and you're just being nice to lull me into a false sense of security."

He holds his hands over his head, outlaw-style, then leans back in his chair, kicking his long legs closer to me. "You've caught me. I admit it. I'm sure the police will have my . . ." He fumbles for the right phrase for a second before saying, "My mug shot stapled to all the telephone poles soon."

He glances over his shoulder, toward the door, then shoots a casual look at my notebook. "You still have that drawing from yesterday?"

Does he not want his family to know I'm drawing him? Instead of asking him about it, I make a quick resolution to shut the notebook if his parents—or anyone—shows up, just in case.

"Oh, now I get it," I say as I turn to the correct notebook page. "You only want me around long enough to draw a flattering wanted poster for you." Why not tease him like I would a normal friend, I figure, since he doesn't know I know who he really is? "I assume you're asking because you want me to finish?"

"I'd like that a lot. But don't make my head too big."

"I'll draw it like I see it," I retort. He grins, and for the next few minutes, we're quiet. I take my time with shading and getting the angle of his jaw just so. Since this one's on request, as opposed to my usual killing-time-in-homeroom job, I want it to be really good.

And I have to admit, I'm getting a Zen feeling sitting with him, not saying anything and just drawing. I wouldn't have guessed I'd be so comfortable with anyone who thinks in German, no matter how good his English might be. It's relaxing, like when I'm with Christie, Jules, or Natalie. They're the only people who seem to get that it's okay to hang out and not talk sometimes. To just *be*.

At least until I told them I was moving to Schwerinborg.

When I finish and hold up the picture, I can't believe how happy Georg looks. Not goofy happy. Touched happy.

"That's awesome, Valerie." His accent nearly cracks me up. It's like talking to the Terminator or something. But I manage to keep a straight face.

"It's all yours." I rip out the page and hand it to him, but he makes me sign it first.

I cannot believe I am autographing something for *him*. It's just wrong.

"I know you have to take the first placement exams tomorrow," he says, his eyes still focused on the picture. "And I'm going to be busy for a few days after that. I have some, um, family things my parents need me to attend.

But I'll look for you before school starts, okay?"

"That'd be great, Georg." It's surreal, talking to someone who's not only a prince, but is named *Georg*. He really should be Scott or Josh or something. But as surreal as it is, I feel like he's invited me into his world.

Once he's out of the library, though, and I'm by myself with the leftover pretzels and sandwiches, I can't help but wonder how long it'll last. Maybe Georg's parents told him to be nice to me. Or maybe he's just bored to death being stuck at home over break and would rather crash in the library with a geeky sophomore than do nothing at all.

I wonder when the bomb's going to drop. Maybe the first week of school. Will he totally start ignoring me? Will he wake up and realize I'm a geek?

Or worse, is he going to drop little hints to his friends that I'm all in love with him so he can look like he's gotten some action over break? Part of me knows this is ridiculous. I mean, he doesn't set off my bullshit detector at all, and I can detect a bullshitter nine times out of ten. But I've seen more than one guy pull that particular trick, especially in the case of older guys talking about a girl who's a couple years younger, so it's not beyond the realm.

As I leave the library I decide my new mission is to find out more about him. Not so I can replace my David Anderson look-alike mission, but so I don't show up at school and find out that no one—David look-alike or not—will have anything to do with me because Georg really is lulling me into a false sense of security.

At least David never did anything like that.

Still, I'm getting tired of having the things I count on in life ripped away from me. And for whatever pathetic, needy reason, I really, really want to count on Georg. I want to believe in the scary-weird-cool connection thing.

Because what if?

To: Val@realmail.sg.com

From: ChristieT@viennawest.edu

Subject: Hottie Heaven

Hey, Val Pal!

Sorry it's taken me a couple days to get back to you. But you would NOT believe what's happened here. Let's just say that there wasn't even CLOSE-to-the-border action with Jeremy, let alone anything *SOUTH* of the border, because David's parents decided to stay in the house during the Christmas party. We all pretty much sat around watching videos and drinking this dumb fruit punch his mom made. Booorrring.

Aside from the videos, about all we did was talk about you. Get this: David said he looked up the Schwerinborg royal family online, and he found all these pictures of them and their palace! Jeremy and I went with Jules into David's room to look on the computer during the party. Val, I don't care how cold you think it is, or whether there are turrets, it looks like a fairy tale!

And you totally lied when you said that Schwerinborg isn't Hottie Heaven. I mean, have you been able to see Prince Georg yet? Apparently, there's a sixteen- (almost seventeen) year-old prince in Schwerinborg. And he's TOTALLY HOT!!! You'll have to tell me if he looks as good in real life if you actually see him. Wouldn't that be something, to see a real prince? Although Georg is kind of a funny name. Do all people in Schwerinborg have weird names like that? Wasn't that the name of the father in *The Sound of Music*?

Anyway, when I said Georg looked hot, David got all weird and clicked on another picture, one that showed the palace's dining room or something. I think he was jealous! It was sooo cute. No one else picked up on it, not even Jeremy, who you'd think wouldn't want me looking at David so closely. But I swear, it's true. And what was David doing looking up Schwerinborg in the first place if he wasn't interested in you??

My cousins are visiting from Tennessee, so my mom's making us all go to the Smithsonian with them. AND we have to do the White House tour. Y-a-w-n.

I'll e-mail you in a couple days, after they're GONE. But

write me again soon. You're the best friend I've ever had, and I miss you lots!!

Hugs and love, Christie

PS—My mom says if you have a phone number you can give me, that she MIGHT let me call you, but it can only be ten minutes because it's expensive, and only if I'm nice to my cousins. SO GIVE ME YOUR NUMBER!!

I've been sick to my stomach all day. No one told me how hard it is to go to a new school.

You'd think, being fifteen, I'd be past all this first-day-of-school-nervousness crap. I'm so *not*. First, I now realize how incredibly sheltered I've been, attending the same school system since preschool. I mean, living in northern Virginia means we get kids moving in and out every year, because there are so many diplomats, military parents, you name it, who move all the time. It's just the nature of being around D.C. But I've never had to move.

And now I'm realizing just how much it sucks walking into a school with a few hundred high schoolers and not knowing ANYONE.

Well, anyone except Georg. And I haven't seen him in over a week, since right before I had to take my placement exams.

Second, I'm having a major guilt trip over each and every new kid at school I've ever ignored. Images of kid after kid who tried to say hi to me are coming back, and I'm thinking I'm going to lose my lunch of (get this!) sauerbraten and carrot salad every single time I think of another face. It's not that I was mean to anyone. I was always nice and said hello back. I just didn't go out of my way to make sure they had someone to sit next to at lunch.

Which is probably why I spent my lunch hour sitting completely, totally alone. God is getting back at me.

I felt like the world's biggest buttwipe, sitting at a cafeteria table eating sauerbraten—which is beyond gross—while all the kids around me yakked about going skiing in Switzerland or shopping in Paris over their Christmas break. I wasn't about to try to introduce myself—again—and tell them that I got to visit the Louvre once. With my *parents*. It'd be like stamping *L-O-S-E-R* in big red letters right across my forehead.

Or however you spell it in German.

On the other hand, classes aren't as bad as I thought. My desk in Western Civilization, where I'm currently sitting, and sketching, is a bit wobbly. But the teachers really are Americans, like Dad promised. Most of them seem to be younger than my teachers at Vienna West too, maybe in their twenties. And they're all *fun*. I mean, when your Western Civ teacher draws a big picture across the chalkboard showing what a pillory looks like, or talks for fifteen minutes about the various disgusting ways suspected witches were tried in medieval times, it's entertaining in a whacked sort of way. Way more cool than listening to Mrs. Bennett lecture in a monotone about the ramifications of the Emancipation Proclamation.

And actually getting to live where all this stuff took place is making it interesting too. Apparently we're going to get to go on field trips to two different art museums this quarter. And we get to take a bus to a place called Rothenburg, in Germany, to see a museum that's completely dedicated to medieval punishments.

Is that not wild?

Still, I'm really glad this is the last class of the day. I don't know why, since it's only three o'clock, but I'm wiped. All I want to do is go home and check my e-mail. Maybe even try to talk Dad into making some magic with his pots and pans. I'm thinking something fried and fatty and totally unhealthy, since I'm never going to have to worry about the size of my thighs or butt again. Judging from today, I may as well be invisible, so there's no way I'm ever going to have a boyfriend.

When the bell rings, I can't get out fast enough. But the minute my way-too-American-looking shoes hit the cobblestoned street, I feel it.

I'm starting my period.

I usually go gangbusters on my first day, so an instant wave of panic is more than warranted. I find a bench next to the sidewalk, sit down (carefully), and rummage through my backpack, hoping that I still have something stashed in the inside pocket from last semester.

Of course, I don't.

I get up and half run, half walk (so I don't look too anxious as I pass by everyone who's leaving) back into the school. Unfortunately the girls' bathroom is no help either. No machines on the wall. Now what? There's no way I'm going to stick my nose into the group of snotty girls standing just outside the bathroom and ask if I can borrow something. If I do, for the next year it'll be, like, "Oh, yeah, I met Valerie Winslow. She was the girl who asked me for a Tampax her first day of school."

Um, thanks but no thanks.

I'm about to race to the nurse's office—I assume there's a nurse's office, but I don't know, which means I'm going to have to embarrass myself further by asking in the main office—when I see a basket on the shelf next to the mirrors.

I peek inside. Halle-freakin'-lujah. At least one thing is going to go right today.

A few minutes later, I'm back outside. Of course, half the kids are still hanging around the outside doors, and the ones who saw me bolting out of class and not bothering to stop at my locker the first time I left school are looking at me now, probably wondering what I was doing back in the building.

I yank my backpack a little farther up my shoulder, put my head down, and blow past them. I want nothing more than to be out of here. Maybe I'll have some e-mail from the A-listers. Something more about David and him being jealous would suit me just fine right now.

Luckily it's not a real long walk home—to the palace, that is. It only takes about ten or fifteen minutes. But there's also a streetcar stop right by the school, and if I hop on, it's only one stop to get to the palace. Since the streetcar is pulling up and Dad bought me a pass yesterday, I jump on. I punch my ticket in the little yellow machine on board and congratulate myself on figuring out something about Schwerinborg without having Dad tell me.

I quickly realize that this is a mistake, because the second the streetcar starts moving, I wobble, fall onto one of the bench seats, and nearly end up in this old lady's lap.

She's in an all-black dress, and she has on—no, I'm not kidding—knee-high nylons, and you can see the tops of them at the hem of her dress. And her legs are all hairy, too.

She waves me off and says something in German that doesn't sound particularly civil, but I have no idea what. And no idea how to apologize. I make an *I'm so sorry* face as I stand up from the too-narrow space beside her, go to the other side of the car, and grab on to an empty pole.

This shouldn't upset me. But it does.

I can feel tears in my eyes, burning way at the back, and I blink to keep myself calm. I so need Jules and Natalie. They'd have made me laugh with some offhand crack about how the Schwerinborgers need an introduction to Nair. Or Christie, who'd have said something miraculous to the old woman to make it all better.

I sure hope Christie got my e-mail with my phone number, and that her mom lets her call me tonight instead of waiting for the weekend. I'm going to go over the edge if I have to wait until Friday to talk to someone about all this.

I mentally pray that Christie will be extra nice to her Tennessee cousins and that they all have a fabulous time at the Smithsonian. I'm desperate.

Then I hear this voice near me speaking German, but it's familiar. *Way* familiar.

"You okay?" Georg asks in English when I turn around.

"Um, yeah," I manage, wondering if my day could possibly go any further downhill. I know how bad I look when I get into almost-crying mode. Before I can take two seconds and think, I blurt out, "What are you doing here?"

"I saw you getting on the *strassenbahn* and decided to follow you."

"Saw me making a total dork of myself." I give the woman I tripped over a weak smile, but she's just staring at Georg.

"I told her it was an accident, and that you're a very nice person but that you don't speak German."

"Or know how to stand up on a *strassenbahn*," I say, trying out the German word for "streetcar." "But thanks."

I think I'm turning red now.

Georg puts his hand on my lower back, and the feel of his fingers through my clothes makes me freak out inside. "We're here."

I look out the window, and sure enough, we're slowing down alongside a street-level platform. There's a canopy over part of it, and in big black letters it says SCHLOSS, which Georg tells me is the German word for "castle."

Schloss doesn't sound like a castle to me, but seeing as the rear gate to the palace is across the street, I trust him that it doesn't mean "sewage treatment plant," which would've been my guess.

I still can't believe that a prince is on this thing. And from the looks other people are giving him—most are more discreet than the old lady, either peeking from behind newspapers or past grab bars—I'm guessing this isn't the usual way he comes home.

Once we're through the gate and we've climbed up the back stairs into the wing where my apartment is, Georg stops.

"What?" I frown. I'm about to apologize for screwing up on the streetcar, but he crooks his finger at me, then puts it over his lips. I follow him down a long hall, wondering what's with all the James Bond secrecy.

Oh, God. I hope I didn't have an accident. If there's a stain on my rear, and he's about to tell me, I am going to call my mom and go home to Virginia. Tomorrow.

No, tonight. I bet I can at least get to Munich tonight.

"Here," he whispers, then opens a door. I realize that we're on a balcony overlooking a huge reception hall. The floor below us is hardwood, with all these beautiful inlays. Big velvet curtains are hanging from windows that are almost two stories high, ending right below the balcony that circles the room. I feel like I've escaped from a White House tour and stumbled into one of the secured areas.

"We're not supposed to be here, are we?"

"It's all right," he says. "But I wanted to get you alone so we could talk."

I start getting a creepy feeling. But excited, too, because he doesn't look upset or stressed, and I know I sure would be if I had to tell a girl she's been walking around with a big red spot on her pants.

This might even be something fun.

I eye the door we just entered through. "The library's not good enough?"

He shakes his head. "Karl will show up the minute we go in there. Or my father will, if he knows I'm home from school. He'll want me to tell him about my homework, what's due, all that. He keeps a very close eye on my assignments."

"That blows."

He lets out a little puff of air, kind of a half laugh. "Well, that's why I wanted to talk to you."

"About homework?"

"No. About the fact you say things like having my father watching me every second blows. You're . . . you're very normal."

"Thanks, I think." I'd rather he told me I'm hot, or maybe that I'm brilliant. At least that I'm a lot of fun. But I'll settle for normal.

"Trust me, it's a compliment." He drops down into one of the straight-backed chairs along the wall at the back of the balcony, and waves for me to do the same. I set my backpack down between my feet, then take the seat next to him.

"So what's up? You didn't need to talk to me alone about that, did you?"

He turns his head to look at me, and since we're less than an arm's length apart, I think I'm going to fall over. His eyes are just amazing. Not as good as David's—on the sparkly-cool scale, at least. But intense.

Georg takes a deep breath. "Do you know who I am, Valerie?"

"An ax murderer." It just pops out. I know he's trying to be serious, but I need *him* to tell me who he is.

He cracks up. "Would you have followed me in here if you believed that?"

"Not unless I had an ax of my own. And maybe a chainsaw."

He smiles, then props his elbows on his thighs and folds his hands in front of him. For a second he looks away from me and stares at his shoes. I want to tell him that for all his dark hair and serious expressions, he looks nothing like an ax murderer.

Or a prince. I mean, a prince who wears Levi's and rides

the *strassenbahn*? A prince who hangs out with *moi*?

He told me I was normal.

I think I'm neurotic. He's probably the normal one.

I'm about to tell him this when he turns sideways in his chair and touches my hand. "I'm a prince. My dad's Prince Manfred." He looks up from where his hand is touching mine, and my heart stops cold the minute his eyes catch mine. "Did you know that, Valerie?"

Whoa.

"Yeah," I whisper. "I know. But I didn't. Not that evening when we first met in the library. I figured it out later."

"So how come you didn't say anything?"

I shrug, but all I can think about is how warm and strong his fingers are on mine. I wish they weren't. And I wish I didn't have such a thing about a guy's hands. It's distracting.

"I don't know," I finally answer. "You didn't say anything to me about it, so I figured it wasn't my business. That you'd tell me when you wanted to."

"But you didn't treat me any differently. You treated me like I was totally normal, even after you figured out who my parents are."

"Was I supposed to bow or something?" Okay, stop me *now*. He's going to think I'm the most evil, most smart-assed—

And then he kisses me.

Not a big, deep kiss, just a quick, soft kiss. Almost polite, but not quite. I mean, there's definitely more behind it than the David cheek kiss, and not just because this one's on the lips.

And the worst part is, it's over before I can even think about it.

"Um, I guess that's a no," I manage.

"It's definitely a no. I hate when people bow." He gives me this lopsided, embarrassed smile, and for a second I wonder if he's going to kiss me again. This time I'm definitely going to kiss back.

Definitely.

"I'm sorry," he says, and he shakes his head. "I probably shouldn't have done that."

I try not to let my mouth hang open. I'm stunned. Why the hell shouldn't he have done it? Because it's improper or something? Because I'm butt ugly and he had a momentary lapse of judgment?

Or because I totally screwed up the simplest kiss and he doesn't want me to think it's going to happen again, because there's no way on God's green earth his lips will ever come within a mile of my icky ones again?

He lets go of my hand and leans back in his chair, tilting on the rear legs so his shoulders are braced against the wall. "It's just . . . everyone I've ever met treats me differently. People who I know, just *know* in here"—he points to his chest—"don't really like me, but are always nice to me. I hate that. I hate that everyone is fake with me all the time. You're the only person I've ever met who's not."

I'm not sure what to say, so I just sit there looking like a total imbecile until he adds, "I just wanted to make sure you knew who I really am. Before you get to know everyone else at school and you see how they treat me, and then think that's how you have to treat me."

I'm trying to absorb what he's telling me, really. But all I can think about is the fact he kissed me, and what I can say to make him realize it wasn't a mistake.

"Hey, no problem," I say, "as long as all the people around here don't mind that I have no sense of what's proper"—I make a gesture encompassing the palace—"which is kind of funny, when you think about it, since knowing what's proper is my dad's whole job."

Georg laughs and stands up, so I do too. I guess in his mind, the conversation's over. There's this look of relief on his face, and I can actually feel the beat of my heart all the way in my ears.

And then he gives me a hug. It's all warm and tight and

I can feel the muscles of his arms against my back.

Do people still swoon? Or is that considered out? 'Cause I feel a definite swoon coming on.

I start to turn my mouth toward his, but before I can, he says, right into my ear, "Thanks, Valerie. You have no idea how much it means to me that I can be myself with you. I really want us to be good friends."

7

To: Val@realmail.sg.com

From: CoolJule@vlennawest.edu

Subject: YOU

Hey Valerie,

You do know that you are living under the same roof as a prince named GEORG, don't you? And that his parents are named MANFRED and CLAUDIA? How whacked is THAT?!?!

While Claudia is okay, I think that Manfred is probably the stupidest name ever given to a human being. Fred is bad enough, but MAN-fred?? How did this guy survive childhood? If he were my brother, I'd have beat the crap out of him.

Anyway, I just wanted you to know I'm jealous as hell,

because Georg looks like he'd be the best kisser in the universe. Track his gorgeous butt down and tell him I want to find out, okay? You're more than welcome to give him my e-mail address and phone number.

But don't tell him I work at Wendy's.

And write back to me soon. Vienna is the most boring place on the entire planet.

Jules

It takes supreme effort not to hit the delete key and pretend I never received Jules's e-mail, sort of because she apparently has the temporary hots for Georg, but especially because the way she and Natalie acted all pissy my last week in Virginia still has me a little peeved.

But since deleting isn't cool—I mean, she's still on my A list, and I guess I can understand her whole *Four Feathers* attitude, in a backward sort of way—my next urge is to ignore her until I get back from school and can say something intelligent about my new classes or some new friend I (probably won't) make or anything at all that has nothing to do with Georg, let alone how good a kisser he is.

That'd lead to a whole discussion of how awful I am at kissing, since I didn't even kiss him back, and I don't want to go there. I really want to talk to Christie first, but she didn't call and I simply *cannot* e-mail her with my whole Georg saga.

Some things just aren't for e-mail.

I stare at the screen for another minute before I click on the reply button. Since I know Jules always sends her e-mails with a return receipt requested, which means she knows who's opened her stuff and when, I can't blow her off. She'll check her e-mail first thing when she wakes up in the morning, and she'll know I didn't respond right away.

For being as tough as she is, Jules can be a real girly-girl sometimes.

To: CoolJule@viennawest.edu

From: Val@realmail.sg.com

Subject: RE: YOU

Hey, hey, cool Jules!

You have no idea how awesome it was to wake up this morning to some friendly e-mail. Did Christie tell you how gray and boring this place is? It totally outbores Vienna. If it wasn't for Dad being lonely, I'd be home tomorrow. I miss you guys like mad.

And don't say you'd beat up Manfred for his name. One, you beat up your brother all the time, and his name's Mike, which is completely normal. Two, Manfred isn't bad-looking, in an over-forty, dadish sort of way. Plus, I get the sense he wasn't the type of guy who let anyone push him around when he was a kid.

Sorry this is so short, but I have twenty minutes to make it to first period and it takes me fifteen minutes to get to school. More later!

Val

PS—I will not spread it around Schwerinborg that you work at Wendy's. But since I haven't even seen one here yet (sorry, only McDonald's and Burger King), I don't think they'd know what it is anyway.

I feel guilty as I shut off my computer. I've never out-and-out lied to Jules before. I mean, I know I didn't tell her the whole truth about my parents' divorce. I just left out the fact that my mom has a girlfriend. So it wasn't really a lie.

But this time I've *really* lied.

For one, Dad is *not* lonely—he's having a blast here, going to parties and meeting new people who take his mind off Mom. And for two, school doesn't start for over an hour. I just figure that if it sounds like I'm in a hurry, Jules won't notice that I blew off the whole Georg topic. Because I lied to Georg, too.

When he said he wanted to be friends, I told him that'd be *awesome*.

Yep, awesome. Right.

Apparently I'm a terrible liar, even when I don't open my mouth. Just *thinking* a lie is enough. I know this because Georg has obviously figured out that I'm crushing on him. He must have realized it even before I did, which was sometime last night while I was lying in bed, trying to focus on David and what Christie said about him being jealous, but really thinking about Georg.

Otherwise, if he hasn't figured this out, what was with kissing me and *then* giving me that whole "I really want us to be good friends" speech? And what was with him ignoring me on the way to school this morning? He left the palace at the same time I did, but walked about twenty steps ahead of me, acting like he hadn't seen me come out the side door.

I think he did, though.

It really bugs me, because after the whole hugging-just-friends thing, we had a great afternoon. I mean, we hid out in the balcony and talked for hours about what kind of music we like and how his parents have such impossible expectations of him. It turns out he has hardly any *real* friends, because the way things work for security reasons—and kind of for etiquette reasons—is that he always has to be the one to call his friends. They can't call him. And he sometimes wonders if his e-mail's monitored or his phone calls, since he uses the same phone line as his dad. So he just doesn't bother.

We also talked about Virginia, and my friends, and somehow we got going on skiing and snowboarding, and where we'd go on our dream trips. It was completely and totally cool. I had so much fun with him I even forgot about the kissing thing for a while.

Which is why the ignoring-me-on-the-way-to-school thing is messing with my mind. And it's still distracting me when lunch rolls around. There's open campus, but other than a little pizza window across the street and a nearby quickie mart (where all the crackers and premade sandwiches are labeled in German, which makes me suspicious of what's really inside) I don't see too many choices. Everyone is pretty much lingering near the school and doing whatever homework they have due this afternoon and still haven't finished.

Skipping the quickie mart, I backtrack to the cafeteria just long enough to buy a premade sandwich and a bag of chips—since here I can at least ask what's in the sandwich—then go back outside. No way do I want to sit alone at a long cafeteria table again. If I'm going to be alone, I want it less obvious.

Of course, I immediately see Georg out on the quad—the school's shaped like a horseshoe, and the area in the middle's called the quad even though it's not exactly square—and he must have eight other people hanging out with him. Maybe more. They're all so blindingly good-looking I don't think I can watch them without damaging my retinas. He's grinning from ear to ear at this incredibly cute blond girl who's laughing at something he said, and of course he looks hotter than hot.

This is way worse than watching David Anderson and all his superathletic friends. Like, times a billion and one. David didn't talk to me very often, but at least he wouldn't have ignored me by walking ahead of me on the way to school. If he saw me, he'd have waited for me to catch up. He'd have kept right on talking to his jock friends for the most part, but still.

Georg catches my eye, and I almost wave, but he gets this *look*, then turns right back to the blonde, who doesn't even seem to notice the hitch in his conversation.

Then it hits me. He *knows*. He knows I'm into him and he doesn't want anyone to know he even knows who I am, let alone that he kissed me.

He seems so comfortable, chatting away with all his perfectly perfect buds, that all I can think is *Yeah, tell me again how you don't have any friends, Georg. Tell me again how awkward you feel all the time.* He sure doesn't look it—especially since he's all dressed up. Not really fancy—he's wearing jeans—but he's a notch above everyone else. He's got on a soft, blue crewneck sweater under this absolutely stunning black leather coat. It makes him look a lot older than sixteen.

There's not an ounce of doubt in my mind that this guy is going to be prom king when he's a senior. He's so popular, it's probably not even going to be a big deal to him, and I can't trust a guy who thinks that way.

I mean, the guy probably has a *real* crown hooked over his bedpost. And can I really trust a guy who has a crown in his bedroom?

Especially one who only seems to be awkward around ME?

I find an empty bench away from Georg and all his fabulous friends and start rummaging through my backpack, trying to ignore the horrible pressure in my chest that tells me I am falling for the wrong guy. Again. I shove my wallet out of the way and find a half-smashed tampon—of course, a day late—then realize that I still need that tampon. I only have four left at home.

Crap.

I'm going to have to stop at that quickie mart on the way home and hope they stock girly products with English labels or some kind of picture, so I don't accidentally buy Depends or something equally revolting. I also have to hope that Georg and his friends aren't stopping into the store for the Schwerinborg equivalent of Twizzlers.

I check my wallet to make sure I have enough cash, then realize I'm screwed. All I have is one euro—which isn't enough—and an American twenty-dollar bill. Since the cafeteria takes a swipe card that deducts from Dad's bank account, I hadn't thought to ask him for any euros other than what I needed for the Coke machine in the Munich airport.

This is bad. Very bad. And I don't want to ask Dad to buy me tampons. That'd just be wrong.

"Hi. It's Valerie, isn't it?"

I bury the tampon under a couple of books in my backpack and smile in the direction of the feminine voice. The quad's pretty crowded, but there are three girls looking at me. I think the blond one spoke—I introduced myself to her in chemistry yesterday. "Hi. Yeah, it's Valerie. You're Ulrike, right?"

She nods, and the look on her face isn't openly hostile or anything, so I figure I'm okay. Ulrike is one of those girls I'm always suspicious of based on looks alone, though Christie tells me this is really shallow. Ulrike's about five-foot-seven, and has this white-blond hair that looks shimmery, even today with the misty weather and nothing but the gray high school building and the snowy Alps behind her. In the sunshine, you just know she's stunning.

"I heard you live at the palace?" she says, still smiling at me.

"Yeah, my dad works for Prince Manfred."

"So you must know Georg?" Another one of the girls jumps in without bothering to introduce herself. She's a teeny tiny brunette, and totally pretty. Of course.

"We've talked a couple times." I drop my backpack onto the bench beside me and make a point not to look across the quad toward Georg. I'm not sure why, but all of a sudden my bullshit detector's blaring, and it's warning me to keep things low-key. "But I just moved here a couple weeks ago, so I really don't know anyone yet."

"Well, now you know us," Ulrike smiles, though the girl who asked if I know Georg doesn't seem all that thrilled about Ulrike talking to me.

They—well, mostly Ulrike—invite me to eat lunch with them, so I do, even though it's more like they're eating with me, since I was the one who snagged the bench in the first place. I wonder if I'm in their spot or something.

Ulrike's okay, I decide after a few minutes. Just from listening to her talk, I can tell she's fairly popular. She's into sports and apparently she's on student council. Her dad's some kind of diplomat from Germany. The third girl, Maya, moved here from New York when she was six for her mom's international banking job. She's a junior, but she and Ulrike live next door to each other and play soccer together, so they hang out a lot.

I keep glancing at the brunette who asked me about Georg, hoping she'll introduce herself. Ulrike finally does it for her: Her name's Steffi, and of course Ulrike says all kinds of nice things about her, including the fact that Steffi's vice president of the sophomore class—excuse me, of *year ten*—and was elected to homecoming court last year *and* this year. I tell Steffi I'm glad to meet her (hey, Dad raised me to be well mannered) and that it's cool she's on student council with Ulrike. Of course, the whole time Steffi just sits there eating her tuna on wheat like what Ulrike's saying is no big thing. Then, when I compliment Steffi on this funky hair clip she's wearing, she only shrugs. Not an embarrassed-to-be-complimented shrug, but a shrug that makes it clear she thinks she's entitled to a compliment or two.

I hate her already.

Finally the warning bell rings. I wad up my trash and Steffi does the same. Then she hesitates and looks up. I think she's actually going to speak to me.

I should have known better.

"Hey, Georg," she says with a megawatt grin plastered all over her face. I turn around, and of course there he is. He's intentionally not looking at me as he gives us a group hello.

Do I have a big, fat letter *L* stamped on my forehead, or what?

Georg asks Maya how much homework got assigned in French IV today, since he's heading there next. While Maya flips through a blue notebook looking for the assignment, I start to tell Georg what it is, since I had French IV with the same teacher right before lunch.

This is the moment Steffi finally deigns to speak to me. "Oh, Valerie," she says in this repellent whisper that's totally meant to be heard, "did you ever solve your little problem yesterday? I saw you headed into the first-floor bathroom after school, and you looked desperate!"

I want to smack her. She is evil, evil, evil. And was she freakin' *following* me or something?

Georg swallows and looks uncomfortable, though his eyes are totally focused on Maya, which means he heard Steffi but is pretending he didn't. When Maya finally finds the right page in her notebook and tells him the assignment, he scribbles it down, then heads to class, with Steffi right at his elbow, because of course her Spanish III class is right next door to French IV.

He doesn't even look at me.

And naturally Steffi never notices that I didn't answer her. Bitch.

The whole way home—I take the *strassenbahn* again, just because I know Georg is still in the school building and can't cross the quad fast enough to jump on the same one—I'm thinking I should e-mail Jules and tell her that to date, my Armor Girl theory is dead on. It's even correct on an international scale, because I am beginning to suspect that Steffi is going to play the role of Shallow Princess to my Armor Girl.

Here's the evidence:

1) Georg liked talking to me over break, when no one else was around. This clearly makes me a safety girl, like the Armor Girl—someone who makes you smile during those trying times when there are no Shallow Princesses around to kiss up to you.

2) I drew a flattering picture of Georg. Armor Girl made Heath some cool armor. Both of us do nice things without expecting anything in return.

3) In public, the hero walks off with the Shallow Princess and totally forgets about the Armor Girl.

I try to think of a number four, but I can't. Truth is, when I push the analogy, it doesn't work.

Heath never kissed the Armor Girl and gave her the let's-be-friends speech. He never acted like he liked her that way at all. Maybe that part of the movie ended up on the cutting-room floor, I don't know. But my gut tells me—despite what happened at lunch today, and despite the fact Georg didn't walk to school with me—that he really is a nice guy. He can't possibly be the type who would kiss an Armor Girl and forget all about it.

And it's not like he told me he's into Shallow Princess Steffi. Heath told Armor Girl flat out that he wanted the Shallow Princess, and he wanted her bad. He even had Armor Girl help him *get* Shallow Princess, and Armor Girl cheered when Heath kissed Shallow Princess. I even think she meant it.

If I saw Georg kiss Steffi, I'd hurl.

Okay, I am thinking about all this way, way too much.

And I'm getting tempted to call Mom and tell her I want to come live with her. Gabrielle, Lake Braddock, tofu dinners, and all.

When I get back to our apartment, Dad's already there. It's only three thirty and he's supposed to be working, so I give him a little grin, even though I feel less than cheerful.

"Now that's not a happy smile." He stops messing

around in the kitchen and frowns at me. "Bad day at school?"

Geez, is every thought I have that obvious?

"Nah." I drop my backpack onto the table, then open the fridge and grab a Coke Light. "Nothing some caffeine and a bowl of chocolate ice cream can't fix."

Dad reaches past me and puts his hand on the freezer door to hold it shut. "I promised your mother that you'd eat healthy foods. I picked up some fresh tilapia fillets this morning, and I'll make some vegetables to go with it. Get a few vitamins into your diet."

"Just give me a carrot to go with my ice cream," I retort, picking up a minicarrot from the pile of veggies he's already chopped into a bowl on the counter. He shakes his head, but moves away from the freezer and starts slicing an oversize yellow squash.

I take a sip of soda, then grab another carrot. "Besides, how's Mom going to know what I'm eating?"

"Maybe when you write her back?"

I freeze with the carrot halfway to my mouth. "Mom wrote me? An actual letter?"

He tips his head toward the Formica table. "It's under the Walmart circular."

"Why did she send a Walmart circular?"

"She didn't. It came in the regular mail."

"They have *Walmart* in *Schwerinborg*?"

"It's everywhere." He laughs to himself as he covers the bowl of veggies with plastic wrap. "So if there's anything you need, remind me and we'll go this weekend. But I'll warn you, their products aren't quite like what you'd find at home. They carry mostly European brand names."

I flip past the Walmart ad—despite Dad's offer to go shopping, I have zero interest in taking him shopping for feminine products, which is all I need, since he bought me a new pillow and a hair dryer already—and see a large, padded manila envelope plastered with U.S. stamps. Mom's neat, rounded handwriting across the front gives me an instant wave of homesickness, as if I wasn't missing Virginia enough after the little episode with Steffi and Georg on the quad today.

"The fish needs to marinate," Dad says as he slides the veggies into the fridge, ready to sauté later. "I'm going to run out to handle a few things for Prince Manfred, so why don't we meet back here at five thirty for dinner?"

Did I mention how cool my dad can be? You'd think he'd be acting like Jules's mom did when her parents got divorced, asking Jules every five seconds what her father said about her. But even though I know he's curious (otherwise, how would he remember exactly where in the stack of mail he'd placed Mom's letter?) Dad's clearly going to give me some space.

I tell him that'll be fine, and once he's out the door, I rip the envelope open. A flat package, wrapped in pink paper with a silver ribbon, falls out onto the table. I resist the urge to tear into it and read the letter first, because I know Mom would want me to.

Dear Valerie,

I hope you're getting settled. I hate that you're so far away! I think about you every day, you know. I miss my baby girl.

Here, I'm getting moved into my new apartment. I'm also getting ready to look for a job. I don't have to do too much to get my teaching certification updated, so I'll soon be interviewing for elementary school positions for the fall. Wish me luck!

Gabrielle has agreed to be a leader for Weight Watchers and she's going through training now, which means that I'm alone at home a lot of nights. So if you're up late, you can call me anytime—you won't be bothering Gabrielle. And if you're feeling uncomfortable there, or school isn't going as you hoped, you know you always have a place to live with me. In the meantime, if you have a rough day, I've tucked in a little gift I hope will help you through.

I guess that's about it. I'm scheduled to get my Internet hookup next week, so I'll start e-mailing then.

By the time you get this, I may be online, so check your computer!

Until then, please know that I'm thinking of you and your dad. I want you both to be happy, despite what you may think.

Lots and lots of love,

Mom

I put the letter down, then flop into the wobbly chair. I can't decide whether to open the gift or to peruse the Walmart circular while I clear my brain.

I feel tears coming, but I grind my fists against my eye sockets for a minute to force them back. I'm not sure if I'm mad or depressed or what. All I know is that my life is royally jacked, and there's not a gift in the world short of a time machine that can fix it. And I'm not sure even that will help, since Mom seems to think she should have come out of the closet ten years ago. If I traveled back much farther than that to try to fix things, I wouldn't even have been born.

It's the kind of thing that only Captain Kirk or Jean Luc Picard would know how to fix. I don't belong here. Mom doesn't belong with Gabrielle, and she definitely shouldn't be teaching a bunch of elementary school kids. She taught fifth grade before she married Dad, but she swore up and down she'd never do it again. She said it drove her insane.

She obviously thinks insanity is preferable to being married to Dad.

I reread the letter, trying to convince myself that Mom really does love me, and that on the inside she's the same person who took me to the beauty salon before homecoming and picked out a cherry red nail polish for Christie and a deep purple for me. Finally I slide it back into the envelope and open the gift. I'm not expecting much, but because it's the first really heartfelt gesture Mom's made since moving out, I figure it's worth a look.

And then I decide it's not. I missed my guess with Dad and the Chicken Soup book. Instead it's Mom with a book telling me not to sweat the small stuff.

She thinks my problems constitute *small stuff*? On which freakin' planet, exactly, was she spawned?

Still, I open the book and flip to a random page in the back, which tells me I'm supposed to notice when my parents are doing things right. O-kay. Well, there's Dad and the fact he wants me to eat healthy and to be happy. That's good.

I turn toward the front of the book, because I can't come up with anything about Mom. She says she wants me to be happy, but . . .

Maybe if I start closer to the beginning of the book I can work my way up to appreciating Mom.

As I go back to chapter 1, a page in the middle catches my eye. I stop and read about the importance of creating my own special space.

I look around the apartment. Ugly furniture and a bad view cannot possibly be the criteria needed for a special space.

Without thinking about it, I take the book and the envelope and head for the library.

8

MY SPECIAL PLACE TURNS OUT TO BE NOT-SO-SPECIAL. Or at least, not special in the sense that I'm the only one who gets to hang out here. Because, wouldn't you know, within ten minutes of me flopping in the chair and burrowing way down—mostly so Karl can't see me from the hallway and decide to come in and offer me pretzels—Georg walks right up to the chair to see if I'm in it.

And he says he's been looking for me.

He starts to sit in the chair beside me, clearly not taking the hint that I'm scrunched up all small into this honking big chair because I want to be alone. But then he sees my not-so-welcoming face and hesitates. My face is hot from crying so I'm willing to bet it looks all blotchy and red—which is pretty scary.

"Hey, you've been crying."

Duh. "Oh, no," I lie. Why not, now that I'm getting in the habit? "It's just allergies."

"Of course. Everyone has bad allergy problems in January." He frowns, then looks down at the letter in my hand. "So what's that?"

I give him the Valerie Shrug. Okay, so I've been crying. I know I'm not a good liar. But I figure it might give him a clue. Apparently not.

"Look," I tell him, "you know how you hate that people treat you differently because you're a prince? They see the castle or your expensive clothes and make certain assumptions?" Or so he says—about hating the attention, that is. It's totally obvious at school that people treat him differently.

"Yeah?"

"Well, people aren't always what you see."

"Meaning?"

"Just because I've been crying doesn't mean I'm trying to get your attention. A lot of girls pull that crap, and if you want to know the truth, it pisses me off. So what you see isn't what you think it is. You don't need to hang out in here because you think I need some attention. I'm just fine all by myself."

He shoves his hands into the front pockets of his Levi's and leans forward so his chest is against the back of the empty chair. The expression on his face goes flat, then he looks right into my eyes, and I know before he says a word that I've gone too far.

"And just because I came in here to ask what happened doesn't mean I think that you're trying to get my attention. And if you want to know the truth"—his mouth curls up at the edges as he parrots my words—"I thought things sucked at lunch today, so I wanted to come down here and talk to you about what happened and apologize."

"You didn't bother trying to talk to me about it at school. You saw me standing by my locker after last period." Not when all his friends were around. Why be nice to the new girl?

"You didn't look like you wanted to be bothered. I assume this all has something to do with yesterday, when we were hanging out in the balcony, which is another reason I didn't bring it up at school. It's nobody else's business."

Okay, I'll give him that. I did turn away from him and his snobby-looking clique to find my own bench when we were on the quad today, though he looked away from me first.

But the *real* truth is that my current runny-nose-scuzzy-crying-face isn't even about him.

"Well, you're right when you say school was rotten today." I try not to sniffle, and I wish I'd been smart enough to tuck a tissue in my pocket. "But I'm dealing with some other stuff and that's why I'm all whacked out right now. It's nothing major or anything, I just have to get past being hyper about the small stuff."

Okay, so I did start reading the book from Mom. And now I'm trying to convince myself that in the grand scheme of life, my parents getting a divorce *is* small stuff. I mean, look at Jules's parents. They got divorced when we were all third graders—well, her mom got divorced a second time after that to remarry Jules's dad—but it all seems like it happened eons ago. Jules is still the same Jules she was before. A little more sarcastic, maybe, but we all knew by the end of our first playdate as little kids that Jules was going to grow up with a major mouth. That's just how she's wired.

Third grade was exactly seven years ago. So I figure that by the time I'm legal drinking age, this won't be a big deal. It'll seem just as distant as Jules's parents' divorce. Small stuff, right?

I mean, I'm only in a library in a freakin' royal palace thousands and thousands of miles from the three best friends I've ever had, I've lost out on possibly becoming the girlfriend of a guy I've been mad about from the moment I first laid eyes on him in kindergarten when we were put in charge of feeding the class rabbit together, and my mother is living with a vegan blond weirdo who attributes her entire life philosophy to Weight Watchers.

Small stuff. Little itty bitty infinitesimal tiny stuff.

Georg comes around and sits in the chair beside mine, though he's moving slowly, like he thinks I'll fling myself at him in a jealous-over-Steffi rage at any moment for ignoring me at lunch. Or maybe he's worried I'll emotionally vomit all over him because I'm just having such a horrid day. (This is a no-no according to the very first page of the small stuff book. It says you shouldn't vomit all over your friends by taking every ounce of your messed-up emotions and dumping them in your friends' laps. I can relate, since I'm usually the one on the receiving end of such vomit.)

"Is the letter from your mom?"

I nod. I'm too worn out to dodge him. And you know, those intense billboard model–like gazes of his are getting to me.

"My dad told me your parents are in the middle of a divorce." He shifts in his chair, and it's obvious he's not comfortable talking about this, but he's making the effort.

"Did your dad tell you why?"

He nods.

"Well, then you know everything."

"You mad at your mom?" He nods toward the letter again.

I am not going to commit emotional vomit. I'm not.

"A little," I say. "I mean, I'm the teenager and she's the adult. I'm the one who's supposed to be figuring out what I want in life, not her. She had it all. And the whole thing just makes me mad at myself."

Georg is kind enough not to agree. "At yourself? What'd you do?"

"I'm just being shallow about it, is all. I need to get over it. I'm just not getting over it as fast as I should, and that's pissing me off."

"I think it'd be hard for anyone to handle, so I don't see how you're being shallow."

"Well, first, I'm not trusting my mom as much as I should. We've always been really tight, and it's hard for me now."

"That's understandable."

"Yeah, but it's shallow. I should be more supportive, but I'm not. I just totally react against it. Like, how about this: Sometimes when I look at you, I think *Gay*-org, instead of *Georg*, and it automatically gives me the willies?"

He puffs out a breath in surprise. "Wow. That's bad."

"That's what I mean. I'm being shallow about it, and it's pissing me off that I'm acting this way."

Okay, I cannot believe I just blurted out the whole Gay-org thing. Despite what I just said, it hasn't occurred to me since the first day I met him. I've gotten used to Georg being Georg. His name doesn't sound odd to me anymore.

It actually sounds kind of sexy and exotic. Of course, that could just be his accent affecting me.

Maybe I told him because I felt guilty.

"So take it one step at a time," he says. "If Georg bugs you so much—which I totally get—you can just call me Jack. My middle name is Jacques, after my French grandfather."

I'm stunned. I know I'm about as shallow as a person can be, but I didn't want *him* to do anything about it. Like tell me to call him something else. This is my problem.

"I'm *not* going to call you Jack," I tell him. "That'd just be wrong."

He holds up his hands as if to say, *Whatever*.

"Look, I really appreciate it. But I'll call you Georg. And I'll eventually get over the whole thing. Honestly, Georg is a perfectly cool name. And I'm not really *that* shallow." At least, I hope I'm not. I never thought so before.

"And I'm not either," he says, his voice dead serious.

I set Mom's letter facedown on the end table and frown. "You think I think you're shallow?"

"Well, I was an ass today at school. I saw you leaving this morning and walked ahead. And then I tried not to look at you at lunch."

"Why?"

He screws up his mouth in this way that's totally cute, despite the fact I so *don't* want to find him cute right now. "I don't know. Maybe because I can't help but spend all my time worrying about what everyone thinks. I don't want to make anyone angry, and if I show the slightest interest in you, people will start with the gossip, and someone's bound to get ticked off. It's been this way since I was a little kid, and I'm not getting any better at it. I try to be nice to everyone, but because I'm a prince, people think they know me. And they all want something from me. If I don't give it to them, then they do things like Steffi did today."

"So you did hear her." I mock Steffi's drama queen fakey whisper as I say it.

"Who didn't? Word of warning—" His eyes sharpen for a split second. "I can be honest here, right?"

"You can with me. I don't want anything from you." Well, maybe I do, if we're being honest here. But I'd want it whether or not he was a prince.

"Steffi's a bitch. Ulrike and Maya are all right, for the most part, but watch out for Steffi. It sounds like I'm on a total ego trip to say so, but she kind of has a thing for me."

Wow. Georg called someone a bitch and did it with perfect posture. He really is getting relaxed around me. And of course, this is driving me insane.

I mean, how do I get over it? He's beyond out of my league. And he said flat out he wanted to be my friend. Nothing else.

"What she did to you today is typical," Georg explains. "I was hoping that if I acted like you didn't exist, she wouldn't think we knew each other and wouldn't pay any attention to you. As nasty as that sounds, trust me, with her it's better not to exist." He looks apologetic as he adds, "But I shouldn't have ignored you. I mean, I might have deflected Steffi a little, but it was still wrong. I'm sorry."

I manage to keep from grinning at his totally whacked pronunciation of *deflected*, and tell him apology accepted, but totally unnecessary.

Which is a lie, too, because I'm glad he apologized.

He kicks his foot out and toys with the leg of my chair. "Look, you're worried about what people will think of you because of your mom. Which is why you never said anything to me about her, right?"

I swallow hard. Damn, but he just cuts to the guts of it. "I never even told my friends in Virginia. I only told them my parents were getting a divorce. No details."

"What if I told you I understand because I do the same thing every single day?"

I just raise my eyebrows. I mean, come on. His parents are about as perfect as you get.

"Did you see the guy in the black leather jacket walking between you and me on the sidewalk this morning? He was carrying coffee, looked like he was headed to work?"

I think for a minute, then nod. "Blond guy."

"He works for *Majesty* magazine. He follows me at least once a week. Usually more."

I can't even respond. I mean, sheesh! No wonder Georg was acting all bizarre and looking over his shoulder while he walked. It didn't have anything to do with me at all.

"I fake my way through school just so I can avoid dealing with people like Steffi, then I hide out at home," he explains, looking more and more frustrated as he talks. "But when I'm home, I'm not completely happy either. I've got my dad on my case about my responsibility to get good grades and to be more mature than most kids my age, because otherwise no one will have faith in me as a leader. And my dad's always showing me tabloid articles about him, or about my mom, and telling me how the slightest thing can get taken the wrong way, so I need to be on my guard all the time."

He looks so serious, and his face is so caring, I believe him. I really do.

"So I guess it's not just a life of going to polo parties or getting any girl you want, huh?"

He snorts. "I've never ridden a horse in my life. And if I did, I'd probably fall off, and the whole world would get it in full color in the tabloids or in one of those royalty magazines. Can't you just see it, a big picture of me with mud and horse manure all over my face?"

"Ouch," I say. Guess I never realized before that he would so get the whole who-my-parents-are-is-ruining-my-life thing.

"And," he adds, leaning forward a little, "I don't get any girl I want."

I roll my eyes and laugh. "Okay, you had me with your life-isn't-always-fun-for-a-prince shtick, but I have to tell you, I don't believe the girl part of it. You're lucky they don't rip your designer clothes right off your body in the middle of the quad."

He cocks his head sideways. "Would *you* go out with me, after the way I treated you at school today? Or what happened in the balcony yesterday?"

I'm about to make a sarcastic reply—I can't help it, it's what I do—but then I realize he's serious. *Completely* serious.

How did *that* happen? Especially when I look like absolute hell?

"Let's make a deal. You talk to your mom, get your

feelings out on the table, try to give her a break," he says. "I think it'll make you feel better, because in your gut, it's what you really want to do. It's what you'd do if you weren't worrying about what everyone will think."

I'm about to protest, but he says, "And I'll do the same. You get honest with your mom, and I'll be honest with you. I'd rather not be just friends."

I think I'm going to hurl. In a good way though. I mean, he just made my stomach do the best kind of twist.

Whoa.

He scoots forward in his chair, and he's sitting so close I can reach out and touch him and make it look like a total accident if I want.

"Meaning?" I don't think I can breathe waiting for him to say something.

"Meaning I kind of flipped out yesterday when we got to the balcony. I was afraid maybe I offended you or I moved too fast . . . I don't know. I didn't even really plan to kiss you yesterday, I just did. And then, after having such a cool afternoon with you, I was a total jerk this morning. I got all hung up on the reporter and Steffi. I just did what I wanted and kind of forgot everyone else. Including you." He does that funky raising-one-eyebrow thing. "So you see, you're not the only one who's shallow."

"I guess that's a good thing," I say, and even though it all seems surreal, I want him to kiss me again. Especially since yesterday I screwed up kissing him back. Maybe this time I'll get it right.

His foot bumps against mine, and he doesn't pull it back. "So does that mean you'd consider going out with me? Since we're both so shallow and everything?"

"As long as we don't double with Steffi." I know. I know. I can't be serious even when it's important. Christie tells me not to get goofy when I'm nervous, but I do anyway. I'm going to have to work on that.

Later, though, because Georg actually laughs at that one.

"Well, I have this thing to go to tomorrow night. I know it's last minute to ask, but I was hoping my parents wouldn't make me go."

"It sounds like fun already," I tease him.

"Well, I thought it might be if you come. It's this dinner and dancing thing. It's in the reception hall—the room below where we were in the balcony. There's a summit on global warming tomorrow in Zurich, and the British prime minister is going to be there. Afterward he's coming here to meet with my dad. So they're doing a banquet dinner, and then there's going to be a ball before the P.M. flies back to London in the morning."

As he's describing who's coming and what the whole evening's about, I start getting concerned that my eyes might pop right out of my skull. This is way, way out of my league. It's my dad's kind of thing.

Dad's probably coaching staff members on what to say and do at this exact moment.

"So?" he asks.

I take a deep breath. "Well, I was kind of expecting you to ask if I wanted to go to McDonald's or catch a movie. Having dinner with a prime minister—not to mention *your parents*—is kind of a big first date."

I hope I don't sound like I'm rejecting him, because I'm actually as psyched about this as I am scared to death. "And my dad is probably going to be there too. Wouldn't that be kind of weird?"

"Maybe we can sneak out after dinner, then."

I can't help but smile at him. "We'd probably get in trouble."

"Nah. I'd just say I was showing you the way to the ladies' room or giving you a palace tour or something."

"I've already had a palace tour."

The grin on his face is downright wicked. "So I offered and you thought it would be rude not to accept."

This is going to get me in trouble, but I could definitely eat this guy alive. I love that he wants to do something risky, and that he wants me to do it with him. "Okay. Then I accept."

I smile, and inside, I hope he's going to kiss me, because he's smiling too, as big as if he just kicked the winning goal in the final two seconds of a championship soccer match. But no. He starts talking about when and where we can meet up beforehand, then he ducks out of the library so he won't be late to dinner.

When I'm alone again, I pick up the book and the letter from my mom to take them back to the apartment. I hope I don't look too blotchy, or Dad's going to think that Mom's letter really messed me up. I sit down for a second to get my head on straight, and suddenly I realize that what I thought was my special place might be *our* special place. Mine and Georg's.

And I'm completely cool with that.

To: Val@realmail.sg.com

From: ChristieT@viennawest.edu

Subject: CALL!!

Val,

You are NOT going to believe this. Natalie got her TONGUE PIERCED yesterday!!! She didn't tell us or even take any of us with her. Can you believe it?

Anyway, my mom said I can call you tomorrow night! Will you be there? It would be right after school for me, about nine at night for you. Let me know. I have all kinds of good dirt for you. Trust me, it's important stuff that you MUST hear, and it has nothing to do with my cousins' visit.

I just couldn't wait to tell you about Natalie, though. Her parents haven't seen it yet (though the way she's moaning and groaning about how it hurts and refusing to eat, you'd think they'd notice).

If they grounded her for a week for Girl Scouts, you just know she's in for it big-time now. I'll let you know what happens. Cannot WAIT to talk to you! Big, big news.

Love, Christie :)

To: ChristieT@viennawest.edu
From: Val@realmail.sg.com
Subject: RE: CALL!!

Christie,

AACK!! You are going to kill me twelve times over. I won't be here tomorrow night!! Any chance you can call tonight (if you get this in time) or day after tomorrow?

I'm DYING to talk to you, and I have a lot of dirt too. You're not going to believe it. Seriously, this is more unbelievable than Natalie's piercing or whatever else it is you have to tell me.

I miss you!!

Val

PS—You do know that Natalie has a tattoo already, right? If you didn't already know, though, I didn't tell you. She has a little heart by her shoulder blade. Her parents DEFINITELY haven't seen it. That's why she "forgot" to pack a swimsuit when her family went to Florida last year.

PPS—I DID NOT TELL YOU, get it?! Pretend to see it yourself next time she's trying on clothes at your place.

To: Val@realmail.sg.com

From: CoolJule@viennawest.edu

Subject: Are you INSANE?

Val,

What do you mean, I beat up my brother all the time even though his name is Mike, which is normal?

It's so not normal. Think about it.

Okay . . . did you think about it?

His name is MICHAEL JACKSON, you freak.

So yes, I would have beat up Manfred for his name. Please. Give me some credit.

Jules

PS—When are you going to write to me about something important? Like that prince you live with and what he said when you gave him my phone number?

I am going on a date with Georg.

I am going on a date with Georg Jacques von Ederhollern of Schwerinborg.

I am going on a date with the guy who has the strangest name in the world and I'm completely and totally okay with that, because I'm learning not to sweat the small stuff.

I am going on a date with a guy who is laid back and easy to talk to and who can see through people like Steffi the same way I can.

I am going on a date with a freakin' prince! Tomorrow!

This is too much. I have to tell Christie about it. About everything. I mean, who has their first date with the British prime minister at the table?

Since with the time difference I know Christie's still at school, I flop in the living room after dinner, half watching the end of a German-dubbed John Wayne movie, half freaking out over how strange my life has become.

And then I tell Dad.

I have to. I mean, he's in charge of protocol. You think he wouldn't find out I have a date with Georg?

He is currently sitting next to me on our not-so-comfy couch trying to absorb it all, and muttering to himself about all the stuff he wishes he'd thought to teach me about proper decorum. I keep telling him it's not a *real* date, even though in my gut I know it is.

That's what makes it so incredible.

"Look"—I turn to Dad and keep my voice as light and sincere as possible—"I talked to Georg about the whole thing, and he says that there's no receiving line. I can meet his parents beforehand, so it's nothing major, and at the dinner itself I don't have to talk to anyone other than him if I don't want to. So I can just lie low, okay?"

Dad picks up the remote and clicks off the movie that's starting on TV, then presses his fingers to his temples. I want to say more—to explain that I won't embarrass him, or that I didn't keep hanging out with Georg on purpose so we could hook up—but I don't think anything I say is going to make Dad any less worried.

I mean, it's one of his favorite movies. He wouldn't shut it off unless he was really concerned.

"Valerie"—he finally sits up straight and turns toward me—"is this something that's really important to you?"

I stare at him for a sec, trying to figure out just what he's asking. "Why? Is this going to make you lose your job?"

He goes from serious to laughing in a nanosecond. "No. Well, unless you do something truly horrific, like start a food fight with Prince Manfred or insult Princess Claudia's taste in clothes in front of a reporter. You're not planning to do that, are you?"

"Um, *no*."

"So you like Georg, I take it?"

Well, duh. "I think he's really nice, Dad. And you said just a few days ago that you think he has a good reputation."

"That's true." He leans back against the arm of the couch and crosses his arms over his chest. "So you can go. But on one condition."

I gesture for him to get on with it, even though I'm dreading the condition. Dad never gives good conditions. It's always, you can go out, but you can't stay out after nine—in other words, late enough to have any fun. And I'm planning on having a lot of fun with Georg.

A *lot*. I'm due.

"I get to play fairy godmother. Help you pick a dress, coach you a little on what to say to Prince Manfred and Princess Claudia."

The idea of my totally buffed-up Dad picking out a dress with me is hysterical. His clothes always look perfect, and totally stylish, so maybe it'll be a bonding experience. And I can always veto his choice if he wants something ugly. I hope.

"Okay. But we don't have much time to shop," I tell him.

"Then let's go now." He jumps off the couch and pockets his wallet before I can even say anything. "I've heard Princess Claudia mention a few places that should still be open. But we'll have to hurry. The stores here don't stay open nearly as late as they do in the States."

I follow him out the door, and I have to admit I'm not nearly as freaked as I was before I told Dad about the date.

And, you know, I didn't even make one joke about Dad using the term *fairy godmother* in reference to himself, which is very tempting given the whole gay Mom thing. I must be learning.

Christie would be proud.

9

To: BarbnGabby@mailmagic.com

From: Val@realmail.sg.com

Subject: Everything

Hi, Mom!

Dad said you called last night and gave him your new e-mail address. Is this an address for both you and Gabrielle, or just you? (I can't really tell from your BarbnGabby handle.)

Anyway, Dad also said he told you about my date tonight. Thanks for being so excited for me. He even helped me find a fantastic dress. Can you believe it? I promise to send you another e-mail tomorrow to tell you how the whole thing goes.

Also, your package arrived yesterday. I know I make fun

of you a lot because you buy so many self-help books, (especially the one about somebody moving your cheese—I'm still not sure I get that one) but it was nice of you to send me the small stuff book. It's really good, and no, that doesn't mean you should buy me more books to balance me emotionally. One is enough, and I am now balanced.

Thank you.

I hope you're happy in your new apartment and that you're excited about teaching school again, though I will say it kind of surprises me. I didn't think you liked it that much. I thought you'd do something else if you went back to work.

I'll write again tomorrow.

Love,

Valerie

Go figure. Dad has really, *really* good taste in dresses. And he's clearly been saving money—now that he's not bringing home little gifts for Mom all the time, I suppose—because he let his credit card take a mighty hit yesterday without flinching. This never, and I mean *never*, happens. I don't even get an allowance. All my money comes from baby-sitting. Well, all my money *came* from baby-sitting. Eventually, I'm going to have to learn enough German to get a job at the Schwerinborg McDonald's or something.

Not that I can think about that right now.

I just hope Mom doesn't find out how much he spent, though maybe she won't care anymore. I mean, she and Dad finally agreed on a lump sum for alimony without having to deal with lawyers, and I know it's plenty, even though he doesn't have to give her any child support or anything.

But I am determined not to hold against her the fact she kept telling Dad (usually with Gabrielle in the room) that he could afford to pay her a hell of a lot more.

Small stuff, right?

I take a deep breath—doing my best to think only good thoughts about Mom or nothing at all, because if I let myself, I could go on all day about her stupid choice of an e-mail address, let alone the money thing—and I turn back around to face the full-length mirror that Dad was brilliant enough to have installed on the back of the door to my bathroom. The bathroom's so tiny I have to stand in the shower to see all of me in the mirror, but it doesn't matter.

I look amazing.

I've always hated my red hair. Not so much because it's different—that's the one thing I like about it—but because it makes me look not-quite-right in clothes and makeup.

Clothes have to stay basic—grays and blacks and other neutrals—or I could seriously blind someone. Contrary to popular belief and my mother's shopping tendencies, jewel-tone greens and blues do *not* look good on redheads.

It makes us look like we belong on the cast of *Dynasty* or *Falcon Crest* or some other corny, over-the-top eighties TV drama. Just picture a pale actress like Nicole Kidman as a teenager in electric pink and you get the idea. *Hideous.* So I limit the colored shirts I wear to my one—*one*—red floral top that Christie bought me for Christmas last year at the Fair Oaks mall and a funky blue halter I purchased myself.

And while clothes can be a challenge, makeup is worse. The chemists at your big cosmetics companies design makeup in shades that look fantastic on your average brown- or blue-eyed, dirty-blond-to-brunette person. Those colors don't work on someone whose face is so shockingly white that wearing reflective gear for an evening jog through the neighborhood is redundant.

But Dad outdid himself here. I mean, our shopping trip was almost like an episode of E!'s *Fashion Emergency* come to life. Only I was the emergency and he was this hunky version of the host and had all the store clerks melting.

First, he got me this killer—and I mean *killer*—dress. As in, the thing is a deep bloodred. Beyond red. I never, ever would have pulled this thing off the rack, but Dad insisted I try it on, and even though I argued with him the whole way to the dressing room, trying to explain the whole ugly-redhead-in-bright-colors concept, I took back every word the instant I got the thing over my head and got an eyeful in the store's three-way mirror.

It makes me look like a *goddess*.

And the thing is, the other reason I wear a lot of black is because it lets me blend in and not look like I'm trying too hard to be noticed. This dress—believe it or not—does the same thing. It's classy and understated. And it's *red*. Go figure!

I turn around in the shower for a final inspection. I'm being pretty harsh on myself as I look in the bathroom mirror, trying to see what I look like if I slouch, when I sit, or if I act flirty. But even if I *try* to look like a desperate girly-girl, which is pretty easy to do when you're standing in a circa 1970s shower stall, I don't.

In this dress, I actually look confident.

How did Dad do that?! It's like he's right up there with the hoity-toity hotel manager from *Pretty Woman* who knew just how to turn Julia Roberts from a total ho into Richard Gere's dream girl.

Now that I think of it, Julia's dress in that movie was red too. Freaky.

Anyway, the best part of the shopping trip came after the red dress, when Dad parked me at a cosmetics counter and told the ladies to go to work. He had them redo my face twice, since he didn't like what they did on the first *or* second go-round. Then he handed the woman behind the register his plastic and gave her a limit, telling her to get me the most essential items needed to re-create the look, while he headed off to the shoe department.

I'm not kidding. Dad picked out my *shoes*.

And you wonder why, if I'd had to peg one of my parents as having gay tendencies, Dad came to mind before Mom.

He brought me these totally fun strappy things to try on—they let him, because they could see me at the makeup counter from the shoe department, plus I think the shoe department lady thought my dad was cute—and even though the shoes were kind of sexy, they weren't so high they were uncomfortable.

It usually takes me trying on, like, ten pairs of heels to find a pair that fits and feels comfy. I'm much more the Skechers and Converse shoe type than one of those girls who wears four-inch heels, and it's usually obvious when I actually *need* a pair of heels how unnatural they are on me. But Dad found the perfect pair on his first try. And now that I'm looking at the whole thing in the full-length mirror, I realize how awesome they look with the dress.

And that's standing in the shower. I cannot imagine how kickin' this is going to look once I'm in that big, fancy reception hall with chandeliers and candlelight.

I might actually look like a girl who is pretty enough to go to dinner with a prince.

When I finally walk out of the bathroom to show Dad, he's standing in the living room wearing his tux. He doesn't say anything. He just smiles.

You'd think I was wearing white and standing at the back of a church about to take his arm, he's so proud of himself.

He has to leave for dinner earlier than me, since he needs to be available to Prince Manfred as soon as the British prime minister arrives at the palace, but I know he's thrilled I got dressed an hour early, just so he could check me out before he has to leave.

All I can do is tell him thanks. And that I am glad I decided to come with him to Schwerinborg, even if I did have to leave all my friends and my entire social life a couple thousand miles away. Because I know he loves me and wants to do whatever it takes for me to be happy—even when that means making me study an extra hour for a geometry exam so I can be proud of how I've done.

He shakes his head and laughs, but it's not an altogether happy laugh. I can tell he wants to give me another warning about Georg. He's totally worried that I'm getting into more than I can handle since Georg's not your typical guy, no matter how much I want to believe it.

Luckily, he knows I know that, and he leaves without saying anything.

I walk back to the bathroom and look in the mirror again, trying to see what Georg will see.

For the first time in my life, I *so* hope I'm going to get more than I can handle.

To: Val@realmail.sg.com

From: ChristieT@viennawest.edu

Subject: I CAN'T WAIT ANOTHER DAY!!!

Val,

Okay, first of all, I cannot BELIEVE you're not going to be home tonight. Second of all, I don't care WHAT you think your unbelievable news is, mine is unbelievable-er.

I got your e-mail too late yesterday to call, because it would have been about 2 a.m. your time. So even though I wanted to tell you everything on the phone, I will give you a hint now.

David spilled his guts to Jeremy yesterday. And I mean SPILLED. And it was about YOU.

Is that enough of a hint about what I need to say to make you stay home so I can call you? Does this not make whatever it is you want to tell me suck in comparison?

I'll try calling tonight just in case, but if you're not there, I'll call again tomorrow night. You MUST hear all my gossip.

You said you could come home if things weren't good in Schwerinborg. I'm telling you, you should seriously consider COMING HOME! Now is most definitely the time.

Details during the phone call.

Love,

Christie, your very desperate, very pushy friend

I can't identify my soup, which is a light, minty green color. I also cannot identify the meat on my plate, which is some kind of fancy stuffed bird I have no idea how to eat. But I can't even think about the food, despite the fact food generally occupies a very high spot on my priority list.

Georg's leg is rubbing against mine under the table, and he's totally doing it on purpose.

And what's worse, I like it. A lot.

But what I cannot get over is that *David Anderson likes me*! For *real*. After all these years. After all this wishing and hoping and fixing my hair just so and choosing at least one class I know he's going to be taking every quarter in the hope that he'll *notice* me as something other than a friend. And now, apparently, he has. Or did.

That has to be what Christie wants to tell me. There can't be another way to interpret her e-mail.

I think I am going to hurl all over the nice white tablecloth and fancy crystal goblets. My stomach is just one big friggin' knot.

I wish, wish, wish I'd just left to meet Georg in the library when Dad left the apartment. I could've found plenty of things to do while I was waiting. I could've sketched while I waited. I could've stared out the window. I could've relaxed in front of the fire with a nice leather-bound copy of Dickens or whatever it is Prince Manfred keeps on the library shelves.

Okay, so I'm not into Dickens.

But what I should *not* have done is go online to read my e-mail and make sure Christie got my message not to call tonight, because she just gave me way more information than I can handle.

What am I going to *do*?!

How is this even possible? How can two guys like me?

And how can I not know which one I really want?

No, I know which one I want. The one who actually talks to me about me and who gets the thing with my mom.

Right?

Then I feel Georg's fingers on my knee. I'm so surprised I bump against the table, even though he's had his leg touching mine the whole meal. He starts making little circles with his fingers, twisting the red fabric of my dress into little swirls against my leg.

Okay, forget David.

I so want to go find a room with Georg. I mean, could he be any hotter? He's wearing a tux, but it doesn't look stupid on him, like on most guys when they're going to the prom. He looks like he wears one all the time. And the best part is that the dark jacket shows off his blue eyes and his high cheekbones, making him look even more interesting and mysterious.

I glance to my left, where he's sitting. His parents are at another table across the room, talking with the British prime minister and smiling for the press photographers—there are about a dozen or so of them crowded along the walls on that end of the room—so I don't think anyone saw me jump. We're stuck sitting with the losers. Okay, not really losers—I mean, they're all fairly important people—but the press isn't clamoring for snapshots of them like they are of Manfred and Claudia. Our table is filled with people like Prince Manfred's private secretary, the minister of the treasury, and a couple of foreign diplomats—one of whom, Georg mentions, is Ulrike's father—who only care about whether they'll get a few minutes' conversation with the P.M. after dinner, and a few random staff members like my dad. Though thankfully, he's three people around the table from me, so he doesn't have a good angle to see me.

The only fairly important person on this whole side of

the room is Georg's uncle, Prince Klaus, who's at the table behind us, with his back toward Georg's. I guess Klaus is Manfred's younger brother.

Could you imagine growing up in a house where the kids are named *Klaus* and *Manfred*?

Well, I've now been in Schwerinborg long enough to find this absolutely believable. I've also been here long enough to realize that the family members who aren't in the direct line of succession—people like Georg's uncle—and other diplomats get about a tenth of the attention someone like Georg does in the press, so they kind of run in their own little worlds. And on nights where politics is the hot topic, like tonight, the only press who show up are from the supersnooty papers and political magazines—reporters who'd rather figure out what the British P.M. tells Manfred about the environment than the fact that Georg brought a date to the dinner.

Of course, this means all of the people on our loser side of the room are talking to each other about their own little lives, and unless they get to meet the P.M., they don't care about being here. It's all same-old, same-old party circuit to them.

And none of them are looking at me or Georg.

I put my napkin up to my mouth and hiss, "Hey, cut it out."

He sneaks a look at the photographers, then at his uncle. Without looking directly at me, he says, "You don't like it?"

And he moves his fingers another inch or two higher.

Oh. My. God.

"No." I blot an imaginary bit of food from my mouth and glance at Dad, making sure Georg follows my point. "I do. But . . ."

He smiles and takes his hand off my knee. He waits a half beat, then gets a hunk of asparagus on his fork before whispering, "Good."

We keep quiet for the rest of the meal, but I can still feel where his fingers were on my leg, playing with my dress. Georg told me in the library, before we came in to the dinner, that he'd told his parents it was a date. However, he says that if it comes up, his parents are going to tell the reporter types that I'm the daughter of a staff member, and they thought it would be nice for Georg to have company his own age at one of these events. Period.

His parents were very cool when I met them too. They sound like they're as laid back as Dad, once they get away from the cameras. So maybe sneaking away after dinner won't be such a bad thing.

And then I feel Georg playing with my dress again under the table.

Oh, this is going to be bad. In a very, very good way.

* * *

"That was beyond boring," Georg says in his completely sexy accent once we're clear of the ballroom and finally feel safe enough to stop running and start walking. "Thanks for getting me out of there."

"You're the one who gave me the idea," I grin at him, trying to catch my breath. Poor Georg had been cornered by two ancient diplomats, and they were not-so-subtly grilling him about what he planned to study in college when I interrupted, as innocently as I could, and told Georg that we needed to go if we were going to finish the "planned tour" in time for him to be back to say good night to the P.M.

Ha!

The diplomats bought it, and the second Georg and I were out the ballroom door, he told me to run—well, as fast as I could in my new heels—and I followed him until I was totally lost. Now that we're finally walking, I realize we're in the long hallway that leads out to the gardens behind the palace. I walked through here on my *real* palace tour the day Dad and I arrived. It's completely empty now, except for me and Georg. And the lights are all off, except for some hidden, faint lights near the floor. Totally romantic, even with the pictures of all the old, gruesome-looking men on the walls and the sour-faced statues scattered here and there beside the closed doors.

"Well, thanks a lot for interrupting when you did. I'm so sick of having all my parents' friends butt into my business, you can't even imagine." He looks angry as he adds, "They weren't asking about school to be friendly. It's that they think they have the right to tell me what to do, like they think I'm not following the correct path for Schwerinborg."

"Like you won't turn out to be as good a prince as your father if you don't take AP Physics next year?"

"Exactly."

"That blows."

This, of course, makes him laugh, which I think is what he really needs.

We walk along in silence for a while. It's a good silence, though, and Georg takes my hand like it's the most natural thing in the world to him.

And the really scary thing is that it feels totally natural to me, too. Exciting and majorly nerve-racking, but natural. Like we're *supposed* to be holding hands.

"Do you think they'll notice if we don't go back?" I ask as he leads me out an unguarded side door.

"Depends. My dad will be too busy to notice for hours. My mom might ask around though."

I almost ask him whether or not his mom will get mad, but the garden is so gorgeous, I quit caring.

"This is fantastic," I say, nodding toward an empty fountain a few feet in front of us. It's surrounded by benches, and you just know that it's full of staff in the summer, sitting and eating their lunches, listening to the water as it cascades down from the vase held by the goddess statue in the center. There's still snow in a few spots, but since today was warm, I'm guessing it'll be gone by tomorrow.

But somehow, the cold and the snow make the garden even more beautiful. Maybe because I know it'll be ours, all by ourselves.

"I come out here a lot," he says. "Especially in the winter. It's a lot nicer in the summer, but—"

"More crowded," we say at the same time, then we laugh.

Georg squeezes my hand, then pulls me a little closer. "You cold?"

I shake my head. I know it's the dead of winter, but I'm not, even in my wispy dress.

Then I realize what a dork I am—because of what he was really asking—and try to cover. "I mean, I wouldn't want to stay out all night, but it's not bad."

Georg slips off his jacket and slides it over my shoulders. I know it's totally corny, and so does he, but neither of us care.

"Better?"

I nod, and he takes my hand again, walking me a little farther from the back door, I think so no one sees us and starts gossiping.

"It's strange. I know we've only known each other a few weeks, but I feel like we understand each other." He looks at me sideways, and I can't tell if he's being flirty or serious. "We're a lot alike."

I think so too, despite the fact that he's dark to my pale, every person in the world is dying to know the real Georg, (like anyone cares about the "real Valerie"), and he's got an accent that makes me want to jump all over him. But I never would have said what he did. I mean, it's fine for *him* to say it. But for me to say I'm a lot like a prince would come off as pretty damned egotistical.

"What?" he asks, misreading my silence.

"Nothing. It's just . . . I feel very comfortable with you too. This"—I wiggle my fingers in his hand—"this feels right. Cool, but scary at the same time, you think?"

"Like when I've got my hand on your leg under the table, with your father sitting right there?" He stops walking and faces me, and that wicked look is on his face again. We're behind a big hedge, so no one in the palace could see us if they tried, which is just *classic*. Even the air around us is cool and still, like it's waiting to see what happens next too.

Oh, I want him, bad.

"Especially then," I say. And I get bold, lean forward, and kiss him.

Because I can tell it's what we both want, but we're both too scared to start.

10

I KNOW HOW TO KISS. GO FIGURE.

After all this time of stressing over whether or not I'd screw it up royally and make a complete and total fool of myself if a guy kissed me, and I mean really kissed me, I find out that I can do it just fine, thankyouverymuch. Georg clearly has no clue this is the first time I've engaged in an intense makeout session. Again, thankyouverymuch.

And kissing Georg Jacques von Ederhollern is nothing like when Jason Barrows kissed me back in seventh grade. For one, Georg knows what he's doing. He is *good*. I mean, there's nothing sloppy or overeager about it. And he doesn't just kiss me with his mouth or his tongue.

I am learning in the best way possible that Georg is a full-body kisser.

Maybe it's supposed to be this way though—I mean, how would I know?

But what I *do* know is that when we hear voices in the garden—apparently one of the waiters and his girlfriend had the same thought we did—and scoot back into the palace, I want Georg to start from the beginning and kiss me all over again, because every single nerve ending in my whole body is doing this funky vibrating thing from wanting him. It's like someone stuck my finger in a socket and left my skin to sizzle.

Apparently Georg has the same thought, because his expression is totally intense as he pulls me along a couple of hallways without saying a word, then through another door.

When he flips on the light, though, every ounce of tension leaves my chest in a whoosh, and it's all I can do not to split my gut laughing.

"Oh, now *this* is totally romantic."

"You like the urinals?"

I laugh even harder, because I just can't help myself. He frowns. "That's the right word, isn't it?"

"Oh, yeah. They're urinals, all right."

"No one ever uses this restroom," he explains, pulling

me past the two regular-size stalls and into the handicapped one on the end. I can hear the music thumping through the floor upstairs, and roll my eyes upward.

"The reception hall is right above us," he says as he wraps his arms around me, pulling me up against him again. "It has its own restrooms, though, so no one will bother us here."

"Good thing we managed to get outta there." I run my finger down his cheek. I love the way his skin feels. Smooth, but a different kind of smooth than mine. Like he shaved right before dinner. "I really prefer to dance to something besides whatever it is they're playing."

"It's Schubert."

"You a big Schubert fan?"

"Him and Eminem." He smiles and kisses me again, but gently this time, all soft and caring. My hip nearly bumps against the siderails of the stall, but he puts his hand there first, anticipating the collision.

"You hang out in these stalls often?" I tease. If he's brought other girls here though, I don't want to know. I don't want anything to ruin tonight.

"Actually, this is the one place I can come to be alone. I've been hiding out in here since I was little. My parents have no clue."

He lets go of me and reaches behind the paper towel

holder that's beside the handicapped stall's sink, half pulling the thing off the wall, and yanks out a pack of cigarettes.

I try to act cool, but I know I must look totally shocked.

"When I'm really, really having a bad day, I sneak down here and grab a smoke." He tosses the pack in the air, catches it with one hand, then tucks it back behind the holder and slams the metal cover back into place.

I'm so surprised I don't even know what to say. I thought Georg was Mr. Perfect. I mean, he plays soccer and gets awesome grades and doesn't even blast his music. Though I know the quiet music is because his parents want him to appear proper and all, I think he'd be smart and basically a clean-living guy without the pressure from his parents.

But he's just normal like me.

"I know you probably think it's disgusting," he says, but there isn't an apology in his voice. "But sometimes, I just need to do something—"

"Like in an emergency situation?"

"Yeah. I hate the smell on my clothes." The wicked grin returns, and he adds, "Plus my parents would kill me if they smelled it. I don't think they'd believe I smoke, but they'd be angry thinking I was even hanging out with anyone who smoked. God forbid some photographer snapped it."

"No kidding." I smile, just to let him know I don't think it's a big deal, and I wouldn't judge him for it.

I mean, he has no clue how relieved I am that he won't judge *me*.

I'm about to tell him that I've had a couple of emergency cigarettes too, and all about the Wendy's Dumpster and Jules and Natalie and Christie. I want to tell him I hate the smell and would never want to endanger my health, but that sometimes doing something dangerous or risky relieves all the pressure and stress at school—just like it took off all the pressure to do something risky tonight and sneak out of the reception—when the door opens so hard it whacks against the tile wall and sends the big letter *H* (which Georg tells me stands for *Herren*, the German word for "men") swinging on its screw.

Georg moves to shut the door to the handicapped stall, but it's too late. My dad has seen us.

Thankfully the tuxedoed man he's leading into the restroom hasn't. My dad eases the guy, who reeks like you wouldn't believe, into the next stall where he proceeds to worship the porcelain god very loudly.

My dad pulls the stall door shut behind the guy and says, "I'll be right here. Let me know if you want a towel."

The guy moans, then begins heaving again.

My dad isn't paying attention though. He's just glaring

at me and Georg. Then his eyes drift past me to the floor, where the cigarettes have fallen from behind the paper towel holder onto the floor.

Oh, *shit*.

"I think you two need to head back to the ballroom," he says very quietly, though I doubt the guy on his knees in the next stall is in any shape to notice he and my dad aren't alone in here.

I want to tell my dad that we were *not* smoking. We weren't doing anything wrong. Not even hooking up—yet—but Georg just nods, then grabs my hand and pulls me behind my dad and out of the restroom.

"How much trouble are you in?" he whispers once we're out of there.

I shrug. "My dad's pretty cool. I doubt he'll rat you out to your parents."

Georg quirks his mouth, like it's no big thing. "I asked how much trouble *you* will be in."

"Truth? I don't know. But"—I feel the same wicked grin Georg gives me spreading across my face—"I got busted last year with cigarettes. My parents know I don't smoke—it was an emergency situation thing—but they weren't exactly doing cartwheels. Getting caught twice could be bad."

"Wow. We really are alike," he says. He looks completely

caught off guard by this, but in a good way. Like I just went up a notch in his mind, even though smoking isn't exactly a quality I want a guy to appreciate in me.

"You'll tell him we weren't smoking, right?"

"Of course," I say. "I'll tell him they were in the stall when we got there. He should know I'm telling the truth. It wasn't like one of us was standing there holding a lighter or the bathroom reeked."

"Not until the minister of the treasury showed up and gave back his quail."

The minister of the treasury? The guy who was sitting with us at dinner? I let out a little laugh, just to let Georg know I think everything will be okay. "If my dad can handle someone that important getting totally smashed, I bet he can handle seeing me in the men's room hanging with you."

"I suppose, if you explain it that way." Georg stops at the top of the stairs, pulling me over to the wall just before I turn the corner into the hall outside the ballroom. The Schubert morphs into Mozart—I think it's Mozart—but despite the fact the music is all classical, you can tell there's a serious party going on. The stairs are quiet compared to the boisterous chatter and clinking glasses of the ballroom.

"Before we go back"—he looks past me to make sure no

one sees us, then back into my eyes—"I want you to know this has been one of the best nights of my life."

"Me too." I grin like a total goof, then take his tuxedo jacket off my shoulders and hand it back to him.

"I really like you, Valerie. A lot. I just—I mean—I want us to be together."

The knot in my throat is threatening to choke me, even more than the bird on my dinner plate did. "Thanks," I say, even though it's probably moronic to thank someone for liking you. "I really like you a lot too. If you didn't notice out in the garden."

He grins at that, and our freaky-cool connection feels stronger than ever. "So would you like to dance with me? In front of everybody?"

"Steffi will have a stroke."

"Steffi won't know." He's lying of course, and we both know it, because of course Ulrike's dad will ask Ulrike who I am when he gets home, and he'll tell her I was dancing with Georg, and Ulrike will tell Steffi. That's just how things work. By tomorrow morning the whole school will know.

What Georg is really telling me, though, is that he likes me enough that he doesn't care what Steffi knows or doesn't know. Or what the world knows.

Which is completely, totally cool.

So we go back into the reception hall, and even though we don't hold hands or dance so close we look like we need to get a room or anything, we have a great time. We're the only people under the age of thirty on the dance floor, but it doesn't matter.

And just when I'm thinking how glad I am Dad made me learn to dance like a proper lady, even though I've always been certain I'd never want to dance to anything like Mozart or Wagner or whatever it is the orchestra's playing, I catch his eye across the room. He's handing the minister of the treasury a glass of water like it's no big thing, but he's looking at me.

And he smiles. Well, until Georg's facing the other way. Then he's not. And it's *not* good.

I can tell from the way he very pointedly shakes his head that we're going to talk later, and it's going to be, as he would put it, a bit *unpleasant*. But he's beginning to warm to the idea of me seeing Georg, I can tell. He doesn't want me developing a smoker's rasp like Karl's, or hanging out in the palace men's room, but he wants me to be happy, even if getting to a happy place involves facing the risks that come with dating Prince Manfred of Schwerinborg's only child. That much I can tell.

Geez, at least I hope so. What if he's *really* ticked off

this time? What if he threatens to send me back to Virginia over this? It's definitely possible. . . .

No. I won't think about that. I'll deal with Dad tomorrow. There'll be *some* way for me to get out of this. I have to. Because now I have a boyfriend.

And I don't want to have to leave him. Let alone live with Mom and Gabrielle and deal with all the crap that's going to be coming my way from Christie, Jules, and Natalie.

Georg grabs my hand and spins me around, and I just can't help but smile to myself.

Who'da thought that my mom announcing she was gay could get me a boyfriend? A boyfriend who isn't a safety boyfriend, like Jason Barrows could have been, or someone like David Anderson either, who'd probably only think of me as his Armor Girl.

Probably.

Christie's my friend, so I'll let her say her piece, and I'll even make myself think through everything she has to say—I owe a girlfriend that much—even though I know in my heart I'm not going to change my mind about Georg.

I cannot believe I have actually found someone who makes my stomach do flippity flops every time I look in his eyes. Someone who *gets* me and doesn't care if I'm popular or that my mother is a lesbian. Someone flat-out gorgeous who can kiss me inside out.

Someone who'll let me see just what it feels like to hook my fingers in the back pockets of his Levi's while he kisses me.

I can't wait to try that.

No matter what it takes with Dad, I'm so not going back to Virginia. This is where I belong.

SPIN CONTROL

For Doug

1

EXACTLY SIX WEEKS, FIVE DAYS, AND NINE HOURS AGO, my mother ruined my life. And even worse, because of her, I am missing a damned good party.

Right this second, I should be over at my best friend Christie Toleski's house, getting ready to watch a parade of hot French and Australian actors (my favorite types) walk the red carpet at the Golden Globes. My friends Natalie Monschroeder and Julia (a.k.a. Jules) Jackson are already there, undoubtedly noshing on popcorn during the television coverage and discussing the plasticity of the host's face while she kisses and disses the celebs and their clothes—or lack thereof.

When Christie's parents aren't in the room, they're also

probably talking about how far Christie and her boyfriend, Jeremy Astin, went on their last date, how far she actually wants to go, and how all of them are sooooo sure David Anderson (whom I've been crushing on since kindergarten) is finally interested in me.

But no. They're doing all that without me. I know because they texted me about half an hour ago to rub it in.

Unfortunately, my failure to attend this year's let's-make-fun-of-celebrities Golden Globes party (not to be confused with our annual let's-make-fun-of-celebrities Oscar, Grammy, and Emmy parties) is because, thanks to my mother, my parents are getting a divorce and I had to move with my dad to Schwerinborg a month ago.

Yes, Schwerinborg's a real country, and yes, my friends all refer to it as Smorgasbord, even though the people here aren't even Scandinavian. The Schwerinborgians—or Schwerinborgers or whatever they're called—speak German. And we're south of Germany, not north. Not that any of my friends care where it is, other than the fact that it's very, very far from Virginia.

So why not live with my mother? After all, she has a nice apartment back in Virginia, where all the important awards shows are carried live. And even though the location of Mom's new place means I'd have to go to Lake Braddock High School instead of to Vienna West, where I've been going, I could still see my friends on a regular basis.

Hmmmm . . . how about because Mom's new apartment is also home to Mom's new *girlfriend*?

Yep, girlfriend. A super-organized, yoga-twisting, vegan Weight Watchers–devotee girlfriend named Gabrielle, who is, no kidding, a decade younger than my mother. And no, Gabrielle isn't a girlfriend like Christie, Natalie, and Jules are my girlfriends.

Gabrielle is *that* kind of girlfriend.

I haven't even had the guts to tell *my* girlfriends about her, and it doesn't take a psychology degree to guess why. It's the kind of thing that takes you a while to work up to telling someone, even your best friends. Telling them about my parents' divorce—and that I was moving to Europe with Dad—was bad enough. Popping out with, "Oh, and by the way, my mom—the woman who took us all out for manicures and facials before homecoming and has definitely seen all of you naked at one time or another when we've gone clothes shopping—yeah, well, she's announced that she's gay!" wouldn't have gone over with them very well.

I know they say they don't care whether a person is gay, and I've never heard them say one derogatory word about anyone's sexual preferences, but I'm not quite sure I want to test their beliefs yet.

And it's not that *I'm* a homophobe. Seriously. I know a

couple of gay kids at school, and they're totally cool. But this is different. This is my *mother*.

It's like the mom I knew disappeared one day and now there's another person inhabiting Mom's body. That's the really hard part. Not the what-is-she-doing-with-that-woman? part. It's that I have to wonder if she's lied to me about who she is my entire freaking life.

You'd think I'd want to find the highest turret—well, if it had turrets—of Schwerinborg's royal palace and toss myself off of it.

But no. I'm not even close to suicidal right now, even though I'm sure about a hundred hot actors look completely droolworthy walking the red carpet in their Armani tuxes and I'm missing it. (Thankyouverymuch, Mom.)

It's because Schwerinborg is completely incredible. I mean, there are definite downsides, like the fact they use mayo on their French fries, that the weather is misty and depressing all winter long, and that I can't watch the Golden Globes live. (Which, come to think of it, makes absolutely no sense—the awards are given by the Hollywood Foreign Press, and if anything's foreign to Hollywood, it's gotta be Schwerinborg.)

It's because I have a boyfriend.

I have a boyfriend who looks like the hottest of those actors, only better. More of a sweetheart, less of a male slut.

I have a boyfriend named Georg Jacques von Ederhollern, *and he is a freakin' PRINCE.*

Yep. I, Valerie Winslow, a totally boring, non-cheerleader, non-athletic, non-popular sophomore redheaded nobody from Vienna, Virginia, have officially hooked up with a European prince. A prince who knows how to kiss in the most knock-me-on-my-ass way, and who is formal and polite and looks beyond hot in a tux, but who also knows how to kick back and be cool and totally un-prince-like when we're alone, if you catch my drift.

And you wanna know a secret? Even though it's the dead of winter and he's always in sweaters and jackets, I've discovered that he has these amazing arms.

Ever see Hugh Jackman in *X-Men*? It's an old movie, but still. THOSE arms.

Okay, Georg's almost seventeen, so he's not quite X-Men caliber yet, and he's a lot more lean and wiry than Hugh Jackman, but he's headed in that direction. His arms are totally ripped and solid—the kind that other guys refer to as guns. A girl could be about to go off a cliff, grab on to those biceps just as her footing slips, and not worry for even a second she's going to fall, you know?

Yes, I know that girls probably go for Hugh Jackman—and every other Aussie actor, for that matter—because of their accents as much as their arms or other, um, physical attributes. But if his name alone doesn't make it clear, Georg *also* has an accent, and it's pretty damned sexy. (However, I will admit that if someone had told me a year ago that listening to a guy speak with a deep, German accent would make me get all gooey inside, I'd have thought they needed some serious therapy.)

But you see, the thing that makes Georg an even better boyfriend than any Hollywood actor could ever be is . . . NONE OF THEM HAS A CROWN! They do not have staff members who polish their shoes before school or ask if they'd like a Coke or finger sandwiches while studying Trig in the palace library. Georg does. And he's not the least bit egotistical about any of those things. In fact, it makes him blush if you mention it. He gets this little pink glow right along his cheekbones, and then he tries to hide his face so you can't see. It's totally cute.

Also, Georg does not care that my mother is a lesbian. He actually tells me I should try to be more understanding of her, and at the same time, he totally gets that while I really do love her, I'm completely ticked off at her for what she did to me and Dad.

Is that love, or what? You don't find that with just any guy. The arms, the accent, and even the crown are simply bonus material. He likes me for me, and David Anderson never did.

Well, unless you believe my friends, who I think keep telling me David likes me to try to make me feel better about the whole divorce thing.

Ha.

Wait until they hear about my prince. Or better yet, wait until I put them on the phone with him so they can hear his accent.

So right now *I'm* on the phone with Georg, and I can hardly follow what he's saying, because I'm so hung up on how he's saying it. All rich and Euro-like, but thankfully without even a hint of that thick nasal sound that you might expect from someone whose native language is German. Georg's voice is smooth and seductive. And it's making me wish he would hurry up and get over here so I can grab him and kiss him the way he kissed me day before yesterday, when we went to this dinner-party-reception-formal thing his father was hosting for the British prime minister here at the palace, then ditched for a while to go make out in the garden. It was icy out there, and all the plants were that generic shade of gray-green that plants get in the middle of January, but between the kissing and him whispering to me in that fabulous accent, I was totally warm. It was our second kiss, but the first serious one, and this time we both knew there'd be more. Lots and lots more.

I can't think about anything else *but* kissing Georg.

"Valerie. Are you still listening to me?"

I sit up on my bed and try to focus. It's difficult, though, when my room is maybe only five degrees warmer than the garden was and Georg isn't here to keep me toasty.

My dad and I live in the royal palace in Schwerinborg because he's the new protocol chief to the royal family—meaning he works for Georg's dad, Prince Manfred—who rules the country—and Georg's mom, Princess Claudia. He advises them on things like the proper way to address everyone from visiting Buddhist monks to the queen of England, and warns them about the fact that when they visit Egypt, they might get served pigeon but that it's perfectly safe to eat.

It's a totally whacked thing to do for a living, but since it once got me a behind-the-scenes tour of the White House (which is where my dad did his protocol thing until the überconservative, up-for-reelection president discovered Dad had married a lesbian) and it's the reason I met Georg and have gotten to hang out with him despite the fact I'm your average American fifteen-year-old, I'm not going to make even one crack about it.

On the other hand, while it might sound cool to actually *live* in a real palace, I'd much rather the royal couple hadn't offered us their, uh, hospitality. Other than the fact that Georg is under the same roof, it pretty much sucks.

Our very ritzy-sounding "palace apartment"—which is actually only three small rooms and a kitchen—is always so cold I have to wear double layers of socks, and it has the decor of a circa-1970s, never-been-renovated motel. Probably because we're in a 150-year-old section of the palace that hasn't been renovated since, well, the 1970s. We'd have been better off living a couple blocks away, in a nice little walk-up.

Preferably one with heat.

"Yeah, I'm listening," I say to Georg as I stare at my tiny, ancient bedroom window and wonder how much cold air is leaking in from outside. "You said you had two assists and a goal at the scrimmage yesterday. But I wish you'd just come over. I can follow soccer talk much better in person."

I'm totally kidding because we both know it's way too late, but still. Does he think a five-minute walk from one side of the palace—the beautiful, *warm,* renovated side, where his family lives—over to the other side, where my apartment is, would kill him? I mean, the guy's an incredible soccer player, so you know his legs work just fine.

They're very nice legs. All tight and muscular and—

Whoa.

This thought zaps my brain back to reality. I have it bad for him. Way bad. I can't stop thinking about his various body parts, and we went out—officially—for the first time, what, Friday night, and it's only Sunday?!

Maybe I'm wigged out because this is the first time I've ever had a real boyfriend (since I don't count Jason Barrows, whom everyone thought I was going out with because he kissed me on a dare in seventh grade. Puh-leeze.). Maybe it's because Georg's a prince, and no matter where he goes, he always has this prince-like aura around him.

But even so, this is not good because Georg and I are trying to keep things low-key, or at least make it look that way for the time being.

Given the way my synapses are firing right now, though, if Georg and I get within fifty feet of each other, I'm going to be all over him. On top of it making me look totally desperate, which would be bad because Georg has no idea I'm a little, um, inexperienced, it would blow the whole low-key thing out of the water.

"I know you're kidding, but if I thought we could get away with it, I would," Georg tells me. "But it's nearly midnight. My father said the fund-raiser would be over around one a.m., which means everyone will be back soon. Until your father's not suspicious about the cigarettes anymore . . . well, we have to be careful."

"I know." I twist one of my sheets into a little whorl

with my fingers, then glance at the bedside alarm clock. "I still can't believe we got busted."

We weren't even smoking them when my dad walked in on us Friday night, and we weren't going to. Really. Georg was just showing me where he keeps an emergency stash, behind the paper towel holder in the handicapped stall of the men's restroom that's below the palace ballroom. He'd even hidden them back away before my dad came in, but they'd fallen on the floor.

Major oops.

I must be pretty desperate, though, because I add, this time only half-joking, "I still think you'd be okay, if you really wanted to come over. Now that Dad's had a day to chill, he's beginning to understand that I wasn't trying to corrupt you with cigarettes."

"And get him fired."

"Exactly." Europeans are pretty lax about smoking, just not when it comes to their royalty. Apparently, Georg getting caught with cigarettes—say, by the press or something—would be a pretty big deal.

I pull the covers up over my shoulders like a cape, then cradle the phone a little closer to my ear. "I told him they were on the sink when we got there, and one of us must have accidentally knocked them off when we were, ah, *talking* in there."

If it's possible to hear someone smile over the phone, I can hear it. "Well, that's good news, at least. So he seems to think it's okay if we're going out?"

"Hey, all we're doing is engaging in a little soccer talk, right? Nothing that will jeopardize your reputation as the next leader of Schwerinborg."

He laughs, but it dies out pretty quickly, which means he's thinking about something serious. "Well, that's what I was getting to. Some of the guys were talking yesterday after we got out of practice."

"Yeah?"

"Well, remember how Ulrike's dad was at the dinner on Friday night? He must have mentioned seeing us together to Ulrike, because the guys were asking me about it."

Uh-oh. I know exactly where this is going. Ulrike is this really nice girl at my new high school who's the president of everything. One of those girls with white-blond hair and a perfect Crest smile, and who I usually write off based on her looks alone, because 99 percent of girls who look like Ulrike are just heinous. Snobby and mean and they think they're God's gift to the world. But Ulrike's actually really smart and friendly—and not just to other beautiful people, but to everyone.

On the other hand, Ulrike has this equally beautiful friend, Steffi, who's the world's biggest bitch. One of those fake, manipulative people no one—especially naive, trusting types like Ulrike—ever *get* until it's way too late.

"Let me guess—"

"Yeah, I'm pretty sure Steffi already knows we're together." Georg sounds irritated by Steffi's mere existence as he talks. "If not, she'll know soon. Thought we should figure out how we're going to handle it when she asks us about it."

Great. It's not that I really care if she knows. Maybe it'll knock her down a peg to realize that just because she's tiny and brunette and popular, she can't get any guy she wants. Like Georg.

But chances are, rather than simply acting like a normal person with hurt feelings when she hears that the object of her crush has a new girlfriend, she'll get totally ticked off, meaning she'll be more aggressive than usual about giving me backhanded compliments when everyone's around . . . making offhand comments about how I must have some wonderful hidden traits if Georg is willing to take the time to introduce me around the school when he's such a busy person.

As if whatever good traits I might have aren't obvious, or as if Georg is doing me this huge favor because I'm clearly not good enough to be around him.

Steffi's like that. You can't really pick apart anything she says as being nasty and call her on it, because she says it in this fakey-nice, syrupy way. But I know she wants me to get the message, especially because she makes genuinely nasty little remarks to me under her breath when she knows no one else can hear. She's so quiet with it, I can barely hear her.

So I say to Georg, "Well, you know how I usually deal with Steffi. I ignore her. But what do you think?"

As much as I'd like to rant to Georg about what Steffi can do with her opinions, I don't, because I know it'll only make me sound like a whiner. Georg tries to be nice to Steffi—since he's a prince, he's stuck trying to be nice to everyone or else risk his family's good reputation, which really sucks if you think about it—but he's the one guy in school who sees right through her.

And I love that about him. We have this funky-cool connection, where we just look at each other and *know* we both see the world the same way. As deranged as it is, the fact we both understand Steffi and her little games—when no one else does—just makes our connection that much stronger.

"Well, I figure we have three choices, assuming she actually asks us what's going on. First, we can play dumb. Second choice, we act like it's no big thing and say we were at the reception together because we both live under the same roof and thought it'd be fun."

"And third?"

"We come clean, and who cares if Steffi knows we've hooked up." I can hear the smile in his voice again. "And that's the fun option, because it means if I feel like kissing you between classes, I can, which definitely has its appeal."

"So what do you want to do?" No way am I making this call. I like option three, for the same reason Georg does. Frankly, a quickie make-out session with Georg—of course where Steffi can see—would totally strengthen my ability to deal with her and all her crap. But Georg knows Ulrike, Steffi, their friend Maya, and all the rest of the kids at school way better than I do. So I figure he's the one who should decide.

"I'd prefer to be honest about it." His voice has that tone that makes it sound like a *but* is coming, and it does. "But the more I think about it, the more I think it wouldn't be smart."

I make a face at the wall. Ooo-kay. Georg was the one who said he didn't care if Ulrike's father saw us dancing together, or who knew about us. And now he does?

"So I shouldn't say anything around school?" I guess it would pretty much be the gossip of the week if we confirmed it to anyone. But why should he care?

Then I realize that I'm the hypocrite of the century. I'm freaked about him not wanting to tell his friends, even though I still haven't told my friends about him, let alone about my mother and everything else. And they're thousands of miles away.

I'm about to apologize, and say we can do whatever he wants, when he says, "School isn't really the problem. It's the people outside of school. Okay, Steffi's a problem, but it's not her attitude around school that worries me. It's who else she talks to."

He gets quiet a second, and the lightbulb turns on in my head. Now I get it. Tabloids.

There's this one reporter assigned to Georg who walks about twenty yards behind him on the way to school a couple times a week. The poor guy's probably the bottom of the food chain at *Majesty* magazine. There really isn't much to report about Georg—his parents crack down on him hard, so he really can't get in any trouble, and he doesn't go out partying. And I'm willing to bet most of the world's population couldn't find Schwerinborg on a map, let alone identify its prince. Not like they could identify Prince William or Prince Harry.

But still, Georg is always careful, so that most of the reports this guy files are about fairly innocuous things, like last week's story, "Teen Prince Risking His Smile," which ran alongside a snapshot of Georg ducking out of a coffee-house on his way to school, but mostly talked about how if you drink coffee or tea for years and years, your teeth can get stained.

"Valerie, I don't want you to think I'm embarrassed to be with you, or that I don't want anyone to know—"

"Hey, no problem. Really." And I mean it. I don't exactly want to be on the front of some trashy rag either. I'm beginning to realize that keeping things low-key goes with the dating-a-prince territory, even if you weren't almost caught smoking.

"You know how I feel about you. It's just that—"

He sounds so concerned about it, I can't help but laugh. I know I shouldn't—my dad would probably tell me it's against some very important rule of protocol—but I can't help it. "I told you, no problem."

He's quiet for a sec, then says, "If I hurry, I can be over there in five minutes, stay for maybe twenty, then get back before my parents are home from the fund-raiser. I just need to watch the clock so I have a five-to-ten-minute cushion."

"And what if we get caught?"

"Have your Chemistry book out, maybe?"

This time I'm really laughing, because my dad knows—and so does Georg—that I'm a total geek and there's no way I'd put my Chem homework off until midnight Sunday. I can hardly stand to have homework that's not done by Saturday at noon.

Is it any mystery why I haven't had a boyfriend before?

His voice is low and completely hot as he tells me, "I'll be there in five minutes, like it or not."

"Not!"

Exactly four minutes and thirty-two seconds later, there's a knock at my apartment door. And I definitely like it.

To: Val@realmail.sg.com

From: ChristieT@viennawest.edu

Subject: Armor Girls

Heya, Val Pal!

Can I just say I'm totally bummed you missed the GGs last night? The red carpet interviewer was wearing a dress that was totally see-through when she stood under the lights. They kept having to cut away from her and back to the person being interviewed, which was hysterical. You'd have made tons of jokes about the woman wanting to show off her boob job.

BTW, Jules told me about your Armor Girl theory—the whole thing about *A Knight's Tale*, the movie where Heath Ledger falls for this totally shallow rich-girl-princess type and ignores the girl who makes his armor. Jules claims that you think you're only an

Armor Girl to David Anderson's knight, and that he's only interested in you until he can find a Shallow Princess.

You are WRONG.

Tonight sucks for me, but you will be home tomorrow night, so I can FINALLY talk to you on the phone, right? I was nice to my cousins for an entire week so my mom would let me call you, and you haven't been there. Now you MUST be. Because I have actually talked to David about you, and you are so not an Armor Girl.

DO YOU GET IT YET?! YOU ARE THE PRINCESS.

I'm tired of dropping hints about this, which is why I'm cyber-yelling. You said you could change your mind and live with your mom if you wanted. I think you should. (I promise I will forgive you for going to Smorgasbord.) Natalie and Jules think you should come home too.

How often do all three of us agree on something? Seriously. Think about it. I know you told Jules that you thought David could never really like you for you, but you are so, so wrong. David is perfect for you. AND HE WANTS YOU.

Hugs and miss you and etc.,

Christie

PS—So what is this "unbelievable dirt" you told me about in your e-mail on Friday night? PLEASE tell me you haven't met someone. And if you did, get over him. He's not David.

To: Val@realmail.sg.com

From: CoolJule@viennawest.edu

Subject: You and your potential ass-kicking

Yo, Valerie!

Five very important things. Are you paying attention?? GOOD.

Number 1: Okay, I will acknowledge, after seeing last night's Golden Globes, that most of Hollywood is constructed of silicone and that the tabloids are probably correct about which celebs have had work.

Number 2: You're still wrong about the Armor Girl thing. I told Natalie and Christie about it, and they totally agree with me that you're the princess, NOT the Armor Girl, so get over yourself.

Number 3: Even Heath Ledger, may he rest in peace, was not as hot as the Schwerinborg prince Christie and Natalie and I read about on the Internet. The one the article said lives in the same palace you do. The one named Georg. (Did his parents forget the "e" in George? Or is that some bizarre Schwerinborg thing?!)

Number 4: You have still not written me back to say what happened when you gave Prince Georg, mentioned in item Number 3, my phone number and e-mail address.

Number 5: If you haven't done it yet, I'm going to kick

your ass. You're on a tight time line here, Val, because we KNOW you're coming home soon. RIGHT? So go accidentally and on purpose bump into my future boyfriend and GIVE HIM MY E-MAIL! I am not joking about the ass-kicking and you know it.

The future princess of Smorgasbord,

Jules

2

I SUPPOSE IF I MARRY GEORG SOMEDAY, I MIGHT actually be a princess. Someday being very, very far away and not even remotely on my brain, especially given the wonderful example of wedded bliss I've witnessed with my parents recently.

But no matter what Christie says, I am definitely not *David's* princess, at least not like Shallow Princess was for Heath Ledger in *A Knight's Tale*. Not even close.

I switch off my computer without answering Christie's e-mail. I know she means well, but I just can't deal right now. I'll think of something brilliant to say while I'm at school, something that'll get her off my case about David but that won't hurt her feelings. Since we're six hours ahead of Virginia, I'll be home long before Christie gets to check her in-box, so she'll assume I answered right away and won't be offended.

And Jules's e-mail just needs to be ignored. For now, at least. Despite her ass-kicking threats, I know she's kidding. Well, I hope.

Geez, I wish they hadn't all popped "Schwerinborg" into Google when I moved here. Or at least that they hadn't found out all about the royal family, and about Georg.

I toss my backpack over my shoulder, give the apartment one last look to make sure I haven't forgotten anything I need for school, then lock the door behind me, since of course Dad was up bright and early this morning to go work for Prince Manfred. He's very efficient. He wakes up at five a.m. most mornings so he can go to the gym. (Yes, my dad is fairly hot, as far as dads go, and no, I try not to think about the way women are constantly scoping out his bod, because the whole idea of some Schwerinborg woman doing my dad is beyond revolting.) Then he takes a shower and gets dressed in one of his expensive suits (always gray, black, or navy blue) and is out the door by six thirty.

Usually, it annoys me that he's so perfectly scheduled, but it worked in my favor last night. He went straight to bed when he got home, so he didn't even realize Georg was in my room when he came in.

I still can't believe Georg and I weren't more careful about watching the clock.

Okay, maybe I can believe it. Georg has this way of making me feel so incredible when we're together—and not just when we're making out—that I have trouble keeping focused on anything else going on around me. This is totally corny, but he makes me feel better about *me*.

As I walk down the palace hall zipping my coat, I realize I have to tell the girls in Virginia about Georg. Somehow. They're going to be all excited by the fact I'm with a prince, but I just know they'll be royally (pardon the pun) pissed off at the same time, partially because of the David Anderson thing, and partially because they're girly-girls and they won't like that I didn't tell them about Georg the very instant I met him—because who meets a prince every day?—let alone that I waited to tell them we're an actual couple.

And even though they won't say it, probably even to each other, they're also going to think it's not fair that I get to live in a palace and date a prince, especially when all three of them are better looking than me. Well, Christie is definitely better-looking. She's tall and blonde and has a gorgeous, zit-free face, not to mention boobage. The kind most women get implanted. Jules and Natalie are fairly good-looking, too. They're your typical cute brunettes.

And Jules has the kind of attitude you'd think a world-wise prince would go for. (Which is probably why she had no qualms about ordering me to give Georg her e-mail address and phone number.)

But me, I'm a red-haired freak of nature. I'm so pale I practically glow in the dark, and I'm pretty ordinary personality-wise. Not great, not bad, just perfectly *average.*

But the thing is—and this is the primary reason I haven't had the guts to tell my friends about Georg—they won't get it. They'll be all starry-eyed, equating Georg with the celebs we drool over during awards shows. They won't realize that Georg is a *real person,* and that Georg and I have conversations about normal stuff like the whacked things our parents and our teachers do, and what kinds of music we like, and how soccer's going for him. They'll think—which, admittedly, I did at first—that his life is full of parties and that he can do whatever he wants, whenever he wants, because he's famous (well, in Europe, anyway) and he has tons of money.

They'll wonder what the hell he's doing with me, and will conclude that I'm just some temporary Armor Girl holding his hand until a mega-wealthy, Prada-wearing, Euro-society girl comes along to hold it. It's also occurred to me that they might think I'm lying, either because I'm lonely over here in Schwerinborg and want attention, or to make them stop pestering me about David.

I guess I can't blame them, though. I pestered *them* about David for years. Like, ever since David and I were assigned to take care of the class rabbit together in kindergarten and I fell hard for the guy and his way-blue eyes and slightly off-kilter smile. Someone who's lusted after a guy the way I've lusted after David doesn't just turn around one day and announce they're seeing someone else, especially when the target of their lust is finally interested. *If* he's really interested.

"Hey, Valerie." Georg's smooth voice makes me jump as I reach for the handle on the door that leads outside, the one I use when I'm walking to school because it's at the back of the palace and cuts five minutes off my walk.

I turn to see Georg leaning against the wall, waiting for me and looking absolutely yummy in his black leather coat, a dark green sweater, and a pair of Levi's. A sudden sour taste—guilt?—rises in my mouth at the sound of his voice, and I mentally chew myself out for even thinking of David.

"Hey back," I say. "Please tell me you didn't get caught sneaking back into your room last night. I was really worried."

He gives me a *who me?* look. "My parents were already in their room, getting ready for bed, talking about some meeting my father's having with the Greek ambassador tomorrow, when I got back. I think they assumed I was already asleep. My door was shut exactly the way I'd left it. I got past without them noticing."

"What about the security guys?" There are two very burly men with guns who stand outside the doors to the part of the palace where Georg and his parents live.

He shrugs. "They're supposed to keep stuff private. And they didn't know I wasn't allowed out, anyway."

I shake my head at him. "Lucky for you."

"Very lucky." He shoots me a grin that's downright sinful, then makes a show of looking past me to see if we're alone in the hall. He pulls me off to the side, behind this big pedestal with a statue of one of his long-dead ancestors on top of it, and gives me a devastating kiss.

A few minutes later, he eases back and whispers, "I missed you, Val."

"It's only been about six hours."

"I know." He leans forward so his forehead's against mine and gives me a slow, incredibly sexy smile, one he knows is going to make me melt inside. "But I missed you anyway."

I shift my gaze toward the door. Since we both have to be at school in twenty minutes, and it's a fifteen-minute walk, we'd better get going. "You want to go first, or should I?"

"Let's walk together."

"I thought we were going to keep this quiet?" Given how close a call we had last night, I'm thinking we should be extra careful today. Last time the reporter was around, Georg walked way ahead of me on the way to school, and nothing had even happened between us then.

"Well, I wasn't planning to hold your hand or make out with you in the middle of the street," he teases, playing with the shoulder strap of my backpack. "We shouldn't appear suspicious if we just walk together like normal friends."

I go to the door and take a peek out. I even stick my hand outside, like I'm trying to determine whether it's raining or just misty, while I'm subtly taking a look around.

"I haven't seen him," Georg says from behind me. "He doesn't usually do Mondays. Tuesdays and Fridays seem to be the days, though he does mix it up sometimes."

I ease the door most of the way shut. "I didn't see him, either, but—"

"Then let's go." He reaches past me and opens the door, then holds it so I can go first.

I can't resist him when he's being chivalrous.

When we're about halfway to school, Georg fishes a few euros out of his pocket and walks up to a coffee stand. The people who live and work along this street are used to seeing Georg every day, so the guy selling coffee and muffins doesn't freak out or anything. He just says hello—well, he actually says, *"Guten Morgen,"* which is German for "good morning"—and hands out a tall latte, Georg's favorite, while I stand a little farther back on the cobblestoned street and rub my shoe over one of the gray stones, wondering how my life could have changed so much in just a few weeks.

When I look up, the coffee guy smiles at me and asks what I want. At least, I think that's what he's asking. I'm about to say, *"Nichts, danke"*—"nothing, thanks"—it being about the extent of my German, not because I don't want any coffee, but because I spaced asking Dad for more cash this morning. But Georg goes right ahead and orders me a cappuccino, just the way I like it, with nonfat milk and cinnamon. He talks a little bit with the coffee guy. Though I can't understand a word of it, I can tell they're pretty friendly with each other.

"You're such a prince," I tease him once we get away from the stand, each of us warming our hands with our paper to-go cups.

"I've heard that before," he says. He's grinning sideways at me, and it's so magical, I try to capture the moment in my head so I can sketch it later. I love to sketch people, and the way he's looking at me now would be so great to draw. There's so much texture—his scarf, wrapped perfectly around his neck and disappearing into the V where his leather jacket is zipped up; the way his long fingers are wrapped around the coffee as the steam curls up out of the tiny hole in the lid; and, best of all, when he looks at me with his head tilted to the side, his cheekbones look freaking fantastic. He's regal and normal at the same time.

"You're making a mental drawing, aren't you?" he asks after he takes another sip of his latte.

I'm about to make a sarcastic reply when he stops short. I follow his gaze down the sidewalk in the direction we're headed and realize the *Majesty* magazine guy is standing right in front of us. His blond hair is messed up from the wind, but he's completely ignoring it because he has out a camera with a monster lens and is snapping away.

Georg puts his head down and starts walking again, so I do the same. But all of a sudden, I'm feeling like I have rocks in my stomach and I can't drink my cappuccino.

"He doesn't usually take pictures, does he?" I ask as quietly as possible, since the guy's only about twenty feet in front of us and walking backward.

"Not very often. He must have space to fill in the paper. Just pretend he's not there." He says this in a whisper, so it's hard for me to tell if he's bothered by this too. I'm guessing we won't walk to school together tomorrow.

We turn the corner onto the street leading to our school. It's an American high school—all the teachers are

Americans—and most of the kids have parents who work for the government or are in the country temporarily for one reason or another. Ulrike's dad's a German diplomat, for instance. Maya is from New York. Her family moved over here when her mother got a job with some big investment bank. There are a few kids who've always lived here, like Georg, but they go to school here because all the classes are taught in English and their parents want them to be fluent.

Thankfully, because it's a private school, the reporter apparently has to stay a certain number of feet back, off school property. Just before we go past the school gate, though, he asks, "Prince Georg, would you care to talk about your relationship with Miss Winslow?"

"Miss Winslow's father works at the palace," Georg says, sounding totally casual. But I'm so shocked, I stop cold. This guy knows *my name*?

"Valerie, you'd better hurry or you're going to be late." Georg says this to me from just inside the gate. He doesn't look alarmed or anything, but I can tell from his tone that he wants me to ignore the guy and get inside the gate, pronto.

I hike my backpack further up on my shoulder and walk in, leaving the reporter out on the cobblestoned street. Once we're out of earshot, Georg says, "He's never spoken to me before, which means he thinks he knows something. Someone's tipped him off."

"He knew my name." How is this possible? I mean, Georg and I had our first real date on *Friday*. And even then, no one but my dad and Georg's parents knew it was an actual date. Georg's parents promised to tell any reporters who asked that we weren't romantically involved, but that they'd invited me to the reception because my father was working there and so Georg would have another teenager to talk to during the event.

We reach the door that leads to where all the sophomore lockers—excuse me, *year ten* lockers—are located on the first floor. Since Georg is in year eleven, he has to take the staircase just inside the door to the second floor, where he has his locker. But instead of going into the building and then us going our separate ways like I expected, he grabs my elbow and steers me a few steps away from the door, so we can talk in private.

"Georg, how could that guy possibly know my name? I'm a *nobody*."

"You're not a nobody—"

"You know what I mean."

"I know what you mean," Georg says with a drawn-out sigh. He takes a long sip of his latte, looking over the lid to make sure no one's watching us too closely. "I've walked to school with friends before—I do it fairly often—and he's never once bothered them or taken their picture. Well, he's taken *mine,* but not theirs."

I'm starting to really freak out now, but Georg says very calmly, "I think he's just fishing, Valerie. That's why he asked his question in English instead of German—so you would understand. He was probably hoping you'd make a comment."

"That still doesn't explain how he knew my name. At the reception on Friday, no one asked who I was. Your parents didn't tell anyone. So . . ." I hold my hands out and give him a *what the hell is going on?* stare.

Georg frowns, and it's clear he has no answer, so I ask the more important question. "What are we going to do now?"

"Nothing," he says, keeping his voice low as a group of guys walk by, give us a quick look, then go through the door on their way to class. "Just act normal and pretend it didn't happen. And if you see the reporter on your way home, ignore him. In the meantime, I'll call my father and let him know about it."

"He's going to be ticked off."

Georg runs his hand over his dark hair, something he does only when he's exasperated, even though he's sounding completely Zen. "He'll be unhappy with the reporter, not with us. And if I let him know about it, he can tell us how to handle it."

"Okay." I take a deep breath just as the warning bell rings. "We'd better hurry. I'll see you tonight?"

He gives me the kind of smile you give someone when you want them to feel better. "Definitely."

But as I scoot into French IV, I realize I don't feel better at all.

By lunch, I feel like I'm ready to hurl.

I grab a very normal-looking turkey sandwich from the cafeteria (usually they have bulkie rolls with unidentifiable contents, which I've taken to calling Unknown Meat of Germanic Origin) and head out to the quad. I want to find Georg. I want to hear what Prince Manfred said about the whole reporter thing. I want to hear that this is just me and my wacky imagination, and that no one knows anything and even if they did, it's no big thing.

What I get is Ulrike, Maya, and Steffi—which would be fine except for Steffi, who's looking at me like I stole my turkey sandwich out of her backpack or something.

"Hey, Valerie!" Ulrike waves me over to their picnic table—there are a few dozen of them around the quad—and offers me the seat next to her. While I unwrap the sandwich and pop the top on a Coke Light (since, here in

Schwerinborg, it's *Coke Light*, not Diet Coke), they all yak and yak about what happened in their classes during the morning, and who saw what movies and who went where over the weekend.

I'm scanning the quad for Georg, and I must be obvious, because of course Steffi asks me about it. I can tell from her face she'd been talking to Ulrike and Maya about Georg before I sat down. Heinous-evil-bitch-girl.

"Yeah, he wanted to talk to me about something," I say, trying to sound as casual as possible while I fumble to make something up. "Probably some palace security thing. Who knows?"

I see Maya shoot Ulrike a look. I want to yell, *What?* but think better of it. Then Steffi gives Ulrike this exaggerated look of concern that's so fake, I want to smack her.

"Valerie, did you see Georg this weekend?" Ulrike turns to me and asks.

"Well, since we live in the same building, yeah," I say. I don't say it in a snotty way at all, more like, *sure, hard not to see him*. But since I'm guessing they already know about the dinner, I add, "And he was at this formal thing of Prince Manfred's Friday night that my father brought me to. I think my dad wanted me to keep Georg company, since he was the only other person there under the age of forty."

Maya's eyes get wide, but she looks down at her Tupperware container and takes a bite of salad.

Now I'm so sick to my stomach I can't even choke down my turkey, so I take a long sip of my soda. Why, why, why did I come out to the quad, when I should have known something like this would happen? And where the hell is Georg?!

Ulrike sets down her sandwich. "Valerie, I hope you don't take offense, but"—she looks at Steffi, as if she needs to know it's okay to tell me something awful—"but at the reception, did you offer Georg drugs?"

I laugh out loud at this. I mean, I know it's not a laughing matter, but are they freaking kidding me?

"Someone told you I gave Georg *drugs*?" Then I realize that they're dead serious. "That's insane! I've never even smoked pot or anything, ever."

I knew there were probably going to be rumors about me and Georg, but at least this one I know I can argue. I look Ulrike—then Steffi—square in the eye and say, "Whoever told you guys that story is the one on drugs."

They all look totally shocked, which makes me wonder who I could possibly have offended when *I'm* the one who should be totally offended.

Geez. Even if I was a total cokehead or pothead or whatever, I'm not stupid enough to give drugs to a freaking prince!

Then Steffi gives me this sad, sympathetic look that I know is for the sole purpose of making Ulrike and Maya think she's all choked up about the situation. "It was the minister of the treasury. He saw you and Georg on Friday night, and he says you were trying to give Prince Georg drugs."

The minister of the treasury? He's the guy who was so smashed at the dinner that my dad had to help him into the bathroom before he puked in public, like, all over Princess Claudia's shoes. I didn't think the guy even saw me and Georg, he was so plowed, but apparently he did.

And completely mistook what he saw for something else.

"Well, he's wrong," I say. "You can ask Georg."

"No, we can't," Maya finally speaks up. "He went home about an hour ago. Someone from the palace came in a limo and picked him up."

"Then ask him tomorrow. Or call him on his cell," I tell them. Now I'm getting angry, because I know the truth. And I know Steffi's going to spread this rumor fast and furious if I give her the chance, because she'd do anything to make certain I don't get together with Georg. "You guys might not believe me—even though you *should*—but you've known Georg forever, and you know he wouldn't lie to you about something like this."

"Please don't think we're mad at you, or that we're accusing you of anything, Valerie," Ulrike says. "I mean, there are tons of people here who are into stuff they shouldn't be. But—"

"Look, I know you're a really nice person, and that you're not trying to hurt my feelings"—I say this to Ulrike, though I'd say the same thing to Maya, too, if it wouldn't make it obvious that I think Steffi's an incredible bitch by leaving her out—"but I would never give anyone drugs, let alone do them myself. The worst thing I've ever done in my life is smoke a cigarette, and it's been ages since I've done that. Seriously."

Well, since I was in Virginia, at least. And even then, it wasn't a regular thing at all. "And all of you had better talk to Georg before you spread any rumors"—this time I look directly at Steffi, because I'm deciding I have nothing to lose, and no way am I going to take her shit—"or you're really going to hurt his reputation and his family."

I wrap my sandwich back up in its plastic wrap, because there's no way I'm going to eat it now. It'd come right back up. It'd be about as ugly as the treasury guy was, hurling all over one of the men's room stalls on Friday night while my dad tried to clean him up and shuffle me and Georg out of the handicapped stall at the same time.

I stand up to leave, but a thought occurs to me and I

turn to Ulrike. "Hey, your dad was at that dinner Friday night. He saw me there, and Georg, too. He'll tell you we weren't doing anything like that."

She blushes all the way from the neck of her peach sweater to the roots of her white-blond hair, and I realize she's the source of the rumor. The treasury minister must've told her father, and he told her.

And Ulrike, of course, told Steffi, thinking she was being helpful or something. Because as nice as Ulrike is, she's too naive to see through Steffi.

"Well, he's wrong," I say. I can feel my throat getting tight, so I force myself to keep my voice steady and calm, the way Georg would. "Very wrong. Call Georg. He'll tell you the truth, even if you don't believe me."

3

"VALERIE? CAN YOU COME OUT HERE?"

I roll my eyes but yell out in a friendly voice, "Just a sec, Dad!"

When Dad calls for me instead of knocking on my door, it usually means he has something serious to discuss. And I have one guess what it is this time.

I wish Georg would call me. I sent him an e-mail and left a message on his cell the second I got home from school, but nada. Nothing. Zip.

I'm guessing he ended up going back to school for soccer practice, in which case he can't call me back, but I have no way of knowing for sure. And how the hell am I going to handle my dad if I don't know what's going on with Georg?

I shove my Geometry book off my lap, stick my pencil and calculator in the page—not that I've been able to focus on it, since I've been replaying my lunchtime conversation over and over in my head, wondering what I should have said—then climb off my bed and go out to the living room.

Dad's standing in our galley kitchen, putting chicken breasts in a pan for dinner. He's humming to himself and smiling, but since he hardly even got mad at my mother when she made her little "It's not you, it's me" divorce announcement out of the blue, the fact he's not growling or anything doesn't give me much hope.

"You need me to chop veggies?" I ask, deciding to play innocent for as long as possible.

"Nope, I'll do it while the chicken bakes. I just wanted to make sure we have a few minutes to talk." He takes a bowl full of some yellowish marinade he's whipped up and pours it over the raw chicken. As disgusting as that sounds, it looks and smells completely delish, and my stomach starts this loud, low rumble. Partially because I know my dad is incapable of making bad food, and partially because, due to circumstances beyond my control, I didn't eat lunch.

As Dad slides the pan into the oven, he asks, just a little too casually, "So school was all right today?"

"Same teachers, same homework."

"And things are going well with Georg, honey?"

Oh, crap. "Sure."

I just know I'm going to hate this conversation. I bet he knows Georg was here last night. He's smart about stuff like that. And that's just going to make him even more ticked off, especially if he already knows about everything that went down at school today.

But I'm still going to eat that chicken and enjoy it.

"I talked to Prince Manfred this afternoon. I understand a reporter followed you two to school this morning?"

I open a cupboard and snag a cookie, even though I know this is tempting fate. Dad hates when I get snacky before dinner. "Yeah. He writes articles about Georg every so often. I think that happens when you're royalty."

He pins me with a stare that I know has nothing to do with the cookie. "But today the reporter asked Georg about his relationship with you. Right?"

I give him my I-don't-care shrug. Dad calls it the Valerie Shrug, which is his way of saying he can see right through me, but I do it anyway. "Georg just told him you work at the palace. After that, the reporter left us alone."

Dad raises an eyebrow.

"Okay, we were at the gate to school, so he kind of had to leave us alone. But it's not a big deal." I don't think.

"Unfortunately, it is a big deal, Valerie. The reporter called the protocol office today and said he wanted to ask me a few questions. I didn't return his call, but I'll have to tomorrow."

Dad takes off his apron and loops it over a hook inside our tiny pantry. I know, it's weird he wears an apron, but he claims all good cooks wear aprons to protect their clothing. Since he feeds me all his wonderful creations, I never say a word about the apron.

I mean, I have serious food issues. Not starvation or dieting issues, or how-fat-do-I-look-in-this-outfit? issues, but you-can-get-me-to-say-or-do-anything-if-you-feed-me-well issues. Dad knows this and uses it to his advantage all the time. It is not a coincidence that he called me out of my room to talk while making dinner. He wants me to smell the chicken.

"So what are you going to tell him?"

"Nothing, not unless Prince Manfred wants to issue a statement. But I wanted to warn you. You're always careful, honey, but it may not be enough to simply be careful."

I polish off the cookie and ask, "Should I not walk to school with Georg?"

"Maybe not every day." He takes a deep breath, then crosses his arms over his chest. "I know you two have just started seeing each other, but dating Georg isn't going to be like dating anyone else, Valerie, and I want you to understand the gravity of that. The media feel they have a right to poke into your life if you're associated with someone who's in the news."

"Like with you, when you were at the White House?"

"Exactly."

The whole media thing is the reason Dad had to move to Schwerinborg. It's an election year, and President Carew is a very conservative Republican. Not only is he pro-gun, pro-life, and pro–big business, he's completely anti–gay rights. And in an election year, you don't want your protocol chief's wife suddenly coming out of the closet. Stuff like that tends to turn up on Fox News, when one of the anchors asks the president how he can be anti–gay rights when one of his employees is married to a lesbian, especially if he's had that employee and his family to dinner at the White House numerous times and they're "personal friends." (We're definitely not personal friends, but Dad says that's how the question would get asked on the Sunday morning political shows.)

So President Carew, out of the goodness of his heart (I think he has a heart, maybe), found Dad this job in Schwerinborg and promised to bring him back to the White House after the election. Dad's worked for three U.S. presidents, so he's the best there is. Even if Carew loses the election, the new president is bound to try to hire my dad back. But still. I know it's tough on Dad not being at the White House, even if he likes working for Prince Manfred and Princess Claudia.

"Well, maybe not exactly like the White House," he corrects himself. He gets a slightly sad look on his face, and I feel guilty for bringing it up. "There, I brought my situation upon myself to a certain extent. I knew when I took the job that I had to"—he hesitates for a second, because he's always careful about how he phrases things—"I had to sanitize my life, in many ways. But I never expected you to have to be so careful, which is why we lived in Vienna, and why I didn't take you to the White House or to government events very often."

"To protect me?"

"Yes." He smiles at me in a way that lets me know he really loves me and views me as an adult, that he's not just saying all this to exert his Dad Authority over me. "Reporters can be very, very nasty about personal issues, whether you're fifteen or fifty. If they suspect you and Georg are dating, they're going to dig into your personal life, and they won't be kinder in their approach just because you're not yet an adult."

"My personal life is boring. I mean, I get straight As, and it's not like they're going to dig up some hacked-off ex-boyfriend to talk trash about me." Because I don't have any.

"But you were in trouble last year in Vienna when you

were caught smoking behind the school." He pauses for a second, and looks me in the eye. This time, he definitely has the Dad Authority look. "And apparently the minister of the treasury saw you in the bathroom stall with Georg. He's mentioned it to at least one other person."

Yeah, no kidding.

So I ask Dad the question that's been bugging me all afternoon. "Why would he do that? I mean, the guy was puking his guts out. You wouldn't think he'd want anyone to know."

My dad lets out a totally uncharacteristic grunt. "That's exactly why he did it. To cover himself. A number of people saw him drinking at the event—drinking heavily—and they know he disappeared for a while. I'd be stunned if a reporter or two didn't notice. But when a friend asked if he was all right, rather than making an excuse or dodging the question, the treasury minister claimed to have been in the restroom longer than usual because he saw something disturbing."

"Me and Georg." And I can guess which friend asked him if he was all right: Ulrike's dad. The guy's probably just as well-meaning and just as naive about people's motives as Ulrike, though you'd think a diplomat—even someone assigned to boring Schwerinborg—would be a little more attuned to people's bullshit.

"Yes. The minister told your friend Ulrike's father that

he saw you and Georg huddled in a bathroom stall, and that he feared you were hiding in there to do drugs. He claimed he stayed in the restroom for several minutes to make sure you two weren't doing anything illicit."

I close my eyes for a sec to absorb this. I had no idea things could be this bad. So much for this being solely Steffi's fault.

"Of course," Dad says, "Ulrike's father knew the whole idea was ridiculous, and told the treasury minister he knew better, since he watched me escort the minister out of the room when the minister was feeling ill. Ulrike's father went to Prince Manfred right away—not to get either of you in trouble, but to ensure that any rumors would be stopped immediately. He knew the treasury minister was intoxicated, and he was worried that the minister might have told the same story to others."

"So Ulrike's dad was trying to protect you or something?"

"He was trying to protect all of us—Georg's family and the two of us. Prince Manfred spoke to the treasury minister this morning. The minister apologized and admitted that he behaved badly at the party, both by becoming intoxicated and by using you and Georg as an excuse to cover his own inappropriate behavior. So the issue has been handled."

I'm thinking, not quite, since Ulrike's dad clearly told

her, and she told Steffi, who has the biggest mouth in the universe. "So no harm, no foul?"

"That's what we thought, until Georg told his father about the reporter following you two to school today. Prince Manfred is worried that something may have leaked. It's too much of a coincidence. Both the minister and Ulrike's father insist they haven't said a word to anyone else, and would never corroborate a news story about it since they know it's not true, but you never know what someone might've overheard, or what that person might be saying to others."

Yeah, like Ulrike overhearing and telling Steffi, thinking she was being helpful by preventing me from trying to get Georg hooked on drugs or something.

I've got to tell Ulrike this was all a mistake. She'll understand. I can't say anything to Steffi, but maybe if Ulrike hears the real story, Steffi will get a clue too.

As I brush the crumbs from my cookie into the trash, my eye catches a book on the table out in the living room. Mom sent it to me—she has this thing about self-help books—and all of a sudden, I have a duh moment.

I turn back around to look at Dad. "You know I'm clean, right? I study and don't cut school, and the smoking thing is totally over, and I've never touched drugs of any kind?"

One side of his mouth curves up. "Yes, I know. You work hard and I'm proud of you."

"Then what are you really afraid of the tabloids finding out? Are you afraid that a reporter might write about you and Mom?"

He gives me one of his *you're smarter than you should be* looks. "It has occurred to me. Europeans are far more accepting of homosexuality than some Americans, but it still makes good tabloid copy. They'll find a way to twist what happened with me and your mother to question Georg's choices, or to question the manner in which Prince Manfred and Princess Claudia are raising Georg."

"That's insane."

"It's reality. Tabloids will print whatever they can in order to sell more papers, and hope that it's close enough to the truth to keep them from getting sued."

I grab two green peppers out of the fridge since I know he's going to chop them and add them to the chicken when it's done, and I carry them to the sink. I have a sick feeling about what Dad's going to say next and I don't want to get all teary. I'm not the crybaby type at all, but I need to not look at him for a sec.

As I turn on the faucet to wash the peppers, I ask, "Does Prince Manfred think it'd be better if I stayed away from Georg?"

"No, but he is concerned about both of you." My dad takes the peppers out of my hands and puts them on the counter. "I didn't tell him about the cigarette incident. However, if the press sees you smoking around Georg, or if he is caught smoking—"

"I told you, we *weren't* smoking. Those were in there when we got there." It's the truth. We weren't, and they were there when we got there.

"You're missing my point, honey. Do you think a reporter would care if the cigarettes were already there? If a reporter sees you smoking, or even with a pack in your hand, he's going to snap a photo. Europeans smoke more than Americans, but they still don't want their princes doing it. Plus, a reporter could use that photo to hint that you and Georg are doing other things you shouldn't be doing, and that'll open all this up again."

I force myself to look at him. I'm completely surprised to see he's not angry with me, just overly worried. "I'll be careful, Dad. Please believe that I'm not smoking, and that I won't."

"I believe you." I see a little muscle twitch in his cheek, so I know he's making an effort not to get worked up about this. "Maybe it was wrong to use cigarettes as an example. It could be anything you do. Anything that can be twisted to show that you don't appreciate European culture.

Speeding. Littering. Treating service providers like waiters or desk clerks badly. Do you understand?"

I nod. If I didn't get it before, I sure do now.

"And I think Georg is terrific. If you recall, I'm the one who took you dress and shoe shopping before your big night out."

"True." And he did a fabulous job, too—when the shoe clerks weren't flirting with him. Of course, the way he's looking at me now, I know there's a big *but* coming.

"But," he says, true to form, "I think you and Georg need to have a long talk about this before you take your relationship much further. All right? Georg isn't going to be like any other boyfriend."

Like I've had any other boyfriend to compare him to. "I'm not sure what there is to talk about, though. We won't do anything stupid, especially in public."

"If you need advice, I know a very good protocol expert." He smiles, but I know he's dead serious. "If anything, anything at all, feels off to you, like that encounter with the reporter this morning, I want you to tell me immediately."

The buzzer on the stove goes off, and Dad grabs his cup of marinade so he can pour the rest of it over the chicken since it's midway through cooking. I'm tempted to tell him about what happened with Steffi—since apparently he doesn't know that the treasury minister and Ulrike's dad were definitely overheard, probably on the phone after the party—but I figure it's probably nothing. Just Steffi being her usual bitchy self. Once I talk to Ulrike, things will be cool on that front. And who knows? Maybe her father's already talked to her if he thinks she overheard, and I'll show up at school tomorrow and everyone will apologize.

It's a long shot, but I'm willing to pin my hopes on it.

Dad glances over his shoulder at me as he closes the door to the stove. "Are we understood?"

"As long as you give me the big piece of chicken."

Because what I really understand is that if things don't go well tomorrow, then I'll have to tell him.

To: Val@realmail.sg.com

From: BarbnGabby@mailmagic.com

Subject: RE: Everything

Dear Valerie,

I hope you and your father are enjoying life in Schwerinborg. As you can imagine, I'm envious of all the rich culture and fine cuisine you must be enjoying there!

Speaking of European food, how did your fancy dinner date go on Friday night? I wish I'd been there to see you in your new dress. Your father said you looked like a movie star. (Of course, I've always thought that.) I'm so excited for you, sweetheart.

You might want to check your mail over the next few days. I know you said not to send any more books, but I saw one I just couldn't resist, and I think it'll help you keep your head on straight where boys are concerned. Not that I'm worried about Prince Georg—I'm sure he's quite the gentleman—but indulge me. I can't turn off the Mom urge simply because you're far away.

I'm still waiting to hear on the teaching job. I'll keep you posted. And you know, if you decide you'd like to come back and visit during Winter Break, you're more than welcome. Gabrielle would love to get to know you better, and I simply miss you.

Lots of love,

Mom

The second sentence of Mom's morning e-mail makes me laugh aloud, because ever since she moved in with Gabrielle she's been living on things like wheatgrass and quinoa. If I were in her place, I'd be envious of my food, too, even if it is wacky Euro-McDonald's half the time as I'm walking home from school. (And really, if she places such a high priority on good food, she should have stayed married to Dad.)

But the rest bugs me. Does Mom really think I need all the self-help books? I mean, she's always had an addiction to them, and I did say nice things to her after she sent me the first one . . . but I also specifically stated that she should not send another.

I so do not want to live life according to the publicity junkie, pseudo relationship expert of the moment. Especially my love life. I mean, if Dr. Phil knows so much about dating celebrities, why is he hawking books on television while wearing a bad suit instead of living in a mansion with some pinup wanna-be and attending pool parties?

And I won't even start on the teaching thing. Mom taught school before I was born and swore she'd never do it again. I mean, I know Dad is giving her whatever she wants in the divorce—he's practically paying for her and Gabrielle's apartment himself. (It's really disgusting and pathetic, if you think about it.) So I don't get why she's in such a rush to get back to work when she could take her time, think about something else she might want to do, and then go do that.

I click on the Reply button to: 1) tell her there's now an official moratorium on self-help books, because even if I wanted them, I have no time to read them and no space to store them in my itty bitty bedroom; and 2) she should really think about it before she starts teaching school again. Because as ticked off as I am about her and Gabrielle and the whole divorce (I try not to be, but I can't help it), I don't want her to be miserable.

Just as I start to type, the phone rings and I grab it. The

only people who'd call me before school are my mom—which saves me typing time—or Georg. And I really, really want to talk to him so he knows what's up.

But it's Ulrike. And I think she's crying.

"Valerie? I just wanted to say I'm so sorry. I hope you're not too mad. I swear it wasn't me, but I might have been the cause of—"

"Of what?" She sure didn't seem this worked up yesterday at lunch. I'm wondering if she got in some major trouble. Or if she called Georg like I asked her to do and he read her the riot act.

Not that Georg would read anyone the riot act. He doesn't get visibly angry about anything. He's totally cool that way.

"Well, you should be mad, but I'm—"

"Ulrike, I'm not mad at you."

At exactly that moment, Dad knocks on my bedroom door, scaring me half out of the chair. It's nearly seven thirty, so the man should be at work. I cover the phone and yell that I'll be just a sec.

"Ulrike, I've gotta go. My dad's knocking on my door."

"But—"

"Hey, we'll talk at school. I'll try to get there early and meet you in the year ten hallway, okay? But it's no big deal, really. I know you were just trying to protect Georg."

"Okay. But I'm so sorry, Valerie."

I roll my eyes as I hang up. Ulrike's too nice for her own good.

My dad knocks again, louder this time, and I'm about to say something I probably shouldn't, like *what the hell?*, when he walks in.

He holds up the newspaper. Not just one of the ratty tabloids, but a regular, honest-to-goodness newspaper. And there I am on the front page. In color.

You'd think the picture would catch my attention, since it's of me and Georg on our walk to school yesterday. Not because it's a good picture—both of us have our backpacks over our shoulders, and my hair is flying all over the place and I look highly annoyed—and not that I didn't kind of expect to see something about us in the paper. It's more the angle. The photo is taken from the side, so it couldn't have been the *Majesty* reporter. In fact, I'm certain I look annoyed in the photo because if it were much bigger, the *Majesty* reporter would be in it, since it looks like it was taken at the exact moment the guy asked Georg about his relationship with me.

But no. I don't give a fly about the picture or the fact that the *Majesty* guy obviously wasn't the only shutterbug around. And I'm guessing Dad isn't concerned about the photo, either.

It's the screaming headline.

4

"OH, SHIT!"

As soon as the words are out, I slam a hand over my mouth, because I can't believe I said what I just said in front of Dad. I mean, as if I haven't screwed myself enough here with the headline alone.

I don't have to know German to translate the two-inch-high type. It says something to the effect of:

THE BAD AMERICAN . . . ?

I think it means bad. Maybe evil or dangerous. Whatever it is, it's definitely not good, even if they did pose the headline in the form of a question, *Jeopardy!* style.

I look at my dad to gauge his reaction, and I realize things must be really bad, because he isn't even pissed at me for swearing, despite the fact I have never, ever said anything like that around him before.

Normally, I'm pretty sure he'd kill me. Martin Winslow is all about polite and proper behavior, and swearing is at the top of his Not To Do list. But instead of jumping all over me, giving me a lecture about how a young lady doesn't use words like that, he just shoots me a *you can say that again* grimace that makes me think he's already uttered a few four-letter words himself.

"Who was on the phone?" he asks, nodding toward the receiver.

"Ulrike."

His eyebrows jerk up. "Was she calling about the article?"

"We just started talking when you knocked, so I don't know." Her tearful I'm sorry's make more sense, though, if she was. "Maybe."

Oh, crap. Not only does the headline mean everyone will know about it—it means half the school already knows about it. They're probably texting one another right now, debating whether THE BAD AMERICAN is really bad or evil or whatever.

I bet Steffi's borderline orgasmic.

Dad takes a deep breath, the kind adults make when they're really worked up about something and are trying to stay calm, where you can actually hear the air whooshing in and out of their nostrils.

"All right. No more telephone for the time being, not unless I hand you the receiver. Let me answer if it rings."

"I was about to leave for school, anyway." I have to be there in about half an hour, so it's not like I'm going to be calling everyone and asking if they saw the gigantic headline.

"Let's hold off for a while. If you go, I'll drive you there. Definitely no walking today."

Wow. I've never been allowed to skip school. I hate to ask, but I do anyway. "So what does the article say, exactly?"

"I assume you can figure out the headline?"

"I think so. Enough to know it's not good."

Dad pushes my door the rest of the way open and hands me the newspaper, then walks over to my bed and sits down while I stare at the front page.

"Prince Manfred says it essentially means 'The Corrupt American.' Of course, they added an ellipse and question mark after it, as if to suggest your level of corruption is open to debate, but I don't think that makes it much better."

I'm thinking not, either. "Well, no matter what the article itself says, I'm not corrupt. I mean, *corrupt* makes it sound like I'm embezzling money from the royal family or something."

Not that I'd have the foggiest clue how to do that. I'm not even sure what embezzle means, exactly, other than something to do with stealing. Guess I'd better find out before the SATs. Now that I think about it, *embezzle* strikes me as an SAT word.

Dad shifts on the bed, and it's clear this whole conversation is giving him a headache. "The article states that there are unsubstantiated—and Prince Manfred said it uses that word, *unsubstantiated*, several times—rumors that you and Georg are close. It doesn't come out and say you're dating, but it strongly hints at it. It also states that you left the Friday night reception together, then were seen entering an unused restroom on a lower floor of the palace."

"Oh." I don't know what else to say. I'm just staring at the words on the page, wishing they were in English. Or even French, since my French is pretty good. I want to read this for myself, and it's killing me that it's just a bunch of funny-looking words I can hardly pronounce, let alone understand.

"So, where does the corrupt part come in?" I can hear the *Jeopardy!* music playing in my head as I stare at Dad, because I just know it's gonna be the whole druggie thing Ulrike talked about.

"The article hints that you and Georg could have been

going into that restroom to take drugs. Again, it doesn't make a definitive claim, but anyone reading the article can draw that conclusion."

And there the *Jeopardy!* music ends. "That's a lie!"

"Well, the bulk of the article talks about who you are, how you came to live at the palace, and then speculates on what influence you might have on Georg. It doesn't actually say you're 'corrupt'—it's written more as a 'what if this person spending time with the prince is a corrupting influence?' and what that could mean for the country."

Like I'm going to single-handedly take down the monarchy of Schwerinborg? Puh-leeze.

"Can't we sue them? I mean, for making it sound like I'm some kind of junkie or something? All I did was walk into a bathroom with Georg. While I'll admit that hiding out in a men's room is not normal behavior, it doesn't mean I'm corrupting him."

I have no clue how suing a newspaper would work, but it's just wrong that they're able to write this when it's totally, completely false. I mean, could this hurt my chances of getting into a good college? Did they even think about that?

He takes another of his loud, deep breaths, then adjusts his tie, and stands up. "No. Litigation isn't an option at this point, so don't even think in that direction, Valerie. Besides, as bad as it sounds, you're not actually being accused of anything."

He gives me a look of sympathy, but thankfully he doesn't say "I told you so." "The next few days are probably going to be difficult, honey. I know you did nothing wrong, and the royal family knows that too. It's been a slow news week, so the papers are just itching for a good story and they're blowing this out of proportion. I think the best thing to do right now is to lie low and let it pass. Prince Manfred has a staff who handle public relations, and they'll advise us as to how we can speed up—"

The phone rings, and Dad reaches past me to grab it, saying that it might be the P.R. guys.

Instead, after a second, he hands the phone to me with a warning look to keep it short. "I'm going to Prince Manfred's offices and find out what's going on. I'll be back in a few minutes. Don't go to school yet, and don't answer the phone."

I nod, hoping he'll boogie, because I am dying to know who's on the phone. Especially since he seems to think it's okay for me to talk to whoever it is.

As soon as Dad shuts the door, I say hello. And thankyou, thankyou, thankyou God, it's Georg. *Finally.*

"What's going on? I've been trying to reach you since yesterday!" I concentrate on my words so I don't sound desperate or ticked off, but I probably do, anyway. Mostly because I am.

"I know, I'm so sorry, Valerie. I wanted to call, but I couldn't."

"It's not your fault," I force myself to say in an understanding tone of voice that'd make Dad proud. "These things happen."

Well, I suppose they do if you're the girlfriend of a prince. But it's only been, like, three days, and already I'm sick and tired of everyone telling me they're *so sorry*. No wonder poor Princess Di was paranoid. I can't even imagine how many times during her life she must've had bad things happen, then everybody calling and apologizing to her after the fact.

And her prince didn't even love her like mine does.

"So what's going on?" I ask again, trying to push the Princess Di images out of my head, since I'm clearly not anything like Princess Di was (rich, pretty, famous, etc.). "My dad just showed me the paper. Is that why you left school yesterday?"

"Yeah. Someone on the newspaper staff leaked the headline to our press office. The source wasn't certain it was going to run, but the P.R. guys wanted to talk to both me and my dad so they could formulate a response in case the story did go to press. That's why they sent the car to pick me up."

"Oh." So they'll work to defend him from nasty newspaper articles, but clearly not me. I suppose that's the way the world works, but having it flung in my face, even though I know he doesn't mean to, sucks rocks.

I hear him messing with something, like he's flipping through the paper. "I'm really sorry, Valerie. I wanted to call you, but after the meeting, they drove me back to school for practice, then they were waiting to drive me home to talk to the P.R. guys again as soon as soccer let out. I didn't get a free minute the rest of the night. I didn't even get my homework done."

Whoa. He's neurotic about getting his homework done—almost as bad as I am. Though in his case, it's mostly 'cause he's afraid if he doesn't, it'll end up in the paper.

How's that for irony?

"Wow." I try to sound sympathetic, because I mostly am. "That totally blows."

"I got in around ten, then woke up at four a.m. so I could try to get my Trig homework finished, but I couldn't focus. All I wanted to do was call you because I was so worried the story would be in the paper. I was hoping it wouldn't be, since you and I both know there's nothing worth reporting. But one of the press office guys woke up my father just before five a.m. to let him know the story ran, and that it was worse than they'd thought. On the front page." He takes one of those deep Dad-like breaths. "I assume your father told you what the headline says?"

"Yeah. Apparently your dad translated for mine." And I'm guessing the conversation that followed wasn't particularly comfortable.

"Well, after I saw it, I really couldn't concentrate on Trig. I've been dying to call you ever since, but I wanted to wait until I knew for certain you were awake."

He sounds so sweet, and so Georg-ish, that I feel a major case of guilt. It's not his fault all this happened or that he couldn't call last night. I mean, it couldn't have been fun spending hours and hours holed up with a bunch of public relations types.

"Well, I'm really glad you called me," I tell him. "Even if it is with lousy news. I've been dying to hear your voice." His accent makes me melt, even if the rest of the world rots.

"I know. I wanted to hear your voice, too. I just don't want you to worry too much. The meetings went forever, but they all seem convinced it's going to blow over." He pauses for a sec, then adds, "That's the right way to use it, isn't it? Blow over? To mean something will go away soon?"

"Yep, you used it exactly the right way." His English is awesome, but sometimes he's not sure of certain phrases. It's incredibly cute, especially because he gets all embarrassed by it.

I really wish I could just shove the newspaper to the bottom of the recycling bin, curl up on my bed with Georg, and lie there. Just to *be*, and to not have to think about school or Steffi or reporters or anything else other than the way Georg talks to me, the way he smells when he's just taken a shower, or how much I love it when he wraps his arms around me and rubs my back.

And, for just a little while, I want to make him forget he's a prince. I want to let him hang out in my cold bedroom with the cracked wall and be normal—maybe watch TV or listen to some music or something—and not have to worry about how every little thing he does gets hyperanalyzed by his family, the palace staff, all our classmates, and even the media.

"Are you going to school today?" I ask as I stuff my homework into my backpack, just in case. "Dad hasn't said whether he wants me to go yet or not, but if we both end up having to hide out inside the palace all day, our parents shouldn't mind if we do it together." Then at least one good thing could come out of all this crap.

"I don't know yet." He sounds a little cagey, and my alarms suddenly start going off. I get a really, really bad feeling. But instead of keeping quiet, I spout off and ask him if something else is wrong.

"It's nothing."

"It doesn't sound like nothing. Just tell me." I know,

bad, bad move. Guys don't like being pushed to talk. Jules is always telling me that when a guy hedges with an answer, to let him hedge or you're not going to like the answer when he finally gives you one. But now I know he's not telling me something, and if I don't find out what it is, I'll go over the edge.

"My parents are worried about us, that's all. I don't think they were expecting things to get so exaggerated in the press."

"I don't think so either." I tell him about my conversation with Dad last night (apparently Dad didn't know about the possible newspaper article then, thank goodness) and about the one this morning. Georg tells me that his parents told him the same thing, basically: to lie low.

"So what did they say about us? Anything?"

He's quiet for a second too long. "Not much. But I think it'd be best if we cool it for a while."

"Cool it? What does that mean?"

"Well, you know what I mean."

No, I really have no clue. I close my eyes and lean back in my chair. "All right, then."

"Really? You're okay with it?"

What can I say if he won't tell me what he means by *it*? And I'm sure not going to ask him to clarify—*again*—since "cool it for a while" is certainly not going to work with my thought of hanging out together today, no matter what he means.

But what's really freaking me out is that I can't read whether he's okay with it—whatever *it* is he's proposing—from the way he asks.

And I can't tell whether "cool it" is his idea, his parents', or what. For all I know, it's the press office's, or the entire population of Schwerinborg's.

"I think my dad's back," I say, even though it's completely untrue. "Maybe we can talk later?"

"Definitely. I'll call you."

He sounds completely sincere, but I still wonder how many teenage angst movies I've seen where someone says, "I'll call you." It has to be a couple dozen. And in every single case, the guy never calls. It's code for something else, something not good.

I'm not sure, but I might've just been dumped.

To: Val@realmail.sg.com

From: NatNatNat@viennawest.edu

Subject: You really are . . .

SMOKING CRACK!

Okay, you KNOW I'm kidding. I know you'd never do drugs of any sort. But People of Earth to Valerie Winslow? Come in,

Valerie Winslow! What's with you and the bathroom? And, let's see . . . hmmmm . . . THE PRINCE OF SCHWERINBORG???

I assume that this e-mail will bounce, because if your e-mail is working, you would have told me about this. RIGHT?!

I'm also assuming you haven't told Jules or Christie about this or they would have told me.

Or could it be you're keeping the world's biggest secret because Jules is gonna kick your ass, since she has a thing for Georg? Or because Christie's gonna be completely bummed because she wants you to hook up with David, who's gorgeous AND totally into you, and what I saw makes it look like you're HOOKING UP WITH A PRINCE INSTEAD?

Lemme tell you, either way makes you a chickenshit.

So if this e-mail DOES go through, and you really have been keeping this from all of us, then I must ask: What kind of crack are you smoking?!

Curious, Natalie

PS—In normal person news, if you haven't heard, I'm grounded again. Bet you're just stunned (Hah!). Mom and Dad found out I got my tongue pierced. (I told you I got it pierced, right?) As you can guess, this did not go over well with Dr. Monschroeder, DDS. He gave me a half-hour lecture on the risks of fracturing my molars with the stud (doesn't "fracture my molar with a stud" sound vaguely kinky?), though he did stop short of reaching into my mouth to remove it. WHY does my father have to be a dentist? In any case, you can e-mail me whenever, 'cause I'm not leaving my room for the remainder of the decade.

To: Val@realmail.sg.com
From: CoolJule@viennawest.edu
Subject: Your Ass Kicking
(Attachment: WashPost74692.jpg)

Oh, Val? Yeah, you. That ass kicking? It's imminent.

I CANNOT BELIEVE YOU!!!! Have you seen this picture? IT WAS IN THE *WASHINGTON* FREAKING *POST*!!

I think you really are doing drugs over there. That's the only way to explain 1) this picture; and 2) the fact you have not said ONE WORD to any of us about this.

Putting on my combat boots (and you can guess why),

Jules

PS—You know I got Schwerinborg right on the Geography exam last semester, right? The one where we were given the map of Europe and had to fill in the names of all the countries? I didn't even write down "Smorgasbord." So don't even THINK I can't find your ass and kick it. I know where you live.

To: CoolJule@viennawest.edu

From: Val@realmail.sg.com

Subject: RE: Your Ass Kicking

Jules,

Okay, I have no idea why the *Washington Post* cares about any of this, but I'm telling you, it's NOTHING. It's just a picture they took of me outside school last week after I happened to walk to school with Georg—which is totally normal since we live in the same building, as you very well know because I TOLD YOU ABOUT IT.

And yes, I will now admit, there might have been a thing with Georg. Emphasis on MIGHT. And emphasis on HAVE BEEN.

And it just now happened. I haven't had a chance to tell anyone. Christie told me she was going to call, so I figured it was much better as a tell-it-on-the-phone thing.

I'm going to e-mail Christie and tell her to CALL. Okay? Will that save my butt from your combat boots for twenty-four hours or so?? Trust me, even if you could afford the airline ticket, you don't want to come to Schwerinborg.

Will explain everything as soon as possible, okay?

Love, Val

The *Washington Post*.

I CANNOT BELIEVE THIS!

I cannot even THINK about it. The picture Jules sent was apparently taken by the guy from *Majesty*, judging from the angle. It's not the same photo they ran in the paper here. And thankfully, the *Washington Post* is not calling me corrupt. I did a Google search on the article, and it's completely different than what was in the Schwerinborg paper. They just have three paragraphs saying that the prince of "tiny Schwerinborg" (and they also show it on the map, because of course no one in the States knows where Schwerinborg is except the twelve of us who actually got it correct on the Geography exam) might be dating an American, and that we were seen sneaking into an empty restroom together.

It does mention that the press in Europe is speculating that Georg and I might have been doing drugs, but that the palace adamantly denies it. And the *Post* article states flat out that there's no evidence, in their words, that "either of these two teens, both of whom are honor roll students with spotless records, were dabbling in drugs."

They actually write about it like it's cool—the American-dates-European-prince-and-is-hounded-by-their-press angle, I suppose.

What's really pissing me off, though, isn't the newspapers, either here or in the States. It's not Jules's threat to put her boots to my butt, or Natalie (jokingly, I hope) telling me I must be smoking crack. It's the whole Georg thing.

Because, as I told Jules, and as the *Post* so eloquently states, it might have been a thing.

As in past tense.

As in, over before it began.

As in I am a complete and total idiot to have thought it meant a *thing*.

When I hung up after talking to Georg, I had a solid two hours to sit alone in my room and ignore the phone's constant ringing before I got distracted by e-mail (since, for once, I thought it'd be wise for me to listen to Dad and not answer the phone, even if every time it rang I was hoping it'd be Georg).

But the whole ignoring-the-phone thing was made much easier by a simple realization that hit me a few minutes after I hung up.

Georg said *I think it'd be best if we cool it for a while*. Not his parents. Not the press office.

I.

To use his own word, *definitely*, he's definitely not calling me again. This much I've figured out.

No wonder I've never had a boyfriend before. I clearly can't keep one for even a week. And come on—if it was him trying to reach me on the phone when it kept ringing and ringing, and if he really wanted to talk to me, then he'd try e-mailing or texting me, too. But so far, nada on that front. Just all my buds from Virginia wanting a piece of me when I'm already as beaten down as I can get.

There's a light knock at my bedroom door. "Valerie?"

"Come on in, Dad." I'm so numb, I don't bother to move, even though I know I look completely lame. I've got one arm slung over my forehead, and I'm sprawled like one of those women who faints in Western movies after some guy dressed in black with really bad whiskey breath shoots the sheriff.

Except in my case, instead of having a totally hot cowboy crouching next to me, trying to loosen my corset so I can breathe, I'm just in jeans and an old sweater on my unmade bed, and I'm covered in Geometry homework.

As if on cue, my dad says, "I thought you finished your Geometry last night."

"I'm so freaking pathetic, I'm working ahead so I don't have to think about stuff."

My dad walks to the edge of my bed and shakes my foot, which he loves to do whenever I'm vegging out. "Don't use 'freaking,' Valerie. It sounds coarse."

I move my arm far enough off my face to look at him. He's clearly back to his old self. I'm not sure if that's good or bad for me.

"You have a package from your mother."

I push myself to a semi-sitting position, then look at the oversized, padded manila envelope with a horrible feeling of déjà vu. She warned me there'd be another self-help book, and this must be it. Dad can tell, too, because he's holding the thing toward me as if it's rat poison.

Kinda makes me wonder if he sort of blames Mom's giant collection of self-help books for her coming out of the closet. We both know that's not the case, obviously, but sometimes it sure feels that way. And there are days I think he wants to blame somebody, or something, for blindsiding him with the whole lesbian thing after nearly twenty years of marriage.

As bad as Mom's decision makes me feel, I know he has it much, much worse.

I pull the string tab on the side of the package, then look at Dad and hold up the book.

It's about cheese. No kidding. About who moved cheese. My mother is clearly getting back at me for making fun of her self-help book about moving cheese, because this is apparently the teen version. Gag.

I flip it over and look at the back cover. It's supposed to help me deal with change in my life. I don't think moving cheese around and having your brand-spankin'-new relationship (if that's what it was) dissected by the Associated Press are equivalent, but whatever.

At least, given the cheese angle, it might be more entertaining than the book she sent last week. That book tried to convince me that my problems were small stuff.

Hah.

I'm thinking no self-help book author ever had a mother come out of the closet and move in with a vegan. Or ever found herself forced to choose between living with her gay mom (and the vegan girlfriend) or moving to Schwerinborg, but that's just a wild guess on my part.

"Write your mother a nice e-mail to thank her," Dad says, though he looks like he's just thankful the book didn't come to him.

"I will," I grumble as I stuff the book back into the envelope.

"And while you're at it, you can tell her you'll be coming home next week for Winter Break."

5

To: NatNatNat@viennawest.edu

From: Val@realmail.sg.com

Subject: I really am . . .

1) NOT smoking crack, or anything else—not even emergency cigarettes;

2) So not surprised you did the tongue-stud thing;

3) Also not surprised about your being grounded (um, DUH, Natalie—did you honestly think you wouldn't be?); and

4) Sitting in my room in the ice palace at this very moment, printing off the confirmation for a Lufthansa airlines flight to Virginia, courtesy of my father.

In other words, I will be there next week for Winter Break.

Please hide Jules's combat boots, if you can. I swear I will explain everything when I get there.

Love, Val

PS—Is Christie gone or something? She hasn't e-mailed. Also, she was supposed to call but never did.

Spin control.

This is how my dad explains the fact that I am now on a plane, taxiing (is that really a verb?) toward the Jetway at Dulles International Airport.

Apparently, after his conference with Prince Manfred and Princess Claudia, Dad worried that things might get out of hand in the press. (I immediately asked if they could possibly get any worse, and Dad assured me they could. He even offered several hypothetical examples that convince me his protocol-wired brain is actually quite warped.)

So for the week of Winter Break, they—they being my dad, Georg's parents, and all the suits in public relations at the palace—thought it would be a grand idea for me to get outta town and let the P.R. office deal with the press. Frankly, I'd rather stay in Schwerinborg to avoid 1) Jules's ass-kicking; 2) dealing with Mom; and 3) making things even worse with Georg.

When I complained to Dad about not being consulted,

he told me that I'm fifteen and should get over it already, though he said it in a more formal, dad-ish way that made it hard for me to argue against.

My dad explained that the P.R. guys would accidentally but on purpose leak a story about how I would spend my vacation in the United States with family (making me sound very goody-goody and non-junkie-like), while Georg and some of the other guys from his year eleven class go skiing in Zermatt. Of course they would also accidentally but on purpose mention that Georg would be stopping to visit kids in hospitals on the way to and from Switzerland. All that nicey-nice prince stuff.

This is evidently what media types refer to as spin control: attempting to change or control the direction that a particular story will take in the press.

So after the week from hell at school—where Steffi gave me these *I'm so so sorry* (fake) looks, Ulrike walked around with a horrible guilty expression plastered to her perfect face, Maya simply avoided me, and my dad drove me to school so the reporters would have to leave me alone—Prince Manfred had his limousine take me from the palace to the Freital airport. Dad gave me a hundred bucks just in case, then sent me off. And now here I am, back in the States, in what must be the world's ugliest airport.

Controlling spin.

According to my father, the hope is that the press will believe that: 1) Georg and I are not together (which might actually be true, depending on what "cool it" means); and/or 2) whether we're together or not, we are good little kids and not the type to use drugs.

Although if anything will drive me to smoke weed, I decide it has to be the sight just past airport security. Yee-gads.

Mom brought Gabrielle.

I kind of figured she would, but seeing them together makes me want to hork up the airplane food. Don't they realize I'm suffering enough already?

"Val-er-eeeee!" My mom is jumping up and down and waving to make sure I recognize her in the crowd, as if her image hasn't been burned on my brain from birth.

I wave back, hoping it'll shut her up, even though I'm disappointed to see that she obviously still thinks her buzz cut is a good idea. She looks freshly shorn. I'd really been hoping she'd grow her hair back out. No woman my mother's age—let alone a woman named Barbara—should wear her hair that short. Does she not own a mirror? Has she not seen a recent copy of *Glamour* or *Vogue*—or, geez, even *Good Housekeeping*?

Once I pass through security, she gives me this monster hug. I suddenly realize that I've missed her hugs, even though she always hugs me so tight it crushes my shoulders because she's one of those super lovey-dovey moms. You know, the kind who hugs you as if she thinks you're never, ever going to hug her again, every single time.

"Oh, Valerie, honey! I'm so glad to have you home!"

"Thanks." I know I should tell her I'm glad to be here, but even though I've had almost a week to get used to the idea, I still can't decide. I mean, Jules refuses to reconsider her threats to do me bodily harm (with Natalie's full support) and that's the least of my problems. Four e-mails to Christie have gone completely unanswered, and all of my texts have been ignored, which is a Very Bad Thing.

Even worse, Gabrielle is looking at me with this dopey, mom-ish smile, and I just know she's going to tell me how much she's looking forward to spending this week getting to know me better. I've gotta give her credit for hanging back and trying to give me and Mom a little space to hug and say hello, but when I give Gabrielle a polite smile—because it's the nice thing to do and I know it's what Dad would expect—I still feel like a total faker doing it. Especially when she gives me this *I'm so excited you like me* look.

Blond freak.

"I'm really happy to see you, Mom," I finally say, focusing on her. And it's no lie—I am glad to see her. Just not her haircut or her girlfriend, particularly. I mean, she's still my mom and I still love her, even if I feel like I don't understand her anymore.

I try to act all happy and smiley as we pick up my suitcase from the carousel, and the two of them ask me about the flight and whether or not I'm hungry. But by the time we're walking out to Mom's green Toyota SUV, I'm only half-listening. My bullshit detector's going off and I can't pinpoint why. Since it's pretty finely tuned, even when I'm tired and grumpy, I figure I'm better off just keeping my mouth shut and watching the two of them.

Or not watching. As Gabrielle puts my suitcase in the back of the SUV and we all climb in, I figure it out: The two of them haven't stood within five feet of each other since I came through security.

This has to be planned. I mean, given how intense they were with each other in the weeks before I moved to Schwerinborg, they must have discussed ahead of time how to act around me. Decided not to hold hands or do anything mushy.

While I know they're doing it so I won't freak out, it's having the opposite effect. It's making me wonder what they're hiding. What they're really like together on an everyday basis. And what they think of my being here.

I'm an intruder in my own mother's car.

I grab an elastic out of my purse, yank my hair back

into a ponytail, then turn and stare out the window. It feels bizarre to be back in the States, even though I've only been gone a few weeks. I've lived in Virginia all my life, but only now am I noticing how wide the roads are and how loud people are when speaking to one another compared to how they speak in Europe. And in Virginia, everything is spread out. We have to drive five miles to the mall, and three to a movie theater. School is nowhere near walking distance for 99 percent of the students.

At the palace, on the other hand, I can walk to anything. School. Shops. Whatever. Even my boyfriend's—assuming I have one. And lots of Europe seems to be that way. City-ish and walkable.

As we slide from one lane into another and the trees and houses of suburbia flash by out my window, I try to adjust mentally to being home. The air even feels different when I crack my car window, and when Mom turns on the radio to my favorite station, the sound of American English and the obnoxious commercials make my new life with Dad feel very far away.

And it makes Georg feel far away too.

I know I shouldn't be so hung up on him, especially when I'm fairly certain I've been dumped, but I can't help it. All week long he's all I could think about. I saw him sneaking looks at me in the halls at school and he didn't seem openly hostile or anything. He even shot me a little smile once when no one was looking, just enough to make me keep my hopes up. On the other hand, he never once approached me—let alone e-mailed me—and I sure as hell wasn't going to walk up to him.

I just wish I knew whether his whole avoidance thing is part of the plan for spin control. I mean, is he avoiding me because his parents say he has to, and maybe it's a temporary thing? 'Cause that would explain the looks and the smile. Or is it because he's figured out for himself that it's not worth it to date me and he wants to extract himself from our relationship while he has a good excuse? Either way, as I lean my head back against the headrest and stare out the window, I feel very much alone.

The pathetic part is that I can't help but wonder if he feels alone too. I mean, if he wants to break up with me, fine. Well, not fine. But it'd be a hell of a lot better if he'd just freakin' say it. Just flat out end it. Otherwise, this whole living in limbo will slowly eat me alive.

But part of me thinks he doesn't. Part of me is convinced that what we have is special, and "cool it" really means that we have to stay away from each other awhile so we can be together later—which, in a way, is totally romantic and totally believable, coming from Georg.

"Valerie, did you hear me?" Mom turns in her seat and

frowns at me as she angles the car down the exit ramp and through the streets of Vienna.

"Sorry, Mom. Guess I'm tired." I didn't sleep well last night (go figure), and the flight has my body clock all screwed up. I left Schwerinborg at noon their time, and now it's two p.m., Virginia time. I think that means eight or nine p.m. in Schwerinborg, but my brain's just not operational.

"I suppose so. You haven't said a word about where we're headed."

"Home, right?" I lean forward and don't see anything unusual. Then it hits me: We're headed toward *my* home. The home where I grew up. Where I lived with Mom and Dad until Mom left to move in with Gabrielle. I'm so used to driving this direction from the airport that I forgot we weren't supposed to come this way anymore. That we should have gone to Mom's new place—the apartment she shares with Gabrielle.

"I thought you might like to see your friends for a while before we go to the apartment. And this gives me a chance to water your father's plants and pay the bills."

"Oh. Okay." I still think it's strange that Dad is having Mom look after his stuff while he's away, but he insists they're still friends despite the divorce and that he's more comfortable with her taking care of things than asking a neighbor or one of his buddies.

I hope I never get divorced and have to deal with this level of weirdness in my life.

"Um, I didn't tell my friends when I was getting in," I tell Mom. "I mean, they know it's today, but they don't know what time unless you told them."

"Of course I did," Mom says, and her voice is just overflowing with happy-happy-happy. "Julia, Natalie, and Christie all agreed to come over. They should be at the house about twenty minutes after we get there. I wanted to give you a little more time, so you could shower or take a nap if you wanted, but your flight came later than scheduled."

"That's okay." For one, the girls have seen me smelly and gross before. For two, even if I look like I just crawled out of the Potomac, they aren't going to notice. They're going to be far, far more interested in telling me off than in whether I've loofahed in the last twenty-four hours.

And despite what Mom thinks, Christie probably won't show. It's completely unlike her to ignore e-mail. And I know the e-mail thing is no accident, because she was all worked up to call me, and on her mother's dime, too. In exchange, her mother made her promise to be nice to her Tennessee cousins for a solid week when they came to visit. She even made Christie take them to the Smithsonian and all the typical Washington tourist sites.

Christie even went along on the freaking White House

tour, which she's totally sick of, so I know she really wanted to talk.

But after the Georg thing hit the *Washington Post*, she didn't even bother to pick up the phone, so it doesn't take superior insight to guess what her attitude toward me must be. She's feeling totally betrayed and I don't blame her. She's the best friend I've ever had, so hiding all this from her is pretty huge.

"You don't look very excited to see everyone, honey." My mom is looking at me in the rearview mirror, and I feel bad because I know she went to a lot of trouble to get everyone to come over. Five bucks says she even went shopping this morning and picked up treats of some sort from Giant. (Well, now that she's living with Gabrielle, I guess they'd get groceries from Whole Foods instead, and I'm guessing Whole Foods does not carry Ho Hos, which Mom always used to keep in the pantry because they're Jules's fave.)

"I'll be fine once I can eat and sleep a little," I say as we pull into the driveway. Thankfully, no one's beaten us here, so as soon as I break away from Mom and the freak, I dump my stuff in my room—which has to be ten degrees warmer than my room in the palace even though no one's even been living here—and take a quickie shower.

Why I even bother, I have no idea.

* * *

Surprise, surprise. When I walk back into my bedroom in one of my mom's old ratty robes, there's Christie, sitting on my bed. She's the same beautiful self she's always been, and I instantly feel horribly, terribly guilty for keeping so much from her.

"Hey." The word comes out froglike, probably because my quickie shower ended up taking nearly half an hour. I think my brain needed to soak. "I didn't think you'd come."

"Well, I did." She doesn't even bother to stand up. She's not visibly mad or visibly happy, just blah, which means she's about as angry as she can get.

"I guess we need to talk." I sound like a total dork, but we've never had a fight before, ever, so I don't know how to deal with Angry Christie. She's usually the peacemaker in our group. "I didn't mean to piss you off, really," I tell her. "You're my best friend. Ever."

"So you keep secrets from me?"

"No—"

"Funny, because I swear the *Washington Post* knows more about your life than I do."

I unwrap the towel from my head and toss it over my desk chair. "Okay, I did keep secrets from you. But I didn't mean to. I was just confused and I needed time to absorb everything. And"—I look her in the eye, which doesn't help matters, because she still looks very blah and unreadable, which, for Christie, is hard to do—"I didn't think you'd understand."

"What I don't understand is what's downstairs." She lowers her voice and points toward the door. "Who is that woman? She's not a neighbor, so I thought she might be from your mom's book club or something, but they don't look like book club buddies to me."

Oh, crap. How could this not occur to me on the ride home?

GABRIELLE IS HERE.

And I can't lie to Christie. Not with everything else. She'd never speak to me again, and right now, I just can't handle having her hate me. "Are Jules or Natalie here?" I ask.

"Not yet. I came early so I could see you alone. Good thing I did, too." Christie leans forward, and she actually looks concerned. "There's a lot more you're not telling me than the fact you're getting busy with some European prince, isn't there?"

I open the curtains partway and stand near the window—not to flash the neighborhood, but so I have warning when Jules and Natalie show up—then I look back at Christie. She's probably figured it out, but even if she hasn't, I have to tell her. "'That woman' . . . is named Gabrielle. And Gabrielle is my mother's new girlfriend."

"Girlfriend." Her voice is dead level, but I can tell what she wants to know.

"Yeah. And so you don't have to ask, she's that kind of girlfriend."

"You are freaking kidding me! Get *out*!" Her voice is low, but I glance toward the door, anyway, to make sure Mom and Gabrielle don't hear. "Your mother . . . is she . . . does she think she's *gay*?"

"Yeah. She is."

All of a sudden, I feel myself getting teary, which I completely did not expect. I manage to hold it in, but when I hear my own voice, I sound like I'm about to completely lose it. "That's why she and my dad are getting divorced. My mom decided—or admitted to herself or however you want to describe it—that she's gay, and announced over dinner one night that she didn't want to stay married to my dad. That it wasn't anything either of us had done, and that nothing would change her mind, it's just that she—and these were her exact words—*needed to be true to herself*, even though she knew it was going to be hard on me and Dad."

Instantly, Christie comes over to the window and gives me a hug. And then I can't help it. The waterworks start and I realize how hard it's been not to be able to tell my friends—Christie, most of all—what's been going on with Mom and Dad.

"That's terrible, Valerie," she says in a whisper, right next to my ear. "I never in a million years would have guessed. I'm so sorry."

For once, I don't care that someone's saying she's sorry, probably because this time I know it's heartfelt. And, of course, that thought makes me snarfle right into Christie's shoulder. "She dumped my dad right in front of me, Christie. It was so awful. I mean, I was beyond blown away, but Dad . . . the look on his face scared me. It was like she'd died or something."

"Why didn't you tell me, Val? It's been weeks and weeks!"

"I didn't think you'd understand. Telling you guys about the divorce was bad enough. And I felt so stupid." I'm totally blubbering now, though it's a restrained kind of blubbering, since I don't want Mom to hear any of this. I'm sure Christie thinks I've lost my mind, but I don't care anymore.

Christie lets me go because she's getting teary too. She reaches over to the top of my desk and grabs a tissue. They look a little dusty, since no one's been in the house for a month, but she shoves it toward me, anyway, then takes one for herself. "Why would you feel stupid?"

"Because I didn't know. I mean, I had no clue. How could I not know my own mother is a lesbian?"

Geez, I hate how that word sounds coming out of my mouth, like I think being a lesbian is a horrid thing. In my gut, though, I don't believe that. It is what it is, and I really do believe Mom when she says it's just who she is, that this wasn't a choice she made. But still.

"I just—I didn't even see the divorce coming, Christie. I actually thought my mother was kidding at first. Who ends a twenty-year marriage on a Wednesday night over Kraft Mac and Cheese?"

"But she wasn't kidding."

"Nope." I snorf into the tissue. I'm sure I look like hell, especially in this nasty robe and with my hair all wet, but whatever. "I'm pretty sure she'd already hooked up with Gabrielle when she made her little announcement, because they had an apartment lined up within days. And then it was so hard telling you guys that my parents were getting divorced that I couldn't bring myself to tell you what was really going on, that it was so much more than that, and—"

"Val. Hey, Valerie." Christie pegs me with a look, one that speaks volumes, letting me know she totally, completely gets it. She knows I'm dying inside, because my mother not only has this whole other existence I had no clue about and feelings toward other women I never could have predicted, but she also cheated on my dad. "It's okay," she tells me. "I mean, it's not okay, but I'm on your side here. I just wish you'd felt like you could tell me."

"Me too."

"Oh, man!" Christie's eyes get huge. "Your mom must think that I already know. And Jules and Natalie, too. That's why she invited us all over."

I swallow really hard and try to wipe my face clean with the tissue. I so do not want Jules and Natalie to see me looking this way.

"I didn't even think about Gabrielle being here until you asked about her just now. I'm having a major brain fart kind of day." Then I get a panicky thought. "There's no way I can tell Jules and Natalie. I just can't."

"Then don't. At least not today. But you should, at some point. They're your friends too. Give them a little credit, okay?" Christie glances out the window, then turns toward my dresser. "Sit. Dry your hair. I'll get you some clothes."

"Thanks. I swear, you're the best friend in the world."

"Keep that in mind next time your life falls apart."

As she tosses me a pair of old jeans, then opens my closet to search for a top, I ask her how she thinks I should explain Gabrielle, since the freak's not going anywhere before Nat and Jules come over.

"Well, maybe they won't notice. They'll think she's just

a girlfriend or something." She looks back at me, and the tiniest smile pulls at the edge of her mouth. We can't help it. We both crack up.

"You're awful, Christie. But in a really, really good way. Seriously, thanks for being cool with all of this."

She does a little hip shake. "I'm always cool."

"You two are awfully quiet. Is everything cool up there?" Mom hollers from the bottom of the stairs.

"Yes!" we both answer, then crack up again.

"Natalie and Julia should be here any minute," Mom calls up. "You should all come down and have something to eat. I even bought some Ho Hos for Julia!"

"Okay!" We both yell back.

"Well, that proves she's still the same mom you had before," Christie says as she picks out a black V-neck sweater from the closet. "She remembered Jules's heart attack in a box."

I let out a deep breath as I start to brush my hair out. "Yeah, I guess."

"Look, if Jules or Natalie ask, you can just lie and tell them she's from the PTA or something—well, as long as neither of them ask right in front of your mom or Gabrielle."

I give Christie a look that says, *you* would lie? Christie is pretty much incapable of falsehood, and everyone knows it. She's that disgustingly pure.

"Just for today," she says. "And if they do ask in front of them, I'll just mention Prince Georg or the *Washington Post* and that'll solve the problem. They'll forget all about Gabrielle."

"Great." I roll my eyes. "And about Georg, it's a really long story—"

"I figured, and I haven't forgiven you for not telling me. Plus, I'm still dying to know what in the world is going on. You'd better tell me soon, too, because whether you like it or not, you're going out with me and Jeremy tonight. I already asked your mom if it's okay."

"I don't want to be a third wheel. I'm here all week, so we can do it another night if—"

"You won't be a third wheel." Her blue eyes light up and I know what's coming even before she says it. "David's coming too. That's why you have to fill me in on whatever you have or don't have going on with His Royal Gorgeousness. Before we go."

"Christie!" I can't possibly go out with them. Not when the whole Georg thing is unresolved. And I'm going to need to explain the spin control concept to Christie 'cause I'm thinking this is a no-no, even if I wanted to go.

As if there weren't enough other reasons to say *no way in hell* to a night out with David—reason number one being I'm David's Armor Girl, not a potential princess.

"Are you going out with Georg? You can't possibly be." Her eyes lock with mine, and in that instant I know she knows. She's been my best bud way too long not to read me. "Omigosh. Valerie, you are. You are!"

"Actually, it's not really—"

"Have you guys been fooling around? Are you committed? Is it serious?!"

I tick off the answers to her questions on my fingers. "Yes, I don't know, and I don't know, but—"

"Then you're coming out tonight. We're going to dinner, and I have tickets for all four of us to a nine o'clock movie. You have to come. You have to give David a chance to talk to you. Please? For me?"

"Does David think this is a date?" I can't go on a date—a real, official *date*—can I?

Even if I've dreamed about David Anderson asking me out since I was learning about two-plus-two and reading books like *Dick and Jane* and *A Duck Is a Duck*, it just feels like it'd be wrong.

But holy smokes. A date with David Anderson? The most gorgeous guy in the whole school? The guy who makes those red carpet actors look only sorta cute in comparison?

The guy whose yearbook picture I photocopied and then taped up next to my bed, where he stayed hidden behind my pillows for over a year just so I could see him every night before I went to sleep?

Okay, I destroyed that photo in a moment of exceedingly good judgment before I went to Schwerinborg, deciding I'd been a total obsessive freak to copy his picture in the first place, but still . . .

No, no, no. It's just wrong. Wrong, wrong, wrong, wrong, wrong!

"It's casual. Sort of," Christie says as I pull on my jeans and the sweater. "Let's just see what happens after you two talk."

"This is a bad idea. Seriously."

"Jules and Natalie are here," she says, looking out the window. "Jules's mom is already backing out of the driveway. And hey, Jules really did wear her combat boots!"

I'm thinking, for the first time, that this might actually be a good thing.

If Jules kicks me hard enough, I won't have to go tonight.

On the other hand, a little tiny part of me wants to go, just to satisfy my curiosity.

"Shoot me now," I tell Christie. "Just get it over with."

"She's not that mad at you," Christie says, making a squished-up face (which is hard for her to do). "She's always this way. I think she's mostly interested in finding out what's up with Georg. A little jealous, but mostly just interested."

"No, I meant shoot me before we have to go out tonight. I can't believe you did this without talking to me first!"

Christie levels her worst stare at me. It's not that threatening if you don't know her, because she can't look violent even if she tries. But I know she's serious. "Like you not talking to me before you hook up with Prince Charming? Hell-o?"

At that moment, I hear Jules yelling up the stairs, and Mom introducing Gabrielle to Natalie.

Oh, crap.

6

I THINK I HAVE SAID ABOUT TEN EXTREMELY HEARTFELT thank yous to God in the last hour that both Jules and Natalie are the type of people who become oblivious to everything but themselves when they're ticked off.

While their occasional self-centeredness is usually an annoying trait, today it's good.

Because I just saw my mother kiss another woman!

Okay, it was on the cheek. And it was when she thought none of us were looking—which I can understand, because we were all sitting in the eating area and she and Gabrielle were in the kitchen, which is nearby, but not in the direct line of vision from most of the table.

When it happened, Jules was tearing open the Hostess

box and Natalie was griping about how she's only allowed out for two hours, and only because I'm home and her parents are granting her a "special break" from the maximum security block (a.k.a. her bedroom) because she's still in trouble for the tongue piercing. And Christie chose the seat facing away from the kitchen, so she saw nothing. But still.

This is beyond bizarre. I mean, Mom and Gabrielle looked all cheery when we came downstairs and plunked down at the table. The two of them stood in the kitchen while Christie yakked about Natalie's tongue piercing and Jules argued that it's probably no worse for Natalie's health than ignoring the trans-fat content of her own beloved Ho Hos, despite all of Dr. Monschroeder's dire warnings about Natalie's risk of breaking a molar or getting an infection.

Mom and Gabrielle were both sipping herbal tea and smiling in that parental sort of way that translates to *I'm so glad my kid is happy in life and has such wonderful friends.* Then Gabrielle turned and said something to Mom very quietly about the Ho Hos—probably agreeing with Jules's trans-fat comment—and Mom's smile got even bigger. Then Mom leaned over and kissed Gabrielle on the cheek—the exact same way she used to kiss Dad when they were having a happy-warm-fuzzy family moment.

For an instant, I just froze. I could not believe what I just witnessed.

It didn't make me angry or anything. It wasn't even that gross (which you'd *think*). It was just . . . *weird*.

But now I can't focus on the conversation around me. I keep sneaking peeks into the kitchen to see if they're going to do it again.

Or if they'll do something else. I mean, what *do* they do in public? I haven't been around to see. Do they hold hands when they go to the movies? Are they lovey-dovey in the grocery store?

I am not going to think about this!

It's all just so wrong, them doing whatever it is they do, and even worse, my thinking about it so much.

"Valerie?" Mom sets down her teacup and leans on the counter to catch my attention. "Didn't you have something to show your friends up in your room?"

I grunt an uh-huh, because I think she means the presents I brought from Schwerinborg. Dad, ever the protocol expert, bought some beautiful bracelets for everyone in a really pricey Freital jewelry shop. (And yes, I wanted to do it myself, out of principle, but I couldn't leave the palace without the press following me. And I couldn't have afforded what Dad spent, anyway, so who am I to gripe?)

But part of me also wonders if Mom is making her suggestion because she wants time alone with Gabrielle.

Though why, when they've had the last few weeks without anyone else around, is beyond me.

Maybe they feel like they're on their honeymoon or something, now that Mom and Dad are separated and Mom's officially filed for divorce.

"Yeah, let's go upstairs so we can talk, Val!" Jules says after licking the last of the chocolate off a Ho Ho wrapper. She not-so-subtly punctuates the remark by bashing one of her boots into my instep. "We have a ton to catch up on!"

Natalie sticks out her tongue and bugs her eyes at me.

"Okay, that is beyond disgusting," I tell her, even though Natalie just being Natalie makes me feel better, in a bass-ackward sort of way. "I mean, ouch."

"Ouch is right," Jules says under her breath, but as we all get up, Christie glares at her, making it clear that she not only heard Jules's comment but that she wants Jules to lay off until she gets the whole story.

Thankyou, thankyou, thankyou, Christie.

"So, things haven't changed one bit with you since the last time we were all in here," Jules says in a totally fake but funny voice once we get into my room and the door's shut. "You're exactly the same old Val we all know and love. You're open, honest—"

"I get it already." I don't even bother to sound apologetic. Although, with the honesty thing, I wonder whether

Jules is referring to Georg, my mom, or both. I'm not sure which topic sucks more to deal with, but since I know they know about Georg—at least as much as they read in the *Post*—I figure I should lead with that. "Look, I really didn't mean to hide anything from you guys. But everything happened so fast."

"You're telling me." Jules fiddles with my hairbrush, then sets it back down on top of my dresser. "I can't believe your mom moved on already. I mean, the divorce can't be final. It's way too fast. Have they even filed yet?"

Natalie sprawled on my bed when we came in, but at Jules's question, she sits up straight and stares at her. "What are you talking about?"

I hate that Jules is such an expert on the whole marriage-divorce thing. And not just because it sucked to be her as a kid, since her parents got divorced when we were all in third grade. Her mom remarried the next year, but that marriage blew up the summer before we started sixth grade. Her parents then remarried—each other, of all people—when we were in eighth grade.

On top of the whole why-won't-my-parents-just-settle thing ruining her elementary school years, the experience made Jules way too perceptive about how adults handle relationships. Well, at least perceptive enough to tell that my mom and Gabrielle aren't just friends.

I make myself face Jules's stare-down. "It was obvious the minute you walked in the door, huh? I should have known you'd figure it out."

"*What* was obvious?" Natalie demands. I know she suspects what we're hinting at now, but she can't bring herself to believe it. She looks at Christie, whose eyes are huge, because Christie's in awe of Jules for figuring it out so easily. Natalie looks at Jules for confirmation, then to me. "No way. NO WAY! Are you serious?"

"Dead serious. Unfortunately."

"Oh, wow. Your mom's a dyke now? Gay?" She pauses for a second before asking, "What *is* the proper word? 'Lesbian,' I guess? Unless she's bi—?"

"Well, definitely not 'dyke,'" I tell her, though I'm really not sure about any of this stuff either. "I think 'lesbian's the most accepted, but 'gay' works, too. And no, I don't think she's bisexual. Just gay."

"That completely blows. I was hoping I was wrong." Jules turns my desk chair around and sits in it backward. "Just for that, I completely forgive you for keeping the Prince Georg thing to yourself. There will be no retribution whatsoever. The boots are off."

"Gee," I say, and I can't help but grin at her. "My ass and I both thank you."

I can tell that Jules and Natalie really do feel bad for

me, which wasn't at all what I expected. I know, I know, they're my *buds*, and I should trust them. But this isn't something any of us have dealt with before. Jules's situation was completely different, plus you never really know where most people stand on the whole gay issue until they're face-to-face with it, no matter what they've said in the past. It's just too dicey for most people to handle.

"How's your dad dealing with it?" Christie asks. "I hope he's okay."

She's always been really tight with my parents, so this can't be easy news for her, either. She's been coming over to my house to hang out and for sleepovers since we were little.

"He doesn't talk about it much." I give them all a half-shrug. "I mean, he's probably got plenty to say, but he wants me and Mom to stay close. I think he's afraid if he gets negative about the situation, it's going to make me more ticked off at Mom than I already am."

"About her being gay?" Nat asks.

"No. I'm not mad about that." I don't think. "Though I'm not *happy* about it, you know? I'm more mad that she was lying to us all this time."

"Did she know she's . . . well, you know. Do you think she's known all along?" Christie asks.

I can tell from the way she's scrunching her nose that

ever since Christie arrived and discovered the truth, all this has been slowly percolating in her head. And now that I think about it, she was pretty quiet when we were having our Ho Ho time downstairs.

She's probably been thinking about all the times Mom has seen her naked, or at least in her bra and underwear. Like when we've gone to the day spa as a treat from Mom, or when Mom stuck her head in my room when Christie and I were changing clothes to go running or to a dance or whatever.

Or maybe Christie's more enlightened than most people, and instead, she's thinking about all the other stuff that had me going berserk the first week or so after I found out. I mean, my mom declaring she's gay is as close as it gets to Christie having her own mother come out of the closet.

Well, except Christie's mom used to be a nun (before she met Christie's dad). And Christie's pretty religious herself. So maybe she's just thinking that my mom's a horrible sinner, and how awful it is for me that my mom might go to hell.

Whoa. I hope that's not what Christie thinks.

I flop onto the bed next to Natalie. Careful to choose just the right words, I say, "I dunno. I think she was lying to herself as much as to me and Dad about her orientation."

I catch Christie's eye, just for reassurance, and I realize that at least part of my hunch about Christie's feelings is dead on. While I can't tell whether she thinks Mom is committing some huge sin, as far as she's concerned, we're in this together. My bad news is her bad news.

I am so so so so glad she's my best friend. No matter what her belief system tells her, she's at least going to *try* to be understanding.

"You're angry because you think your mom cheated on your dad," Jules says before Christie does. "Otherwise, how could she have hooked up with Miss Thang down there so quickly, right?"

I just nod. The whole room suddenly fills with this whispered chorus of *I'm so sorrys* and *oh that's terribles*, and I can't help but not want to hear it anymore.

"Can we talk about something else?" I ask, even though I know what they're going to want to talk about. "Not that I'm blowing you guys off, but another topic would sure make me feel better. I'm sick of thinking about the whole my-mother-is-gay thing right now."

"Hmmmm . . . Georg the Gorgeous?" Jules gets a wicked grin on his face. "You know if he lived within a twenty-mile radius of here, he'd be mine."

"Yeah, yeah, yeah," I say, as Natalie tosses one of my pillows at Jules's head and tells her to give me a break.

So I fill them in on everything—starting with my meeting Georg and our flirting a little, then our date to his dad's fancy event. I tell them about making out in the palace garden and in the public restroom, though I try to be casual about that part, as if I've kissed lots of guys and making out with Georg that night is just another part of the story and not the absolute best, most mind-blowing thing that's happened to me in my life.

I also tell them about the cigarettes (that we were *not* smoking) and about my dad catching us. I finish up with all the stuff about the *Majesty* reporter, the bizzaro conversation at lunch with Ulrike and her buddies, the photos in the European papers, and the entire concept of spin control.

"So you don't know if you and Georg are together or not?" Christie's incredulous as she asks this. "You have to have a gut instinct—I mean, you don't even have a hint, like from his tone of voice or anything?"

"Nope. Not a clue." Was she not listening? I mean, I suppose I could tell them about the little smile he gave me in the hall at school, but then they'd tell me I was giving him credit where credit's not due, or they'd tell me I'd imagined it. Either way, I don't want to hear it.

"How well do you really know him?" Natalie asks. "Not to be harsh on the guy, because it does sound like he's pretty damned incredible, and I mean, he's a freaking *prince.* But how can you not know if you're together?"

"Look, things were kind of crazy right before I left. How many relationships have you been in where the entire staff of a press office wants to weigh in on every little thing you do? It changes things."

Not that I have any basis of comparison, and neither do they. Jules and Natalie are both short-term-relationship types. Their modus operandi with guys is to go out, make out, and then get out.

And Christie's had one—ONE—boyfriend. They've been together for quite a while now, which explains why she responds: "But if you two really like each other, and want to be together, that shouldn't matter. I mean, look at Jeremy and me. If we're separated, like when he goes to running camps in the summer to train for cross-country season, we're still a couple. We don't have to talk about it or anything, it's a given."

"So you guys are telling me that 'cool it' means Georg has dumped me?"

They all look at one another, then Jules shrugs. "Maybe. I mean, we weren't there, and since you left us out of the loop it's not like we can give you a fair assessment."

"What I think," Natalie tells me in a very deliberate tone, "is that you need to decide whether *you* want to be with *him*. That's what really matters."

I frown at her, because she's sounding like my mother or, more accurately, like one of Mom's self-help gurus. "I can't be with him if he doesn't want me, so I don't know that that's helpful. I mean, what if I *do* want him, but he doesn't want me?"

"Then forget him," Jules mutters, "and I'll have a crack at the boy."

I ignore her. In the most unemotional and firm voice I can manage, I say, "Well, we can debate it all day long, but there's no point. I won't know anything for sure until I get back to Schwerinborg and Georg and I can sort it all out."

Assuming the spin control plan actually works and we're allowed to have more than a five-minute face-to-face conversation alone, that is.

"That's not true," Christie cuts in. "Just go out with David while you're here. I bet you decide pretty quickly whether Georg is really the guy for you once you're out with David. Even if Georg is a prince and you think he 'gets' you."

Right. I can tell what she's really saying is: 1) Georg *doesn't* get me, or he would have known to explain "cool it"—or to not even say "cool it" in the first place; and 2) David *does* get me, so who cares if Georg does or not, since I've been crushing on David practically my whole life?

"I agree with Christie," Natalie says. "What can it hurt?"

Well, it can hurt Georg. But I'm not going to say that aloud because it's clear to me that they're all in David's corner.

"Okay, fine. I'll go out with David." I point a finger at Christie. "But it is not a date. Casual really has to mean casual, okay? Make that crystal clear to David and to Jeremy. I still believe I'm the Armor Girl."

"You're wrong," Christie says. "But you can wait and see for yourself."

To: Val@viennawest.edu

From: GvE@zasucafe.ch

Subject: Are you there?

I know this is your old e-mail address from home, but I thought I'd try to send to it on the off-chance you'd get it.

I'm at an Internet café in Zermatt. I managed to get over here from my hotel without anyone from the press following me. I think I can safely send you a message, but you know how that goes, so I'll keep this basic.

I just wanted you to know I meant what I said after the dinner. The way things happened afterward, I wasn't sure you'd know that anymore.

Don't respond—this is only a temporary address—but I promise we'll talk as soon as possible after we both get back. I'll find a way. Even if I have to sneak out at midnight to do it.

G—

I forgot how completely, totally, unequivocally gorgeous and witty David is. I had a crush on him for nearly a *decade* for a very, very good reason.

I keep peeking over at him in the next chair, watching him watch the movie (and hoping he doesn't see me doing it), and thinking about how his surfer-blond hair and smooth, tanned-even-in-the-winter skin makes him look like he belongs in a movie himself.

And speaking of the movie . . . yeah, it's one with an Aussie actor in the lead. And it's one of those historical dramas. Christie knows I get all hot and bothered by a guy with an accent wearing a fancy costume, so this is totally intentional. To top it off, David bought me a Diet Coke and a small popcorn, no butter, which is exactly what I like to have. He bought himself Reese's Pieces (which I love but never buy, because everyone will think I'm an oinker) and made a point of offering me some.

I feel like there's a massive conspiracy going on around me. Massive. It's not normal to have everything fall into place so perfectly. We laughed our asses off at dinner, talking about all kinds of things over TGI Friday's buffalo wings and Caesar salad—fun topics without a mention of Schwerinborg, my mother (I still assume that Jeremy and David do *not* know), or David's father's ultraconservative politics.

David brushed my hand a couple times under the table, and he even made the same jokes about the ketchup I always make. He kept grinning at me with his perfect mouth and his perfect eyes, both of which sparkled. (Okay, that might have been the TGI Friday's lighting, but they sure seemed to have a sparkly kind of shine whenever he looked at me.)

It was *all* perfectly perfect, and anything that perfect makes me suspicious.

Especially since I am feeling incredibly guilty now. To take my mind off the fact my evening—let alone my *life*—has been planned without my consent, I spent this afternoon going through all my e-mail from Vienna West, since I discovered that the high school didn't close my account like they were supposed to when I transferred to Schwerinborg.

And there it was. It almost made me call Christie and back out of the date-that's-not-officially-a-date.

Actual communication from Georg.

His e-mail was dated yesterday, the day he got to Zermatt, and it said everything I've wanted to hear from him ever since the whole tabloid-newspaper-spin-control mess started.

He wants me. For real.

I know because that's what he told me the night of the dinner. We had that same aura of everything-tonight-is-perfect around us that's now being created between me and David in the movie theater. But that time, it didn't feel like a conspiracy. It just *happened*.

I shouldn't have come. Even before Mrs. Toleski showed up in her minivan to drive me (well, all of us) to TGI Friday's, I *knew* things would be okay with me and Georg. But then I figured nothing bad could happen if I just went along with Christie's plan and played it cool. David couldn't really be *that* interested in me. Half the girls in school would kill to go out with him, and I'm headed back to Schwerinborg in a week. And by not canceling, I keep Jules, Natalie, and especially Christie from giving me any more grief about it.

But now I'm feeling the vibe. The aura. The psychic whatever-it-is that makes me think this thing between me and David actually might be a *thing*.

Just like I felt with Georg.

I think.

They can't both be true, can they? I can't possibly have feelings like this—that a relationship is cosmically ordained—for two completely different guys at the same time. It's just wrong, at least with one relationship, and maybe with both.

"You know that's completely inaccurate historically," David leans over and whispers in my ear as the main character strolls down a street that looks vaguely European and knocks on a weathered door.

I glance at David and smile, because I like that he's so smart and that he assumes I'm smart, too, since he's not bothering to point out what the on-screen inaccuracy is. "They didn't wear those until the late eighteen hundreds, at least," I whisper back, trying not to think about how solid David's shoulder feels where he's leaning it against mine. Must be all that rugby he plays. "No way would they have 'em in the Middle Ages, anyway."

"Bet Mrs. Bennett wouldn't have caught it," he says, close to my ear, and I try not to laugh aloud since we're smack in the middle of the movie and everyone in the theater's hush-hush.

We both turn our attention back to the screen, because the movie's really good (despite the costume inaccuracy), and a few seconds later he reaches across the armrest and puts his hand over mine. He's a little tentative (can he tell I'm totally freaking out?), but after a few seconds he laces his fingers through mine. He does it loosely so I can still pull away without being obvious.

But I don't. His fingers are long and warm and strong and feel fabulous in between mine.

Most of my friends look at a guy's eyes, or at his shoulders and arms. With Jules, it's the way a guy's rear fits just so in his jeans. Me? I like a guy's hands, and I've always thought David's were the best. Well, except for Georg's. Maybe.

David doesn't look at me, but when I glance over at him he seems totally comfortable, like this is the normal course of events. I try to focus on the main character and the guy he's arguing with in the movie, but I've lost track of what's going on.

All I can think about is David. And Georg. I mean, doesn't David know there might be a thing between me and Georg? Is he kidding himself by holding my hand? Everyone else saw the newspaper, so I *know* he must've. He reads it every single day, first, because he's a natural news junkie, and second, because his dad's in it all the time. (All part of being a powerful Republican lobbyist, Dad once told me when I showed him an article about David's dad.)

And who am *I* kidding? There is a thing between me and Georg, and if I hadn't been so crazy about the whole "cool it" phone call and had just freaking *asked* him to clarify things (even though, at the time, given the way our conversation went, I thought it would have sounded bizarre to ask him twice), I wouldn't be here. Feeling guilty.

Oh. My. God.

I am *cheating*.

Is this how Mom felt? Totally ripped up inside? Guilty? Or did she even care?

Because even though I know I love Georg, I'm feeling a total pull toward David. A *normal* girl wouldn't drool over a guy like I've drooled over David, then decide to yank her hand away when he finally holds it, would she?

Or when he tightens his fingers around hers, the way David's doing now? Because it feels really good.

Maybe it's just that I'm not a normal girl.

"I'm glad you're home," he leans over and whispers. "I missed you, Winslow."

"Thanks—"

And then I feel it. Just the softest, most romantic kiss, right next to my ear. And I have no idea if this is a good thing—the thing I've wanted forever and can now get—or if it's the worst thing possible.

7

I AM SO GLAD WE'RE IN THE BACK ROW OF THE theater and no one can see us without turning around and being obvious. With my luck, a reporter flew over from Schwerinborg and followed me into the flick so he could snap a few more pictures. Or worse, maybe there's a private eye lurking in here. Someone hired by Steffi, because that's just the sort of thing nasty girls on soap operas always do when they want to get back at the nice girls. They make it their life's mission to prove the nice girls aren't so nice.

Steffi watches soaps. Lots of them. I think imitating soap opera bitches is how she became the evil demon spawn that she is.

Okay, I know my mind is going from highly unlikely

possibilities (reporter) to downright whacked possibilities (Steffi), but given what's happened to me in the last few months, and what's happening *right now* . . .

I turn to give David a friendly warning look to discourage further kissing, since even though I like it, it's wrong, but before I can get a word out, he leans in, his lips meet mine, and he's kissing me. This time, for real.

So I kiss him back.

Really, what can I do? I mean, he's right *there.* And the kissing's not bad.

In fact, it's actually pretty good. Deliberate and kind of daring, since Christie and Jeremy are sitting on my other side, plus who knows who else might get up to go pee and see us, since this theater's the closest one to Vienna West High School. But it's obvious from the way David's kissing me that he doesn't intend to have one of those grope-heavy sessions you always see other teenagers engaging in during the movies. Thankyou, thankyou, thankyou, David has more taste and class than that.

I guess, since his father's a semi-public figure, he's learned the tabloid lesson too.

But as his hand squeezes mine tighter for a split second (making me all warm and gooey inside), I can't help but wonder, *is this really okay?*

Of course, I've dreamed of kissing him forever. I've had

it so bad for him, I've even pretended that my pillow was David. (I did not kiss my pillow—puh-leeze—but I did go to sleep at night many, many times imagining I was putting my head on David's shoulder instead of a bunch of Poly-fil with a flannel cover.)

So I know if I could turn off my brain and forget that I theoretically have a boyfriend waiting for me a few thousand miles away, I would enjoy this immensely. David definitely knows what he's doing, though it's not as if I have much basis for comparison. Not even Christie suspects that Georg is the only guy I've ever kissed (well, besides Jason Barrows, which doesn't count).

It's totally pathetic, since I know people who are sleeping together, but there you go. I fake experience well, I guess.

David eases back and says in a voice barely loud enough for me to hear, "I've wanted to do that for a long time."

Not nearly as long as I have, but whatever. Hearing him say it makes all those years of lusting after him soooo worth it.

If he really means it.

Careful to play it cool, I just give him a little smile before turning my focus back to the movie (and trying to figure out what's going on, since now I'm completely lost).

A little over an hour later, we're in the back of Christie's mom's minivan. (I can't wait until one of us can drive and Mrs. Toleski doesn't have to accompany us on every single evening out.) David and I are in the back seat, while Christie and Jeremy are in the middle, behind Christie's mom.

David let go of my hand right at the end of the movie so it wouldn't be obvious to Christie and Jeremy what was going on, even though I think Christie was probably trying to watch me out the corner of her eye as much as she was trying to watch the movie. But now, while Christie is telling her mom about what we had for dinner and Jeremy is picking something off the bottom of his shoe, David's making it clear he really is serious about this. He reaches his foot under the seat in front of us and hooks mine, where no one else can see, then gives me this very cute, slightly devious smile that makes my insides do a little dance of joy.

"You like the movie, Val?" he asks loud enough for everyone to hear.

"Sure, what wasn't to like?"

He shifts so he's slightly closer to me on the seat, and I realize what he was *really* asking me with that question. Geez, but I'm a dork.

"Which way is it again, Valerie?" Christie's mom asks, looking at me over her shoulder just before turning into the apartment complex where my mom and Gabby have their place. "I think I came in from the other direction when I picked you up."

"Take your first right—by the stop sign—then it's the second building on your right. Middle stairwell."

As she pulls into an empty parking spot along the curb in front of Mom's building, David asks, "Want me to walk you to the door?"

The sidewalk from the street to the stairwell door is about a hundred feet long, but I'm perfectly capable of walking by myself, even though it's midnight. I mean, we're in a nice part of town, and Mrs. Toleski can see all the way from the van to the front door. It's no dark alley or anything.

"I'm fine," I say as Christie and Jeremy scoot over so I can climb past the middle row of seats and out the sliding door.

"I'd feel better if David walked you up," Mrs. Toleski says, which I suspected she would (she's cautious—probably comes from having been a nun), so David hops out of the van behind me before I can argue.

Secretly, though, I'm kind of glad he's with me. Not because I think there's a wacko lurking in the bushes, though. Just because.

I thank Mrs. Toleski, say bye to Jeremy and Christie (while trying to ignore the self-satisfied grin on Christie's face), and turn toward the apartment, with David right off my elbow. I can tell from the way he's walking, close to me but with his hands very carefully tucked into his front pockets, that he's hyper-aware of our proximity and the fact we're on a mostly dark sidewalk with all the stars out overhead. The clear skies and the soft breeze around us make the atmosphere totally romantic in a way you usually only see on sappy TV movies.

I've always known when David was within a shouting distance of me—I've developed a well-honed radar regarding the guy—but this is the first time I've been positive *he's* really noticing *me*.

And it's pretty cool.

We step up onto the wide stair outside the heavy glass door leading to my mom's new apartment and I fish around in my purse for the key Mom gave me—mostly so I don't have to stand there feeling awkward, wondering if he's going to kiss me good night.

"Must be hard seeing your mom living in an apartment all by herself," he says. "I couldn't imagine having to deal with a divorce or trying to choose between parents."

"Yeah," I say. He clearly doesn't know the whole story, which means Christie has kept her word—so far. I'm tempted to tell David the truth about my parents, even though we only have a minute. First, I want to be certain he hears it from me instead of from gossip central, and second, I'm curious about how he'll react. But I keep my mouth shut. Just for tonight, I don't want to know.

He bites his bottom lip, which I've never seen him do. David Anderson isn't the nervous type.

"What's wrong?"

He shrugs. "I just wish you weren't going back to Europe, I guess. That you'd consider staying here with your mom. I know living in the apartment means you'd have to go to school at Lake Braddock instead of Vienna West, but it'd make Christie real happy. She's been moping around like you wouldn't believe since you left." He hesitates for a second before adding, "It'd make me happy too."

Whoa. If it was possible for a person to make one wish and have it come true, this is what I would have wished for. But why-oh-why-why-why couldn't he have said this to me a year ago? Or on any day at all since, oh, kindergarten? I was just getting over him, coming to terms with the fact I'm his Armor Girl, and that being the Armor Girl isn't such a bad thing.

Does he not realize what he is doing to me here?

"They're watching us," I say, rolling my eyes in the direction of the curb. Part of me wants him to kiss me, *now*, but common sense (and the fact I can see Christie staring at me through the side window of the minivan) tells me that this is sooo not the time.

"I know. Otherwise, I wouldn't be standing here with my hands in my pockets. They'd be somewhere else."

Now I think I'm going to die. Right here on the front step of a suburban, ugly-ass apartment building.

And I'd die a happy girl.

As I slide the key into the lock, he takes a step down so he's on the sidewalk leading back to Mrs. Toleski's van. "Maybe we can get together tomorrow night? I can ask my brother to drive us somewhere. I know it's lame, but I bet he'd—"

"Can I e-mail you tomorrow?" I need time to clear my head.

"You have my address?"

I nod. He gave it to me a few days before I left for Schwerinborg and asked me to keep in touch, but I never wrote. It didn't feel right, since I'd never e-mailed or texted with him while I was living here.

But that doesn't mean I didn't memorize his info the second he gave it to me.

"Before you go back, I think we should at least talk."

I swallow hard. Wow, but I can tell from his face that he really means what he's saying, and it's making me insane because if I stand here one second longer, I'll grab him and kiss him first. Christie watching and all.

"I'll e-mail in the morning," I say, surprising myself with how calm I sound.

I turn the key and walk into the lobby as casually as I can. When I turn to take the stairs up to the third floor, where my mom's apartment is, I see David strolling toward the van. His hands are still in his front pockets, which makes his jeans pull across his rear just enough to make me take a good, long look.

Yee-ow.

I have no clue what I'm going to do.

"How was your night, honey?"

"You're still up?" My mom's never been a night owl—she usually goes to bed at nine thirty, sometimes ten if there's a good TV show on. But it's past eleven thirty now, and since she's sitting in an armchair with her reading lamp on and the rest of the apartment's dark, I figure she's up for one reason and one reason only.

Me.

"I wanted to get some time alone with you," Mom says with a smile. She sets down her book—I notice she's barely started it, which means she wasn't really reading—and reaches out to pat the arm of the chair next to hers. "Sit and tell me about it."

I leave my purse by the door, then drop into the empty chair. "The movie was great. Wasn't your style, though. Very commercial and big budget." My mom loves indie flicks—all the stuff they show at festivals—that usually have choppy editing and too-deep-for-normal-people-to-understand hidden meaning. Dad and I always used to tease her about it. Most years, she hasn't seen any of the Best Picture nominees for the Oscar.

"Was it the historical film with that British actor? The blond one?"

Historical film? She's making it sound like it should be on A&E. I keep a straight face and reply, "Yes. He's Australian, though."

"Bet he looked pretty hot, too."

Come again? She's mocked my obsession forever, but I have to wonder, does *she* actually think he looks good? And then I totally crack up, because I can see from her face that she said it to be funny.

"You looked like you could use a good laugh," she says.

"Definitely."

I know, I know. It's a strange thing to bond over, but I'm gonna take what I can get.

"Gabrielle's asleep already. I thought it might be a good time for the two of us to just sit and chat if you're not too tired."

"Sure." I'm beat, even though I took a nap after the girls left this afternoon just so I wouldn't crash at the movie, but I figure now's as good a time as any to talk to her—especially if she's in a jokey mood.

She looks a little uncomfortable even though she's still smiling, and I get the impression she wants to talk about Dad—how he's getting along in Schwerinborg, if he's seeing anyone, if he's making sure I'm eating healthy food, all that type of information.

Since the absolute last thing I want to do is report to Mom about Dad, or vice versa (mostly because Jules warned me about this happening and says not to even think about telling one parent about the other), I decide to make a preemptive strike. "You know, this afternoon I saw you kiss Gabrielle on the cheek in the kitchen when I was talking with the girls."

One of Mom's eyebrows arches up at this, but I keep going. "I know you two are trying to keep things low-key so you won't freak me out. I mean, it was obvious at the airport. You never got within arm's reach of her, but you kept giving each other looks when you thought I wasn't watching."

"Was that upsetting to you?"

"No. Not really." I pick at a piece of lint on the arm of the chair, then make a face. "Well, maybe it was. But I think you two should just act normal around me, even if

I'm only here for a week. Dad says we'll move back here for good after the next election, no matter who wins the White House, so I'm going to have to get used to you guys being together sooner or later."

Mom reaches over and puts her hand on top of mine. "Gabby and I are doing our best to make this transition as painless as possible for you."

"I know that."

"But you're still pretty uncomfortable with it?"

I nod. "I don't have a problem with you being gay, I don't think. It's more that you found someone else so fast. I mean, even if you'd hooked up with a guy, I'd be torqued by all of this."

Mom is quiet, and I know she wants me to look at her. When I do, she just tilts her head and gives me one of those looks that says she knows better.

"Fine, I'm uncomfortable with the gay thing too. But I'm trying very hard not to be. I don't *want* to be."

"I appreciate that. More than you can ever know." She gives my hand a squeeze and her eyes get all watery. "It might not seem like it sometimes, but you're the most important person in my whole life, Valerie. I'd do anything for you and I want you to know that."

"I do."

"But I can't not be who I am."

In a completely non-snarky voice, I say, "You made that very clear."

"I never wanted to hurt you or your father. I love him very much, and I always will. But when I met Gabrielle, I realized why I've been so . . . well, that's probably a whole different conversation. Suffice it to say I realized that I'd been living a lie, and I finally understood, deep in my soul, why my marriage to your father never felt quite right. It wasn't easy for me to do what I did, and it took me a long time to work up the courage to leave. Mostly because I was afraid of how it'd affect you and your father. I didn't want you to be hurt."

"It did hurt, though." It *still* hurts. "But I know it wasn't on purpose. And Dad's been great about it all. He's never said one bad thing about you."

"Well, that's something, I suppose." She wipes her eyes with the back of her hand and stands up. "I think we woke up Gabrielle."

At that moment, I hear the toilet in the hall bathroom flush. "Sorry. I was probably talking too loud. She won't be pissed, will she?"

"Don't say 'pissed.' Your father will kill me if you go back to Schwerinborg using that kind of language," she says, though she's smiling. "And no, she won't be."

A minute later, Gabrielle comes out into the living

room. She has a sleepy look on her face and her hair's looking pretty bad, but she seems agreeable enough, so I doubt she overheard anything. Not that she isn't already aware of everything we talked about, anyway.

"How was your date, Valerie?"

I give her the Valerie Shrug. "Okay, I guess." Like I'm going to discuss my love life with Gabrielle when I can barely talk about it with my parents—though I do give her props for being courteous enough to ask.

"Your friends seem pretty cool. I really like Christie. Jeremy and David are nice, too."

Damn straight. "Thanks, I've always thought so."

Mom gives my shoulder a quick squeeze—probably for being polite to Gabby—then starts organizing the magazines on the coffee table, which is always the signal she's about to go to bed. "Gabrielle and I wanted to take you someplace tomorrow as a surprise, but I just had another thought. If I can get appointments, how about if we go to that day spa we always liked in Vienna first?"

"That'd be cool." I haven't had a manicure in ages and ages, and I love getting them. Maybe, if Mom's feeling particularly guilty and they have an opening, I can get a facial, too. That'd rock.

But then I see a little look pass between Gabrielle and my mom. I get the feeling that wherever else they were—

or are—planning to take me isn't going to be something I'll like.

"So what's the surprise?"

Mom gives me a grin that's way too perky for this time of night. "Just that. A surprise. But I promise, you'll like it."

Right.

"What do you think?" I lean forward, pulling the seat belt to its max so I can extend my fingers into the gap between the two front seats of Mom's SUV to show off my manicure.

"Love that red!" Gabrielle says, inspecting my nails. "What shade was that? I must've missed it."

"It's called Rock the Vote Red. It's one of the Nicole colors." I usually go for pinks, but the name of the polish screamed out to me. I figured picking Rock the Vote would be a good luck charm to make doubly sure whoever wins the White House in November hires (or remembers to rehire, in President Carew's case) my dad.

I can only hope.

"Very pretty," my mom says. "Which did you end up with, Gabby?"

"It's called Blushingham Palace." She waggles her pink-tipped fingers in the air, and her whole attitude reminds me that she's a freaking decade younger than my mom, at least. "I think I like your Rock the Vote color better, though. I'm going to have to remember to look at the Nicole colors next time we go back. I love supporting them, since the company gives so much money to charitable causes."

Of course.

"I bought a bottle so I could do touch-ups," I tell her. "I'm probably not going to take it on the plane, so you can have it if you want."

"Are you sure?"

"Sure." The more people who wear get-Dad-his-job-back polish the better. Plus, for my mom's sake, I figure I'm going to have to be nice to Gabrielle eventually. She might be a mom-stealer, and she might've made me eat whole-grain pancakes for breakfast (made with soy milk, which gave them a bizarre aftertaste—and pancakes should *not* have an aftertaste)—but maybe, if I try really hard, I can convince myself she's not so bad.

I see Mom smile to herself. "Maybe I'll try out the color, then, too."

"I've never seen you use color." I look at Gabrielle. "She's worn nude polish or had a French manicure for as long as I can remember. Red would be a serious departure for her."

"Well, life's an adventure. We'll drag your mother along kicking and screaming if we have to, right Valerie?" She reaches back to rub my head, like I'm in kindergarten or something. "She needs a little change in her life!"

Okay. Bonding moment over. The whole life's-an-adventure philosophy is too much like that moving cheese book's philosophy (yeah, I flipped through it, so sue me) and I do *not* need to be reminded of the cheese book.

"So will you tell me where we're going now?" We're headed out of Vienna, toward Burke. "Or is it still a surprise?"

"Hang on for another five minutes, honey, and we'll be there." She's still smiling, but the smile's not reaching her eyes anymore. Wherever we're going, I can tell she's worried I might not like it.

And if she thinks that, I can safely assume I won't.

Mom turns the SUV onto a suburban street, taking us through a neighborhood of colonial and Tudor-style homes, all with yards kept pristine by landscaping services. We pass a neighborhood park, then she slows down as we approach a church. Apprehension gets the better of me as we pull into the parking lot. There are six or seven cars parked by the back door, and that's where Mom pulls in too.

"Um, Mom? You're Episcopalian." And I'm guessing Gabrielle believes only in Evangelical Vegetarianism. "You might've deduced from the red flag draped over the cross and the big sign out front that this is a Methodist establishment. And it isn't even Sunday."

"I'm well aware of the date and our location."

"Are we going to a Bible study?" A gay Bible study, maybe? If so, this would take the cake. And it's the kind of thing I can totally see Mom wanting to bring me to, hoping it'll make me feel better about her and Gabrielle, and to keep me from believing the Religious Right types who are bound to tell me that Mom and Gabby are going to hell, or that what they're doing makes them not good Christians anymore.

We always went to church together—me, Mom, and Dad—until Mom moved out. Dad only goes sporadically in Schwerinborg, and I've gone with him, but I figure Mom's been going all along. And she definitely believes in God, so I know she's not going to hell.

But a Methodist church? Are they more open to gays or something? I know there were a few articles in the newspaper a while back about some gay pastor (or bishop?) in New Hampshire, but I can't remember what kind of church it was.

Or if it was even New Hampshire. Could have been Vermont.

"It's not a Bible study." Mom shuts off the ignition and gestures for me to unbuckle 'cause she apparently wants me to come into the church. As she opens the back door for me, she says, "It's a pee-flag support group meeting."

As I follow Mom and Gabrielle across the parking lot, I shoot her a look that says, *support group*? And *Pee Flag*? "A what?"

"P-F-L-A-G. Parents, Families and Friends of Lesbians and Gays."

"We thought you'd enjoy sitting in on a meeting while you're home," Gabrielle adds, pushing open the back door and leading us down a semidark hallway. I'm getting a real queasy feeling, and she must be able to tell, because she looks over her shoulder and adds, "You don't have to participate, just listen. I think, if you allow your heart and mind to stay open to the discussion, you'll come to understand that you're not alone in your world experience. That your mother is better for coming out and that you'll be better for it, too, in the long run."

I'm so not wanting to hear Gabby's psychobabble. As if my mind needs more opening to world experience. I mean, what does she think I got being shipped off to live in *Schwerinborg*?

And better for it? How in the world did she say that with a straight face?!

I put my hand on Mom's elbow to attempt a last-minute appeal. "Can't we—"

"Don't worry, it'll be fine." Mom opens the door to a brightly lit room with about a dozen people mingling inside and drinking coffee from a big silver urn. A guy who I'd put at about seventeen years old waves to Mom. She gives me a little push into the room, then introduces me to "John" before I can even argue. "I'm sure you two will have a lot to talk about," she says.

I mumble something vaguely polite to John, because Dad has drilled *polite* into my head from birth, but I can't focus on John at all. I'm still trying to process Pee-Flag and the fact I'm here and simply *do not* belong. I mean, please. My mom has definitely flipped out this time.

This is way worse than a self-help book.

"Hi, Valerie!" one of the women says as she bounces—and I do mean bounces—across the room to stand beside John Boy. Her smile is Hollywood fake—as in I'm wondering if it's been surgically uplifted—and it's clear she knows Mom (and who I am) and that this whole PFLAG ambush has been planned.

"Great, you're here!" Mom says to Bouncy Lady. "I'll be back in an hour for Valerie. I know she's in good hands."

"You're leaving?" I hiss, trying not to be rude but really not caring at this point. How can she leave me here?

But she and Gabrielle scoot out the door without even bothering to answer me, and I'm stuck all alone in a room full of strange people. Worse, every last one of them is staring at me like I'm the newest attraction in the National Zoo's primate exhibit.

Great.

I glance toward a wooden rack on the rear wall of the room. It's filled with brochures about the church. I focus on one with a little cross on the front, mostly so I don't have to look at Bouncy Lady and John Boy and let them see my panic.

God, get me through this, please, I scream inside my head.

Because if I don't end up on some psychiatrist's couch soon, it truly will be an act of God.

8

"I'M YOLANDA. I'M THE GROUP LEADER," BOUNCY LADY says. I wonder if she's on uppers or something, but decide that no, she's just one of those fidgety people who hops around like a little kid her entire life. Like she's on a permanent Kool-Aid rush.

"Hi, Yolanda. Nice to meet you." I shake her hand, but I feel like a complete idiot. A *trapped* idiot. I tilt my head toward a bunch of gray metal folding chairs, which are arranged in a C-shape in three rows at the other end of the room. A couple of people are sitting there with their coffee, but most of the chairs are empty while everyone stands and yaks in little groups. "Um, should I just sit?"

"Sure, make yourself comfortable. We'll be starting our

meeting in just a minute. There's coffee and soda, if you'd like a drink."

I tell her thanks, I'll grab a Diet Coke (because I need one, bad), but then she gets all squealy as someone else—a woman about my mom's age—walks through the door.

It's the freaking Twilight Zone in here.

John pops the top on a Diet Coke and hands it to me. In a hushed voice he says, "Yolanda's always like that. The rest of us are much closer to normal."

I take the drink and give him a grateful smile.

"Your mom just dumped you here without warning you, didn't she?"

"It's that obvious, huh?" I can't help but like the guy. I get the impression he's being genuinely nice and that he hasn't been coached to say this just to make me comfortable.

He shoves his hair out of his face. It's scruffy brown and too long to be stylish, and he's wearing an old Kenny Chesney T-shirt. He's not bad-looking—he's got a killer bod and a decent enough face—but he's definitely not the kind of guy who hangs with the in crowd.

Which, of course, means he probably realizes I'm not exactly cool either.

"My parents brought me without telling me what it was

all about the first time either," he explains. "My mom's not here today, but she still comes sometimes."

How do I ask this? "So, is your dad, um—"

"No. My older brother, Brad. He came out last year."

"Oh." I can't imagine a buffed-up, grungy guy like John with a gay brother, let alone a gay brother named Brad, which sounds like a pretty non-gay name. He just doesn't look the type.

Then again, what's the type? Do I look like the daughter of a lesbian? And what's a non-gay name?

I take a long sip of my Diet Coke, telling myself that I must be way more shallow than I thought for making such an asinine snap judgment about John. Or for making judgments like that about anyone.

"The group's not so bad," he says, keeping his voice low. "The first time I came, I was pissed off like you wouldn't believe. Couldn't believe my parents were dragging me to something like this. So I know where you're coming from."

"And you're here by choice now?"

One side of his mouth crooks into a smile. "Yeah, believe it or not. I don't come to all the meetings, but most of 'em. I'm going to NYU next year, and between making college plans and everything that's been going on with my brother, I'm completely stressed out. This helps me keep my head on straight." He pauses for a sec, then adds, "So to speak."

Did he just make a gay joke? In a room full of people who are probably sensitive to the issue?

"I was planning to share an apartment with Brad in New York, since he's already at NYU, but now I'm not sure, you know? I mean, what if he gets a boyfriend or something?"

"Yeah, I can understand that." That would suck way worse than my situation.

Yolanda starts herding everyone toward the folding chairs, so I quickly grab a seat as far back as possible. It's a small room, though, and with only a dozen people in it, I can't really hide out.

Especially since Yolanda is now pointing at me. "We have a new member today." Her voice reminds me of a varsity cheerleader. Or worse, a wannabe varsity cheerleader. "Everyone please welcome Valerie!"

There's a murmur of hellos, then Yolanda says, "Valerie, why don't you tell us why you're here today?"

"Ummmm . . ." Because my mother tricked me? And what about Gabrielle telling me I didn't have to talk if I didn't want to? I want to give Yolanda the Valerie Shrug, but every single person is staring at me.

I'm going to *kill* my mother.

"I guess I'm just here to listen," I finally say.

Thankfully, Yolanda seems to accept this, and moves on to talk about her week. Apparently, her daughter, Amy, is gay. Sounds like they get along well enough, but Yolanda's worried about Amy moving into a new apartment complex, and that Amy's older, more conservative neighbors will treat her differently or will say nasty things when they discover she's not coming with a nice young husband, 2.5 kids, and a minivan.

"Amy doesn't seem too concerned, though," Yolanda tells the group. "She admits that the neighbors will probably react badly, but she doesn't think they'll pay enough attention to her to figure it out right away. So I'm just trying to trust in Amy, and trying not to worry."

A few people offer encouragement, which makes Yolanda smile. "So, anyone else with something to share? Anything happen in the last two weeks?"

She points to a guy in the front row with his arms crossed over his chest who's raising a finger in the air. Not a hand, just a finger. He says his name is Mel (for my benefit, I'm sure, though I can guarantee I won't remember his name five minutes from now). Mel, a balding guy with a beer gut and tattoos on his knuckles, talks about meeting his son's new partner for the first time last weekend. How he felt strange seeing his son kiss another man, even though there wasn't full-on tongue action or anything.

"Caught me completely off-guard, I'll tell ya. I guess I should've seen it comin', though," he says with a sarcastic laugh. "Ever since Jake was little, I figgered the day'd come where he'd call and tell us he met a young lady—someone from college or from his fancy office—and that he wanted to get married and give me and my wife a bunch of grandchildren."

Mel scratches his chin for a minute, then adds, "I've adjusted to the fact he ain't never gonna have a wife. But seeing him kiss another man just—" He stops for a second and closes his eyes. When he opens them again, he says, "I guess it just hit home all over again that everything I pictured for my boy ain't gonna come to pass. I drove home from the restaurant mad. Real mad."

I start thinking about Mom kissing Gabrielle, and I can totally identify with this guy. Even if he is, like, sixty or so. And I'm willing to bet he has anger issues regardless of his son's sexual orientation, if his deep frown lines and rough voice are anything to go by.

"Did the kiss make you question your love for your son?" A woman sitting in the front row, on the opposite side of the C-shape from Mel, asks.

Mel thinks about it for a moment. "I don't think so. I

love the kid, no matter what. But I sure was angry. I wanted to take a swing at his . . . his *partner* . . . just knock the fag's head off. Never would, course. I know in my gut that this is all *my* problem—not Jake's, and not his partner's. But ya know, people just didn't *do* this sort of thing where I was raised. Ya went to school, worked hard, and got married. Period. I guess what I'm saying is, I still have days where I feel like Jake's intentionally trying to ruin *my* life. So that's why I came this week, even though I ain't been here in a couple months. To try not to be so damned angry."

To my left, I hear John clear his throat. "I was really ripshit a few months ago—you know, wondering if I was going to have a place to live after I made all these plans. I wanted to call up my brother in New York and just tell him off."

Wow. I wouldn't use the word "ripshit" in this crowd—let alone that we're in the basement of a *church*—but no one even blinks when John talks this way. As I look around and listen to the people whispering, I realize they all pretty much talk however they want to, and all seem to accept how everyone else talks. Even Mel calling his son's partner a fag, which is another word I'd never use.

Not that I'm going to actually *talk*. But it is interesting.

"Anyway," John says, "I read somewhere that a good exercise is to put all the things that bother you about a person down one side of a paper, and all the things you love down the other side. So I made myself do that before I picked up the phone."

"Like a pro and con list?" someone asks.

He nods. "It sounds stupid, because you sort of know it all in your head already, but when I listed everything out on paper, I could see exactly what was bothering me about my brother, in black and white."

"And it helped you deal with those issues?" Yolanda asks.

"Exactly. And it's been good having a concrete list of things I love about my brother, 'cause I can read it whenever I need to remind myself to chill out."

He leans forward in his chair and pushes his hair off his face again. "Having a gay brother is really small stuff when I think about it. I mean, I'd choose having him tell me he's gay over telling me he has cancer any day. Like Mel said, it reminds me that I'm the one with a problem, not him. It's just part of who he is."

John's use of the phrase "small stuff" reminds me of the self-help book Mom sent to me in Schwerinborg a few weeks ago, and of course, that reminds me of the ridiculous cheese book. The one that said I have to anticipate change in the same way I'm supposed to anticipate that the cheese in the fridge will go bad, and go out and get new cheese. Or something.

But now that John's talking, I'm thinking that even though the cheese book sounded pretty bizarre, the small stuff book was kind of useful. Maybe I should give John's list idea a chance too.

I'm not one for exercises. I mean, I hate taking those quizzes in teen magazines that are supposed to tell me what kind of guy would be perfect for me, what kind of clothes fit my personality, or all about my dosha. But this exercise seems to make sense, because as John tells the group about what he wrote on his lists, I find that I'm mentally making lists for Mom. When I can't keep track anymore, I pick up a Methodist church flyer that's lying on the floor under the chair in front of me and scribble, keeping the print super-small so no one else can read it.

The Cons

- *Gabrielle (I think. Jury's still out.)*
- *Probably lied to me (about being gay, about cheating)*
- *Put Dad through hell, and he did NOT deserve it*
- *Explaining everything to my friends blows*
- *Sends self-help books in (misguided) attempt to make me happy*

The Pros

- *She loves me.*
- *Didn't mean to lie to me (or lied for the right reasons?)*
- *Brought me here when I never would have come on my own (Possibly a con? Probably a pro, since I'm making this list.)*
- *Trying to be open with me now*
- *Trying to treat me like an adult (with exception of today's kidnapping)*
- *Told me I could choose where to live, with her or with Dad (understanding that the choice should be MINE)*
- *Cool to my friends*
- *Took me for manicure (though as a possible setup)*
- *Tried to make marriage work for years so she wouldn't hurt me or Dad*

As I keep scribbling to the bottom of the page, I realize that while the cons on my list are biggies, they all have to do with me and my attitude.

Okay, I'm not happy that my parents don't live together anymore. I can add that to the cons list. But otherwise, as John discovered when he made his lists, most of the cons have to do with *me* being angry or uncomfortable or disappointed.

The pros, on the other hand, have to do with my mother herself: that she loves me, and that she never would have come out if she hadn't felt like she absolutely had to. The pros are all things that won't change. And five years from now, the cons look like things that might not matter so much.

Well, maybe not the cheating.

Maybe I need to just suck it up, deal, and grow up a little. Though, apparently, judging from Mel and the rest of the room, it's one of those things that's easier said than done.

I'm egotistical enough to think I have better emotional management skills than Mel, though. And if John can learn to deal—or at least try to deal—maybe I can too.

"How was it, honey?"

"Not as bad as I thought," I admit as I climb into the back of Mom's Toyota. I never did talk, but at the end of the meeting, I did check out the table of books Yolanda had on display. Some weren't for me, like *Our Trans Children* (sheesh, I really hope I never need that one, though I did see one woman pick it up and she looked relieved to have found it), but there was one called *Is Homosexuality a Sin?*

I grabbed that one.

Before I went outside to meet my mother, though, I hid it under my shirt. Totally immature, but I don't care. I don't want her to know I'm worried about this.

I mean, I'm *not*. I don't think she's committing a sin against God. I figure He wired her the way He did for a reason. But I still want to read the book. I have a feeling other people *do* think Mom is living a sinful life, and sooner or later, they're going to tell me so. Some may just be concerned, like Christie (and maybe Christie's mom—I don't know). But what about the serious gay-bashers? The kind of people Yolanda was worried might harass her daughter when she moved into a new apartment, maybe egging her house or yelling at her to repent? I have no idea how to handle that kind of thing.

Mom puts her key in the ignition, but before she starts the engine, I lean forward into the front seat, totally ignoring Gabrielle, and give my mother my toughest stare. "But don't ever, ever spring something like that on me again. I mean it, Mom."

I know I shouldn't talk to her this way, but I have to get it through her head—and Gabrielle's—that leaving me at the PFLAG meeting without telling me what I was about to face was totally uncool.

"I know we probably could've handled it better," Mom

says with a big sigh. "We've talked about it ever since we heard from your father that you were coming to visit. And we talked about it the whole time we were waiting for you."

"You waited outside?"

"Down the street." Gabrielle has the good sense to look embarrassed. "Your mom and I didn't want you to see us out the window and come running back to the car."

"Very mature of you both." Freaks. I'm in a Toyota SUV with freaks.

"I'm really sorry, honey," Mom says, sounding mostly sincere. "But I knew you'd never go otherwise, and I wanted you to try it out at least once just so you'd hear what other people in your situation are doing to deal with their concerns, and to see that you have resources."

"Yeah, I kind of got that."

"Well, I won't do it again. All right?"

I just give a little huff as I sit back in my seat and buckle my belt. I forgive her, but only if she keeps her word and doesn't pull this crap again. Even if it *was* helpful.

She flicks her gaze toward me as she puts the Toyota in reverse. "So was it helpful?"

Can she read my mind?

"I guess." Doesn't mean I'm all happy happy happy

about her being a lesbian, but I do feel better than I did before I came to Virginia. Well, about the whole gay-mom thing. The who-the-hell-am-I-dating? issue is something else entirely. Coming home made that a lot worse.

"Well, when you come to visit me during your school break this summer, maybe you can go again. Just for reassurance, or if you have anything you need to talk about. I promise not to spring it on you." Mom's face squinches into a grimace when I shoot her a death look. "Sorry. I'll drop the whole subject. I'm just glad you went and I hope you'll consider going again next time you come."

I shrug. Maybe.

"So," she says as she turns the SUV out of the parking lot and back toward the apartment, "what did you think of John? He seemed very nice."

"He's fine."

"Maybe if things with David don't work out, or with that boy in Schwerinborg . . ."

That *boy*?

"Mom, I don't need you playing matchmaker for me. I have enough trouble with Christie, Jules, and Natalie as it is."

"All right, all right," Mom says. "But did you notice that he's a Kenny Chesney fan? I love Kenny Chesney."

"Mom? No."

To: Val@viennawest.edu

From: BarbnGabby@mailmagic.com

Subject: FWD: FOR VALERIE

Valerie, this is from your father. Mom.

To: BarbnGabby@mailmagic.com

From: MartWins@realmail.sg.com

Subject: FOR VALERIE

Barb, I don't know if Val still has an e-mail account there, or if she can access her Schwerinborg e-mail from your apartment. Either way, would you please forward this to her at the proper address? Hope all is well. Martin

---

Dear Valerie,

Sorry I had to send this via your mother's e-mail account. I know you'll be back here in a few days, but I wanted to touch base with you before you return, and I'm usually working during the hours when you're home to take a phone call.

I've met with the press office, and things here look positive. They pinpointed the source of the leak. It seems one of your schoolmates overheard a conversation and told several friends. That student's father has the situation in hand and has dealt with it.

The only story that's been in the press since you left simply mentioned that you flew home for vacation. There has been no more speculation about anything questionable where you're concerned. The press about Prince Georg's trip to Zermatt and his charity stops at hospitals has all been positive.

So please, do not worry. And if you do keep in touch with your friends here, I think it best to not mention the incident. They understand that they were wrong to gossip in the school halls about these matters and that what they believed happened at the palace was, in fact, not true.

I'll pick you up at the airport when you arrive. I'll meet you just outside the security gate.

It'll be good to have you home again. I want to hear all about your trip, and I have quite a bit to tell you, too.

Love, Dad

To: RugbyDave@viennawest.edu
From: Val@viennawest.edu
Subject: Hi

Hi, David.

First, I must ask—RugbyDave? I know you play rugby,

but I have never heard ANYONE call you Dave. Just David.

Second, if you're still interested, and if your brother is willing to drive, I can go out tonight. Have to be home by 11:30.

Valerie

To: Val@viennawest.edu

From: RugbyDave@viennawest.edu

Subject: RE: Hi

Hey, Valerie.

To answer your question—I definitely prefer David to Dave. My family calls me Dave, though, and I thought "RugbyDavid" sounded stupid. So there you go.

And yes, I'm still interested.

Yes, my brother can take us out and pick us up in time to get you home.

How about if I get you at 6:30? I remember how to get to your mom's place. We can go out to dinner near the mall, if you'd like, so we can walk over for a movie if we want afterward. Or do whatever.

See you tonight,

David-but-please-not-Dave

To: RugbyDave@viennawest.edu

From: Val@viennawest.edu

Subject: RE: Hi

6:30 is fine. I'll watch out the window and come down so you won't have to buzz. (Believe me, you're better off not coming inside—my mom will ask a zillion questions.)

And I promise not to call you Dave. You're definitely a David.

Later,

Valerie-who-IS-also-Val

To: Val@viennawest.edu

From: ChristieT@viennawest.edu

Subject: WHOO-HOOOOOOO!!!!

Valerie,

Did last night not ROCK? I saw you and David holding hands in the movies, and I THOUGHT I saw him kiss you. Did he? Does this mean you're going to give him a chance? (And does this all make you feel better about everything with your mom?)

Just a sec, Jeremy's on the phone. . . .

WHY ARE YOU NOT CALLING ME THIS SECOND?!?

Jeremy says David just e-mailed him and said that the two of you are going out again tonight!

I KNEW IT!!! I am SO FREAKING THRILLED FOR YOU!!

I just knew this would work out. You two belong together. Jeremy says David sounds totally pumped about the whole thing too. (It's about time—this should have happened in jr. high, if you ask me!)

Anyway, call me FIRST THING tomorrow morning to let me know what happens, 'kay? I am DYING.

AND—I really hope this makes you feel better about everything that's going on with your mom. I'm here for you if you EVER need to talk about all that, okay? No judgments, no worries—got it?

Your extremely happy friend,

Christie

9

"LADIES AND GENTLEMEN, YOU'RE ABOUT TO HAVE your asses kicked by two sophomores."

I can't help but grin at David's remark as we huddle over a sticky round table in the bar area of TGI Friday's. We just ate here last night, but we figured it'd be easiest to eat here again since it's next door to the movie theater. (Plus, I've had a serious craving for American French fries for a while now. They just aren't the same in Schwerinborg.)

In the end, though, we skipped the movies because, with the obvious exception of the one we already saw, they all sucked. Plus, TGI Friday's has a trivia game running on the television screens (well, on the TVs that aren't showing college basketball, which I don't give a rat's ass about), and tons of people are playing. This presented us the opportunity to do what the two of us do best and show off our geeky smartness—without Christie or Jeremy here to make fun of us—and we couldn't resist.

"You just *know* we're the only ones who'll get this," I say, carefully tapping the D key for *Badajoz* on the answer pad, because we both (naturally) knew that was where the British surrounded a French fortress in March 1812.

"I dunno." David studies the rows of restaurant booths on our right, then slides a look to our left, toward a married couple sitting at the bar with a trivia pad in front of them. "I think they're the ones who got that question about Henry the Eighth right."

We decided earlier—judging from their intense focus, expensive gray suits, and the leather bags they have tucked in front of their barstools—that they're lawyers or investment bankers or something else requiring a fair amount of smarts. And that they're probably our toughest competition.

"Yeah, I think so too. But this question is way more obscure. I wouldn't have known it if it hadn't been drilled into us in European History last year."

We watch the television as two of the wrong answers, the Falkland Islands (as if!) and Trier disappear from the screen, leaving Badajoz and Casablanca.

"Not many people know that Jane Seymour was Henry the Eighth's third wife, though," he argues, eyeing the couple at the bar. "They only know the actress Jane Seymour. If they knew about the original Jane Seymour, they'll know Badajoz."

"No way. Remember how we learned about Henry's wives back in eighth grade?" I reel them off on my fingers, along with the little ditty our teacher taught us to help memorize what happened to each of them. "Divorced, beheaded, died, divorced, beheaded, survived. Every kid learns that one. And since only one wife died—well, other than from having her head lopped off—she's easier to remember."

"You get off on knowing this kind of useless information, don't you?"

His smile is so perfect, I have to smile back. "Yeah. And you do, too, so shut up."

David puts his hand over mine on the table. He gives it a subtle tug, urging me to look at the couple again, so I do, just in time to see them switch their answer. They must've had Trier.

The television flashes the correct answer: Badajoz. Then the scores pop up, and we were the only ones to get it right.

"Do we rock, or what?" He sounds totally shocked. "There's only one question left, and unless we completely blow it, they can't catch us."

The couple at the bar look around, scanning the rest of the people sitting at the bar with drinks and trivia pads, then past us to analyze the players at dinner tables.

"They can't figure out who knew it," David says. "They assume it's one of the other groups of adults. Or someone who made a lucky guess."

"You'd think they'd know better." I look up at the scores, which are still flashing. David put our team name in the trivia pad as V.D.—totally juvenile, but also kind of funny, since it's hysterical hearing other teams speculate about the identity of V.D. And whether V.D. actually has venereal disease or doesn't know the abbreviation's usual meaning.

We get the last question right—what does a milliner make? (hats)—but so do a lot of other people. Doesn't matter, though, because we just beat at least ten other teams.

"I feel like such a geek," I tell him.

"You've got a pocket protector I don't know about?"

"No."

"You sit at home trying to come up with new scientific theories, just for fun?"

"Definitely not."

He scoots his chair closer to mine. "Then you're not a geek. And neither am I. We just like competition, is all."

"You're way too popular to be a geek," I tell him. And

too gorgeous. He's wearing a pricey-looking heather-green shirt that makes the gold flecks in his eyes stand out, and his jeans fit his body as well as they would any gym-ripped model. "No matter how smart you are or what kind of grades you get, your cool factor will always outweigh any geek tendencies. But when I was stressed out one afternoon last week, you know what I did? Worked ahead on Geometry. I actually used Geometry to relax."

He laughs aloud and runs his thumb along mine. I look down at our hands and it puts my brain into hyper-spin. It's the whole thing I have for guys' hands.

I have to stop.

I start to glance up at the TV screens, but freeze when I see he's totally studying my face. "That's not geeky, Winslow, that's disturbed."

He's got a crooked smile as he says this, and I feel him pulling my chair closer to his with his foot. When I ask him what he's doing, keeping my voice light and jokey, he answers back, "I think you need a better way to relax."

Then he kisses me. Nothing too racy, but the promise of what he'd like to do later—when we're not in a crowded restaurant—is definitely there, messing with my mind enough for me to ignore his corny line about better ways to relax. (Did he get that from a movie, or what?)

He eases away, letting go of my hand a few seconds

before the waitress comes to refill our sodas and ask if we're finished with our dinners. I don't even answer, I'm so distracted. I just let her take my plate.

A new trivia game starts, and David and I decide to defend our first-place finish. The couple at the bar's still there to give us a challenge, and a group of kids I vaguely recognize from Vienna West (I think they're seniors) are scooting into one of the booths with menus and a trivia pad. They keep looking at us. Probably wondering what Mr. Popular Smart Guy is doing out with the red-haired, pale-skinned goober girl.

We get the first question right, but don't get the second until they eliminate two answers, since we forget exactly how many men rode into the valley of death in Tennyson's "Charge of the Light Brigade" (six hundred). Then the third question pops onto the screen:

What's the capital of the European country of Schwerinborg?

A) Baden-Baden

B) Zurich

C) Freital

D) Interlaken

David cracks up beside me. "Well, I'm guessing you know this one. It's not Zurich, and I think Baden-Baden's in Germany, so it's either Interlaken or Freital . . . Freital, right?"

I nod, even though while he wasn't looking I went ahead and punched the button next to choice C. Of course we're the first ones to get it right, so we get the highest score on that question.

"Way to go, Winslow." He drapes one arm around the back of my chair. I don't object, but as he puts his hand on my back, tracing lines up and down, I start to get a funny feeling. Like something's wrong with this picture.

But what, I can't pinpoint. There aren't any reporters or photographers in here (because, being paranoid, I keep looking for them), and when I think about it, this actually fits my idea of a perfect date. Playing trivia games, talking about nothing in particular with a hot guy who's, from all indications, totally into me. Being competitive without having to do it on a sports field, where I'm liable to get bashed and bruised. Hanging out and chatting and not feeling like we have to be anywhere at a certain time.

And the best part is that David really seems to like doing this too. Maybe, after dating super-popular types for so long, he's gotten sick of having to show up at all their parties and put on a show for their friends.

Maybe.

I try to shake the feeling something's off and just enjoy myself as we answer the next few questions. We're in second place, behind the seniors. I know it's them, because David says he's seen them playing here before and they always use the same team name: MONSTER. In all caps. To make them extra scary or something, I suppose.

There's a break in the game, and a couple of the guys from the other table walk by on their way to the restroom and say hey to David.

"They're on the rugby team," he explains after they pass. "Well, some of them. I don't recognize the two guys on the end."

"Oh."

I look over and instantly get why I'm feeling so uncomfortable. The guys who are still in the booth are staring at me, trying to be as inconspicuous as possible while they either peek out from behind their menus or pretend they're watching basketball on the TV behind me.

All except for this one guy with long brown hair who's fidgeting with the plastic-encased menu that shows all the desserts. He puts it down and shoves his hair back from his face, and I realize it's John.

PFLAG John.

He's ditched the Kenny Chesney shirt for a navy blue NYU shirt that's actually kind of cool. But more than the shirt or the fact that his hair looks cleaner than the last time I saw him, it's his attitude that's setting off my inner alarms. The way he's intentionally not looking this way when all the other guys are.

Did he tell them about me? That my mom is gay? Is that why they keep looking over here?

I don't think we're supposed to talk about the stuff that comes up in meetings, and John didn't strike me as the type who *would* tell, even if there's no rule against it.

But if he did, will the rugby guys turn around and tell David?

Should I say something first? Make a pre-emptive strike?

Before I can decide, David (who's totally oblivious to the fact that the MONSTER guys are watching us) starts talking about what's going on at school—who's going out with whom and all the other gossip I've missed since I transferred. I'm interested, but I have a hard time keeping up because, on the inside, I'm totally freaked about what the rugby guys may or may not know. Then David gets off on a tangent talking about Christie and Jeremy and whether they've done it.

I know for certain they *haven't*. There hasn't even been any south-of-the-border action. But from the way David is talking, Jeremy hasn't confirmed the occurrence of full-blown sex one way or another to any of the guys, so they're all starting to make assumptions. Assumptions I know Christie—who quietly prides herself on being a good Catholic girl—would not want them to make.

"So what about you, Val?" David asks.

"What about me what?"

"What do you think about the whole sex-before-marriage thing?"

"Why, you wanna do it on the table right now or something?" I try to sound funny instead of defensive, but I'm not sure I succeed. I mean, where did *that* question come from?

Guess I'm really more worried about David's opinions on sex between women at the moment.

Oh, ick. I can't believe I just thought that.

He raises an eyebrow. "You making the invitation?"

I don't say anything (what can I possibly say?), and just grin like I made a big joke.

"Seriously, Winslow. Give me your ten-second opinion."

Is he trying to get me into bed? After, like, a date and a half?

"I don't have a problem with it." How can I have a problem if it's never even come up? "The whole sex-before-marriage thing, that is. Not the sex here on the table thing. That, I cannot do. Sorry."

He laughs. "Same with me."

"Which part?"

"Both."

The way he says it makes me think he's testing me, though. Like there's a question behind his question.

"Why do you want to know?" Maybe I'm misreading the I-want-a-relationship vibe that's coming from him, which is usually different (or so Christie and Jules tell me) from the I-just-wanna-get-laid vibe. Besides, he can basically point to any of the girls in school and they'd be happy to give it up to him if all he wanted was a quickie hookup. No point in pursuing me, in that case.

"Well, I heard about that guy you've been seeing in Schwerinborg, and I just . . . I guess I wanted to know what your expectations would be if you decided you wanted to go out with me instead."

Come again? "I don't get it."

"Well, I imagine Prince Georg what's-his-name is the type who has certain expectations when he's going out with someone. Right?"

He's so *not* that kind of guy, but I'm not going to tell David that. I want to know his point. "And?"

"And you know what my father does for a living." He lowers his voice, as if he's embarrassed. Or worried someone might overhear. "I just can't—I can't risk doing anything that's going to reflect badly on him. So I wanted to let you know that up front. He's on Capitol Hill this week lobbying to take condoms out of public schools, since he thinks they encourage teenagers to have sex, and next week he has a meeting with two senators to discuss the gay marriage issue."

He reaches past me to punch the D button on the trivia pad, because while I was listening to him, a new question has popped up on the television screen.

He looks back at me. "It's not that I have a problem with condoms in schools. Or Christie and Jeremy doing whatever they do. Or even if you did it with that guy in Schwerinborg. I figure that's your business, you know?"

"I guess—"

"It's just that it's really important for my dad to be successful in his job. To encourage Congress to support President Carew and his policies, which will help him get reelected. So I can't go around using the condoms from school, if you catch my meaning."

Uh-huh. "You're saying it'll undermine his work if anyone finds out. And the wrong people *always* find out."

"Exactly." He gives me a flirty grin, but I have no idea how to interpret it.

I can't believe I'm having *two* relationships where the guy's dad's job is a major impediment to my happiness. But Georg, who has a lot more pressure on him than David does, seems to handle it way better.

And it's pissing me off.

"So you think I'm here with you because I want to get busy? That's a pretty freaking big assumption you're making." Even if I have lusted after him for years and he knows it. (I'm guessing Jeremy's told him about my mondo crush, since I know Christie's told Jeremy.)

His face gets completely red. "That's not what I'm saying. It's just that I like you a lot and I don't want you to think . . . well, I just want you to know where I'm coming from. I'm in kind of a weird position. Plus, my dad's trying to line up an internship for me in the Senate this summer. I can't ruin that opportunity."

He moves his hand to play with my hair where it's hanging down my back. "But I don't want to ruin this opportunity either. Even if you are going back to Schwerinborg in a few days, I know you'll be back for good after the elections, right? At least, that's what Christie told Jeremy—that your dad plans to come back to the White House then."

"Well, it's not a firm plan or anything." I don't know why, but I feel like I shouldn't give him a straight answer. I mean, as far as I know, the whole Dad-returning-to-the-White-House thing isn't supposed to be public knowledge.

"So you understand?"

"Yeah." I understand better than he knows. It's like Georg, Take Two.

"So why did your dad leave the White House in the first place, if he's considering coming back after the election? There had to be a reason—something political, I'd guess—that might've made him want to leave for a while?"

He sounds totally casual about it, but I give him the Valerie Shrug. I'm not about to tell him my dad was temporarily "placed" with Prince Manfred because President Carew thought having an adviser going through a divorce from a lesbian could be an election-year liability.

I reach over to hit the A button on the trivia pad for *Michelangelo* (person who painted the ceiling in the Sistine Chapel), since—while I wasn't even paying attention—we moved into first place ahead of MONSTER, and now I don't want to lose the game.

I glance over at John. He's still not paying attention to me.

Once David and I answer the next question with *John Glenn*, I turn and ask him what's really on my mind: "So your dad's dealing with the gay-marriage issue next week?"

"Yeah."

I'm not even really sure how I feel about it—I think I'll hurl if Mom gets married to Gabrielle—but I ask anyway. "What do you think about all that?"

"About gay marriage?" He glances sideways at me. "Why, are you for it?"

Okay, I cannot believe I'm having this discussion on, like, our second date. But since I kind of started it, I say, "I haven't really thought about it. I'm not up on politics as much as you are. But I don't think someone who's gay should be discriminated against."

"It's not discrimination. It undermines the whole institution of marriage to allow gay couples to marry." He makes quotemarks in the air with his fingers as he says the word "marry." "I mean, where do you draw the line? What happens when these so-called married couples have kids? Will those kids grow up to marry the opposite sex? Will they think marriage is a joke?"

"A joke?"

He makes a face of disgust. "You bet. If gay marriage is legitimized, a hundred years from now marriage as we know it will cease to exist."

"I don't think that would happen." Geez, but this is a weird conversation. And freaking uncomfortable.

"Sure it will. Marriage wouldn't be valued anymore." He doesn't sound judgmental at all, just very matter-of-fact. "Think about it. We'd be changing thousands and thousands of years of history by legitimizing homosexuality. If we, as a nation, say that anyone can marry anyone else, man or woman, then what's special about marriage?"

Plenty, I want to tell him. But I don't. He sounds so sure of himself, and frankly, I'm not sure at all. About any of it.

And it's creeping me out to have PFLAG John only a few tables away while David and I are having this discussion.

"Hey," David says, taking his arm off the back of my chair and pointing to the screen, "I think we're about to win again. MONSTER missed that one entirely. Look!"

Sure enough, they did. The next question appears at the same time the waitress drops our check on the table. It's about Pickett's Charge, which we studied last semester in Mrs. Bennett's class.

David picks the correct answer, then gives me a killer smile that makes me want to ignore our entire discussion about gay marriage. How can he possibly be so hot and so smart but so set on ideas that maybe aren't so cut-and-dried?

"We make an awesome team, Winslow." He gives me another quick kiss before grabbing the bill.

Unfortunately, we miss the last trivia question—about an obscure 1960s football player—and end up in a tie with MONSTER. Probably for the best. I really don't want to tick them off.

After we put on our coats to leave, David pulls me over to their table. He introduces me, but instantly gets into a conversation about rugby. John looks up—since it'd be rude not to, I think—and he gives me a nod that lets me know he wants to say hello but that he's not going to acknowledge that he knows me. Or, at least, from where.

I give him a little smile of thanks when no one's looking. Then, when all the other guys start high-fiving one another over some big rugby play they made in their last game, John mouths, "No problem."

As grungy and strange as he is, I decide right then and there that John's a good guy.

But the something's-not-right-here feeling is still sticking in my gut, like I shouldn't be doing what I'm doing. But since we're about to leave, I force myself to ignore it.

After a few more minutes of rugby reminiscing, David puts his hand on my back and steers me out of TGI Friday's, since it's time for his brother and his brother's girlfriend to pick us up. David has them drop us off at the entrance to the apartment complex instead of at the door, so we can talk for a while as he walks me home.

And, I can tell, because he wants to kiss me again without his brother seeing. His brother gives us an *I know what you're doing* look, but I notice he's not exactly protesting having to wait for David. It gives him a few more minutes alone with his girlfriend, presumably to do the same thing.

As we start down the sidewalk, David grabs my hand. "I didn't want to say anything at dinner, but the guys at the other table were staring at you the whole time."

"Really?" So he did see.

"Yeah. One of them was trying to set me up with a friend of his, and I told them I couldn't—that someone I really liked was coming to town and that I thought I might be otherwise occupied."

"Oh."

"I just wanted to tell you in case you were wondering why they were staring. They were probably curious."

We get to one of the darker places on the sidewalk, in between the glow of two streetlights, and he stops walking and pulls me right into his arms. "Thanks for keeping me otherwise occupied."

I let him kiss me. This time, since we're alone, it's finally a real kiss.

And after all these years of dreaming about it—of dying every time he looked at me or slowed down on the walk to school so I could catch up to him and his friends—the whole kissing-David thing just doesn't do it for me.

"You're the best, you know that, Valerie?"

"Thanks." I want him not to say any more. It's making me feel horrid.

"I always thought we'd be good together, you know? I kind of suspected you might have a thing for me, but I didn't know for sure until Christie told me a few weeks ago."

The blessing of a friend with a big mouth. At least she didn't tell him I've wanted him like mad since I was five. Geez, I hope she had that much sense.

"But I was stupid and I never did anything about it." He twists a few strands of my hair around his finger, then lets go and starts running his hand along my shoulder. "I kept asking out other girls, thinking that they were what I wanted."

Yeah, the future prom queen types. Who wouldn't want them?

"So why me?" I ask, even though I'm not sure I really want to know.

"I think it took hearing you were going away to realize that, in the end, all I've wanted is someone who thinks like I do. And Winslow, I believe you're it."

Hoo, boy. If he only knew.

I let him give me a few more quick kisses, then say, "I think your brother's waiting."

"I doubt it. But I don't want you to miss your curfew." He walks me to the door and says he'll call me—he wants to see me as much as possible before I have to go back to Schwerinborg.

I thank him for dinner and trivia, then duck in the door. As I watch him walk back toward his brother's car from the glass windows of the stairwell, I feel tears burning up in my eyes. After they drive away, I sit down on the stairs.

I realize that I want the same thing David does: Someone who thinks like me. Or, more accurately, someone who understands me. Who doesn't just spout his opinion and expect that I'll agree. Someone who will listen to and respect my opinion, even if he doesn't agree.

Someone who won't expect me to be his Armor Girl.

I let myself into the apartment as quietly as possible. Mom left on the reading light in the living room, but it looks like she's gone to bed.

Good thing, because I know she'd want to talk. And I need time to digest what has happened.

Maybe I'll make a list. David in one column, Georg in the other. Just to be certain. Although, in my gut, I know what the answer will be.

No. Too *Glamour* magazine. Although it did help when I did it at the PFLAG meeting, so maybe—

"What's wrong, honey?"

I jump about a mile. What's she doing lurking in the

kitchen without the light on? "Mom! You scared the crap outta me!"

"Sorry. I was just getting a glass of milk," she says, holding it up as proof. "I was reading in the living room, waiting for you to get home."

Of course she was.

"You look upset. Did something bad happen on your date?"

"No, we had a good time." At least, until I woke up to reality. And now I feel horrible. I never should have gone out with David tonight. Going to the movies was one thing. That was supposedly casual. A favor to Christie, sort of, and because I'd committed to it when I thought Georg and I might still be "cooling off," even though apparently he never meant it that way.

But tonight—tonight was a massive, no, make that a monster (ha-ha), mistake. Because if I'd taken a fraction of a second to think about it, I'd have known I want Georg, not David. And I never would have David that e-mail telling him I'd meet him.

Why did I do that?

Why did I not realize that's the reason I felt wrong all night? I should have been here, either thinking about Georg or hanging with the girls. Doing anything except going out with David.

"You don't look like you had a good time, Valerie. You look disturbed."

"I don't want to talk about it, Mom."

"Okay. But it might help to get it off your chest." She walks past me and picks up her book—the latest bestseller by her favorite self-help guru—from the end table and gives me one of her *I'm an understanding mom* looks before sitting down. "And Gabrielle's not here. She went out to dinner with some of her friends from Weight Watchers after their meeting tonight."

"So they can pig out on pizza?"

Parallel lines of disapproval appear between Mom's eyes. "Valerie—"

"I'm *kidding*. I know Gabrielle takes it seriously."

Mom just stares at me. Doesn't start reading her book, doesn't give me the usual spiel about how Gabby lost a ton of weight a couple years ago with the program, and how she now feels she owes her low cholesterol levels and Earth-friendly vegan lifestyle to the good folks at Weight Watchers.

Clearly she's not going anywhere until I spill about my date. But I just can't.

I feel too rotten to talk to anyone, let alone my mother. I mean, what does *she* know about staying loyal to someone?

I toss my purse on the counter because I know she's not

going to let me go to bed. And I don't know that I can sleep, anyway. "Mom, stop staring at me."

"No, I don't think I will."

Fine. Two can play this game. I put my hands on my hips. "Okay, then answer a question for me. Did you cheat on Dad?"

10

I LET MY HANDS FALL TO MY SIDE.

Where in the world did *that* come from? What is *wrong* with me? The way I'm acting tonight, I have to wonder which circle of hell I'm destined to occupy.

"I'm sorry, Mom, it's totally none of my—"

"I didn't cheat on your father. Nothing happened with Gabrielle until after I told you and your father I wanted a divorce." She takes a deep breath and fiddles with the ties on the front of her robe until they're pulled tight. "Is that what you're upset about?"

Wow. This was so *not* the answer I expected to hear. "You didn't cheat?"

"No." She doesn't look the least bit uncomfortable with

this topic—when, if our roles were reversed, I'd kill me for asking—so I figure she's been planning her answer for a long time. "But when I met Gabrielle, I knew. Sometimes, you *just know.* In here." She taps her chest as she talks. "And it woke me up. I realized that I wanted Gabrielle in my life, most likely for the rest of my life, and to pursue that, I needed to leave your father first."

"How did you know Gabrielle would want you?"

This draws a smile out of her. "I had my suspicions. Well, they were more than suspicions, I suppose. She'd been flirting with me a little, and I with her. But neither one of us acted on our attraction—we never even spoke of it—because I was married. But even if she'd never flirted, I knew that I couldn't be with your father anymore. Staying with him when I felt that way about someone else—anyone else—would be cheating both myself and him. And you, too. I've always wanted you to be true to yourself, and if I lived a lie, what kind of example would I be to you? How could you respect me if I couldn't respect myself?"

She lets out a little sigh, then continues. "So before things got out of hand, I told Gabrielle how I felt about her, and that whether she returned my feelings or not, I'd decided to leave your father that night. It was a huge, huge risk for me to do that. Not just emotionally, but financially, too, because I knew leaving your father also meant I'd have to go back to teaching. And I wasn't sure I could do that and enjoy it."

I am beyond stunned. I cannot picture my mom having all this angst without my realizing it. Ignoring the teaching thing for the moment, I say, "But Gabrielle returned your feelings?"

Mom nodded. "She said she had fallen in love with me and that she wanted us to be together. She just knew the same way I knew that we belonged together, and for the long term. But, again, neither Gabrielle nor I acted until *after* I came home and told you and your dad. It would have cast a pall on our relationship to have taken that first step physically before I'd ended things with your father. And Gabby and I wanted to start clean."

Wow. She sounds like she's been reading way too many self-help books (probably because she has been), but still . . . I never realized how hard all this has been for her. And how much she worried about what *I* might think.

I cross the room and sit on the arm of the chair next to hers. "So you didn't *just know* with Dad? Before you married him?"

She gives me a sad little smile and wraps one of the ties to her robe around her wrist, then unwraps it. "I wanted your father to be the love of my life. I really did. I wanted a nice life in the suburbs with kids and the whole shebang."

"But . . . ?"

"But no, there was never any lightning bolt, *aha* kind of moment. I always had fun with your father—I liked him a lot, and will always love him on some level—but I know in my heart that I'm attracted to women and I'm just not capable of loving any man the way I should." She takes a long drink of her milk, then sets it on top of the book on the end table.

"I just wish I'd been honest with myself about it sooner," she adds. "I could have saved us all a lot of pain."

"But then you wouldn't have had me. *I* wouldn't even have me."

Her face splits into a wide grin at this. "No, and I don't know what I would have done without you."

"I'm sorry I thought you were cheating," I tell her. "I should have known better." I think.

"It's all right. I figured you'd have questions after you went to the PFLAG meeting. That's why I've stayed up late the last couple nights, so you could talk to me if you wanted to. You're not visiting for long, and I wanted to make the most of our time."

"Well, I'm not asking because of PFLAG. I'm asking

because of me. I—I feel like I'm cheating, and I guess I needed advice." I wave my hand in front of me, as if I can erase the words from the air. "That just came out all wrong. I'm not saying that—"

She frowns. "How, exactly, do you think *you're* cheating?"

So I flop backward into the chair and tell her everything. Well, not everything. But I do tell her about Georg's "cool off" call, and then the e-mail from Zermatt, and how I went out with David, anyway—that the first time was theoretically casual, even though I let him hold my hand in the theater and I could have pulled away and just stopped everything right there. But then I was even worse and went out with David a second time. Where it was just the two of us and it was definitely a date.

And I tell her that now I feel like I'm being one of those evil, bitchy types of girls who cheat on their boyfriends, and that's just beyond wrong.

"Valerie, how old are you?"

"Um, Mom, you should know."

"Fifteen, honey. *Fifteen.* And, to my knowledge, you and Georg aren't married."

"Not to my knowledge either."

"And you made no promises to each other. So you're not cheating. In fact, you're perfectly normal. You and Georg have only been together a short time, Valerie. Far too short a time to be committed, even though the connection you felt with him sounds pretty intense."

Intense? "Mom, don't try to sound cool."

"I'm not. I'm just trying to get it through your head that you're doing the right thing. Think—what if I'd taken the time to date around, to make sure your father was really the right guy for me? What if I'd taken the time to be certain about my decision? That's all you're doing."

"So going out with David was a good thing?"

She grins and reaches over to grab my foot where it's hanging over the side of the armchair, then gives it a little shake, exactly the way Dad does. "Yes. It sounds like you've learned what you don't want, at least for now. And in many cases, learning what you don't want is as important as learning what you do want. Or *who* you want."

"I think I know who I want."

"For now." She lets go of my foot. "Remember, you're fifteen. You have plenty of time to learn as much as you can—about Georg, about other boys. About yourself. Use that time wisely."

I must still look uncertain, because as she stands up to go to bed, she says, "And trust in your friends. Jules and Natalie will understand. And so will Christie. Make the choices that are best for you, not the choices you think will please them."

As she walks down the hall, I say to her back, "I don't know what you're thinking about teaching, Mom, but if you do go back, you're going to be great."

She stops, looks back at me, and says, "You know, I think I will. I wasn't ready when I was young. Now I'm looking forward to it." Her face splits into a big grin, and she adds, "Proves my point that it takes a while to learn what you really want in life."

To: Val@viennawest.edu

From: ChristieT@viennawest.edu

Subject: David, of course

WELL?!?

To: ChristieT@viennawest.edu

From: Val@viennawest.edu

Subject: RE: David, of course

WELL . . . it went well. We played trivia, we acted like the total geeks we are, we had a good time.

But—and please, please, do not kill me for saying this—

as great as David and I get along, and as much as we have in common, I don't think there's a spark.

No cosmic connection, no yo-baby-do-I-belong-with-this-guy. Nothing like what you have with Jeremy.

In my gut, I still believe I'm David's Armor Girl. It just took going out with him a couple of times to know it for sure.

And, in many ways, maybe he's my Armor Guy. Someone I can enjoy being around, someone who gets along with my friends and who looks fantastic and says all the right things to everyone.

But he's not THE guy.

I promised to tell you the truth from now on, so there it is.

I'm really sorry!!

Of course, now I have to figure out what to say if (when) he asks me out again. I already have e-mail from him . . . opening that one next. . . .

Val

To: Val@viennawest.edu
From: RugbyDave@viennawest.edu
Subject: Last night

Hey Valerie-who-is-also-Val,

Did we rock on trivia last night or what? Want to do it again before you leave, just so we can prove our utter geekiness?

Or—a bunch of the rugby guys are getting together at this guy Kevin's house for a party the day before you leave. Might be fun.

Later,

David-not-Dave

To: RugbyDave@viennawest.edu

From: Val@viennawest.edu

Subject: RE: Last night

David-not-Dave,

One: Yes, we did, indeed, rock on trivia. Did you expect any less than us dominating the entire TGI Friday's crowd?

Two: While I'd love to do it again, I can't. Well, more accurately, I think it'd be a bad idea. I really do like you a lot—just ask Christie, since you know she's painfully honest about everything—but my life is in a chaotic mess right now, and I don't want to lead you on. I just can't do the whole relationship thing.

Three: I really am very, very sorry. You do know you're pretty much the hottest guy in school, right? And that you should NOT take this personally?

I'm sure I'm messing this up, and should probably do this in person, but I am a wimp. Please forgive me?

Valerie-who-is-also-Val

To: Val@viennawest.edu

From: RugbyDave@viennawest.edu

Subject: Valerie Winslow ((Attachment: valemail.doc))

Jeremy,

I must've blown it, man. She thinks I'm a "bad idea" (I've attached the e-mail she sent me). If it wasn't for my dad getting on my case about everything, I'd just tell her to bite me.

Whatever. Maybe I'll see if Melanie Fergusson wants to come to the rugby party.

David

To: Val@viennawest.edu

From: RugbyDave@viennawest.edu

Subject: BIG mistake . . .

Okay—huge apology. I meant to send that to Jeremy. I accidentally hit Reply instead of Forward.

And even then . . . you know I would never tell you to bite me (no matter what my dad says), so please, please, forgive me. I was suffering from Temporary Pissed-Offedness.

And I do forgive you. So I hope that makes us even.

Friends?

David

To: RugbyDave@viennawest.edu

From: Val@viennawest.edu

Subject: RE: BIG mistake . . .

Yes, friends. And you can tell me to bite you if you feel the need (but don't expect me to actually do it!). Consider Temporary Pissed-Offedness as a total defense.

Besides—I'd hate to have to play against you in trivia when I get home from Schwerinborg for good. I'd much rather you were on my team.

Val

To: Val@viennawest.edu

From: ChristieT@viennawest.edu

Subject: LOL!!

Oh. WOW. That e-mail exchange between you and David was TOO TOO FUNNY. (Yes, David forwarded it all to Jeremy, who forwarded to me.)

I already forgive you for not going out with him again. Even temporary anger is no reason for a guy to say "bite me" to YOU. Really. You are the coolest person on Earth.

AND . . . I just loaded up a movie. Want to come over? My mom says she can pick you up. We can talk about David and Jeremy and your mom and whatever else you want. I've missed you so much!!

See you in an hour?

Love,

Christie

PS—Jules thinks you should walk up to David next time you see him and actually bite him.

PPS—Natalie says she will not make any comments regarding violence one way or another until she is out of the maximum security block or the prison guards might not recommend her for parole.

The pilot's voice comes over the speaker, waking up half the people on the flight. We're starting our descent into Munich, so he says anyone who wants to go to the restroom should either go now or hold it until we land in Germany.

I glance at my watch, then back at the huge screen covering the wall at the front of coach class. It alternately flashes a map showing the plane's location over Europe with a list of our airspeed, altitude, and the distance to Munich.

I've been watching it count down the miles (and kilometers) ever since the in-flight movie ended an hour ago.

Thankfully, we're on time and I won't miss my connection to Freital, because I cannot wait to get there. Dad will be waiting, and he says we're going straight back to the palace because he has to work today. Prince Manfred's hosting the president of Taiwan tonight, so Dad needs to do his protocol thing.

Fine by me. The sooner I get to the palace, the better.

I glance down at the piece of paper on the tray table in front of me. I read nearly all of the *Is Homosexuality a Sin?* book, though I was getting some strange looks from other passengers and I finally put it away, figuring it'd be better to read the rest at home. Sometime when Dad's not around.

So to kill time, I started making a list. Just to help me see everything in black and white.

David Anderson

- *Driven to do well in school (like me)*
- *Has lots of the same friends I do*
- *I've known him forever*
- *Smart and polite*
- *The body. The hands. The eyes.*
- *CONS: Anti-gay. Is careful with his behavior because of his dad's job.*

Georg

- *More adventurous than me, in a good way*
- *Good-hearted and polite*
- *The body. The hands. The eyes. The arms. The ACCENT.*
- *CONS: The press office wants to sanction our every move. Is careful with his behavior because of his dad's job.*

Georg's list is way shorter than David's, probably because David and I have so much in common. Their cons are similar—they both have dads whose jobs change how they have to act when they're with their girlfriends.

Except Georg doesn't have the major cons that David has. Georg doesn't care about my mom's lifestyle. And even though he's someday going to have his father's job (as I suspect David will also, or something like it), he doesn't let it change his everyday behavior or who he is on the inside.

And he doesn't let it change what he feels about me.

I crumple up the list, push up my tray table, then yank the airsick bag out of the seat pocket and stuff the list inside. I glance toward the back of the plane, and since there's no line, I unbuckle, walk to the minuscule airplane lavatory, then push the airsick bag through the trash slot.

In exactly fifty-three minutes, the plane will land and

nothing I wrote on paper matters. All that matters is that I'm dying to see a certain prince named Georg Jacques von Ederhollern. Even if I have to sneak out of a palace apartment to do it.

I want to be his princess.

I cannot believe it. No Dad. Anywhere.

I scan the entire area where passengers exit the security gate, but no luck. A half-dozen or so people are dressed in black outfits, holding their driving hats and clutching signs bearing the last names of passengers other than me. Otherwise, it's pretty darned empty.

The plane from Munich to Freital ended up ten minutes late due to the perpetual rain in this country, so even if Dad is running behind, which he never is, he should definitely be here.

I walk across the open area of the terminal to a huge wall of television screens showing arrival and departure information. Yep, they got my flight correct. It shows us right there in green and says this is the proper terminal for meeting passengers. Even though it's all in German, I can understand that much.

"Excuse me," a low voice says next to me. Since most people flying into Freital speak various European languages, I'm wondering how this person can possibly pinpoint me as

American. But then I take a good look at the guy—who's wearing a baseball cap pulled low over his forehead—and drop my duffel bag on the ground.

"Georg!"

"Shhh!" He grins at me, then looks over his shoulder toward the passengers from my flight as they filter through the security gate to meet up with their rides. "I had to see you, so I talked your father into letting me come along."

"Where is he?"

"Baggage claim."

"Oh. Thanks." I want to hug him right there, but I'm not absolutely positive where things stand.

"I think I made a huge mistake," he says. "When I called you and said we had to cool it, I didn't call back or e-mail you to explain."

"That's okay."

"No, it's not." He looks at the floor while a young French-ish-looking couple with backpacks slung over their shoulders walks past us. "My parents were all on my case." He frowns, then asks, "Is that how you say it? 'On my case'?"

I think the smile on my face must be the dorkiest ever, but the way he always has to ask me about his English is delicious. "Yes, that's it."

"Well, they were all on my case about the newspaper

article, and telling me I had to call you that instant to make certain we weren't seen together in public for a while, and all the press guys were in our apartment, discussing it with my father, and I caved."

"I understand."

He lets out an exasperated grunt. "It's fine for us to keep things cool in public if we need to, but it's not fine for you to think I don't want to be with you. Because I do. And I told my parents that when I got home from Zermatt."

He picks up my duffel bag and loops it over his shoulder, then reaches for my hand with his free one and leads me toward the escalator to baggage claim.

"I think the cold air on the ski slopes cleared my brain," he says as we descend. "I couldn't stop thinking about you—about how funny you are, or about how you tell me what you think and not just what I want to hear. And I kept thinking about our night in the garden, and how much I like hanging out with you and just talking. And I realized we belong together. If we really want this, we'll find a way to make it work. I just hope you feel the same."

My heart is thumping about a hundred miles an hour as we step off the escalator toward the rows of baggage claim carousels.

Man, do I want him. Bad. And not just for long, slow

kisses. For everything—walking to school, talking about the world, laughing at each other. Every freaking thing.

"But what about the reporters?" I look at the faces of the people passing through baggage claim—mostly dour-looking Europeans my parents' age juggling their suitcases, trying to figure out how to find the taxi stand or the parking garage. "Didn't your parents freak when you told them you were coming to the airport?"

"I promised to keep a low profile. But I had to see you. And what can reporters possibly say or photograph if your father is with us?"

"Or if you're in that baseball hat," I tease him. "You know you've gotta lose that. You're not the baseball hat type."

"Great. But you're not answering my question," he says.

"Which one?"

"Do you still want to be with me?"

I try to give him a serious look, like I have to think it over, but I just can't. I'm giddy-happy-scary in love with the guy—even more than before spin control happened—and every second I wait to tell him is killing me.

Who knew going out with David would actually strengthen what I feel for Georg?

I tilt my head so I can see into his eyes despite the silly baseball hat. "What if I told you I really want to kiss you like you've never been kissed before? Right here, right now, in the middle of the Lufthansa Airlines baggage claim?"

"Please don't."

I spin at the hissed words coming from behind me in a way-too-familiar voice. "Um, Dad. Hi."

"Hi, yourself." He has a welcoming sort of smile on his face, so I hope that means I haven't made him mad by wanting to jump Georg, especially given the fact I'm supposed to be controlling spin. "I have a car waiting at the curb, if you can hold off on your plans for about two minutes. This is a public area, you realize."

I can feel myself turning bright red all the way to my ears. There are certain things a father is just not supposed to hear.

"Thank you, Mr. Winslow," Georg says, sounding all princely and polite despite his casual clothes.

When we get to the car—a black Mercedes with tinted windows that, believe it or not, doesn't stick out in Schwerinborg, since everyone here drives high-end European cars—I realize that Dad is driving. No one else from the palace came.

"You guys really are trying to be discreet," I say to Georg as I look around for reporters lurking curbside, but see none.

"Just get in," Dad says, so I do.

I cannot freaking believe it. Dad and Georg have

McDonald's for me. And a huge bouquet of flowers. All of it's in the middle of the backseat.

"I figured you've been eating Gabrielle's vegan food all week," Georg explains.

"You're bribing me?"

"Whatever it takes."

As we pull out into traffic, heading away from the airport, he leans across the seat (well, as far as his seat belt will allow, since Dad's a stickler for seat belts), puts his hands on my cheeks, then pulls me toward him for a major mind-blowing kiss.

"Ahem. This isn't a limo. There's no privacy panel."

"Sorry, Mr. Winslow," Georg says. He leans back in his seat and winks at me, making me feel completely warm inside despite the drizzle hitting the windshield and the gray Schwerinborg skies. Then, just so I'm completely happy, he opens the Mickey D's bag and hands me the fries, which smell absolutely decadent.

"Fortification against Steffi," he says. "Though I think we'll be able to deal with her better now. Ulrike's on our side, too, since you left."

I see my dad grin to himself in the rearview mirror.

"That's something." Though I couldn't care less about the girls at school right now. All I can think about is Georg. I offer him a few of my fries, but he waves them off. Instead, he reaches back into the bag and offers me my favorite—a McChicken. And it's fixed just the way I like it.

"True love," Georg mouths to me.

I think I'm going to cry, but I manage to hold it in long enough to smile and mouth back, "I love you, too."

Because I do. I just know.

DO-OVER

For all the readers who've sent me letters and e-mails or posted to my message board to say you like my work. You've made a good gig great.

1

I'M IN LOVE! I'M IN LOVE! I'M IN LOOOOOOVVVVVE!

I'm in love with a guy who I think is completely and totally perfect—he's got brains, he's funny, and best of all . . . he actually likes me. He's one of those guys who, if he were famous, everyone would constantly mention how hot he is and flip through copies of *People* looking for a really good pic of him, but if he happened to be the guy sitting next to you in Chemistry every day, you'd describe him as being decently good-looking (if you took the time to actually think about him) but not drool-worthy.

But the thing is, he *is* kind of famous. At least in a small, German-speaking part of Europe.

That's because I'm in love with a prince. And I don't mean that I'm in love with a prince from seeing him in a magazine and thinking he's gorgeous. Oh, no.

I'm actually going out with one.

I kid you not. With a prince. And it's not like I love him because he's a prince. I love him and he *happens to be* a prince.

And sometimes, I love him *even though* he's a prince, because there can be some serious downsides to dating a guy who actually has a "lineage" instead of plain ol' relatives like the rest of us.

Since my English teacher back in Virginia was always trying to bash into my head that stories all have to have a beginning, a middle, and an end—I tend to jump around from place to place in my essay assignments—I'll start at the once-upon-a-time beginning before I get into the whole love part.

Once upon a time, there was this not-quite-cool, average-looking, redheaded girl named Valerie Winslow, or Val for short. (That'd be me.)

One night, over a dinner of Kraft mac and cheese, Val's (my) mother, Barbara, announced that she wanted a divorce from her husband, Martin (yep, my dad), thus ending their storybook relationship. Barbara claimed she'd discovered her True Self and needed to follow her destiny.

And she did . . . right over the rainbow.

Her True Self, it turns out, had fallen in love with someone she'd met at the gym, a skinny blond vegan named Gabrielle, about ten years Barbara's junior.

Yes, it's a strange fairy tale. And yes, Gabrielle is a female.

By a cruel twist of fate, Martin just happened to have a cushy job as the chief of protocol in a very conservative White House, where having your wife step out of the closet is frowned upon, particularly when the president decides to run for reelection and tout his family values on *Meet the Press* and during campaign trips to all fifty states. So Martin quietly relocated to the tiny European principality of Schwerinborg (yeah, don't even try to pronounce it), where the royal family agreed to do the president a favor and employ Martin until after the next U.S. election, at which time it was understood Martin could return to his duties in the good ol' U.S. of A., advising the White House on such important topics as the appropriate colors to wear while attending a state funeral in India or whether it's okay to serve lamb chops to dignitaries from the Seychelles.

In the meantime, this situation left Val (yup, still me) with quite the fairy-tale-ish dilemma: where to live?

Staying in northern Virginia held its appeal, namely Val's best friends, Christie, Jules, and Natalie. Then there was this gorgeous guy named David Anderson, whom Val had been crushing on since they met on the first day of kindergarten, and who had finally noticed her in *that* way.

However, unable to handle living with her mother and ultravegan Gabrielle in their new apartment, which involved being forced to switch to a different high school—not to mention live on a diet of things like Tofurky and bulgur wheat—Val (again, me) opted to go to Schwerinborg, where everyone speaks German. There she lived in a tiny palace apartment with her father, which isn't as swanky a setup as it sounds. Val and Martin discovered that properly heating—let alone renovating—the wing of the palace that houses the employees isn't exactly a high-priority use for Schwerinborg's tax revenue.

But then, because this is a fairy tale and I forgot to start at the beginning, everyone already knows what happened next. When Val was feeling lower than low (in other words, holding a pity party for herself), she bumped into a guy her own age who had a knack for making her laugh.

More precisely, she bumped into Prince Georg Jacques von Ederhollern of Schwerinborg. Not George, but *Georg*. Pronounced "*gay*-org." Like the uptight Austrian Julie Andrews fell for in *The Sound of Music*. Watch it sometime and you'll understand. Needless to say, Prince Georg was (and is!) totally, completely hot. Val really liked Georg, despite his strange name, and it turned out that Georg liked Val back and could kiss like nobody's business.

And right now, they're living happily ever after. The gorgeous prince and the ordinary American girl with freakish red hair. Well, except for the fact that the tabloids once snapped a pic of them (us) and claimed that the country's future leader might be hooking up with a "corrupt" American girl. Since we were seen coming out of a bathroom together, the paper speculated that there might have been drugs involved. (*So* not my style. Please.)

But that was just a blip. And things are really good between us now.

I know, because at this moment he's knocking at my door with his homework-filled backpack slung over one shoulder and a bag from McDonalds—my nutritional Achilles' heel—in his hand. I'm feeling very happily-ever-afterish watching him through the peephole, wondering how long I can torture him before I open the door.

Or how long I can torture myself, because I really want to plant one right on those delicious lips of his. Well, and then snag that Mickey D's bag to see what fattening, artery-clogging delicacy he's brought me.

I think this is how all fairy tales should be, really. No mean stepparents (much as Gabrielle drives me insane, she's really okay), no evil witches with poisoned apples (though there is this one girl at school, Steffi, who's determined to snag Georg for herself, not that she'll ever admit it in public), and lots of fast food and making out.

"I know you're looking through the peephole, Valerie," Georg says.

Shoot. *So* not what Prince Charming would say to Cinderella, even though Georg says it in the most delicious European accent.

I pull the door open and, as much as I want to play it cool, especially given that my very protocol-minded dad is just a few steps away in the kitchen—and it *is* literally a few steps, since this apartment is dinky—I can't. Georg's simply too phenomenal for words and too willing to kiss me blind during the few seconds I have the door open behind me, blocking Dad's view of us.

And, thankfully, the door is also blocking Georg's view of Dad. Dad's been acting strange ever since I got home from spending my winter break in Virginia, and I don't think Georg needs to witness any of the strangeness.

Dad is totally straitlaced—I mean, the guy accompanies VIPs to the royal ballet, and he knows the difference between a shrimp fork and a salad fork without even having to think about it—but a few minutes ago, he was dancing while he diced tomatoes for dinner. *Dancing.* Shaking his forty-something groove thang and the whole bit. When I asked him what was up with that, he just shrugged and said it was because "Modern Love" was on the radio and everyone has to dance to David Bowie.

Um, I think not.

The only times I've ever seen my Dad dance before tonight have been at state functions where there are waltzes and such—no Bowie. While Dad seems to have a decent sense of rhythm when it comes to eighties tunes, I'm hoping he'll keep it under wraps now that Georg's here.

"What'd you bring me?" I ask Georg once we stop kissing and I wave him inside.

"Sundaes. So we'd better eat fast." I shut the door and he instantly looks past me to the kitchen, which is open to the main room. "Hello, Mr. Winslow."

My dad nods, acting all proper now. "Good evening, Prince Georg."

Georg takes in the sight of my dad working his culinary magic and hesitates. "I apologize if this is inconvenient. I didn't realize I would interrupt dinner—"

"It's no problem. If you'd like to put those in the freezer for the moment and sit down with us, you're welcome to stay. I made plenty."

"I just ate, but . . ." Georg glances at me, then at the counter, where Dad is ladling a yummy-smelling tomato sauce over chicken. "If you don't tell my parents, I could eat again. That smells terrific."

They are so polite to each other I could hurl. Guess that's what you get when you put a prince and a protocol expert in a room together. They fight to out-nice each other. Thankyou, thankyou, thankyou God, Georg isn't that formal with me in private, or I bet we'd never have hooked up.

"If your parents would prefer—"

"No, they really wouldn't care. They'd just tell me not to, um, mooch." Georg says "mooch" as if he's not certain that's the word to use in this situation. He does that a lot with American slang, which totally cracks me up. Even though his parents have him at the same private American high school I attend so he can improve his English—he's going to be running the country someday and good English is apparently key to diplomacy in the Western hemisphere—he still gets confused about certain words.

"It's not a problem," Dad assures him with a smile. Good thing, because I'd have been an eensy-weensy-tiny bit upset if Georg had gone back to his rooms on the opposite side of the palace just so I could eat dinner with Dad.

We spend most of dinner rehashing what we did over winter break. Georg went skiing in Switzerland but stopped at a couple of hospitals along the way to visit little kids, which is the kind of thing he does every time he goes on vacation.

I talk about my trip home to Virginia, where I spent a week with Mom and Gabrielle. Not my choice of winter break destinations, but I got to see my friends and tell them about Georg in person. And although I'm not sure what Dad really thinks of Gabby, I suspect he's glad I made an effort while I was there to get to know her at least a little. And I know he's definitely happy I'm getting along okay with Mom again, even if she is a zillion miles away and continues to mail me dorky teenage self-help books in an effort to fix my perceived shortcomings in life.

"I probably suck at skiing compared to you," I tell Georg, though using the word "suck" garners me a warning frown from Dad. "I'm barely in the intermediate category. I do a few green runs to warm up, then blue runs most of the day. Though I have to go back to the easy greens again if I get tired. Otherwise it's wipeout city. But I'd love to be able to try a black run soon. If I can work up the guts, anyway."

Georg raises one dark eyebrow. I love when he does that. It's goofy and sexy at the same time. "We don't have green runs here. Blues are the easiest, reds are intermediate, and blacks are the expert runs. But they're probably equivalent."

"Oh." I'm such a clueless American. "Well, I should be able to see what it's like to ski here soon. Right, Dad?"

His mouth is full of chicken, but he's nodding. He *did* promise to take me skiing when I agreed to move here from Virginia with him. I mean, we live in the middle of the Alps now. Ski resorts everywhere. Back in Virginia, we'd have to drive all day just to get to a decent slope. Hence my ski suckage.

"I was planning to talk to you about that later tonight, Valerie, but now's as good a time as any," Dad says, once he's swallowed. "I thought we could go to Scheffau this weekend. It's a rather quiet resort in Austria, without so much of the glitz or attention that St. Moritz and some of the other Swiss ski areas have."

"I've been to Scheffau before," Georg says, sounding excited. "It has some great runs. You'll like it."

"*This* weekend?" I just got home a few days ago, and things between me and Georg were a little rocky right before break, due to the whole tabloid fiasco. They're great now (I've never had to make up with a boyfriend before—probably because I've never had a boyfriend before—and I've discovered that making up is way, way fun), but the last thing I want to do is spend another two or three days away from him. Even if it is to go skiing in the Alps.

"What's wrong with this weekend?" Dad asks. "Do you have something scheduled at school?"

I glance from Dad to Georg, then look back at Dad. "No, but—"

"I see," he says with a grin that's totally embarrassing. I hate that I'm so transparent. "Perhaps I can speak to Prince Manfred and Princess Claudia about having Georg come along. We'll need to make some arrangements regarding the press, since it's possible they'll use the opportunity to take photos if they figure out Georg is in Scheffau, especially if they believe he's there with you, but I'm sure we can work something out."

Do I have the best dad ever, or what?

I look at Georg, who's eating his chicken as if he hasn't had food in days. "Don't you have soccer this weekend, though?"

"Nope," he says. "Bye week." But I can tell from his guarded expression that he's not sure about going. Probably because of his parents. They're just a tad overprotective.

When Dad gets up to grab some more chicken and salad from the kitchen, I lean in close to Georg and whisper, "You can say no if you don't want to go. I won't be offended."

Well, I probably would be offended, on the inside. But I've resolved not to take things like that personally. Before break, he told me he wanted us to "cool it," and I got upset and jumped to the conclusion that he wanted to break up. In reality, he just wanted us to quit making out where we could get caught by some crazy photographer and end up on the front page of the local paper. But when I took offense, it almost screwed up our relationship for real.

"It's not that," Georg says. "I just figured you might want some time alone with your father."

I shake my head, and the smile he shoots back renders my breath immobile in my lungs for a moment.

I resolve to always, *always* give Georg the benefit of the doubt from now on.

Dad comes to clear away our dishes and asks, "Are your parents in their apartments, Georg? I can give them a call while you two enjoy on your sundaes."

Georg tells him to go ahead, so after finishing in the kitchen, Dad takes the phone into his room to make the call—presumably because he'll be talking with Georg's parents about stuff he doesn't want us to hear. What, I can only guess. Probably reassuring them that he won't put me and Georg in the same bedroom or something.

"This is heaven," I say after my first bite of chocolate sundae. I can almost feel my butt and thighs spreading, but I don't care.

"Nope," Georg replies, leaning over and giving me a

quickie kiss. "Skiing in Austria with my girlfriend. That's heaven."

"If your parents let you."

"If," he agrees.

At noon the next day, I still don't know if Georg can come to Scheffau. His father, Prince Manfred, was in the middle of some conference call about tourist-industry legislation when Dad rang their apartment. Princess Claudia seemed to think it would be fine if her son came along with us—given some quick planning—but first she wanted to talk it over with her husband. And their security team. And the public relations office.

It's the unbelievable drawback of dating a prince. Every freaking thing you do has to be cleared by what essentially functions as a behavioral review board.

So even as I'm sitting at the lunch table in the cafeteria—it's too cold to eat outside at our usual spot in the quad—listening to my friends Ulrike and Maya talk about an upcoming school dance (where I'm guessing they won't play David Bowie), my brain is totally focused on Georg and skiing.

Well, and on cuddling with Georg on the chairlift. Or in front of a big, warm fireplace. Or over a steaming cup of Austrian hot chocolate while we sit on a balcony and watch the sunset over the Alps and tangle our feet together under a blanket. Just spending some time alone, away from school and the palace and the city and the behavior police.

Yum.

"The tuna's not that good," Steffi says to me as she plunks her tray down across the table from me. She tells Ulrike and Maya hello, then looks back at me. "So what's 'yum,' huh?"

Did I actually say it aloud?

I give Steffi the Valerie Shrug. It's what my parents say I do when I want to make it look like I don't give a rip about whatever's going on around me even though I really am paying attention. It's usually enough to put people off. But not Steffi.

"I missed breakfast," I lie. "Guess I'm hungrier than I thought or something."

I learned my very first day of school that Ulrike and Maya are all right, but that Steffi, despite her innocent brown eyes and delicate appearance, usually has ulterior motives if she's being nice to you. Since she's good friends with Ulrike and Maya and they seem to be clueless about girls like Steffi—in other words, manipulative types—I figure my best option is to tolerate Steffi while staying below her radar. However, the below-the-radar part is becoming tougher and tougher to do now that everyone's suspicious that Georg and I might be together. Mostly because Steffi thinks *she* and Georg should be the ones going out, and God forbid anyone get in the way of what Steffi wants. She instantly sees that person as a threat to be annihilated.

Steffi seems to take my word for it on the "yum" thing, since she turns toward Ulrike after I take a stupidly huge bite of my tuna salad. "So, you guys talking about the dance?" she asks. "Who are you going to ask?"

Ask? It's a girls-ask-guys thing? Gag.

Ulrike pushes her tuna salad around her lunch tray. She's one of those impossibly skinny girls who hardly ever eats, and not because she's obsessed with fitting into a negative clothing size. Sorry, but I abhor standing in a mall dressing room trying on normal-sized clothes while girls in the other booths are whining aloud to their friends—who are usually standing outside the dressing room doors being total poseurs with their cell phones, checking for messages from their unfortunate boyfriends—about how they're sooooo fat they're almost out of a size zero and omigod their life is over! I want to rip the clothes out of their hands and tell them to get the hell out of my range of hearing. Maybe go to the food court and have something other than a head of lettuce for lunch.

But Ulrike's not that way at all. She just gets focused on other things—like the dance—and forgets to eat much.

She would probably have to stop and check her clothing tags if you asked her what size she wears, since she's not that into clothes shopping. Of course, she's also really tall and has this shiny white-blond hair that makes her look like a movie star no matter what she has on.

Good thing she's one of the sweetest people I've ever met, or I'd really have to hate her based on nothing more than her looks.

"I've been so busy with the planning committee, I haven't even thought about who to ask," she says, and glances across the table to Maya, who's sitting next to me. "How about you?"

"I'm still thinking," Maya mumbles in a way that makes me think she wants to go alone but doesn't want Ulrike or Steffi harassing her about it. She's a junior—excuse me, a *year eleven*—but since she lives next door to Ulrike, she hangs out with us lowly year ten types. Maya pushes her dark hair back over her shoulders so it doesn't hang in her lunch tray, then focuses on Steffi. "Why do you ask? Is there someone you're planning to take?"

"We'll see. No firm plans yet."

Georg is unavailable, I mentally telegraph in her direction.

As if she can hear my thoughts, Steffi looks straight at me. "And how about you, Val? Are you going to try to ask Prince Georg?"

I hate her. Really I do. Because she says this in a tone that sounds nice to everyone else, but that I know is meant to make me feel like dog crap. It's that use of the word "try." She just slid it in there. Like it's sooooo cute that I have a thing for the prince and I'm going to be pulling a real goober move by "trying" to ask him to the dance.

"I haven't really thought about it, with the trip to Virginia and everything," I answer honestly. She has to know there's no one else I'd ask, which means she's sniffing around to see how serious Georg and I really are. We've worked hard to keep things low-key just so we're not the main topic of school gossip—and to try to overcome our recent tabloid snafu and the way it affected his parents—but all that secrecy does have one nasty side effect.

Namely, that Steffi still thinks she has a chance with him.

Before Steffi can say anything else, I ask Ulrike, "When is it, anyway? This weekend?"

I hope so, 'cause then maybe I'll be off skiing with Georg and I won't have to worry about Steffi giving me backhanded compliments all night while she tries to latch on to my boyfriend.

"Next Saturday," Maya says, since Ulrike has finally taken another bite of her tuna salad and is too polite to talk with food in her mouth.

"Only ten days," Ulrike adds, dropping her sandwich

back onto her plate. "And I'm panicking. We need to sell a lot more tickets. You guys have to promise me you'll come, even if you don't bring dates. Okay?"

We all promise. Steffi and Maya are fairly enthusiastic, but the last thing I want to do is go to a school dance. I've always felt like a loser at these kind of events, and even though I (finally!) have someone to go with, it's not like we can go hide in a corner like other couples do and make out.

It just doesn't work that way when *Majesty* magazine has a reporter whose sole job is to take photos of your boyfriend. The school is off-limits to the press, but still. We're both bound to hear a "remember that you're in the public eye" lecture from our parents before we set foot out the door, and we've learned the hard way that we actually need to take those lectures seriously.

On the bright side, it'll be a night out where we can listen to good music and see who's hooking up with whom around school (even if we don't get to be all lovey-dovey with each other while we're there) and we can always hide out at home and do something fun afterward.

"Great!" Ulrike's smile is cotton candy sweet as she sets down her fork. "And if you feel like coming early to help me set up, I'd really appreciate—"

"Not me." Maya holds up her hands like she's warding off Satan. "When I set up, someone has to come through after me and redo it the right way. I'm awful at that kind of thing and you know it."

Steffi says she'll try to make it there early but isn't sure what her plans are yet.

In other words, she's hoping she'll find something better to do, but she's hedging so she won't upset Ulrike.

Before my mind can stop my mouth, I pop out with, "I'll help you."

I'm totally not the school dance volunteer type, but the look on Ulrike's face when both Maya and Steffi act like they're gonna bail is too much for my guilty conscience to handle. I turn to face Ulrike and add, "You're just going to have to be very specific directing me what to do so I don't screw it all up. All right?"

"Thanks, Valerie!" Ulrike looks so grateful and Steffi so anxious, like this is eating her up inside, that I know I made the right choice.

"No problem." Take that, Steffi.

"Can you be at the hotel at six?"

Hotel? "Um, which hotel?"

She says something very German-sounding, so I ask her to repeat it slowly. Since German is Ulrike's and Steffi's native language, this kind of thing just rolls off their tongues all the time. Maya's lived here long enough (and taken enough German) to understand them, but not me. After taking French all through school (with straight As, thankyouverymuch) anything in German still sounds like someone horking up a loogie to my ears. I know maybe five or six words other than what I've figured out from road signs and reading the McDonald's menu, and that's only because Dad drilled them into me. Things like "excuse me," "please," and "thank you." Typical Dad words.

Ulrike grabs her backpack out from under the cafeteria table and scribbles on a piece of paper. "Here's the address and the hotel's name. It's only two blocks from the school, over on Blumenstrasse, so you should be able to find it."

I study the page. I can't begin to pronounce the hotel's name. It looks kinda like Jagger, as in Mick and the Rolling Stones, but that's not what it sounded like when Ulrike said it. "This is where the dance is?"

"They have a great ballroom. Prom is there most years, too," she explains.

In other words, the press will have a much easier time getting in than they would at the school.

And Georg is going to be that much less likely to go.

To: Val@realmail.sg.com

From: GvE@realmail.sg.com

Subject: Skiing

Just got a call on the cell from Mom. Dad says I can go to Scheffau. See you at home after I'm done with soccer practice? Love, G-

He signed it *love*!

I think I'm going to pop right out of my seat in computer lab. Knowing Georg, he'd never say it unless he meant it either. Whaaa-hoooo!

I mean, once he handed me a McDonald's bag with my fave sandwich in there, and when I thanked him, he said something about how it was "true love." But that's not the same, I don't think.

I keep seeing all these articles in magazines about how relationships are doomed if one person likes the other one more, and it's always the one who's more head over heels who gets hurt. They make me wonder if I'm stupid, letting myself become more dopey in love with Georg than he is with me. But now I'm thinking we might actually be equally googly-eyed for each other.

I try not to look too obviously happy about what I'm

reading, since I don't want anyone in the computer lab getting too curious. From the time stamp, it looks like he must have been here at lunch. He has a paper due in his English Lit class next week, so I'm guessing he was here working on it. It also explains why I didn't see him anywhere in the cafeteria at lunch, though I probably wouldn't have noticed anyway, what with Ulrike talking about the dance and me off in la-la land, daydreaming about skiing with my boyfriend.

Oh, shit. Skiing.

With my *boyfriend*.

What in the world was I thinking? I drop my head against the keyboard. The girl sitting next to me asks me if I'm all right, and I mumble something nonsensical but reassuring-sounding back to her. She gives me an "uh-huh" before turning back to her own e-mail.

How could this not have occurred to me before? Like, the exact minute Dad suggested we bring Georg along?

I'm going to have to wear ski pants. The ultimate in how-big-is-Val's-ass fashion. And not only will Georg see it, photographers are bound to immortalize it. In print.

Oh, man. It might even end up in some media database, where anyone who wants to can pull it up at will, print copies, and plaster them all over the school. Knowing Steffi, she'd show the absolute worst picture to everyone and say,

"Doesn't Val look so cute in this picture? Isn't it so lucky for her that Georg's parents let her tag along on his ski trip?" or something like that.

I raise my head and start tapping out an emergency missive. I'm tempted to put "Save My Ass!" in the subject line of the e-mail, but I know Dad won't appreciate my language or the humor. And I've gotta stay on his good side, since he's the only person who can help me now.

Assuming I handle this correctly.

I settle for "Major Emergency" and type a note explaining the situation in the nicest language I can muster (since this is going to the palace, after all). Then I hit send.

2

FOUR HOURS AFTER I GET HOME FROM SCHOOL, STILL no Dad.

Georg has come and gone. I've not only finished my homework, but I've worked ahead, super geek that I am. I've been forced to find dinner for myself (horrors), and worst of all, even if Dad walks through the door right this very minute, I'm going to have seriously limited shopping time. Unlike stores in the United States, most of Schwerinborg's shops tend to close right around dinnertime.

Unable to distract myself with food, I leave my microwaved carnage on the table and go check my e-mail for the zillionth time.

Nothing.

Not even the usual spam offering me low mortgage rates or asking if I want to increase my size to please my partner (and those messages never do mean my pathetic barely-B cups.)

How is this possible?

I open my sent mail folder to make sure I used the correct e-mail address for Dad. Of course I did.

I groan out loud. The man clearly doesn't understand my emergency. It's Wednesday. If we leave for our ski trip on Friday right after school . . . well, the clock is ticking. Even if he had some government event to attend tonight, you'd think he'd take two secs to e-mail me back and let me know.

Just to cover my ass (so to speak), I decide to e-mail my best buddy Christie in Virginia. Like Ulrike, Christie is one of those perfect people I could hate based on looks alone if she didn't possess an uncommon cool quotient. Since her fashion sense is as good as my Dad's—and Christie's a lot less likely to ridicule my ski pants dilemma—I figure she'll be able to steer me in the right direction.

Since she's six hours behind me, if I'm really lucky she'll be sitting at a computer at school. At worst, she'll check e-mail when she gets home in a couple of hours. Either way, she's probably going to be able to help before Dad.

To: ChristieT@viennawest.edu

From: Val@realmail.sg.com

Subject: Fashion Assistance, Please!!

Hey, Christie!

Three things: First, I'm really glad I got to see you, Jules, and Natalie over winter break. You have no clue (and I mean none) how much I've missed you guys while I've been here. I'm making friends, but it's just not the same as hanging with my A-listers.

Second, things with Georg are going way better than when I arrived there for vacation. Remember how I told you he met me at the airport when I came back to Schwerinborg? Well, we're totally on track and back together now.

Which brings me to number three: Dad is taking me skiing this weekend and he said Georg can come. (I know! I'm totally psyched . . .) However, I have a major fashion problem. Ski pants. I e-mailed Dad at work and asked him to take me shopping tonight, since he's usually good at helping me find stuff that doesn't look hideous. (Remember I told you about that killer dress I wore to that palace dinner I got to attend with Georg? That was all Dad.) But if you have any suggestions at all . . . HELP!!! I'm gonna have to shop either tonight or tomorrow, ’cause we’re leaving on Friday.

Freaking out in Schwerinborg,

Val

PS—How’s everything with Jeremy? He’s not mad that you hung out with me, Jules, and Natalie for most of vacation, is he? If he is, just blame me. Tell him I had a boyfriend crisis and a mom crisis at the same time (both of which are totally true) and he should be good with that.

To: Val@realmail.sg.com
From: ChristieT@viennawest.edu
Subject: RE: Fashion Assistance, Please!!

VAL!!!

This is really Twilight Zone, because I was writing an e-mail to you at the exact second yours appeared in my in-box. (I’m in the library . . . we’re supposed to be doing research on World War I for Mrs. Bennett’s class.) I was worried about you and Georg, so I’m thrilled everything is cool on that front. He sounds incredible (and I know he looks incredible!)! Lucky you!

Jeremy was totally okay with me hanging out with you

over break. He's all obsessed with training for a marathon, if you can believe it, so he has zero time for me these days anyway. It was a big deal when we all went to that movie together while you were here.

Yeah, I know. I wish he'd chill out over the marathon too.

On the ski pants thing—the ones you already own aren't that bad. Does your mom have them? E-mail or call her and have her overnight them to you immediately. It's probably pricey to send them from Virginia, but I bet it's cheaper than buying new pants.

Now, I'm not saying you can't do better. What you need to look for are black ski pants (pretty much all they sell anyway). Skip the overalls type. Too hard to pee. Look for something with a good boot cut and that hugs your rear end and lifts. I'll send you a few links to web pages to show you what I'm talking about. And if you have to wear your old pair, no big deal. Besides, I bet Georg won't care.

BTW—you did tell him you went out with David Anderson a couple times when you were here over break, didn't you?

He must've handled it pretty well!

Write soon!

Christie

To: ChristieT@viennawest.edu

From: Val@realmail.sg.com

Subject: RE: Fashion Assistance, Please!!

Christie,

1—Checked web pages. Gotcha. Will also have Mom overnight the old pants (though I think they might have a hole in a bad location . . . will have to check.) Thankyou, thankyou, for saving my tail on this one, literally and figuratively. Will report back on what I end up wearing.

2—What is up with Jeremy? He's always been obsessive about running, but a marathon is insane. Think of the chafing!

And has he not looked at you lately? Does he not realize that you are beyond beautiful and that some other guy will snag you if he doesn't pay attention? (Okay, you and I both know you'd never break up with Jeremy for another guy. But Jeremy doesn't know that. Work it just a little bit. Seriously. Like, compliment another guy on his shirt or something where Jeremy can hear you and that'll be enough to wake him up.)

3—No, I didn't tell Georg. It hasn't come up. AND IT WON'T.

4—Dad's finally here. Gotta go. Will write soon!

Love, Val

My dad is a freakin' miracle worker. As I pull on my ski helmet just outside the lodge, I shoot him a smile. He's sitting on a bench about fifteen feet away, closing the latches on his boots and watching me at the same time. I mouth a "thank you" and give a little pull at my pants so he knows what I mean. He just winks at me and goes back to work on his boots.

Not only did he come home with dinner for me on Wednesday night (leftover cordon bleu from some government dinner that was way better than the preprocessed hunk o' meat I nuked in the microwave and ended up tossing in the trash can), he also brought four pairs of ski pants. He took part of his afternoon off from work to buy them, then rushed back to the palace for an evening meeting with Prince Manfred about an upcoming state visit from the Georgian President (not Georgia as in plantation tours and the Atlanta Braves, but Georgia as in the former Russian republic, and apparently a very important trade partner of Schwerinborg), meaning no time to call or e-mail. He walked into the apartment around eight thirty, right after I fired off that last e-mail to Christie, and tossed a shopping bag at me like it was no big thing, telling me to choose whichever pair fit best and he'd return the others.

And I look incredible. In ski pants! The ones he chose are even better than the ones Christie suggested. When I sent her a pic of me in the new pants, she got all excited about them.

Good thing, because I need something to distract me (and Christie) from the David Anderson issue, which has been plaguing me for two solid days and is now threatening to ruin my Saturday, too.

Somehow I've gotta get over it. Just forget Christie ever brought it up.

"You ready?" Georg asks. He looks completely comfortable with his ski gear, like he could go down any slope without worrying that he'll crash and burn the way I worry. He has his boots on and he's carrying his skis over his shoulder, pointing toward the nearest chairlift with one pole. "We can put our skis on once we're closer to the lift line."

He's so gung ho, I just know he's going to be disappointed by my skiing skills. I hope he doesn't get too annoyed waiting for me when I panic at the top of every section that looks the least bit icy or steep.

"Sure," I say. "Let's wait for Dad and what's-her-name, though. They'll want to know where we're going."

Georg grins, letting his skis slide down in front of him so the tails rest in the snow. "Her name is Fräulein Putzkammer. But she said you can call her Miss Putzkammer if you want."

I roll my eyes. I cannot, cannot say "Putzkammer." Please. It's hard enough just to think of her as The Fräulein—which is now my mental nickname for her—because *fräulein* is a strange enough word itself. The French *mademoiselle* is so much cooler. "I still don't get why the press office felt like they had to send someone along."

I'm sure The Fräulein is nice enough. She's probably in her late thirties or early forties. She's also way prettier than her name makes her sound, with blond hair and a fairly athletic bod—nothing sagging too far south—which I assume also means she can keep up while we ski. And she seemed okay on the way here last night. She let me and Georg choose what music to listen to in the car, and she didn't seem to mind when I took longer than everyone else at the gas station, trying to count out the euros correctly to pay for a candy bar so I could get my chocolate fix. She even translated some of the wall signs for me when we checked into our cutesy little guesthouse last night here in Scheffau.

But something about her isn't sitting right with me. It's more than the fact that she's obsessive about telling Georg to keep his ski cap on whenever he's not wearing his helmet, just to improve the odds that no one will recognize him this weekend and we can have a more relaxing, private vacation. More than the fact that she flirts with my dad, because pretty much all women over voting age flirt with my dad.

Scary, I know, but the guy *is* decent-looking in a parental sort of way. He goes to the gym every morning to keep his buffed-up muscles, plus he has the whole etiquette thing going for him. Women get into that.

I glance over as the unnaturally blond Fräulein brushes a piece of lint off the side of her ski jacket, resolve to be my nicey-nice self and not make a crack about how lint won't matter once she's skiing, then turn toward Georg, who's messing around with the bindings on his skis. Without even looking up, he whispers, "Don't worry about her, Val."

"Easy for you to say."

My bullshit detector is pretty finely tuned, so it doesn't usually go off without reason. The fact that I can't pinpoint why is driving me bonkers. But I don't want to get all bitchy about her and then find out I'm way off base, either.

"She's been working for my parents and traveling with them for almost five years now. She even came on my Zermatt trip over winter break to keep an eye on me. She's cool." Georg's voice is low enough that she can't hear him from where she's sitting on the bench, pulling on her ski gloves. "And she's really helpful, Val. If any media types show up, she'll work with them to arrange a time where they can ask me questions or take photos somewhere here at the base lodge. Otherwise, they'll all buy ski passes and try to snap pictures on the slopes, which is dangerous for everyone. Or worse, they'll try to follow us in the evenings to see if something is up with you and me so they can write about it." He raises his head and his eyes meet mine for a brief moment. "I don't know if my parents would have let me come without her."

"Yeah, yeah, yeah, I know." Dad explained it all last night, once we'd checked in and Georg was in his room next door to ours and The Fräulein was in her room across the hall. "But it still sucks. I was hoping it'd just be you, me, and Dad. Mostly just you and me."

"It will be," he assures me. "We'll split off from them when we get to the summit. As long as we check in every so often, we should have plenty of time to ourselves."

The smile he gives me as we follow Dad and The Fräulein to the lift line makes me want to crumple right there in the snow. Especially when he adds, "Hey, nice ski pants. Those new?"

Gotta love a guy who notices.

Dad and The Fräulein are ready to go, so we head to the lift line. As we snap on our skis, Georg asks me how Christie, Jules, and Natalie are doing, just because that's the kind of guy he is. And he's never even met them.

He's just so amazingly perfect.

And I'm so *not*. Just thinking about Christie ties my stomach up in knots again.

How could I possibly have cheated on Georg?

Okay, it's not like I was *cheating* cheating on him in Virginia. He did tell me he wanted us to cool it (his exact words) right before I went home on break, so what did he expect? And my friends set me up with David, totally without my knowledge, so it wasn't as if I initiated the date at all. And they did it in a way that would have made it rude for me to back out.

We only went out one time after the initial setup date, and that was it. Over and out. I figured out pretty fast that, for one, I was still crushing pretty bad on Georg even if he did want to cool it (and even if it turned out I misinterpreted what he meant), and for two, once I actually went out with David, he just didn't do it for me. Even when he kissed me, it wasn't anything as good as Georg's kisses. No zing. No flair. No ooh-baby-do-I-want-you-now.

I think David and I would still be really good friends if I lived in Virginia. However, even if he kissed better than Georg, we're too different on the inside to be an actual couple. I firmly believe this, despite the fact that I had a massive crush on him for so long, it could probably be in *Guinness World Records*, assuming they covered such things.

David simply looks at the world in a different way than I do.

Specifically, in a way that wouldn't include my mom.

I can't blame David for his views, especially since he idolizes his father, who's this hotshot Republican lobbyist I'm constantly seeing on CNN talking about the importance of strong conservative Christian families in holding together the fabric of society. (Really, he said that. In prime time.)

Frankly, I don't expect anyone to be all happy-happy-happy that my mom's a lesbian or anything like that. I'm still having trouble dealing with the fact that my parents aren't together anymore, let alone the whole Mom-is-living-with-another-woman thing.

But the entire David incident drove home to me that I really need to be with someone who can understand my family and its quirks and still be okay with it all. Someone who can be okay with *me*, exactly the way I am. Even on the days when I'm not okay with who I am.

And that someone is Georg. My heart has been with him the whole time. If he'd intended to break up with me during our whole "cool it" thing, I know deep down inside that I'd still be devastated.

Mom assured me that it was fine that I went out with David while I was home and told me not to feel the least bit guilty. She said I wasn't cheating on Georg. That I was learning what I don't want in life, which is as important as learning what I do want—or some psychobabble along those lines.

At the time, it made perfect sense. After all, it's not like I'm thirty and married to Georg and still trying to figure out what I want by messing around with another guy. I'm fifteen, I just started going out with my first-ever boyfriend, and we haven't been together very long at all.

But now, waiting in the lift line with Georg next to me and Dad and The Fräulein behind me, I have to wonder if I handled things the right way. If I really should have been listening to Mom, the Self-Help Book Queen of the World, instead of my own gut. And if I should have 'fessed up to Georg the minute I got home and realized that he didn't want us to be broken up, but simply wanted us to keep things low-key.

Georg and I get up to the front of the line. Thankfully, I don't take a header as I scoot to the red STOP marker and wait for the chair to come around behind me so I can sit. Once we're airborne and Georg has pulled the safety bar down in front of us, I close my eyes, enjoying the morning sunshine and the soft breeze blowing on my face. I can hear the swoosh of skis against snow as we sail over the heads of the skiers who arrived here before us and have managed to squeeze in a run or two already.

This is so much better than just hanging out in the palace scribbling essays for school or killing time vacuuming the apartment for Dad while I wait for Georg to get home from a soccer game.

That thought instantly makes me picture Georg in his soccer shorts. Yummy, yummy, yum, yum, yum. His legs are all muscular without being bulky. The kind you can just run your hands over and—

Georg's arm bumps against mine. "Perfect day, huh? The snow's just glittering. And it's not too cold, either."

I turn and look at him. He's so gorgeous I can't stand it. His helmet is covering most of his dark hair and he's pulled his goggles down over his eyes, but I can still make out a devilish gleam through the lenses that makes me go all loopy. Mostly 'cause I know that gleam is one hundred percent for me.

"You know I love you madly, right?"

It just blurts right out of my big mouth, right there with my dad all of twenty feet behind me on the next chair.

We've never done the "I love you" bit. I made a pact with Christie, Jules, and Natalie years ago that if any of us ever felt that way about a guy, we'd wait for him to say it first. But I couldn't help it.

And now that I've had two shocked seconds to think about what I just said, I don't want to take it back.

Even though we're totally in public here on the lift and Dad and what's-her-name are on the chair right behind ours, Georg eases his hand across the seat and slips his gloved fingers over mine.

"You have no idea how much I want to kiss you right now," he whispers.

Oh, I can guess.

I scoot just a little closer to him on the chair, lace my fingers up through his, then squeeze. We let go quickly, since neither one of us wants a lecture from Dad or The Fräulein about how inappropriate it is for a prince to engage in a public display of affection.

"We'll find an empty section of the trail after we ditch them." There's enough urgency underlying Georg's scrumptious accent to have me scanning the slope immediately, trying to see what areas are in view of people riding the chairlift so we don't do anything stupid in any of those places.

We get off the lift and decide to take one of the easy runs, just to warm up.

On the good side: Even after nine months off, I pick up right where I left off from skiing. I glide right along. I don't fall or even wobble on the way down. I manage to do this even though I know Georg's watching me and even though I can practically feel him kissing me, I want him so bad.

On the not-so-good side: Dad and The Fräulein stick to us like glue the whole way down. Even when I pause at the side of the trail and fake like I need to adjust my goggles, they stop and wait.

Can they tell Georg and I are dying to jump each other or what?

When we get to the lift, I tell Dad that I think Georg and I are going to head to another part of the slope now that we've done a practice run, but we'll make sure we don't draw any attention to ourselves. Georg adds that we can meet them for lunch and that if they need us before that, we'll both have our cell phones.

Dad agrees (hooray!), but then he maneuvers in the lift line so I end up riding with him this time while Georg's stuck with The Fräulein.

I feel bad for Georg, but better him than me.

"You looked pretty good there," Dad says as we take off. "Must be the new ski pants."

"Very funny."

"Look, Val, I wanted to ride with you for a reason." His voice is quiet, like he's afraid what he's saying might carry to Georg and The Fräulein on the chair behind us.

Damn. Time to do a preemptive strike against his fatherly instinct to lecture me. "I promise, Dad, Georg will keep his helmet on. I don't think anyone will realize who he is. And we'll definitely behave if we go—"

"It's not that," Dad assures me. "I trust the two of you."

He's quiet for a minute, using his pole to pick some loose snow off the side of his boot as the chair ascends. Once he's settled again, he says, "It's just . . . do you remember when I e-mailed you in Virginia to let you know I'd be meeting you at the airport when you returned home from break?"

"Sure."

"I said I wanted to hear all about your trip, but that I also had news to share with you."

"Oh. Sorry . . . guess I forgot." Duh. I totally spaced that he said he wanted to talk about what happened with him while I was gone. Or maybe I just assumed he was saying he wanted to talk because he *always* wants to talk, and it's usually just to nag me about proper behavior. Or to tell me all about what dignitaries he had the chance to meet while he was at work that day. Then it occurs to me. "Are you going to have to travel for work?"

I knew that travel was a possibility when I moved here with Dad. Part of why we're living in the palace instead of some apartment in downtown Freital (the capital city and, frankly, the only real town in Schwerinborg) is so that if Dad needs to go along on any official trips with Prince Manfred, I'll be where other adults can check up on me.

Make sure I eat decent food and don't skip school and all the usual stuff Mom did whenever Dad traveled during his last job, working for the president. And being at the palace—as Dad has pointed out on numerous occasions—means no one can get to our apartment (or to me) without going through metal detectors and showing ID first. It's like being a well-guarded dignitary myself. Or a prisoner in lockdown, depending on how I feel on any given day.

"No, it's not travel. This is more, ah, personal."

"Oh." At his tone, my throat instantly tightens up. This cannot be good. He never talks to me about personal stuff. At least not about his *own* personal stuff. He barely said two words when Mom made her off-the-cuff declaration that she was leaving him for Gabrielle. He hardly even got snarky when they were trying to divide up their stuff, even though I know Mom took a few things he really didn't want to hand over. He's the king of sucking it up and moving on, even when I know he's pissed off and hurt. "Um, what is it?"

"While you were in Virginia, I started seeing someone." He rushes to add that it's nothing serious; they just went out a couple of times. "I thought you should know. I didn't want you to hear about it from anyone else. And I want it to be clear that this isn't a situation like your mother has with Gabrielle, where they're now living together. I have no intention of getting remarried. Or even getting into a serious relationship. At least not anytime soon."

I'm tempted to point out that he couldn't remarry even if he wanted to, since I don't think the divorce is final yet. But I can't say anything. This is so out of left field.

It's a good thing there's a safety bar on the chairlift, or I might fall overboard.

"Valerie?"

"I'm processing." I stare at the white snow beneath me, studying the patterns of ski tracks weaving through it and admiring the way a sun-reflected sparkle will appear and then disappear as my viewing angle changes along with the movement of the lift.

What would happen if I did raise the safety bar and lean forward?

He shifts in the seat, which makes it swing a little in the breeze. "You're not going to ask who it is?"

"Um . . ." He knows so many people—VIPs, their staff members, palace employees, political reporters who are assigned to follow Prince Manfred around during the day—I can't even begin to guess. But I oblige him anyway. "Who is it?"

"Anna."

He says it like "On-na." Not like we'd say it in the States. More Euro-sounding.

"She's from Schwerinborg?" I ask. For some reason, now that there's a name attached, I'm curious.

He turns and frowns at me. "Anna Putzkammer, Valerie. *Fräulein Putzkammer*. Her first name is Anna."

No. Way.

No. No. No. Is he friggin' insane?

"Her?" I try not to sound screechy, but I know I do.

"Shhh. Sound carries up here." He takes a deep breath through his nostrils, then says, "And yes, *her*. That's not why she's on this trip, though. Prince Manfred and Princess Claudia have no idea we've been seeing each other. As I said, it's a very casual thing."

Somehow, I get the feeling Blondie back in the chair behind us isn't hoping for casual. And now I know why my bullshit detector's been pinging like a Geiger counter at a nuclear waste dump every time I look at her. She not only has the hots for Dad, like every other woman on the planet, but she's the first woman to actually go out with him since my parents started dating way back in the dark ages.

"You okay?" Dad sounds concerned, but I can't bring myself to reassure him.

It didn't occur to me he had any interest in dating, let alone that he'd actually go out and find someone. "I dunno. How am I supposed to be?"

What I really want to say, though, is something along

the lines of, *Isn't she a little young for you?* Or, *You know she needs to touch up her roots, right? Because that wouldn't do at a state dinner.* Or maybe even, *Tell her to keep her hands to herself, 'cause you're on the rebound and I don't want you to get hurt.* But I don't think any of those statements would go over very well.

We're nearing the top of the lift, so he raises the safety bar and shifts his weight forward. "You're supposed to be worrying about yourself at this stage of your life, not about me," he says. "And you're supposed to know that you're my priority and always will be."

I mumble an okay. Before we can say anything else, our skis are hitting the snow, and we're being propelled forward off the lift. Georg and Fräulein Predator Putzkammer ski up right behind us.

"Make sure your cell phones are turned on," The Fräulein says, looking first at Georg and then at me, all business. "We'll meet at noon at the bench where we put on our boots. Ja?"

Georg tells her no problem, then indicates that I should follow him down a side run, toward the intermediate slopes. I glance at Dad, who nods that it's okay, then I turn my skis in the direction Georg's going. He skis about fifty yards to where the trail goes around a corner, then stops and waits for me to join him. When I pause a few feet above Georg to loop the straps of my poles around my wrists, I look back to where Dad and The Fräulein are standing at the summit. They're studying the trail map and Dad's pointing at something.

Oh, shit. They're probably trying to figure out where they can ski that's out of sight of the lift so they can make out or something. Or at least I bet that's what she's planning. And I have to wonder—does my dad understand women enough to know their ploys? Will he see through her? It's not like he's been out on a date in nearly twenty years. And that was with Mom, who was never the flirty, game playing type, and who's now batting for the other team, so to speak. He might know how to deal with flirty women like the ones in department stores, but this is a whole 'nother thing.

He's probably way out of his league here.

At the moment that thought enters my brain, The Fräulein leans in so her head is closer to my Dad's.

I think I'm gonna yorck up my breakfast.

"Let's go back," I say. It's uphill, but I think if we hurry, we can sidestep up to the summit and catch them before they take off.

I turn my skis to go, but Georg catches my elbow. "What? Why?"

"I just, um, I don't want Dad to think I'm ditching him. It'd be rude, wouldn't it?"

"You're kidding, right?" He pushes his goggles up on top of his helmet and stares at me. I turn away, looking back uphill just in time to see Dad and The Fräulein disappear, heading down from the summit in the direction opposite the one Georg and I started down.

No chance of catching them now. No way of knowing what they're up to anymore.

I turn my skis back downhill and wave to Georg that we can go. He shakes his head and pulls his goggles back down. "He's an adult, Valerie. If he'd really wanted you to stay near him, he would have said so. I think he and Fräulein Putzkammer will have a good time without us."

Yeah, that's what I'm afraid of.

3

AS I SHIFT MY WEIGHT FROM HIP TO HIP, ATTEMPTING to carve out semidecent turns over the immaculate, perfectly parallel tracks Georg's leaving as he glides downhill in front of me, I decide that being unable to keep up with him isn't all bad.

I'm guessing my speed (or lack thereof) is probably holding him back and making him cranky, but for one, there's the view from back here (smokin' hot, especially when he's in a crouch, getting some speed on the open downhill sections of the run) and for two, there's the fact that he can't see the angry tears that keep fogging up my goggles.

How could I have been so worked up over what kind

of friggin' ski pants I wore this weekend? How could I not have realized that I had bigger issues to handle?

How could Dad dancing in the kitchen to David Bowie and singing "Modern Love" not have worked like a knock upside my thick head to make me realize *dear God, he's found himself a woman*?

I know I shouldn't be so upset about this. I didn't get all snot-nosed and crybabyish (too much) when Mom left, and that triple whammy (divorce, Gabrielle, and the whole fact that Mom's gay) gave me a reality check from completely out of the blue. I should have anticipated that Dad would eventually find someone. In fact, I'm pretty sure that deep in my gut I knew he would. He's a decent-looking adult whose job revolves around socializing, after all.

And it's not like this changes my universe the way Mom leaving Dad did. When that happened, I had to move out of the house where I had lived my whole life, leave behind the best friends I've ever had . . . the whole shebang. I witnessed Mom getting hot and heavy with someone other than my father (and not even the same sex as my father) and was forced to stand by and watch as she loaded all her stuff into cardboard boxes and crammed them into the back of her Toyota SUV. The SUV that should have been ferrying me and my friends around to school and sports and shopping.

I crouch and lean on my inside leg to go around a corner, trying to ignore my sniffly nose so I can focus on skiing. If I get too distracted, I'm bound to catch an edge and wipe out. I really don't need to compound my problems by breaking bones.

Besides, if I'm in a hospital bed, there's no way I can keep tabs on Dad. Or on *her*.

I make it around the corner—barely—then straighten up and look for Georg, but he's nowhere in sight.

He probably turned down some black run, expecting me to bump over moguls and barrel down icy steeps after him. Expecting me to be a way better skier than I actually am.

I am *so* not going over moguls. Huh-uh, no way.

"Val!"

I do a quick turn, skidding to a hockey stop, but I have too much momentum and end up doing a lame, sideways sit-down in the snow. Georg skis up beside me and offers a hand to pull me up.

"I waited by the tree back there, but you blew right by me. Didn't you see me?"

"Sorry. Corner," I mumble. I bend down, using the excuse of brushing snow off my rear and my side to blink and clear my eyes.

"This looks like a quiet stretch," he says. "And see that

trail heading off through the trees?" He raises a pole and points toward the other side of the run, where a narrow path slices into the woods. "Total privacy. You thinking what I'm thinking?"

"Perfect." I sound so convincing, I surprise myself. It's not like I don't want to go find an empty spot and sneak in a few kisses, especially since I just passed the momentous relationship milestone of telling this guy that I love him.

Maybe kissing is what I need. Just enough to make me forget that Dad's probably doing the same thing with that scuzzy ho, Fräulein Putzkammer the Predator.

Arrrrgh! So not the image I want burned into my brain. I know I'm being completely immature, thinking that blond equals predator, since she's really done nothing out of the ordinary for a normal female trying to find herself a little TLC. But still . . .

Kissing Georg. Yes, I need a lot of that. Enough to keep me from saying something rude to The Fräulein that I'm bound to regret later.

Georg reaches over and puts one gloved hand against the side of my helmet, studies me, then raises my goggles. His gorgeous mouth thins into a hard line and I know he can tell I've been crying. Any other time, I'd find his concern sweet, but right now I don't want to deal.

"I'm fine," I tell him. "Just had a cramp. It's gone now."

"Right." He yanks off his gloves and then lifts his goggles to the top of his head so he can study me. "Half an hour ago, when we were riding the lift together, you were smiling and having a great time. Now you're all worked up about something. What changed?"

I pinch the bridge of my nose and squeeze my eyes shut. "You don't cut me a moment of slack, do you?"

I can tell that he's not quite sure what "cut slack" means, but he's figuring it out from the context. "Was I going too fast? Just tell me . . . I can slow down. I don't mind—"

"It doesn't have anything to do with you," I assure him. At the look of doubt in his eyes, I say, "Honestly!"

A few skiers whiz by us. Georg watches them disappear, then says, "Come on. Let's cut across to that trail and find a better place to stop."

We look uphill to make sure it's clear, then ski across the run and into the woods without bothering to put our goggles back on. We bump along between the trees until we get to a place where it's wide enough for someone to pass by if they happen to come through, but isolated enough that we'll hear anyone coming long before they see us.

As I stop alongside him, Georg plants his poles. "Is this because I didn't say 'I love you' back?"

What? "No! I told you, it's not about you at all."

In fact, until he mentioned it just now, it didn't occur to me that he didn't say it back.

But it's clearly occurred to *him*, because he looks like he's upset about it. "Seriously," I assure him. "It's not you. It's Dad."

"Excuse me?"

I'm not at all ready to get into this. But since Georg's not going to believe any excuses and he's going to stand there thinking I'm afraid he doesn't love me, I just blurt out, "Did you know my dad's seeing someone?"

"That's why you're so unhappy you had puddles in your goggles? Why would it even matter?"

I jam my poles into the hard-packed snow. "Why would it *not* matter?"

Georg takes a slow breath, then reaches over and puts his hands on top of mine, which are gripping the tops of my poles as if they're the only things in the world keeping me on my feet. "He told you on the lift, didn't he? Is that why you wanted to go back and ski with him?"

I nod.

"Don't let it upset you, Valerie. You know, she's really cool, and—"

"Whoa! Hold it right there." I yank my hands out from under his, pulling my poles to my side. I don't even know where to begin. With the fact that Georg thinks I shouldn't be upset by my Dad getting all hot and heavy with someone or the fact that he seems to know that it's The Fräulein Dad is getting all hot and heavy with.

Georg huffs out a breath. "I'm sorry, Val. I just assumed you knew already and that it wasn't a big deal."

I feel my face getting red—and not from the cold. "No, I didn't know. Does the whole freaking *palace* know my father is going out with that woman? Am I the last to find out?"

"No! I didn't even know for sure until you said so just now."

I hate his tone of voice. Like he's pissed off about me being pissed off, and I really don't want my Dad's demented hormonal urges to result in a fight between me and Georg. Not when we're just getting over the whole "cool it" catastrophe.

As calmly as I can, I say, "I'm not blaming you. But you suspected something was up? I mean, with my dad and what's-her-name?"

"Not really. Well . . . maybe. I guess I did." He must sense my fear of getting into an argument, because his voice levels out. "When I was skiing in Zermatt over break, Fräulein Putzkammer came along to handle all the public relations stuff. I stopped and visited hospitals on the way, remember? Played Monopoly and cards with the kids, made balloon animals, that kind of thing. Trying to cheer them up."

"Her job was to handle all those appearances?"

He nods. "While we were on the way up to Zermatt after leaving the last hospital, she asked me a few questions about you and your father. I figured it was work-related—you know, since stories had started showing up in the tabloids about you and me right before I left for break, speculating that maybe we're a couple. Not a big deal. But then when I got back from Zermatt, I saw your father and Fräulein Putzkammer heading out of the palace together, walking toward the downtown area. And I started to wonder."

Oh, please, please, please, God, don't let them have been holding hands or being gooey. Not where anyone—especially Georg—could see. "Do you know where they were headed?"

He shakes his head. "They were wearing casual clothes, not suits like you'd wear out for a business dinner. I got the feeling that it wasn't work. Not for any reason I could identify, though."

"Why didn't you tell me?"

"Like I said, I was only wondering. I wasn't certain. After that night, I didn't even think about it again." He holds his hands out, palms up, like he's asking for forgiveness. "I figured if there was a relationship there, you'd tell me about it."

"Assuming Dad bothered to tell me."

"Yeah. I hadn't thought about that part." He leans over and kisses me on the cheek, which isn't easy when we both have on ski helmets. "I'm sorry, Val. You gonna be okay?"

"I don't have much choice."

His blue eyes lock onto my face, and he couldn't look more sincere. "Well, I'm here for you if you need me. I would never do anything to hurt you, you know that?"

"I know."

I feel lower than low right now. Even with him standing right here with me, being so incredibly wonderful. Or maybe *because* he's being so incredibly wonderful and I'm such a lowlife—jealous of a woman at least twice my age because she's getting my dad out of his funk over Mom and I'm not—and I'm unable to admit how angry I am about it all.

Not to mention how screwed up I am with the whole David issue.

I so do not deserve Georg.

"I love you, Valerie Winslow."

I blink in total surprise. I hadn't expected *that* to come

out of his mouth. And I can tell he means it. Like, he's even getting all emotional.

"No one has ever understood me the way you do," he says. "Everyone expects me to be this magazine-model, cookie-cutter freak of nature just because of who my parents are. But you don't. And I love you for it. And I love you for just being your perfect self. You're smart and you make me laugh at the craziest things. You see people the way they are and you aren't afraid to say so. And you treat me like I'm any other person."

I fake shock. "You're not like any other person?"

One side of his mouth twists up at that. "I want you to feel better, Val. I want you to stop worrying about your father and just have a fun vacation. With me."

And then he kisses me for real. With snow falling on us from the branches of the trees at the side of the trail, with no noise at all other than the breeze blowing down the side of the mountain and the crinkle of his ski jacket brushing against mine.

It's like a scene out of some movie, only I am so, so, so incredibly not the right person to be cast in this part.

Because what's he going to do when he figures out that I'm not the perfect person he thinks I am?

* * *

"How was your morning?" The Fräulein asks, all perky and red-cheeked from spending the last few hours on the slopes. Or maybe from spending the last few hours engaged in various extracurricular activities with my dad that didn't involve skiing.

"Fine," I mumble, then hide behind the cup of hot chocolate Dad bought for me.

I know I should have gotten this whole Predator Putzkammer mentality out of my system. Skiing all morning and stopping for quick kisses on the slopes should have made me relax. But instead, it's left me feeling like I'm building up to the world's worst case of PMS ever. And like she's the cause.

Georg, on the other hand, sounds just as chipper as The Fräulein, going on and on about which runs we skied, how long we had to wait at each lift, about how his skis (apparently new) handled, and a whole lot of other blah blah blah I tune out. Mostly because he sounds like he's sincere, and I'm just not in the mood for sincerity where The Fräulein is concerned.

We're sitting in a quiet section of the main ski lodge, not far from the concession area, but out of the way of most foot traffic so we don't draw any attention to ourselves. By the time Georg and I had locked our skis to the racks outside, Dad and his little blond friend had already locked up their skis and gone ahead through the line to buy food for all of us. The Fräulein explained that they thought it best if they handled everything at the concession area so Georg wouldn't have to stand where he was more likely to be recognized. Apparently, it's not that big a deal if he is (according to The Fräulein), but our trip will be easier if he's not.

I said all the appropriate thank-yous for the food (Dad, being Mr. Protocol, appreciates it when I remember to say thanks), though I'd have preferred to choose my own lunch. Something's gotta be better than bratwurst with spicy mustard and a bowl of (no, I'm not kidding) salad made of shredded carrots and cabbage. But no way am I leaving Georg alone here with my Dad and his new girlfriend (who probably picked this specific meal for me in an effort to give me horrible gas) now that I know what's going on. And now that I'm seeing Georg's reaction to everything.

The way Dad, Georg, and The Fräulein are chatting, if I dump the bratwurst and cabbage and go buy a cheeseburger, I'm liable to come back and find them all calling each other by their first names, holding hands, and singing "Kumbaya." That'll make me more sick than the bratwurst ever could.

"You know, you two should call me Anna," The Fräulein says, looking from Georg to me. "At least when it's just us.

At official events or when there are media present, perhaps it's best to simply refer to me as—"

I'm not listening, I'm not listening, I'm not listening! How does she *do* that? Can she freaking read my mind or something?

I feel her hand on mine. "Is that all right with you, Valerie?"

I assume she means the whole "call me Anna" thing—since *I'm not listening!*—so I give her the Valerie Shrug.

I get a discreet glare from Dad about the Valerie Shrug, but The Fräulein doesn't catch on, since she just goes on yammering all happy-like, as if this is the best lunch she's ever had. As if it's never occurred to her that I might not be wildly ecstatic about her shouldering her way into my life. Or that I might mentally be calling her The Fräulein or Fräulein Predator instead of Fräulein Putzkammer.

Or *Anna*. Gag. Yuck. Spit.

How in the world does this woman do public relations if she's so dense? I mean, I know I'm not acting openly hostile or anything; I'm actually being very nice to her. But doesn't she get that vibe you get when you know the person you're talking to isn't really enjoying the discussion?

As Dad starts talking about what runs he and Anna might try in the afternoon, I get more and more pissed off.

Logic says I shouldn't be. I should be happy for Dad—

glad he's found another adult to hang around with. But I just can't, and knowing I'm being bitchy about this is making me even crankier.

She *is* perfect for him on paper, aside from the horrific last name. (I have to wonder—what does *Putzkammer* mean, anyway? It can't be good.) I suppose she's nice enough, aside from wanting to get some action with Dad. She's young. Pretty. Outgoing and social for a living. Fairly open-minded, from what I can tell. Athletic, like Dad, so I imagine if they're having fun skiing together, she'd be up for a lot of the other things Dad enjoys doing.

It's like she gets a check mark for every item on the What Dad Likes list. So if I absolutely had to pick someone for Dad to take out on a hot date, it'd probably be her. Well, other than Mom, but that's not going to happen short of me majoring in chemistry and creating a potion that'll wipe both of their memories clean. Oh, and change Mom's sexual orientation at the same time. (Of course, David's father would probably tout any such potion as a Miracle Cure for the Immoral next time he's on CNN. . . .)

So what in the hell is wrong with me?

And why do I feel like Georg's totally on their side, even though he told me all that "I'll always be there for you" stuff? I mean, I know I'm in the wrong here and I really should suck it up and change my attitude. But that doesn't mean I want Georg acting the way he's acting. Like this is just peachy keen and swell. Another happy day with the Winslow family.

Five hours later, as we're unloading our car at the guesthouse and carrying our boots inside to dry out, I'm still feeling sullen. You'd think the fact I actually made it down a red run at the end of the day—going Georg's speed, with pretty good form, and without chickening out on the steep part—would cheer me up. Or maybe the fact that the private guesthouse where Dad got us rooms looks like it was constructed straight out of an upscale Hansel and Gretel fairy tale—the sloping roof, the dark wood beams, the romantic balcony and view of the Alps—would distract me enough so I'd mentally start composing an e-mail to Christie to tell her all about it. Or that I'd mellow out given that I can actually hear cathedral bells tolling nearby.

But . . . no. None of it's working to get me out of my funk.

And apparently my gloom-and-doom mood shows on my face, because the instant Georg and The Fräulein get settled into their rooms and Dad and I close the door to ours, leaving us alone for the first time since we were on the ski lift this morning, Dad lets loose. "Care to explain your attitude, Valerie?"

I frown and look at him like I have no clue what he means. "Come again? What attitude?"

"You've been wearing a pout all day. I thought you wanted to ski."

"I do!" I pull the liners out of my boots like the guy at the ski shop taught me, then prop them near the fireplace so they dry out. "Georg and I had a lot of fun. I even kept up with him on our last run instead of having to go back to the green trails at the end of the day."

"Then why so crabby?"

As if he doesn't know. And frankly, I thought I was being pretty noncrabby, considering the bomb he dropped on me this morning. But the Valerie Shrug doesn't get me anywhere with him this time. In fact, I think it pisses him off worse.

"Don't give me that. And don't give it to Anna again, either." He makes a little sucking sound with his mouth, like he's trying to pull back words.

I ignore him and yank off my stinky socks, then rifle through my suitcase, trying to figure out what I want to wear to dinner. I think I can get away with sweats, since this is a ski town and everything, but I'm not sure.

"You're angry because I'm seeing Anna." He says it as a statement, not a question.

Whatever.

I assume we're not going anywhere fancy or crowded, what with trying to look inconspicuous and everything while we're here. Maybe I should call Georg's room and see what he's going to do.

"Valerie, look at me. I'm waiting for an answer."

I grab a pair of sweats, zip my suitcase closed, then turn to face Dad. He's standing near the door to the room, his boot bag still slung over his shoulder.

I spread my hands in a sign of surrender. "Look, Dad, what you do is your business. My opinion doesn't count for anything."

"It does count." He sets his boot bag down without opening it. I'm tempted to tell him he'd better air those dogs out. If my boots are gross from a day on the slopes, his have gotta be downright nasty. But before I can think of a polite way to phrase the suggestion—and hopefully change the conversation to a different topic—he continues on, "I'm not going to end things with Anna just because you don't like the idea of me seeing someone. That's not fair to me and it's not fair to her."

How rude does he think I am? "Geez, I didn't tell you to quit seeing her, Dad. I wouldn't do that." I don't think.

"Good." He glances at the alarm clock on the night-stand between our two beds. "We have an hour until we meet Anna and Georg for dinner. The guesthouse owner recommended a restaurant across the street that serves traditional Austrian food. It sounds like a great place. If you want to take a shower first, why don't you go ahead?"

I figure that's a pretty strong hint, so I blow by him and take a super-short shower. When I'm done, I pull on my sweatpants and a warm sweater, then yank my wet hair back into a loose ponytail. I can't work up the energy to blow it dry and make it look good when all we're doing is eating dinner at one of the laid-back places here in town, then coming back up and going to sleep.

As Dad takes his shaving kit into the bathroom (probably to make sure he looks nice for The Predator), I flop on the bed and start channel surfing. Since I can't find anything in English, I pound on the bathroom door and tell Dad I'm going to check out the Internet room the guesthouse owner told us he had downstairs and that I'll meet him near the front door before we head across the street.

I hesitate at the top of the stairs, then take a few steps back down the hallway, past the room I share with Dad, to knock on Georg's door. He doesn't answer. I listen for a second, hear water running, and decide to head downstairs without him.

Knowing him, he'll probably take a nap after he's done showering, anyway. If I get lucky, maybe The Fräulein will take a nap, too. And oversleep.

To: Val@realmail.sg.com

From: CoolJule@viennawest.edu

Subject: You, Idiot

Hello, Val Pal,

Notice the subject line? I couldn't decide whether to make it "You, Idiot" or "You Idiot."

Note the difference in meaning without the comma.

Note that I opted for the more polite meaning, which is rare for me. But I still want you to take this seriously.

Yes, I think you're being an Idiot. Christie and I went to the movies last night and she mentioned that you haven't told Prince Georg about David yet. Are you beyond STUPID? Did something happen to your brain's oxygen levels from all that time in airplanes?

What's he going to think when he finds out??

And you know he's going to find out.

Take my advice: Come clean. Make it clear that you are NOT interested in David, but that you felt it would be dishonest not to say something. And don't get all "I'm so sorry" about it, either. Be sorry that you hurt Georg's feelings (if it turns out that his feelings really are hurt), but don't tell him you're sorry for going out with David, like you committed a crime or something, because you didn't. Act like the thing with David wasn't a big thing at all, and simply say you wouldn't have done it if you didn't think you guys were cooling it or whatever it was you were doing. Does that make sense?

Remember: I still know where you live. And my combat boots still work just fine for kicking your ass if you need a good kicking in order to fess up.

I say all this in love, you know. And because you are one of my dearest friends and I don't want you to get yourself in trouble. Again.

Don't screw this up.

Jules

To: CoolJule@viennawest.edu

From: Val@realmail.sg.com

Subject: RE: You, Idiot

Jules,

1—I asked Christie to steal your boots when I was home for vacation, so forget about kicking my butt. Besides, violence is never the answer to the world's ills.

2—I'm thinking of the right way to tell Georg. I realize you have my best interests at heart (most of the time), but I've only been home a week, okay?

3—Why was Christie out with you on a Friday night? She said Jeremy's been busy training for a marathon (so don't call me the idiot . . . I think Jeremy's the idiot), but they *always* go out on Friday nights. What gives?

4—My dad has informed me that he has a girlfriend. Or a "something." He says it's casual but I'm so not buying it. And get this: Her last name is *Putzkammer*. Go ahead. Start the wisecracks now. I simply think of her as The Fräulein. I'm afraid if I even think the name Putzkammer while I'm talking to her I'll start laughing out loud.

5—I'm in Austria skiing this weekend—with Georg, Dad, and *her*—but will be home tomorrow night.

Trying not to flip out over any of items 1-5, as listed above,

Val Pal

To: Val@realmail.sg.com

Cc: CoolJule@viennawest.edu; ChristieT@viennawest.edu

From: NatNatNat@viennawest.edu

Subject: Who the hell is JOHN?

Hey Val,

I'm still grounded for getting my tongue pierced—I swear, it sucks sometimes having a dad who's a dentist and is obsessed with oral health—but I did get my computer privileges back today (whoo-hoo!) so write to me, okay?

Anyway—I had the most bizarre thing happen this afternoon, which is why I'm cc'ing Jules and Christie on this one.

So I'm at the grocery store with Mom, hanging out in the book and magazine area while she goes to inspect the produce or whatever. I'm flipping through the latest copy of *Self* (which has a great article on how to do self-tanners right . . . check it out if you can get a copy in Smorgasbord or wherever the hell you are) and this guy I've never seen before comes up to me. He asks if I'm a friend of Valerie Winslow's.

Strange, huh?

I was like, "Um, yeah. Why?" and he says he was wondering if he could have your e-mail address. He says he knows you through your mom but wouldn't say from where. And he said he really wanted to talk to you.

It was just weird, even though he was totally and completely polite. He was actually kind of hot, in a slightly older sort of way—I'd guess he's a senior or maybe even a college freshman. He had brown hair that was longish and I'd say he's six feet tall, maybe even a little more. Anyway, he says his name is John and that "Val will know who I am." Then he said if I didn't feel comfortable giving him your e-mail address, would I give you his? I didn't have any paper in my purse, but he scribbled it on the magazine, since I figured I was going to buy it at that point anyway.

Val, do you have any clue who this guy is? Because he looks a little too scruffy to be your type (though very much my type . . . assuming he's not a lunatic of some sort and stalking you).

Christie? Jules? You guys know anything?

I swear, Valerie—fifteen years and you couldn't get the guy you wanted to save your life. Now in a mere eight weeks, you not only got him interested (and dissed him), but you're going out with a prince (which I'm still shocked about) and you have this hot older guy named John after you?

Tell me again—what kind of drugs have you been taking to make you irresistible to guys? Where can I get my hands on some?!

Color me jealous,

Natalie

PS—He was wearing an NYU sweatshirt, if that helps. And his e-mail address is JPMorant@viennawest.edu.

To: Val@realmail.sg.com
From: CoolJule@viennawest.edu
Subject: WHAT THE HELL?

I was about to answer your e-mail but then I got the one from Natalie.

Um . . . JOHN?

Care to explain that one? Yeah, I'm thinking you're in it over your carrot-topped head. Again. And apparently Natalie will catch on at some point that he must go to our high school (given that his e-mail address is from Vienna West). I bet that tongue stud is causing magnetic disturbances with her brain waves.

I am so gonna kick your ass.

Jules

PS—On a side note to the ass-kicking, I am very sorry about your Dad's casual "something." And even more sorry he's doing that casual something with someone bearing the world's most hideous last name. That's even worse than my brother's name—I still say no one with the last name Jackson should ever name their son Michael. I don't care how common a name it must be.

PPS—When you're back home and can e-mail me again, give me all the dirt on this Putzkammer chick, okay? (But realize the Putzkammer Issue does NOT give you a free pass on the David Issue. You've still gotta tell Georg.)

To: NatNatNat@viennawest.edu

Cc: CoolJule@viennawest.edu; ChristieT@viennawest.edu

From: Val@realmail.sg.com

Subject: RE: Who the hell is JOHN?

Hiya Nat (and Jules—again—and Christie),

I don't have much time, 'cause I'm on a ski trip with Dad

and Georg AND this chick from the palace public relations office named Anna Putzkammer. (No, I'm not kidding about her name, and no, I'm not happy about having her along. Christie and Nat, have Jules fill you in since I just e-mailed her with the early report.) I have to meet them in exactly one minute for dinner.

But long story short: JOHN IS A FRIEND.

More later, I promise . . . I'd write more but you know how Dad is about punctuality.

Advising you ALL to relax,

Val

4

PFLAG JOHN. THE JOHN WHOSE LAST NAME I DIDN'T even know (though now I'm guessing it's Morant. And his middle name must start with the letter *P*.)

The guy I met over winter break when Mom and Gabrielle pretended like we were driving to church on a random Wednesday night, but ended up dumping me in the church basement—without access to transportation—in the middle of a meeting of Parents and Friends of Lesbians and Gays (*so* not where I wanted to be) with no polite way to escape. Because they thought it would help me with my *issues* with their relationship.

Okay, so the meeting ended up being more normal

(and actually more helpful) than I thought it would be when Mom abandoned me there with nothing more than a wave goodbye. But only because John—a normal human being my age—was there. He's dealing with a situation similar to mine, since his brother, Brad—who's supposed to be his roommate next year at NYU—came out to their family last year.

What can I say? We bonded. But I never in a million years would have predicted he'd approach Natalie Monschroeder in a grocery store to get my contact info. I haven't talked much with him about my friends, which means he was probably asking around to see who I hang with when I'm home. What could be so important that he needs to talk to *me* when he has a whole freaking support group right there in Virginia?

Plus, John and I have this whole unspoken thing where we don't acknowledge that we know each other outside of the PFLAG meetings (well, the one meeting I actually attended) because we don't know whom each other has told about the whole I-have-a-gay-family-member thing. I wouldn't want to say something like, "Hey, how are Brad and his boyfriend?" to John in front of some guy from the rugby team only to find out John hasn't told his teammates yet. Or that he never wanted them to know.

The fact that he walked right up to Natalie in a grocery

store and introduced himself is just . . . well, as Nat said, weird.

"Valerie?" Georg's accented voice cuts into my thoughts. "You tired? Or is dinner not what you thought it'd be?"

I blink, realizing that the waitress brought out our meals and set them down while I was trying to mentally run through the possible reasons John might have for talking to Natalie. All I could come up with was that he thought Nat was cute and mentioning me was the only way he thought he could meet her, since Nat usually gives off a "leave me alone" vibe, especially if she hasn't done her hair or anything. "Sorry. Just daydreaming, I s'pose."

I pick up my fork and poke it into a french fry. While I munch on it—and wow, do the Austrians make their fries warm and salty—I eyeball the hunk of breaded mystery meat on my plate. My dad says it's schnitzel and Georg tells me I'll like it, but I dunno.

It looks like a monster-sized chicken nugget, though apparently schnitzel is veal and is a very popular food here in Austria. (In all German-speaking countries, actually, though somehow I haven't encountered it in Schwerinborg yet. Go figure.) But Gabrielle would have a fit if she saw me right now. She'd probably talk about the method by which veal is processed and how awful the conditions are for the animals.

In other words, she'd make me feel heartless for eating it.

I cut a tiny square, mentally ask Gabrielle and the cows to forgive me, then take a bite. And . . . Georg was right. It's awesome. Pretty much like a zestier, heartier version of a chicken nugget, and the exact thing to hit the spot after skiing all day.

"What do you think?" Dad asks.

"Pretty good." Way better than the bratwurst or the carrot crap I had at lunch.

The Fräulein smiles at me—one of those overcompensating type of smiles that you know is intended to make you feel at ease but actually has the opposite effect—and starts telling me how marvelous it is that I get to have the experience of living abroad and how lucky I am as an American teenager to see other cultures. Yak, yak, yak.

I resist the urge to give her the Valerie Shrug and smile right back—probably looking just as stupid as she does—and tell her that I do feel very fortunate. I manage to work some serious gratitude into my voice, too. Dad looks down at his plate, probably because he knows I'm full of it, but I can see that he's happy I'm trying to be polite.

I want to retch.

When we get back to the guesthouse, Dad says he's going to stop by the front desk to ask about other area restaurants so we can try a new place for dinner before driving home tomorrow night. Anna offers to go with him, so after I grab the key from Dad, Georg and I head back toward the rooms without them.

"You handled that pretty well," Georg says as soon as we're out of hearing range.

"Don't get me started," I tell him. I glance back over my shoulder to make sure they aren't behind us before we head up the stairs, then add, "And what was all that trash she started spewing about how lucky I am to live here? Do you think she's working to convince Dad and me that it's all fabbity-fab-fab here for her own reasons? Because if Dad decides to stay in Europe instead of going back to his job at the White House after the election, then she'll have a shot at marriage and kids and all her little dreams—"

"Don't you think you're getting carried away, Valerie?" Georg sounds odd, like he's ticked off at me for talking about Anna as if she has ulterior motives for being nice to me, but now that the thought has entered my mind that she might want *kids* with my Dad—because the fact is, she doesn't have any that I know of and her biological clock's gotta be ticking fast—it makes total sense.

Oh, shit. Dad and Anna with *babies* . . .

I stop in the hallway near the door to my room and lean my head against the wall. The image of Dad changing a poopy diaper . . . or playing with a toddler who looks up at him and calls him Daddy . . . I just can't handle it.

"Georg, I know you're trying to be supportive of me, but telling me I'm getting carried away isn't the way to do that. I don't think you get how it feels to see my Dad with another woman. How awful this is for me."

I hate the way I sound. I hate the direction my thoughts are going. But careful to keep my voice down, since we're in a semi-public place, I spew out what's on my mind anyway, committing what I know is going to be a horrible act of Emotional Vomit.

I can't stop myself.

"Georg, your parents are perfect. They never argue. They're totally happy with each other and with their life. They aren't going to get divorced and hook up with other people and possibly have children with those other people. Especially people named *Putzkammer*."

I swipe a hand over my face, trying to calm down, but it doesn't work. I look into his confused eyes and say, "Look, Georg, this is nothing against you and nothing against your parents. But you just don't get it. You've never had to deal with the kind of stuff I've dealt with over the last few months, so you don't know how you'd feel or how you'd act if you saw your parents with someone else. Nothing is stopping my Dad from getting married again or from having kids with someone else. So don't tell me

I'm getting carried away, because *you just don't know*."

I glance back toward the staircase to make sure no one else is heading this way—I really don't want Fräulein Predator to hear us—and add, "Plus, if he decides to stay here with Fräulein Putzkammer, it means I might never get to move home to Virginia and be with all my friends. To graduate high school with them or to hang out at our favorite places, except maybe on a vacation here and there, which isn't the same. And I'm trying to adjust to that fact. It's a lot to wrap my brain around, okay?"

He's quiet. Staring at me like I've grown horns.

I push off the wall and step toward him, 'cause I know from his expression that I've gone too far. None of this is his fault at all. "I'm sorry, Georg, it's just—"

"Stop, Val." He holds up a hand to keep me from touching him. "You adjust to whatever facts you want to. Me, I'm trying to adjust to the fact you won't even consider the possibility of staying in Schwerinborg. If you find it *so* awful living here, and you find it *so* awful seeing your father happy—"

"That's not what I meant at all!"

"It sure sounds like it. It sounds like you'd much rather be with your friends in Virginia than here with me. And I don't know what that means for us. Or if you really meant it when you said you loved me this morning."

"I did mean it. I *do* mean it." And I wish I knew the magic words to make it all better.

We both look at each other, unwilling to say much more. Partially because each of us seems to be scared of the path this conversation is taking, and partially because we're in an open hallway where the owner of the guesthouse or his wife could overhear us and tell who-knows-who.

Georg puts his hands on his hips and hooks his index fingers through the belt loops of his jeans. "In that case, I think the smartest thing we can do right now is go to our own rooms and go to bed early. We have to be up before seven for breakfast if we want to get to the slope when the lifts open, and it's a long drive back to Schwerinborg after dinner tomorrow night."

There's no way I can sleep with so much on my mind. But before I can explain that, he nudges my foot with his. "Maybe we'll both see everything more clearly after we get some sleep. Okay?"

I glance down at his foot, then look back into his eyes. They're so blue against his pale skin and dark hair—the way he looks right now, at this very moment, reminds me of the day I first met him in the palace library. When I didn't even know he was a prince, and all I saw was a friendly, ultra-polite guy I was dying to sketch. Just so I could see if

I'd be able to capture his cheekbones and all the shading of his features on paper.

"Georg, I—"

He leans over and kisses me on the cheek, lightning-fast, his hands still at the waistband of his jeans, then leans his forehead against mine. "We'll figure it all out tomorrow. We have all day to ski together, out where we can be alone. So relax, get some sleep, and be nice to your dad."

I want to kiss him again, but he pulls away, giving me a wink I think is meant to reassure me. Then he walks past me and keys into his room.

I just stand there, leaning against the wall, playing with my room key. I'm not ready to let go yet. I want him to wrap his arms around me and tell me that everything with Dad will be okay. That everything with *us* will be okay—and to know that he's on my side.

I want him to kiss me the way he usually kisses me good night. The way that lets me know his thoughts are going to be with me until morning even if we can't physically be in the same room.

I close my eyes and breathe in through my nose, then out through my mouth, the way one of Mom's self-help books said to do when you feel overwhelmed (not that I think her books are helpful enough to justify what she spends on them, but they do have the occasional useful tip, like reminding you to breathe).

How the hell did I screw things up with Georg—again—so fast?

I try to tell myself that it's not that bad—a temporary emotional tic that's making me hyper—and that Georg is right. We'll figure everything out tomorrow, when we have time alone and we're not so tired.

Though once I deal with today's disaster, I still need to find a way to tell Georg about David. But first things first.

I open my eyes and walk the last few steps to the door of the room I'm sharing with Dad. As I get ready to stick the key in the door, I hear laughter coming from the stairs.

I can't help it. I walk back to the staircase and peek over the railing. Sure enough, it's Dad and The Fräulein. They're standing at the base of the stairs, totally oblivious to the fact that I'm up here. She's laughing about something Dad said, but they're not all touchy-feely with each other or anything.

They're talking like normal people do. Normal friends.

And then I tell myself that it shouldn't matter if they're normal friends or normal whatever-else.

Feeling like a voyeur, I back away from the staircase and

go into the room. I kick off my shoes, take the elastic out of my hair and fling it toward my suitcase, then wander to the window to wait for Dad.

It's snowing again. Just a light snow, so I can barely make out the flakes against the lights of the restaurants, ski shops, and other guesthouses scattered along the street. I crack the window and lean out. It's so beautiful and romantic—the smell of smoke from guesthouse fireplaces mixing in with the odors of restaurant kitchens and the fresh snow—that it seems fake. Like what my senses are taking in can't possibly be my reality.

It feels a million miles away from Virginia—from Mom, from my girlfriends, from John and everyone else—but I have to wonder: Is Georg right? Do I dislike Europe so much that staying here is unthinkable?

I hear Dad in the hallway telling The Fräulein good night, then the sound of his key in the door lock.

"Hey, sweetie," Dad says.

"Hey, Dad." I don't bother turning around. I'm fixated on the snowflakes and the way the metal signs hanging over the shop doors swing in the breeze if you watch them long enough.

He comes to stand beside me, leaning his elbows on the windowsill so the backs of his arms are grazing right up against mine. I can feel his triceps through the thin fabric of his shirt and decide he spends way too much time in the gym in the mornings.

I wonder if The Fräulein has noticed his arms. Probably. Guess she can't miss 'em.

"I expected Georg to be in here," he says. "Or for you to be over in his room."

Me too. "I think he wanted to get some sleep. You know, since we have to be up so early tomorrow."

"Smart guy." Dad stretches out a hand to catch snowflakes as they flitter down from the sky. They're so small, they melt the instant they hit his open palm.

"I'm not sure I can sleep yet," I admit.

"Me either."

I look sideways at him. The goofy grin on his face has me responding with one of my own. He asks if I want to watch a movie, assuming we can find something in English. When I tell him sure, we reach out at the same time to close the window and bump into each other, like Moe and Larry in the middle of a Three Stooges skit. I step back and let him shut it, since I'm bound to miss getting the latch tightened the right way. When he turns around and tosses the remote to me, giving me the choice of what to watch, I know there's an unspoken peace treaty between us. Like no matter what happens with The Fräulein, or with Georg, the two of us will always be solid.

And wouldn't you know, one of his favorite flicks is on TV. So of course that's what I choose.

"You didn't go to sleep right away, did you?" Georg asks as the chairlift comes around behind us.

I can't answer him right away because I'm yawning. Worse, I tangle my poles in front of me at the very moment the chair sweeps under us, so I barely manage to sit without tripping forward over them and face-planting in front of the attendant.

"You all set?"

I can hear the laughter in his voice as he waits for me to straighten out my gear so he can bring down the safety bar.

"Your Highness?" I put a saccharine-fake flirtiness in my voice. "I kindly beg you to shut up."

He cracks up, since I don't think I've ever called him Your Highness. Probably because I'm not even one hundred percent sure he is a highness. (Maybe he has some other title? I'm going to have to ask Dad sometime.)

"Okay, so you didn't go to bed right away." He swings his skis beneath him as he talks, letting them wave back and forth in the air. "But you seem like you're in a better mood today."

"I attribute that to the coffee."

"At breakfast you started joking around with your dad before the coffee even came."

I elbow Georg, though it's hard to have any impact with our pouffy ski jackets on. "You're way too observant."

"I'm not observant at all. It's just that I can't help watching you. I try not to, but . . ." He lifts his shoulder, then lets it drop. "Like I said, I can't help it. I'm just too aware of you and everything you do when we're in the same room."

Omigosh. I think my heart is going to physically up and quit right now. I mean, I watch him all the time. Even if I didn't like him, I'd study him simply because he has this interesting, unique look that appeals to the artist in me. But what really grabs me is that he has this aura about him that reaches out and demands my attention anytime he's within a hundred yards of me. It's something I noticed before I even knew he was a prince. But I never thought he would feel one iota of that same awareness about me.

I mean, do people ever admit it when they're that obsessed? I know I couldn't have told him I felt that way without coming off as a goofy, lovesick dork.

In an attempt to play it cool, especially given the way Georg and I left things last night, I say, "I talked to Dad after you went into your room. Okay, correction—Dad and I actually didn't talk all that much. But we stayed up and watched a movie together and it went really well."

We get to the halfway point of the lift, and Georg looks over the side, taking note of the snow conditions on the run we plan to take, then looks back at me. "What'd you watch?"

"*The Matrix* was on. The original. It was in German, but since we both know the lines by heart, we made fun of the dubbing. The guy sounded nothing like Keanu Reeves." I want to reach over and grab Georg's hand, even though we're technically in public and I probably shouldn't anyway, given my performance in the hallway last night. "Thanks for telling me to be nice to him. Even if I am still cranky about the whole girlfriend thing."

I resist the urge to make a Putzkammer joke, since I can tell Georg really likes her.

"I'm glad you and your dad aren't fighting anymore. And I'm glad I went to bed early, even if you didn't. I think we're both in better moods this morning."

I grimace. "Yeah, I think that conversation would've gone downhill quickly. Thanks for suggesting we call it a night even though I didn't want to."

He leans back in the chair, which makes his thigh bump up against mine. I'm not sure if he's aware of the contact, but I'm hyperaware—and wondering what it means. Is he okay with me? Is he going to forgive me for my ranting last night?

After a long yawn, he meets my gaze. "You were right

yesterday, you know. My parents have a good marriage, so it's hard for me to see things the way you do. I can't imagine seeing anything that makes them happy as being a bad thing, the way you see Anna. But I can't picture them being happy with anyone besides each other, either."

"You were trying your best to understand," I say, since I know he was. I scoot a little closer to him in the chair, trying to work that thigh-contact thing to make sure he knows we're touching. To see if he stays put or shifts away. "I'm sorry I flipped out on you. I really don't want any of this stuff with my Dad to mess up the two of us."

"It won't if we don't let it." His voice drops lower as he adds, "But I still wonder if you'd rather be in Virginia than with me."

"It's not that simple," I tell him. "I want everything to be the way it was a few months ago, when I went to a high school I loved and saw my friends all the time and when my parents were together and happy. But I'd want you there too. I want it all."

"But even if all that could happen, it was still a fantasy. Your parents weren't really happy."

"No, they weren't." I have to accept it now, like it or not. "And in reality, you couldn't exactly transfer to high school in Vienna, Virginia. You think the culture shock I had moving here was bad . . . you in Virginia? Ouch."

Here there's almost a small-town feel to Georg's existence. People who live in Freital—or anywhere in Schwerinborg—are used to seeing him. He's out and about, and they generally respect his privacy. He'll walk into a local cafe for a sandwich on his way home from school, talk to the old guy behind the counter, be friendly and ask about the guy's kids. Sure, there are always people who gawk, but they at least try to be discreet. And while the European tabloid guys follow him on occasion, there hasn't really been any dirt to report (other than me). They're more interested in his parents' day-to-day activities, since Prince Manfred runs the country.

Suburbia might kill Georg. Americans wouldn't be so casual about the fact he's a prince. Once it got out that an eleventh-grade European prince was visiting, it'd be sensationalized to the extreme. He'd take one step into a Starbucks and get mobbed by people wanting his autograph or shooting pics of him on their cell phones to e-mail to friends.

The minuscule Schwerinborg tabloids would be nothing compared to what he'd face in the U.S. The Fräulein, especially, would have a complete conniption fit if she had to make those kind of media arrangements.

"So let's make the most of what we do have," he says, sounding very Zen. "Because the way things are right now, your mom's already happy, your dad has a chance at happiness, and the two of us can be together. Don't you think?"

Georg scoots his thigh away from mine. I can't really read anything into it—we're nearing the top of the lift and he always scoots away so I don't wipe out. I glance toward the top of the lift to see if we're near the spot where we have to raise the safety bar, but just as I register that we still have a little way to go, I feel Georg's hand on my cheek, turning me back toward him. Then he leans in and gives me the kiss I really wanted last night.

The one that says he loves me, even when I'm crabby and whacked-out. The one that makes me want to curl up in his arms and kiss him like crazy and make them stop the lift so we can stay here forever. The one that says he forgives me—or at least mostly forgives me—for my outburst in the hallway last night.

The one that makes me think, *Screw Virginia and all my friends there—I want to be like this forever.* And I'm sure that's exactly what he intends, too.

Especially when I hear a loud cough come from the lift chair behind ours.

Dad, of course. And Anna.

Sheesh—did I just think of her as *Anna*? My coffee must have been spiked this morning.

"We need to get off," he says, pulling away from me and reaching for the safety bar.

I choke, I start laughing so hard, which makes him frown at me. I wave him off, 'cause I am *so* not going to explain the double meaning of his words. It'd be too, too cruel when he already worries about his grasp of English slang.

Plus, I don't want him to know I have a dirty mind.

Once we're at the summit, Georg and I endure the requisite lecture about public displays of affection from Dad and Anna, promise not to do the kissy-face thing again, and point out exactly where we'll be skiing on the trail map. They take off down one of the intermediate trails, but not before Dad looks backward over his shoulder one last time to give me a warning glare with a very clear *Don't make out in public* message.

I simply give him the same glare back. But unlike yesterday when I watched him disappear down the trail with Anna, I'm not so worried about it actually happening.

By the time we're ready to meet Dad and Anna for lunch, I've managed to actually make it down a black run. Not gracefully (and probably not quietly, since I think I screamed when I started going too fast on one steep part), but at least with all my bones intact.

"Yes!" Georg shouts as we sail down the very bottom of the run, heading toward the ski racks outside the base lodge.

Once we finally stop, I use my poles to release my bindings, then keel over and do an over-the-top act of grabbing my quads.

"The pain! The pain! Somebody call an ambulance!"

He just smiles and shakes the snow off his gloves, like he wonders how I could possibly be sore. Probably because he cruised down the run like it was no big thing. He even skied backward on one of the not-so-steep sections, just so he could face me and see if I was doing okay.

Show-off.

"You did just fine," he assures me once our skis are locked and we're clonking along like Abominable Snowmen in our heavy boots, doing the same heel-to-toe walk into the lodge everyone else is doing. (Someday, someone will invent ski boots a person can actually walk in. And they're going to make a kazillion dollars on the patent, too. If I had better science skills, or anything close to real ski skills, I'd be all over it.)

"Use lunchtime to rest up, then we'll take a few of the intermediate runs when we're done," Georg says. "We can try that black run again later. Now that you've done it once—"

So not happening. "Do you know how much snow I

got up the back of my jacket when I fell on that icy part? I don't even want to risk it."

"But you know where the ice is now. And you're not *that* sore. You could go dancing right now, I bet, and you wouldn't be able to tell you've been skiing for a day and a half."

I spy Dad and The Fräulein in the concession line at the same time Dad sees me. He points to a table near where we were yesterday that's covered with his gear. I pull Georg over, shoving Dad's hat and gloves out of the way as we sit down. "That reminds me," I say, speaking quickly because I'm afraid we won't have much time to talk, "you know there's the dance at school next weekend, right? Ulrike's working on it for Student Council."

"Sure." He yanks off his gloves and tosses them into the pile with Dad's and The Fräulein's.

"Well, I volunteered to help set up. Ulrike was talking about it at lunch a few days ago and she sounded like she really could use the help."

"Will Steffi be helping out too?"

His voice is completely polite as he says it—years of having "polite" drilled into him by his parents, I'm sure—but we both understand what kind of person Steffi is, and I know that's why he's asking. To watch out for me.

"Nah. She didn't seem interested. I actually told Ulrike

I'd help after Steffi and Maya both turned her down." I give him a guilty grin. "I wasn't all that interested either, honestly. But I felt bad for Ulrike, trying to round up help and getting no takers."

"You like her, don't you?"

"Yeah, I do. She tries hard, you know?" I can tell he's about to say something about how it's cool I'm finding a new group of friends here in Schwerinborg, but I cut him off. I don't want to go down the whole road of why I should like it here as much as I liked living in Virginia. Plus, I have a more pressing issue to discuss. "But that's not why I brought it up. It's a girls-ask-guys dance. And I was hoping, since I have to be there anyway, that you'd come with me."

"An official date?"

Official? "I guess. I mean, I don't think it has to be government-sanctioned or anything."

Oh, somebody smack me. Bad, *bad* joke. It probably does have to be government-sanctioned, since we'd have to tell Dad and Georg's parents. I bet The Predator would want her say, too, since the public-relations people at the palace are always worried about Georg's image. We'd be coached on how to behave, how to answer questions if anyone asks . . .

Okay, asking a guy out *sucks*. It's just wrong, no matter what the situation. But in this situation, it sucks double.

And I wish that for once in my life I would have canned the first smart-ass comment that came to me and counted to ten before speaking.

Georg doesn't say anything. He keeps his focus riveted on his jacket as he unzips it and then hooks it over the back-rest of his chair. I know he's trying to buy time to decide—and I can understand why it's a tough decision—but all of a sudden, I realize that I really want him to come with me.

I want us to be public. Loud and proud.

I mean, we did have one out-in-public date already, at a palace event with his parents. But they simply told anyone who asked that they'd invited me—the daughter of a palace employee—in order for Georg to have someone his own age to talk to. So it wasn't really like anyone other than my Dad and Georg's parents knew there was something going on with us.

Ditto for this weekend. It's all so officially *un*official, because as long as no one took pictures of us kissing on the slopes (and other than that quickie on the chairlift—assuming they could even identify Georg with his helmet on—they wouldn't have had a chance) it's easy to explain this weekend away by saying we're just on a friendly trip.

Up until this very second, I've been fine with keeping the whole boyfriend-girlfriend thing under wraps. In a way, it's been romantic keeping things secret—sneaking in kisses when we're positive we're alone, shooting looks at each other across the quad at school when no one's looking. Hiding out in our apartments, where no one from outside the palace could possibly know what's going on.

Plus, acting like we're simply friends when we're in public has made us that much more lovey-dovey when we are alone together. There's a risky edge to it all.

But looking at him now, knowing how I feel about him and how I'm pretty sure he feels about me—well, assuming he's truly over my little hissy fit of last night—I don't want to hide anymore. Tabloids and speculation that I'm a corrupting influence on Georg or whatever be damned. I don't care if they say that I'm too stupid or ugly or nonpedigreed or just too flat-out American to be going out with him.

Or if they say I'm pregnant with an alien baby. Or that I *am* an alien baby.

I just want us to be together whenever we want. To walk down a street and hold hands if we want. To live our lives like normal high schoolers do. Eventually, the press types would lose interest, wouldn't they? I mean, Prince Harry has some hotsy-totsy long-term girlfriend, and I haven't seen *them* in the papers together in a while. And Britain's Prince Harry is far better known than Schwerinborg's Prince Georg.

Before I moved here, I didn't even know there was

such a person as "Schwerinborg's Prince Georg." I'd have thought somebody made him up, it sounds so whacked to say it aloud. *Schwerinborg* all by itself sounds plenty whacked, but that's the German language for you.

I notice that Georg's looking past me, toward the concession area. I follow his gaze and see that Dad and The Fräulein have finished paying for our food and are at the condiment counter, loading minuscule paper cups with ketchup and piling napkins and straws onto the trays.

"Looks like lunch is on the way," I say. I want him to give me an answer, but since he's obviously hesitant, I figure the kind thing to do is to give him an out. Let him give me his answer later, after he's had time to think about it. "So, wonder what they got us?"

"Probably bratwurst again." He squints at the trays they're carrying, then mumbles something about how he can rule a country but can't pick his own lunch. It's so out of character for him that I can't say anything.

Besides, maybe he'll take that sentiment and run with it—and start dissing The Fräulein. Not that I'm holding my breath on that one.

"Look, Val," he says, looking at me again. His brows are pulled in, and I know what he's going to say even as the words come out of his mouth. "The answer has to be no. I'm sorry."

"It's no problem. I mean, that's what I figured." I try to act like it's no big thing, but I'm dying to know why. *Exactly* why. I'm that kind of a glutton for punishment. "So do you—"

"Lunch is served!" The Fräulein practically yodels the words as she plops a plastic tray down on the table. Seriously—I wouldn't be surprised to hear a singsongy "yoo-hooooo" out of her.

"Great. What'd you get today?" Georg asks, ever the polite one.

"Soda, bratwurst, Kaiser rolls." She flashes a smile in my direction. "I even brought some extra mustard, since I know you like it, Valerie."

I don't. I just used a ton yesterday to kill the taste. But she babbles on. "And for a special treat, when we're done with this, your father and I are going to grab some warm strudel for everyone. They had a fresh pan in the oven, and it'll be ready about the time we're finished eating. How does that sound?"

I glance at Dad, trying to gauge his reaction to the strudel announcement. I swear, I am living one totally demented fairy tale. The Brothers Grimm never wrote anything this warped. Eventually, Hansel and Gretel got away from the mean witch, Sleeping Beauty woke up from her nap, and most important of all, the whole kingdom learned about Cinderella hooking up with Prince Charming. Right?

So when do I get my happy fairy-tale ending? And is there a way it can *not* involve strange foods?

I can tell from his hopeful expression that Dad expects me to be enthusiastic about the freaking strudel, so I look at The Predator and utter one of the few words I know in German. *"Wunderbar!"*

Wonderful.

5

"LISTEN," GEORG SAYS ONCE WE'RE ON THE CHAIRLIFT again, keeping his voice low since Dad and Anna are right behind us and—as Dad pointed out—voices carry on these things. "I'm sorry about the dance. But it's being held at the Hotel Jaegerhof. The hotel's a beautiful place, but . . . well, it's not the same if the two of us go to a dance together as it is when we go on a ski trip where your dad and someone else from the palace staff are along. It'd be hard not to—"

"Don't even worry about it." I can tell—despite the fact that he's wearing his ski helmet and has his goggles pulled down—that he's wigging out, thinking that I'll think he doesn't love me.

I know he loves me. I'm just tired of hiding.

However, as I choked down the bratwurst and gushed to The Fräulein about the strudel (which should earn me some serious brownie points since it's not like she made it herself—she freaking bought it, at a *ski lodge*) I resolved to take the high road regarding the dance, no matter how much this let's-lie-low situation bugs the snot out of me. Give Georg the benefit of the doubt and all that stuff I swore I'd do after getting back from vacation. I want Georg to know that I love him, that I trust him, and that he can trust me.

Well, before I drop the David bomb—if I can figure out the right time to do it—and Georg wonders all over again if he can trust me.

"I do worry," he says quietly.

I give him the Valerie Shrug, hoping he thinks it's genuine this time and that I really don't give a fly because I understand his position. Keeping my tone as relaxed as possible, I say, "I'm going to be busy helping Ulrike, at least for the first part of the dance, so it's no big deal. Besides"—I shoot him a grin that's meant to blow him away, though whether it works or not, I have no clue—"I know exactly where you live. I can find you whenever I want."

"Maybe when you get home from helping Ulrike we can do something completely laid-back. Rent a movie or play

Scrabble. Share some popcorn. We can make it a date night, just not at the hotel with everyone else."

We're going to get burned out on watching movies in our apartments every night, and even I can only eat so much popcorn, but it's not like I can really object to one more in-the-palace date night, can I?

"Come on," he says once we're at the summit and have gotten our goggles adjusted and looped the pole straps around our wrists. "Let's go halfway down on this red"—he points out a trail on the map using his pole—"and we can cut over to that black run we did before lunch. Just do the bottom half of it and see how you're doing."

Right. I'm tempted to say, *hey, if I make it down without a major wipeout, will you reconsider the dance?* But since I know that's not gonna happen, I keep my mouth shut and follow him.

If Georg wasn't being Mr. Ultra Nice and letting me sleep on his shoulder now that we're finally off the ski slope and heading back to Schwerinborg, I swear I'd smack him. Hard.

Well, assuming I could find the energy to lift my hand to do it.

He's been asleep for at least an hour. It's dark on the road, so all I can see are the vague outlines of trees and mountains. Occasionally there are the far-off lights of some tiny Austrian village. You'd think I'd sleep, too, seeing as I'm actually getting the opportunity to do so with Georg's arm slung around me in the backseat of the black Mercedes the palace let my Dad borrow. It's totally cozy, and I can feel Georg's heart doing its muffled *thrum-thrum-thrum* against my ear, but every time I start to drift off, Dad changes lanes or hits the slightest bump or turn and I jerk awake in pain. My quad muscles are so tight from doing that insane black run three times that I'm pretty sure I won't be doing any dancing for weeks. Even if Ulrike pays me to do it. Even if Georg shows up at the Hotel Whatsits and begs me to get my groove thang going. As it is, I can barely sit still in the car.

This is all Georg's fault. Georg and his insistence that I could do that black run again. And *again*.

I desperately need to get out and stretch.

This is just wrong. I finally, finally have the chance to get all snuggly-buggly with Georg (who somehow manages to ring my chimes even when he's asleep), and it's so physically torturous I can't enjoy it at all.

Not to mention the fact that my rear end hurts. I think I bruised it hitting that ice patch this morning.

I'm about to say something to Dad—point out that we just passed a sign saying there's an Esso station two kilometers ahead—but he whispers first. "It's gorgeous out, isn't it?"

"Sehr romantisch," The Fräulein whispers back before I can respond.

I have zero grasp of German, but *that* I understand. Gag. She is truly The Predator. I wonder if that's what *Putzkammer* means. Wouldn't be surprised.

Dad glances in the rearview mirror, sees Georg's sleeping face, but I can tell he's having trouble seeing me, so I close my eyes, fast.

A half minute later I crack open a lid to check out what's going on in the front seat. Dad is gazing straight ahead, eyes on the road rather than checking me in the rearview mirror. But as my gaze drifts down, I see the unthinkable—or maybe not-so-unthinkable—and literally bite my own tongue in shock.

Dad's hand is no longer on the gearshift. It's resting comfortably on The Fräulein's knee.

Eeewwwwwwwww!

This is so not happening. No, no, no. I close my eyes again, certain my retinas have suffered irreparable damage.

This is almost as bad as when I saw Mom and Gabby kissing in the kitchen while I was home for winter break. (I say "almost" since I have to give Dad credit for checking to make sure I was asleep before putting the moves on his new chick. Mom and Gabby didn't bother, and I was sitting right in the next room with my A-lister girlfriends—Christie, Jules, and Natalie—when they kissed. But *still*.)

Now I have a serious dilemma. Not only do I not want to be in the car behind *that*, faking sleep so I don't have to watch, but I have to do something about my aching legs. And I want to look at my tongue in a mirror, 'cause now I think it's bleeding.

Geez, I'm an idiot.

Georg's stomach rumbles, giving me an idea.

Ten minutes. Ten minutes and I'll fake being carsick.

That should do it.

To: CoolJule@viennawest.edu

From: Val@realmail.sg.com

Subject: I've grown a conscience . . .

Hi Jules,

I know, I know. It's not the kind of thing you'd recommend, but maybe Christie will appreciate that I actually did the grown-up thing for once.

On the way home tonight, in the car, I saw my Dad put his hand on Fräulein Putzkammer's knee. In his semi-defense, he did think I was asleep.

But can you IMAGINE?!?!

Anyway, I was going to do something you'd totally endorse: wait a decent amount of time, then fake like I was carsick and needed to hurl. I figured that'd not only get them to stop the car so I could move my legs (they're wrecked from skiing) but it'd also get them to cut the groping.

Instead, at the last second, I actually grew a conscience. To the detriment of my quadriceps muscles, I faked sleep for the last hour and a half of the drive home because I decided that if Georg had seen everything, he'd have told me to be nice to my dear ol' dad.

Plus, faking nausea struck me as being somewhat juvenile.

Of course, now I can't sleep (despite the fact I have school tomorrow and it's two in the morning) because the image of Dad with his hand on this bottle-blond chick's leg is making me nauseous for real.

I know, I know. The whole situation's whacked. (And please don't lecture me about how I'm obviously discriminating against women with dyed hair. I have no such prejudice—as you know since I did your highlights last year—but I have the emotional need to pick on SOMETHING about her, and I wouldn't have picked her hair if she'd kept up with her roots.)

But I had to share and knew you'd be appropriately ticked off on my behalf.

Val

To: NatNatNat@viennawest.edu

Cc: CoolJule@viennawest.edu; ChristieT@viennawest.edu

From: Val@realmail.sg.com

Subject: RE: Who the hell is JOHN?

My dear, imaginative friend Natalie (and Christie and Jules, too),

Sorry I didn't have more time to e-mail when I was in Austria last night, but I'm home now. So I'll let you in on a fat, juicy secret: John was telling you the truth. He is someone I met through my mom. If you look around next time you're walking through senior hall at VWHS, you just might see him. (Did you or did you not look at his e-mail address, Nat? Duh!)

And another fat, juicy secret: There is nothing whatsoever going on with him. He probably just wanted to talk or something. Seriously. For one, no senior would be interested in me, let alone from so far away. As you guys are constantly pointing out to me, I look even younger than I am (which is *so wrong*). For two, there's this guy named Georg . . . I believe I've mentioned him? And for three, while John may be cute, I think you're right, Nat—he's definitely more your type.

I got back from skiing a few hours ago and it's just after two a.m. here, so I'm about to go to bed. But I wanted to remind you that Georg came along with me on the ski trip and things are just wunderbar with him.

In fact, THE L WORD WAS SAID!

So you can quit imagining anything happening with John.

Your thoroughly tired pal,

Val

To: JPMorant@viennawest.edu

From: Val@realmail.sg.com

Subject: What's up?

Hey John,

My friend Natalie said she saw you at the grocery store and you gave her your e-mail address to pass along to me. How's life in Virginia? Schwerinborg—as you might guess—is cold, snowy, and mountainous with an abundance of schnitzel.

Let me know what's up with you,

Val

The e-mail to John was the hardest. Way harder than phrasing my L-word explanation to the girls (because no way am I going to tell them I said it first).

But even after I wrote and rewrote the e-mail to John six times, I still wasn't sure what tone I should take. Casual? Friendly? Worried? I ended up attempting casual-yet-concerned, which I then tempered with a pathetic attempt at humor before hitting send.

Now that it's gone, though, it occurs to me that it'll probably end up getting deleted as spam with the generic subject line I used. I am beyond lame.

I stand up and reach around the computer to shut it down so I can take another crack at going to sleep, when my instant message box pops up.

CHRISTIET: Hey, you there? Is this working?

I blink at the screen in disbelief. Of course I immediately sit down and start typing like the wind.

VAL: Christie!!!!!!

CHRISTIET: Yay! You're awake! Just got your e-mail. I'm so psyched about Georg and the L word! That rocks!

VAL: thx!!!

CHRISTIET: So anyway, I know things are crazy for you right now with your dad and all, but I'm having a meltdown and had to talk to you.

VAL: ?????

CHRISTIET: Jeremy passed on our Friday date night for the second week in a row. I'd already stopped by the theater and bought the movie tickets because I thought the show would sell out, but it didn't matter. He said he was just too tired from running and he knew he'd fall asleep during the movie. I ended up going back to the multiplex to get a refund.

CHRISTIET: I dunno . . . I know he's telling the truth about being wiped out, but it's like he's not even interested anymore. Could he possibly be THAT tired?

VAL: no way! what r u gonna do?

CHRISTIET: I don't know. I can't flirt with anyone else. I just can't.

CHRISTIET: I don't expect advice or anything—I just needed to talk to someone. You like Jeremy. You can be neutral. Jules and Natalie like him, but it's not the same. If I whine about this to them, they'll want to corner him and ask him what's up. Right to his face. Probably in the middle of sophomore hall.

VAL: so not your style . . .

CHRISTIET: I KNOW!!

VAL: I think it's a phase . . . just be patient, ok? u know u rock.

CHRISTIET: Thanks. Hey, I gotta finish a paper tonight, so I'm going to have to sign off. Talk to Georg about David, okay? Because I bet you haven't yet.

CHRISTIET: He loves you, and he sounds like such a fabulous guy, so I know he'll understand. Just be honest with him. I want things to work out with you two.

VAL: ditto for you . . .

CHRISTIET: I hope so. I'll try to talk to Jeremy soon. Before the marathon, if I can.

VAL: HUGS!

CHRISTIET: Hugs to you, too. I miss you tons. I'll keep you posted.

VAL: miss u 2 . . . TTYL.

Christie is the strangest person on IM. She has no concept of abbreviations, which means her messages pop up veerrrrry slowly, since she's not exactly the world's fastest typist. At the same time I'm reading her IMs, two new e-mail messages appear in my in-box.

Jules and Natalie, of course.

I glance at the clock. Two in the morning here is eight in the evening there. I should've known they'd all be online. Five bucks says Jules and Natalie got on the phone with each other the minute my John e-mail hit their in-boxes. Sheesh.

I know I should go to sleep, but I can't help it. I click open the message from Nat, decide to answer tomorrow (well, technically later today), then open the one from Jules, only to realize that she put an auto-confirm on her e-mail so she'd know the second I opened it.

Meaning—if I don't answer Jules immediately, she's going to fire off another message meant to send me on a guilt trip. And then she'll tell Nat that I replied and Nat will wonder why I didn't answer her, too. So I'm stuck answering both.

I swear, Jules has no conscience whatsoever.

To: Val@realmail.sg.com

From: NatNatNat@viennawest.edu

Subject: Private re: JOHN

Val,

I'm only writing this to you this time.

First—are you serious? Prince Georg said the L word to you?! (Not to rain on your parade, 'cause I don't know the guy at all, but is this a common thing with him? I mean, he is a prince. But don't read into my question that I'm unsupportive, because I'm very supportive! I just want to make sure you're not going to get hurt.)

Second—assuming you're giving me the full scoop (unlike when you hid the whole fact your mom is gay from us for WEEKS), then would it be totally rude of me to flirt with John when I see him, assuming I'm someday not grounded anymore? I mean it—tell me if I shouldn't. I do NOT want to step on toes, okay?

Third—John really is hot. No offense, but he's way hotter than your prince (although I do give Georg bonus points for having an actual TITLE.) And when John saw me in the grocery store, he told me he thought my tongue piercing was cool. (I left that part out when I cc'ed Jules and Natalie. Didn't want them to comment, you know? And no, my parents haven't made me take the tongue stud out yet even though they're totally snarky about it all the time.)

I'm rambling, but you know what I mean by all this. I can't stop thinking about that John guy and how cute he is and how he didn't immediately go away even though I was being kinda grouchy with him.

Catch you soon,

Nat

PS—If you haven't already, you might want to e-mail Christie to see what's up with her. She says things with her and Jeremy are fine, but I'm getting a bad vibe. She's more likely to talk to you.

PPS—I could be all wrong. I don't get to see her outside school as much lately, thanks to Dr. Monschroeder, DDS, and his strange obsession with incarcerating me (a.k.a. grounding me) for what I consider to be only minor infractions of the house rules.

To: NatNatNat@viennawest.edu

From: Val@realmail.sg.com

Subject: RE: Private re: JOHN

Natalie,

With Georg: I have no idea if he's said it before. But I can tell he means it.

With John: Go for it.

With Christie: I'm on it.

With your parents: Fuggedabout it, girl. You're screwed on that front. Maybe consider stopping with the curfew violations and the unauthorized piercings and tattoos until you're in college?!

Your pal,

Val

To: Val@realmail.sg.com

From: CoolJule@viennawest.edu

Subject: Yeah, right.

Val,

You say you've grown a conscience. I think not. I bet you an extra-large Frosty you haven't told Georg about David yet. I'll raise you a Biggie Fries that you've been angst-ing about it even though you're acting like it's no big thing.

Yep. That's right. You owe me and you know it.

Jules

PS—I think you should've faked that you were sick. Georg would have forgiven you because it would have been so funny to watch.

PPS—He'll forgive you for the David thing, too, but ONLY IF YOU TELL HIM. Use that conscience you claim to have for good.

To: CoolJule@viennawest.edu

From: Val@realmail.sg.com

Subject: RE: Yeah, right.

Jules,

Totally unfair. You work at Wendy's, so what kind of bet is that? You can eat Frostys and Biggie Fries all you want. And anyway, after being totally wiped out by skiing, I've decided I need to eat better. Yep, me. Weaning myself off of fast food (at least most of the time).

Oh, and you know what else? GET OVER THE DAVID THING ALREADY. I'll deal with it when the timing is right.

Going to bed now,

Val

"So, what'd you do all weekend?" Steffi's question sounds casual to everyone but me as we're eating lunch at our favorite table in the quad. There's snow on the ground, but it's bright and sunny out (for once! hooray!), and the tables and benches are dry, so we headed outside with our lunches. Until Steffi decided to up and speak to me, I'd been enjoying myself out here, watching a group of freshmen attempt to make a snowman, complete with a carrot nose they probably swiped from the cafeteria. The sun and excitement have kept me from falling face first into my food, exhausted.

Still, I'm sharp enough to know Steffi isn't the least bit interested in what I did this weekend. Other than to confirm that it didn't involve Georg.

Sorry, sister.

"Not much," I say. "Went skiing."

"Where'd you go?" Ulrike's head swings up, and she shoves her open notebook away. She's really worked up about the dance and has been quiet until now, making a list of all the stuff she needs to do. "I didn't even know you skied."

"We went to Austria." I'm not going to get too specific. What if Georg has told his friends he went to Scheffau? As much as I'm dying to go "nya-nya-nya" to Steffi, I need to respect the fact that Georg's not ready for us to be a public couple at school yet.

"Really? Where?" This from Steffi. Of course.

"I can't remember the name of the place—you know me and the German language—but it was really pretty. I'm totally bruised, though. I wiped out a lot. Get this . . . I have a bruise the size of an apple on my rear end."

This brings a few sympathy comments from all three of them (guess Steffi figured she'd have to join in or risk looking like a total bitch) and a story from Ulrike about her first ski lesson and how she ran right into the instructor, sending the guy to the first aid shack for the afternoon.

I subtly glance at my watch. Five minutes to go. Gotta strategically keep Steffi off the Georg topic. I'm about to say something about the freshmen and their snowman when I hear a familiar voice behind me.

"Hey, guys."

"Hi, Georg!" Ulrike, Maya, and Steffi all say it at once. Of course, Ulrike's "hi" is chipper, Maya's is pretty normal, and Steffi's . . . well, The Predator could take a lesson from Steffi. Her sultry little "hi" is barely out of her mouth and she's asking him if he's ready for the exam he and Maya are having in French IV right after lunch. Just to get him talking to her.

Naturally, he's polite, and she soon manages to turn the conversation to a direction she'd prefer. Nodding toward Ulrike's notebook, she says, "Poor Ulrike here is working her tail off, getting ready for the dance this weekend. Did you get your tickets yet?"

I know she's just dying, waiting for him to say, *Isn't it girls ask guys?* or something along those lines, because that would give her the confirmation she's dying to hear—that he doesn't have a date with the big event less than a week away. Apparently, most people here do the who-are-you-going-with thing at the last minute, but she's gotta know Georg's not a last-minute planner. His life doesn't allow it for the most part.

I'm cringing on the inside, waiting for Georg to fall into her oh-so-subtle trap.

I need a way to save him. Fast. I stand up, thinking I can get him moving toward his French IV class (since the warning bell is going to ring any second), but just as Steffi opens her mouth to speak again, he says, "I can't go. I have a party to attend that night."

He does?

"You do?" Steffi's eyes meet mine and then look away so fast I doubt anyone else even notices. "Is it a palace event?"

"It's an Oscar party. You know the Academy Awards are this weekend, right?"

Omigosh. The Oscars are *this* weekend? Every year, the A-listers and I make a huge deal out of it. Since fifth grade, our parents have let us stay up really late to watch it. We rate all the gowns and gossip about our fave actors—debating who's the hottest on the red carpet, who needs style lessons, and who's probably not going to be invited next year because their career is tanking. It's such an important ritual with us that last year our parents agreed to let us all spend the night at Jules's place so we could watch it on her monster-size TV, despite the fact we had school the next day.

Which reminds me. "Isn't it always on a Sunday?"

"Not this year." Georg explains, "They're switching venues and decided to host the ceremony on a Saturday night instead."

Ulrike looks from me to Georg. "Um, do you get to fly to L.A.? Like, to the actual event?"

I'm about to say something along the lines of, *Are you kidding?* but as I look from Ulrike to Georg, it hits me that Georg's father probably gets invited to events like the Oscars all the time. If not to the actual awards ceremony, then to one of the zillion Hollywood shindigs that follow it. He knows all those Hollywood types. And now that I'm thinking about it, I remember Dad once mentioning that Prince Manfred has put some of his personal money into funding independent film festivals. Encouraging the pursuit of the arts and all that.

"No, no trip to L.A. this time," Georg says. "It's a private party here in Schwerinborg. I have school and soccer, so I couldn't go to the States even if I wanted to."

This time? I try not to stare at him or look surprised, but now I'm dying to ask if he's been before (and if he knows any famous actors and actresses and what gossip he has about them . . . mostly so I can give the scoop to Jules, Nat, and Christie). His tone makes it clear the topic is closed, though. He even asks Maya if she'll walk with him to French IV so they can quiz each other on the way.

After Maya loads up her backpack and heads off with Georg, Steffi looks at me with the most overacted sympathetic look I think I've ever seen on a human being—assuming she's human, that is. "Bummer, Val, huh? I guess it wasn't meant to be."

I give her the Valerie Shrug. Whatta bitch. Thankfully, I'm saved by the bell from any other catty comments she might add.

We wad up our trash and toss it into a nearby can, which gets Ulrike griping to Steffi about the obscene hour the garbage truck showed up on her street this morning, with the sanitation workers clanging cans around and revving the engine of the truck.

In other words, it's the kind of conversation I can tune out.

Careful not to let Steffi see what I'm doing, I steal a glance toward the door where Georg and Maya disappeared.

And that's when it hits me.

Georg never mentioned that he had to go to a party this weekend. Not even when I asked him to the dance.

In fact, he said the reason he didn't want to go was because the Hotel Whatsits is a public place, yadda yadda. He even said it might be fun for the two of us to do something afterward. How could he possibly have meant any of that if he has another party he's attending?

I frown as I hitch my backpack higher on my shoulder, careful not to let Steffi see that I'm suddenly bothered.

As with Hamlet in Denmark, something is totally rotten in the state of Schwerinborg. And I have to wonder if the prince is involved.

6

I SIGN ON TO THE COMPUTER IN THE LIBRARY, shove my Diet Coke—technically Coke Light here in Schwerinborg—off to the side so the librarian doesn't see it and slap me with a warning, then open a blank document.

Problem is, I can't figure out what in the world I want to type.

I got the library pass so I could (theoretically) work on an essay for English Literature. I know I'm going to have to show that I was actually doing work while I was here, but I'm just not being productive. I can't wax poetic about *Pride and Prejudice* when I have more pressing issues futzing with my gray matter.

I have to know where Georg is going this weekend.

Mostly because I've worked myself up to the level of total freak-out about his Oscar party statement despite my own resolution not to do this to myself anymore.

I click into the browser and do a Google search for "Oscars" and "Schwerinborg." All it brings up are the television listings, showing which network is going to be airing it here (one broadcast from Germany is being picked up locally, which is swell, 'cause I can just imagine some burly German announcer trying to describe the fluid drape of an Armani gown).

I try again, this time using the search terms "Academy Awards" and "Schwerinborg." No dice. Whatever party Georg is going to must not be one that's at a location the press will be covering, like at a hotel or restaurant. He did say it was a private party, but generally most "private parties" the royal family attends get at least a little publicity.

It occurs to me that maybe there's no party at all. Maybe he was onto Steffi's game, and he was afraid *she* might ask him to the dance?

I push the thought from my brain as soon as I consider it. It just isn't Georg's style. He's not deceptive enough to make up a party story as an evasion tactic. He'd just tell her straight out he didn't want to attend. And he'd do it in that way he has of convincing people to drop the subject and discuss something else while still being completely tactful.

Though now I'm *really* wondering why he didn't tell me about his Oscar party. And what he meant by what he was saying on the chairlift about maybe having us make it a movie night when I get home from the dance. Was he just tossing out general ideas? Did he forget he had a party? Not that I was dying to have another hot date where all we do is watch movies, but still. And it's not like he could go to his party and then meet up with me. The Oscars run late, especially here, given the time difference.

I scoot back from the computer and close my eyes, trying to do that Mom breathe-in-breathe-out thing. Maybe Georg got more pissed at me over my guesthouse hallway comments than he let on. Maybe he was trying to take the polite way out, turning me down for the dance because he really didn't want to go at all.

I reach forward, grab my Diet Coke, and drain it. The rush of caffeine does nothing to bring down my freak-out level, though.

Since the librarian is looking at me now and I don't want her to see the Coke can, I lean toward the computer to try and look busy. Since *Pride and Prejudice* ain't happening, I sign on to my e-mail to whine to Christie about Georg's mystery party—since she'll understand—and to ask her if she'll look around for an Oscar Internet feed in English so I can watch the show after I get home from the dance. She's great at finding that kind of thing. But when my mailbox screen pops up, I'm stunned to see a bunch of new mail.

And I'm *really* stunned by the return address on the first one in the box. Guess the spam filters let my mail get through after all.

To: Val@realmail.sg.com

From: JPMorant@viennawest.edu

Subject: RE: What's up?

Hi Valerie,

If I'm interrupting your schnitzel, I apologize. I'm sure it's a critical component of your survival in Schwerinborg. (I hate to ask, but what IS schnitzel, anyway? Is it some kind of sausage?)

I hope you don't mind that I talked to Natalie at the Giant a few days ago. She was standing there reading some health magazine, looking very bored. Since I wanted to give you an update, I figured it would be okay to give her my e-mail address. (Though I wasn't sure she'd actually pass it along.)

Here's the thing—I think I'm out a roommate when I head

to NYU in the fall. My brother wants his new boyfriend to move in with him. Or—to be perfectly clear about the situation—he wants his new boyfriend to move in with *us*.

He insists the apartment is big enough for three—he and his boyfriend would have one bedroom and I'd have the other—but I don't want to do it. I haven't told him no, since I'm afraid he'll think it's because I'm a homophobe or something. But I wouldn't want to live there even if it was a girlfriend, you know? I have no desire to be that close to someone else's relationship.

And no matter how big he says this apartment is, it's in *Manhattan*. Brad doesn't have a ton of dough, so how big could the place really be?

I guess I'm just having trouble with the whole situation and knew you'd understand better than some of the adults at the PFLAG meetings might. They'd just tell me to find a nice dorm room or something.

So . . . if you can think of a good way for me to tell Brad I don't want to live with him next year (at least not if he has a significant other in the apartment), I'm open to suggestions.

Of course, then I have to find another roommate, which is a whole new problem.

Hope you're having fun over there, eating what sounds like interesting food,

John

PS—I wasn't going to ask this, but what the hell. Is your friend Natalie with anyone? After seeing her the other day at the Giant, I'm noticing her all the time in the hallways at school now. She seems like she'd be a lot of fun.

PPS—*If* she's not with anyone, and *if* she'd even think about going out with me . . . have you told her about your mom? How'd she handle it? What would she think about Brad? I wouldn't want to say anything to her and find out she either doesn't know about your mother and Gabrielle or is super-conservative about that kind of thing.

To: JPMorant@viennawest.edu
From: Val@realmail.sg.com
Subject: RE: What's up?

Hi John,

Wow—bummer on your brother. It's great he's found someone, but I wouldn't want to live with them, either. (Hey, I ended up in Schwerinborg because I wasn't mentally up to living with Mom and Gabby, so I completely understand where you're coming from. And I bet that Brad's apartment in NYC is way smaller than the place my mother and Gabby have in Virginia.)

I wish I could tell you what to say, but I've learned the hard way that I suck in these situations.

Maybe honesty is the best policy here? Just tell Brad you want to give him and his boyfriend some space and that you don't want to intrude. If he starts acting all pissed, you could tell him what you told me—that you'd feel this way whether his significant other was male or female.

And about Nat—she knows about Mom and Gabby and she's cool with it. She's actually been really supportive. And Natalie is completely and totally single, so if you want to ask her out, go for it. (Though I'll warn you, she might not be able to do much for a while. She keeps getting into trouble. Nothing major, but enough that her parents are keeping her on a tight leash lately.)

I'm at school, so I'll have to write more later. Good luck,

Val

To: JPMorant@viennawest.edu
From: Val@realmail.sg.com
Subject: Another thought . . .

Hi again, John,

I'm supposed to be working on an essay on *Pride and Prejudice*, but I just had another thought. Your situation's not totally the same as mine was when I was trying to figure out if I wanted to live with Mom.

I had two equal choices—Mom or Dad.

Of course, I had to move to Schwerinborg with Dad, which was a big consideration, but I would have had to move if I'd chosen to live with Mom, too (and living with Mom would have meant transferring from Vienna West to Lake Braddock, if you can imagine). I think both of my parents wanted me to live with them, but both of them would have been cool if I'd gone the other way, you know?

You don't really have the same choice. Mine was "who do I live with?" Yours Is more, "do I live with Brad or not?" So maybe you need to ask yourself how important it is to him. Just tell him what you're thinking, see how he reacts, then go with your gut.

I know this probably doesn't help you at all—it might even make things more confusing—but I know you'll be fine no matter what you decide to do.

Keep me posted.

Val

PS—Schnitzel is not sausage. It's more like a giant chicken nugget if you get the plain, breaded kind of schnitzel (apparently there are lots of other kinds). It is not made from chicken, though. Any more info than that would probably gross you out.

To: Val@realmail.sg.com

From: CoolJule@viennawest.edu

Subject: Mmmmmm, good!

Good morning, Val Pal!

Okay, so it's probably the afternoon where you are. But I'm e-mailing you instead of messing around with my curling iron and getting pretty for school ('cause does it really matter?) because I wanted to let you know that I'm eating a Ho Ho.

Yep, right now. As I type.

It's chocolatey and delicious and the filling just melts in your mouth . . . I bet you want one. Don't you?

It's really, really, REALLY delicious. . . .

My point: What the hell are you doing giving up fast food?!?!?! Please. You're totally skinny, but even more important, quitting is not going to affect the size of your ass or your skiing ability. Seriously.

Last time I checked, you lived with a gourmet chef type. (You do remember your father, right? Nice guy, great cook?) I guess what he makes is fairly healthy, but I know if I had him prepping my dinners every night, I'd double my weight in a year because I'd eat so much. And I happen to know that you eat like a horse when he cooks for you, too.

Plus, don't even THINK you're gonna get out of buying

me that Frosty and Biggie Fry. (Not unless you talk to Georg about David. Like, within 24 hours.) I'm not taking it out of my employee allowance when I have you to treat me.

Off to school with bad hair and Ho Ho breath (yet blissfully happy!),

Jules

"Wow. Think Ulrike's overdoing it a bit?"

Georg is staring at the large sheet of paper I have unfolded across my bed. Literally *across* my bed. Ulrike must have stolen it from one of those flip charts in the corner of the art room. The whole thing is covered with her scribbles, though I'm too tired to analyze all the detail she's put into it. More than half the paper is a hand-drawn map of the hotel ballroom, complete with little circles and rectangles showing where I need to put chairs and tables outside the main doors, and diagrams of where the refreshment tables will be and the area we need to cordon off for the DJ and his equipment. She's even marked in where the speakers will be located.

The rest of the page is one honking big to-do list. Actually, it's three to-do lists: one for her, one for me, and one for the two guys she roped in to do the heavy lifting.

"I know." I can't get over it myself. I mean, did she

make extra copies of this thing for herself and for the guys? "I told her when I volunteered that she'd have to be specific with me, but I didn't mean this. I think she needs to get a life."

"This *is* her life."

"Well, now it's my life too." I fold up the piece of paper—which feels like folding a bedsheet given its insane size—since I don't want to think about item number one on my to-do list, which is to call the DJ and ask him a long list of questions about things like his music selection, his preferred speaker volume, and when he expects to take his breaks.

I mean, what if he doesn't speak English? *Good* English?

To distract myself, I ask Georg how soccer practice went. He was wearing his sweats from soccer when he got here, but since our apartment is now broiling (the heat is never right—it's either like living in Antarctica or the Sahara on any given day, and Dad and I can't predict which we'll get), he's pulled them off and is only in his practice shorts and a T-shirt. I point to a row of evenly spaced scrapes on the side of his calf and ask what happened.

Tragic to mar that gorgeous bod, I tell you.

He shrugs like it's nothing, though. "Got knocked into the wall trying to steal the ball. I missed and tried to change direction to catch the guy, but I was off balance and fell down." He adds, "I, like, wiped out totally."

I laugh so hard I snort. A genuine, sitcom-type snort. "You've been listening to me talk too much."

He has the good sense to blush. "It's good for me, though, isn't it? I want to sound more natural when I speak English. So whenever I go to the States, I don't stand out."

I am so not going to tell him that his attempts to sound natural have the complete opposite effect.

"You're going to have a lot to do at the dance, from the looks of it." He takes a seat on my bed, leans back against the pillows (man, how I wish I could whip out my sketch pad and capture him just like that!), then says, "How late are you going to be there?"

"Probably until the end." Which sucks rocks. "But you've got that party to go to, don't you? So it's not like you'd be home anyway. Unless it's here at the palace."

He shrugs but doesn't say anything, which naturally makes me think he's trying to keep the details of this party hush-hush. Since I just can't leave it alone, I decide to go fishing. "It must be before the awards actually air, since we're so many hours ahead of California, right?"

"I guess. I haven't paid attention to what time the telecast starts." Even though he pauses on the word "telecast," he's being casual, not giving me a hint of info. Dammit.

Did I do something wrong? Why is this such a big fat hairy secret?

"Anyway," he adds, "I was curious about when you thought you'd get home. You'll probably get back about the time the—what do you call it when all the nominees are shown entering the theater? The preshow?—when that starts."

When I tell him that's my plan, he says, "That's good. So you'll be able to watch at least part of the show. I couldn't believe when the Golden Globes were on last month that you stayed up almost all night to keep checking the winners online."

"I know. I think Dad wanted to kill me, since it was a school night. But I felt like I was hanging out long-distance with Christie, Jules, and Natalie, since I was e-mailing them my comments. I think Dad kind of felt sorry for me, and who was I to tell him not to? The A-listers and I always watch together, and there was no way I was going to miss out."

"Yeah, you mentioned how you guys do the awards

shows." As he talks, he flexes and then points his toes, like his calves are sore from soccer. Judging from how beaten up he is, it's no wonder. If he didn't have to be a prince, I know he'd want to attempt a pro soccer career. He likes it that much.

"You planning to do that this weekend, too?" he asks.

"I guess. We haven't really talked about it. I s'pose it depends on when I get back from the dance." And on what Georg is doing then.

"Maybe going to the dance will distract you from the fact you can't watch with your friends this time. Don't you think?"

"Maybe."

Geez, but this is an awkward conversation, at least for me. He really shouldn't be reminding me of how much I miss home. Or about the fact that I'm going to be stuck at this wacky Schwerinborg-type dance without him, so I won't even have him to console me as the girls watch an awards show without me. Again.

I take Ulrike's attack plan and stick it under the stack of books and binders piled on my desk. I don't want to look at it.

Because it's more than the fact that I'm missing the Oscar party with the girls in Virginia, or even the fact that Dad will probably take advantage of my absence and disappear for the night with Fräulein Predator that's got me feeling so mopey and blah.

It's the fact that Georg will be celebrating with who-knows-who—dancing and chatting and being oblivious to the fact that all the cute Steffi types are desperately trying to hook up with him—when if he'd *really* wanted to, he could be spending the evening with me.

For some reason, he doesn't. And he doesn't even want to tell me why.

To: CoolJule@viennawest.edu

From: Val@realmail.sg.com

Subject: RE: Mmmmmm, good!

Jules, Jules, Jules,

I am simply trying to be healthy. That's all. If I won the Frosty/Biggie Fries bet (which, you may notice, I've never officially agreed to), then you'd be off the hook. So what's the big deal?

Besides—if I so much as tried to take a single Ho Ho from your precious stash, you'd steal your combat boots back from Christie and use them on my head. No amount of chocolate—no matter how delicious—is worth that.

Your clean-living friend,

Val Pal

To: Val@realmail.sg.com

From: CoolJule@viennawest.edu

Subject: RE: Mmmmmm, good!

Val,

Clean living? Oh, PLEASE. Take a look at the clock.

Yep, that's right. You're e-mailing me at what hour over there? Get your delirious self to sleep!!

Jules, who knows better about all that clean living stuff you're spouting, because I know you're using it as an excuse to procrastinate on the David Issue

PS—BTW, I just got home from school and you won't believe what I saw on the way out of VWHS. Natalie was talking to that John guy in the parking lot. (She pointed him out to me at school right after the incident at the Giant, so I know it was him.) What's with that??

To: Val@realmail.sg.com

From: ChristieT@viennawest.edu

Subject: Trying to stay positive . . .

Hi Valerie,

So Jeremy just cancelled our Friday night plans—for the THIRD time in a row. The ones he promised he wouldn't back out on. We were going to go bowling, but he says his quads are really sore and he just can't crouch down with a bowling ball without risking injury to himself.

I wanted to point out that it's probably not the smartest thing to try running a marathon if he's so sore he can't even bowl, but I am trying to be positive.

Anyway—I won't see him on Saturday, either, because my grandparents are coming up from Tennessee and I promised Mom and Dad I'd stay home all day. Then Saturday night's the annual Oscar party at Jules's place. Since Georg said you'll be at a school dance, I guess you won't even be able to get online with us, will you?

This is just awful all around.

Remind me again that Jeremy loves me,

Christie

To: ChristieT@viennawest.edu

From: Val@realmail.sg.com

Subject: SHEESH!

Christie,

Get it through your head already: Jeremy loves you. He's just being stupid right now. I bet all that running is messing with his electrolyte levels and making him act weird. He'll get over it soon enough. Forget about him for now and enjoy the Oscars.

And, more important than your Jeremy issue . . . YOU E-MAILED GEORG?!?!?

Val

I swear, I am going to have a freaking coronary, right here at my desk. Dad will knock on my door in the morning to harass me to eat a healthy breakfast before I head out to school. He might even whip up some oatmeal or an omelet before coming back and knocking a second time. He'll open the door, intent on reading me the riot act, only to find me slumped over my monitor, mouse in hand, dead from shock.

What the hell is Georg doing e-mailing with Christie? How would they even have each other's e-mail address? What is this all about?

Oh, no. No, no, no. Could the girls be feeling him out about David? This is the last thing I need right now!

I know Christie wouldn't be sneaky that way, but for all I know he's also e-mailing Jules and Natalie. I don't think they'd tell him about David, either, but they might drop hints if they thought it'd push me to tell Georg about David myself.

I do *not* want them dropping hints. I do not want them to have anything to do with this.

I wonder if he knows already? Maybe that's why he suddenly had this Oscar party thing. . . .

I'm just about to text Christie, since I simply must know about the Georg thing, when a new e-mail from her pops up in my box.

To: Val@realmail.sg.com

From: ChristieT@viennawest.edu

Subject: RE: SHEESH!

Hi again, Val! (You're up late, aren't you?)

NO, I didn't e-mail Prince Georg. And he sure hasn't e-mailed me. Could you imagine, getting an e-mail from a real prince?? (Okay, maybe YOU could. But I sure can't!)

I am obviously so stressed out by the Jeremy thing, I must've put "Georg" in that e-mail when I was thinking about YOU telling me about your school dance.

Sorry! I didn't mean to freak you out!

Christie, clearly needing to decompress . . .

To: ChristieT@viennawest.edu

From: Val@realmail.sg.com

Subject: RE: SHEESH!

WHEW! Geez, Christie. Please don't do that again.

Val, also clearly needing to decompress

* * *

"So, did you call the DJ yet?"

I should have known Ulrike would pounce first thing in the morning. It's Wednesday, and since I managed to avoid her all day yesterday (it's amazing how something can come up, say, in the computer lab, right at lunchtime, therefore saving me from a solid hour of listening to Ulrike fixate on the tiniest details of this dance), I knew I couldn't hide from her today. Not without being really obvious, and the whole point of helping her was to keep her from having hurt feelings.

Now that she's nabbed me at my locker between first and second period, I figure the only reason it's taken her this long is because I didn't stop here before school. Five bucks says she was waiting for me then, too.

"No, I wanted to do it when I got home from school today." It's sort of the truth. I was *thinking* about calling then, but I don't exactly *want* to. "Though, are you sure you want me to make the call? It might be better—"

"No, you're the best person for the job. My hands are full, and I just know the guys wouldn't ask the right questions. Even when they have a list, they don't do what they're supposed to."

I close my locker and spin the combo lock, but Ulrike puts a hand on my wrist to stop me from leaving. Her face is earnest as she speaks. "Val, this really means a lot to me.

Thank you. It's a relief knowing I can count on you. You're such a great friend."

Well, crap. Now I have to call the DJ.

"Thanks, Ulrike. I'm happy to do it." I even keep a straight face as I say the word "happy."

"Great. Promise to call or e-mail me after you talk to him, okay?"

As soon as I promise, she blasts off in the direction of senior hall—well, year twelve hall—presumably to harass the guys.

I glance at my watch and realize I have all kinds of time before I have to be at my next class. Since it's only a few feet down the hall, I walk to a quiet spot near the doors to the quad so I can pull out my cell phone and the scrap of paper with the phone number.

Maybe if I call the DJ now, he won't be there. I can see if his voice mail is in German or English, plus I'll know I've done my duty for Ulrike (at least for the moment), and I won't have to think about it all day.

I'm just about to dial when I hear Ulrike calling my name. I look up to see her jogging back down the hall toward me, her white-blond hair bouncing all over the place and her backpack smacking against her shoulder.

Great. She probably thought of more DJ questions.

"What's up?"

"I forgot to tell you!" she says on a gasp. "You won't believe who's coming to the dance!"

"Really?" Please, please let her say Georg. Maybe she talked to him during first period? Heard some juicy bit of news that he's canceling his party appearance so he can come be with me? I force my breathing to remain as calm as possible and ask, "Who?"

"Well, I was talking to my dad yesterday—you know he's coming as a chaperone, right?—Well, he said he ran into your father yesterday at the palace. I guess Dad had some kind of economic meeting there."

Since Ulrike's dad is a German diplomat and he's at the palace a lot, this isn't really a shocker. "So what happened?"

Her grin gets even bigger. "He told your father about the dance and mentioned that they needed more chaperones. And your dad said he could do it. Volunteered on the spot, just like that! He even said he knew someone else from the palace who'd be able to come—this woman from the public relations office my dad's worked with a few times before who has all kinds of security clearance—so now I have all the chaperones lined up. Isn't that great? I was so worried we wouldn't get enough and I'd have to go begging teachers."

"That's great, Ulrike!" Man, can I fake enthusiasm. "One less thing on your to-do list, huh?"

She says something appropriately giddy, then flounces off

toward her class once more. Me, I just sink against the wall.

Not only is Georg not coming, but now I have to endure a dance with my father there? I guess it's not that bad, since it's not like I'm going to be dancing with anyone.

But I can just guess who else from the palace is coming.

They're going to be at a dance. Together. With slow music and glowing crystal chandeliers and a general aura of romance all around them.

If Dad gets all kissy-face with his girlfriend at this dance, I'm gonna be humiliated. Not that he's gotten kissy-face with her in public yet, but there's always a first time. I mean, he's not in the same situation I am—it's not like Fräulein Predator is being followed by tabloids.

Dad might be one of the world's leading experts on protocol, but with my luck, he'll get all starry-eyed over The Fräulein, forget his professional training, and do something stupid at the exact moment my new friends are there to see it. Like planting a big one on The Fräulein.

Or worse, he'll do it when Steffi's around, since it'll give her the perfect opportunity to make a comment about how wonderful it is that someone in my family is getting some action—though she'll say it in a much less crass way, one that'll make it impossible for me to say anything back without looking like I'm just another American lacking in good taste.

"Hi, Valerie!" Speak of the she-devil.

"Hey, Steffi!" She looks all perky and tiny and perfect. Her brunette hair has every curl in place, but it's not obvious she spent the time on herself I know she must take.

False advertising, if you ask me. Any guy who asks her out is going to think she's low maintenance and find out pretty fast that she's not.

"Just saw Ulrike," she says, playing with the shoulder strap on her designer—no, really, *designer*—backpack. "She said your dad volunteered to chaperone at the dance. That's so cute!"

I thank her, then head past her to class. I can feel her staring at my back as I walk, like she's checking to see if she's mortally wounded me with her "cute" comment.

I have to pay better attention to who's around me in the halls so I can take evasive action next time.

7

"GUTEN TAG. DARF ICH IHN HILFEN?"

"Um, hello?" I can tell already this is going to rot. After the "good day" part, I have no idea what the guy said. "Is Helmut there?"

I know it's pronounced like "Hell-moot" and not like "Helmet," but I still don't like saying it aloud. I can't fathom how anyone gives their kids these wacko names non-German-speaking people can't begin to say without wanting to crack up.

It's taken me weeks to get used to *Georg* and *Manfred*. Adding *Helmut* to the mix is like God daring me to say something snarky aloud, probably at whatever time it can get me into the most trouble.

Still, I figured it'd be best if I got on the phone and got the whole call over with the second I got home from school, before I gave myself any more time to think about the joke potential of the guy's name. Or to think too much about the call itself and what I'll do if Helmut the DJ doesn't speak English.

If I tell Ulrike she's going to have to do this herself, I think her stress meter will smash right through the red zone.

There's some mumbling in German on the other end of the line—maybe the equivalent of telling me to hold on?—and then the voice comes back on. "*Entschuldigung* . . . uh, sorry. My dog was scratching for outside. May I help you?"

Yes! His accent is pretty thick, but he's understandable.

I quickly introduce myself and run through Ulrike's list. The guy seems friendly enough—as if he was expecting all the questions—and he doesn't act like I'm being obnoxious for speaking in English to him, even though I sure feel that way. Before I know it, I'm set. And since Helmut has apparently worked on dances for Ulrike before, he even asks me to tell her he'll be there for the sound check in plenty of time, so she shouldn't worry.

I immediately fire off an e-mail to her. It's a quarter to

four, so she's probably just getting home from school herself. She's going to be relieved to know she can put a check mark next to one of her to-do list items. I know I'm relieved. The only items I have left are things I have to do at the dance itself.

The real question, of course, is whether those are going to be enough to distract me from everything that's going on—or *not* going on—around me.

It's so pathetic when the most successful ten minutes of my day consist of making a phone call to a guy named Helmut.

To: Val@realmail.sg.com

From: JPMorant@viennawest.edu

Subject: RE: Another thought . . .

Hi Val,

I'll take your word for it on the schnitzel. I really have no desire to try the stuff. I'm not that big a fan of chicken nuggets, so I can't imagine I'm missing out.

I called Brad, but I'm not sure how well the whole conversation went. I told him that if he's in a serious relationship, I should probably live elsewhere. Nearby, if I can afford a place close to his, but not in the same apartment.

He was pretty quiet and said he'd think it all over and call me tomorrow. He has an important accounting exam this week, and I know he's stressed out about that (I caught him in the middle of studying) so I'm not sure how much of the "call you tomorrow" was exam-related and how much was him being pissed off at me. Guess I'll find out soon enough. But no matter what he says, I'm glad I called and told him. Thanks for pushing me in the right direction.

And . . . you probably already heard it from her, but I talked to Natalie Monschroeder yesterday after school. Even asked her out. She said her parents are ticked off about her getting her tongue pierced and that they've been keeping her in the "maximum security block" (her exact words) but that they're offering her a few furloughs. So she's going to ask them if she can go out this weekend.

I assume she meant it and it wasn't an excuse. She did seem a lot less hostile than when I saw her at the Giant. But can you casually mention to her that if she's not interested, that's cool with me? She can just tell me no. (Though if she truly wants to go out, I'm willing to wait until she's out of prison. No pressure.)

Keep me up to date on the goings-on of life in the beautiful country of Schwerinborg, schnitzel and all,

John

To: JPMorant@viennawest.edu

From: Val@realmail.sg.com

Subject: Natalie

John,

Trust me when I tell you that Natalie has no problem telling people no. If she said she'll try to get out, it's 'cause she wants to. Congratulations! (You obviously passed inspection.)

Let me know what Brad says. I bet he understands.

Val, having something non-schnitzel-ish for dinner tonight

To: Val@realmail.sg.com

From: NatNatNat@viennawest.edu

Subject: That John Guy

Val,

So that John guy asked me out. We ran into each other after school in the parking lot. You're right—he's a senior here at Vienna West. And I have to say . . . now that I've really had a chance to look him over . . . he's even hotter than I thought when we were talking at the grocery store. He's got that brown hair flopping in his eyes, so it's not something you notice right away, but his face is really fantastic without being too Pretty Boy. (You know I hate the model-type look on guys. So not my thing.)

But here's the bad part: I don't know if I can go! Friday's out, since my parents are having a dinner party here at the house with Dad's dental partner and his wife. I'm expected to help Mom (in her words) "clean the house from top to bottom" and get the food ready. Then I have to sit there and be Wonderful Teenage Daughter for the evening. You know what I mean . . . where Mom and Dad brag to Dr. and Mrs. Petrie about how I'm doing sooo well in school and I have lots of friends and they're sooo proud of me. (I ask you, could there be anything more hideous than attending a dentist dinner party? And on a Friday night?!)

Then Saturday's the Oscar party at Jules's house, which I'm not even sure Mom and Dad will let me out of the prison block to attend. And do I really want to take John to that? We've never had the guys there before—not even Jeremy—so I hate to even ask Christie and Jules. I'd feel like I was violating a Sacred Awards Show Trust or something.

Yeah, the dirty words are flying through my brain fast and furious.

I'm thinking maybe the dinner party will end early and I can sneak out. Or maybe I can fake being sick and sneak out even earlier (I'm a lot better at faking sick than you are).

Help!

Nat

To: NatNatNat@viennawest.edu
From: Val@realmail.sg.com
Subject: RE: That John Guy

Nat,

Don't make me fly back there just to smack you. You cannot sneak out. CANNOT. Got it? Promise me?! DON'T DO IT!!!

John will wait. Really. I realize that you think he's an amazing guy. I also realize that you have been incarcerated a long time and are probably at your desperation point. (Don't get pissed at me . . . it's true and you know it.) But if you get caught sneaking out, the warden (a.k.a. Dr. Monschroeder, DDS) is gonna throw away the key to your prison cell this time and then you'll never see John.

My advice: Kiss up like mad at the dinner party. Be so nice to your parents they'll feel guilty for keeping you locked up for so long. *Then* figure something out.

Val (who could've faked sick but knew it'd be WRONG!)

To: Val@realmail.sg.com
From: NatNatNat@viennawest.edu
Subject: RE: That John Guy

Val,

FINE. I will not sneak out. I will be Daddy's Little Darling at dinner. I will even chew with my mouth closed and be careful when I speak so Dr. Petrie doesn't see my tongue stud and ask Dad how he could "let me do that" to myself. (Which would inevitably be followed by a dental debate on the possible damage tongue studs can do to one's teeth.)

In the meantime—you'd better tell Georg about David. It's been, what, like two weeks already? And I assume you've convinced Christie that Jeremy's not about to dump her, right?

Nat

To: NatNatNat@viennawest.edu
From: Val@realmail.sg.com
Subject: RE: That John Guy

Nat,

FINE. I will talk to Georg. Soon.

And I'm working on Christie. You know how she is.

Now stay in the house!

Your well-meaning friend,

Val

"And you're sure you talked to the DJ?"

Ulrike's totally frantic on the phone. It's T minus two hours to liftoff (that is, dance time), and despite the fact that Helmut isn't supposed to show up at the hotel for another hour, she's suddenly certain that he's not coming. (Probably because she didn't talk to him herself. For all her nicey-nice tendencies, she's a serious control freak.)

"Ulrike, I talked to him. He's probably not answering his phone because he's trying to do what I'm trying to do right now. Finish eating dinner so I have time to get ready."

For the last forty-eight hours, she's been in a state of constant motion. Selling tickets like crazy in the school halls. Putting up extra signs to encourage people to attend. Calling the hotel over and over to make sure they have the lighting right, the electrical hookups for the DJ correct, the room cleared properly. . . . Not to mention trying to finish the paper on the First Crusade she had due today in her history class.

It's exhausting just thinking about it all.

"I'm sure you're probably right. I just wish I knew for sure. And I forgot to have you ask if we need to provide him with drinks while he's working. I can't remember what we did last time. Do you think I need to assign someone to him as an assistant or something? To get him water or—"

"Ulrike"—I put my fork down, because there's no point in trying to get in another bite until I'm off the phone—"take a deep breath. Maybe five deep breaths. You only have an hour, so nothing you do now is really going to matter, right?"

"But—"

"You'll be a lot better if you find yourself something to eat so you don't pass out halfway through the evening. Then put on that outfit you bought on your trip to Italy and do your hair like a normal person would before a dance. Everything will be fine. I promise."

She takes an in-and-out breath loud enough for me to hear, then in a calmer voice says, "Okay, okay. You'll be there in an hour, right?"

"Same time as Helmut. Don't worry. Now let me finish eating so I'm not late."

I feel like I'm talking her down off the ledge the same way I have to talk Christie down after every little Jeremy-related panic moment she has. It's a total feeling of déjà vu.

It makes me miss Christie. At this very moment, Christie's probably trying to figure out what to wear to Jules's house for the Oscar party, even though her brain is totally fixated on Jeremy and why he's more obsessed with running than with her.

Ulrike finally hangs up, sounding reassured, though I'm sure the slightest thing is going to set her off again.

She's being *such* a party-obsessive girly-girl. I know it's the most sexist thing in the world to think—especially since I like to think of myself as being an unprejudiced type—but in her case, it's true.

"I didn't think you'd still be eating, Valerie. Are you going to be ready on time?" Dad asks, strolling in from his bedroom. He's all dressed up in beige pants and a stylish, well-fitted shirt, though I guess that's not dressed up for *him*, since he frequently wears tuxes when he works in the evening. But he's not exactly greeting the Canadian prime minister tonight over caviar and champagne. He's going to be watching three hundred teenagers dancing and partying.

"I'm wearing what I have on," I tell him. "And don't look at me that way. It's totally fine for a school dance." Especially when I don't have a date and I'm not even remotely trying to impress anyone. And it's not as if I haven't *tried* with my hair and makeup.

"Shouldn't you wear a dress?"

"Bite your tongue." Hell, no!

A pair of wrinkles mars the space between his brows. I have to admit, he looks pretty damned good for a school dance chaperone. Not like the usual dowdy parent or substitute gym teacher they rope in for these things. But that doesn't give him permission to nag me.

To change the subject, I gesture toward the garment bag he has looped over his forearm and raise a brow. He'd better not be changing into any outfit requiring a garment bag. What he has on is uptight enough.

"Oh, this is Prince Georg's tuxedo. I was just about to take it over to his family's apartments."

"Why do you have his tux? I thought all his good clothes were done by the cleaners downstairs." One of the perks of being a prince is having a dry cleaner right there in the palace to get his clothes looking good at a moment's notice. Of course, the downside is that Georg actually has to wear tuxes. Regularly. The dinner parties he has to attend with his parents are nothing like Natalie's with her dad's dentist pals.

Dad grabs his wallet from the kitchen counter and pockets it. "I offered to pick it up while I was getting my own suits this afternoon. He mentioned that he had an Academy Awards party to attend tonight and I suggested he wear Dolce and Gabbana. Don't you think he'll look good in it?"

Great. Now Dad's offering Georg style tips? I suppose it does come with his job, but it's just wrong for my own father to go making my boyfriend look good when he's going to be out without me. And where there'll probably be a bunch of gorgeous—and rich—chicks flirting with him.

"I guess. So, um, where's this party Georg's going to?" If Dad's dressing him for it, maybe he has some info.

"I'd have to look at my calendar; I can't remember offhand," Dad says, heading for the apartment door. "I'll be back in ten minutes. Whenever you're ready, we'll go pick up Anna and we can head over to the hotel. All right?"

"All righty!"

My enthusiasm is so obviously faked that Dad pauses with the door open to glare at me. "I think this evening will be fun, Valerie. Don't write it off as a waste of your time until you've given it a chance. Attitude is everything." He even has the gall to hold up Georg's tux and tell me that Georg's making the most of the night and that I should follow his example.

I plaster a smile on my face and wave him out the door.

The sooner he goes, the sooner we can get to the dance and the sooner this whole wretched night will be over.

I decide to do one last e-mail check while Dad's gone, just to see if the A-listers have sent me their last-minute Oscar picks (since half the fun of the evening is seeing who's best at predicting the winners). Nada from any of them. But there is one from a familiar address.

To: Val@realmail.sg.com

From: JPMorant@viennawest.edu

Subject: The great catching-up e-mail

Hey, Valerie,

Heard from Brad. He told me he's bummed that I don't want to live with him and his boyfriend, but he understands.

And better yet—he has an apartment for me! His boyfriend has a fantastic studio (he sent pics) about two blocks from where Brad's living now, and he hasn't sublet it yet, so it's mine for the asking. (And I suppose if Brad and the boyfriend ever break up, we can swap places back again.)

I'm still not sure about Natalie. She says she has "an idea" for tonight if she can, and I quote, "convince the jailer that a furlough is in order." So I suppose until I hear from her, I'm going to hang out at home. (She mentioned that you have a dance to go to tonight . . . have to say, I'd rather hang out at home waiting for a call—or not—from Natalie than go to a school dance. Not my thing at all. I bet you have a great time, though.)

More later,

John

"Ulrike really did a fantastic job. It's beautiful in here and insane at the same time," Maya tells me. And she's right. The doors have opened, the place is packed, and everyone is jamming to Helmut's (surprisingly modern and dance-y) tunes. But despite the kickin' music, there's a surreal air to it all. There actually are chandeliers in this place—and they're amazing. I keep catching myself staring at them, analyzing the way the light reflects off the hundreds of tiny crystals. Even the walls in this place are beautiful. They're a rich nutmeg color with gold-painted trim. There are heavy velvet curtains tied back with gold cord alongside each of the floor-to-ceiling windows. Other than the thumping music and the fact that everyone's dressed like they just walked out of the trendiest European shops, you'd think the place was taken straight from the pages of "Cinderella."

If Georg were here, I'd be having the time of my life.

As it is, I have to admit that things aren't that bad. I've been hanging out at the refreshment table (put in the proper place at the proper time by the guys, just as their to-do list instructed), and Ulrike has finally relaxed now that everything's in full swing. Maya's been dancing like crazy, even to classic Snoop Dogg. (I can't believe they have old Snoop Dogg in Schwerinborg, but they do . . . and everyone knows the words just as well as they do to the bizarro German pop songs I couldn't begin to sing.)

I hand Maya an extra-large glass of the free punch Ulrike convinced the hotel to provide. As she slugs it down, I say, "You ought to tell Ulrike. I think she's just now figuring out that this is all going to be okay."

Maya laughs. "Remember how I said I wouldn't volunteer because I thought I'd mess up? Total lie. I've seen Ulrike put these dances together before. I know how she gets. I volunteered last time and swore I'd come up with an excuse if she asked again. Did she make you call the hotel a million times asking the same questions?"

I shake my head. "Nope. DJ."

"Well, I'll go find her and tell her it's all marvelous. You get out and dance, okay? I know Prince Georg couldn't make it, but . . ." She looks around, like she's expecting Steffi to pop up. "Well, if he'd come, I bet he'd have danced with you. I think he kind of likes you, even if he acts like he doesn't."

I try not to give myself away by smiling too big. "Thanks for the vote of confidence."

"Just don't tell Steffi I said so. You haven't seen her, have you?"

When I shake my head, Maya says, "Wonder where she is tonight? Guess we'll hear on Monday if she doesn't show."

She flips her empty punch cup into the trash bin, then waves a good-bye as she sways back onto the dance floor. It's a mass of people out there, but she fits right in.

I wish I could. Maybe I could forget about Georg for a while. And about Steffi's mysterious absence. Not that I want her here, but it's odd. It's making me wonder if she figured out where Georg would be and finagled an invite somehow.

I grab a cup of punch and sling it back. I've gotta stop my imagination from taking over my good sense.

"I think we're going to manage without any major glitches," Ulrike says, walking up behind me. "Do you think?"

She still sounds nervous. Unbelievable. "Ulrike, you *think*? Look around you. Everyone's having a blast!" Well, everyone except me. I'm just counting off the minutes.

"I know, I know. I get a little uptight about having things turn out okay. But if I didn't, who would?" She puts an arm around my shoulders—easy for her to do, since she's so much taller than I am—and gives me a quickie hug. "Thanks for tolerating me the last couple days. I know I can be a pain, but I couldn't have pulled this off without you. Helmut's really good, isn't he?"

I agree that Helmut's keeping the place on fire. I look over to where he's set up near the front of the ballroom. I expected someone named Helmut to be hairy and very hippie-ish, I guess. But he's actually pretty young—maybe college-age or a little older—and decent-looking, too.

I take a step to the side so I can get a better look at him and I realize he's talking to none other than Fräulein Predator.

Geez. She's probably telling him his music has inappropriate lyrics or something.

"You know Fräulein Putzkammer, right?" Ulrike says, following my gaze over to the DJ and Anna. "She's the chaperone your dad suggested."

"Yeah, I do," I say, trying to keep from spitting as I talk. Thinking about The Fräulein makes me want to do that, though I know it shouldn't.

"She was so excited when she found out Helmut was going to be the DJ," Ulrike says. "Can you believe they already knew each other? How's that for a coincidence?"

"Wild," I say, totally not caring. Besides, doesn't it figure that someone named Putzkammer would hang out with a guy named Helmut?

"By the way," I ask her, "you know how last names have meanings? Like someone told me last week that Schmidt in German is the same as Smith in English."

"Sure."

"What in the world does *Putzkammer* mean?"

One side of her mouth hooks up in a grin. "*Putz* has a lot of meanings, but in this case, I would guess it's closest to the English word 'clean' or 'fine.' *Kammer* is, literally, 'chamber.'"

"Like 'house cleaner'?" Not predator? Or ho?

"Not really." She frowns for a sec, then says, "*Putzkammer* is a lot more formal than 'house cleaner.' More like, um . . . what's the English word? Oh . . . 'chamberlain'! That's it. Same idea, though."

Leave it to The Fräulein to actually have a name that's hoity-toity in German. "Thanks."

She smiles. "You'll start getting better at German. It's great you're working so hard at it."

I mumble something nonsensical, 'cause I'm gonna let her go right on thinking that.

After a few minutes, I urge Ulrike to take a break and go dance, assuring her that I can handle giving out cups of punch by myself and that I won't allow anyone to sneak over with a bottle of liquor and pour it in the bowl. But despite my promise, I have a hard time keeping my undivided attention on the punch bowl. I can't stop sneaking peeks at Anna and the DJ. How they're talking over the music is beyond me, but they seem to be laughing it up, like hanging out together at a high school dance is the coolest thing in the world.

Guess it'll keep her from doing something to embarrass me. Like asking Dad to dance.

I force myself to grab a stool from the wall so I can sit facing away from them. I stare out at the mass of bodies on the dance floor, watching everyone shake their hips and wave their hands in the air as they sing along with the music.

I know I look pathetic. It's like I'm the ultimate wallflower, hanging out dateless at a girls-ask-guys dance, handing out cups of Schwerinborg's knock-off version of Kool-Aid. And what's worse, even though everyone's required to speak English when we're at school (that's the whole point of

English immersion, I suppose), there's no such restriction here. So most of the conversations are in German, the one language God never intended for me to speak.

I can't help but feel distinctly apart from it all.

If my life were a movie, this would be the point when the whole dance floor would go silent and everyone would turn toward the doors. The crowd would part and I'd see Georg standing there in the open doorway, scanning the crowd for someone. Everyone would wonder who, but then his gaze would fall on me.

And he'd smile. A cheesy, movie-moment type of smile.

Everyone would ooh and aah as he strode through the room (and he really would stride, what with his soccer muscles and all), and he'd sweep me onto the dance floor and the whole world would know that he loves me.

But no. Instead, I get Dad. Sneaking up behind me.

"Are you having fun, honey?"

"I dunno." I gesture toward the DJ's setup. "She gonna request Bowie?"

He must've been expecting a cynical comment out of me, 'cause he grabs an empty stool, pulls it up beside mine, and says, "Oh, don't be that way."

"What way?"

"Fifteen and female and pouty."

"Well, I am fifteen and I am female, and there's nothing

wrong with that. And I won't even address the pouting."

I'm *so* not pouting. I *feel* like pouting, but I think I'm actually doing a good job of appearing to be a perky little volunteer here, handing out punch and selling the occasional bottle of water.

"It's not so bad having me here as a chaperone, is it?"

I slide a sideways look at him. I can't help but crack up, because he looks so stiff and formal compared to everyone here, even if he is more laid back than most adults. "No, Dad, you're fine. Just don't try to dance, okay?"

"Not to worry. Not my kind of music."

So long as The Fräulein doesn't finagle a special request. Although—as both of us glance over at Anna—I find myself wondering if Dad and Anna have ever danced together. If he has visions of himself sweeping her off her feet and onto the dance floor, kind of the way I was fantasizing about Georg.

Though it's possible he's simply thinking about sweeping her away from Helmut.

"She seems like she's having a good time, doesn't she?" Dad says, sounding pleased.

"Um, yeah."

"The DJ's her cousin's boyfriend. They've known each other for years. I think she's getting caught up on family gossip."

So much for sweeping her away from a rival.

"I guess things are going pretty well with you two, if she agreed to come to the dance as a chaperone," I venture. I have to admit, ever since Ulrike told me about Dad volunteering to come—and bringing The Fräulein—I've wondered how fast things are going between them.

"They're still casual," he says, knowing where my thoughts must be going. "We're not even exclusive. But if it gets more serious, I'll let you know."

We're not even exclusive? I turn to face him. "You know I don't mean to be a butthead about it. If you want to go out with her—exclusive or not—I'll try to be happy for you. I'll even call her Anna if she really wants me to."

As long as I don't have to think about Dad and Anna having kids together, I think I can push the pause button on my Opposition to The Fräulein mentality.

Dad fakes like he's going to knock me off the stool. "I didn't raise you to use words like 'butthead.'"

I'm about to say, *Like you could stop me*, but he continues, "You haven't been a butthead, though. You've had a lot happen to you this year. I could easily see how hearing that I'm dating someone could be the last straw for you."

"Really?"

"Really. But you have to realize that it's been a hard year for me, too."

We drop the conversation as a group of freshmen come up and grab cups of punch. A few of them produce euros for bottled water, which I pull out of a cooler stashed under the table—a little extra fund-raiser to help the student council coffers.

When they're gone, I climb back onto my stool. The music switches to a slow song, but the dance floor stays packed. Even the people who came alone seem to pair up.

"If you want to dance with Anna, Dad, go ahead." It's not like I can be any more humiliated than I am right now. Dateless. Sitting with my own father during a slow song.

If Steffi were here, she'd be thinking of all kinds of things to say to me.

"No, I think she's busy catching up with Helmut. She's been so swamped at work lately—and spending her free time with me—that I think she feels out of touch with her family. Family's important."

I can tell he's working up to a mushy father-daughter moment, and sure enough, that's what comes next. "You know, Valerie, I meant it when I told you in Scheffau that you're the most important person in the world to me."

"I know."

"And the fact that I'm seeing Anna won't change that. It's been good for me to go out with her." His voice gets lower, so quiet I can barely hear him over the music. "It's good for me to know that I can be appreciated for who I am. To know that just because your mother walked out on me, my romantic life isn't over. And I'll admit," he lets out a chuckle, "it's also good for my ego."

"I bet. Isn't she, like, way younger than you?"

"I haven't exactly asked to see her driver's license. It wouldn't be proper, you know. . . ." He shifts on the stool, then shakes his head. "But I'd guess I have at least five years on her. Probably more."

"Sorry, Dad. I couldn't resist."

He smiles at me, and I know we're cool.

"I'm sure it's a nice ego boost, having Georg in your life."

I don't say anything. It's not like he's in my life at this particular moment. I mean, sitting here without him is, like, the opposite of an ego boost, whatever that is. Ego dive? Ego plummet? Ego crash? I think it's gotta be ego crash.

"It's a challenge, I realize. He has to be very careful about appearances. I happen to know he asked his father if he could come tonight—if there was some way he could be out in public with you."

No way! "How do you know?"

"Because Prince Manfred and I discussed it."

My love life? Dad discussed my love life with my boyfriend's father, who also happens to be *the ruler of this country*?

Whoa.

8

I HAVE TO STAND UP TO HAND OUT ANOTHER CUP OF punch, but I get back to Dad as fast as possible. "You discussed it?"

"We know how hard it is for you and Georg. But after the tabloid story . . . well, it's just too soon. Georg's going to be the leader of this country someday, and that means that—despite the fact that three quarters of the world's population can't find Schwerinborg on a map—he's under intense scrutiny. He's not just going to be a ceremonial head of state. He'll be the actual head of state. But Prince Manfred and I don't want that scrutiny to ruin your relationship."

Manny has a point. It almost did tank our relationship when that article came out.

"I know you hate when I use the word 'sucks,' Dad, but I have to say, as much as I know that Prince Manfred's right, it sucks."

He bites his lip, like he wants to tell me I'm not funny, but he can't quite bring himself to do it. Especially after my earlier "butthead" comment.

"I know it does, Val. But that doesn't mean the two of you have to hide forever."

"No problem. We can always do the Oscar thing another night. Maybe even next weekend?"

I swear as I look at Dad that he's trying to hide a smile at my sarcasm. "Well," he says, "Prince Manfred and I agreed that we want the two of you to be able to see each other—either in the palace or on vacations, where you'll be away from the press—as often as is feasible, so long as you two behave yourselves and keep your grades up."

I roll my eyes. "Sure. Like I'm going to let my grades take a nosedive." I'm a total straight-A geek. I don't need my parents to nag me about my grades and Dad knows it.

I'm the kind of wacky person who flips out over a B the way Ulrike flips out over dance details.

As the slow song winds down and Helmut manages to weave in the first beats of a hip hop tune, a few people start to leave the dance floor and wander toward the refreshment table.

"You're on," Dad says. He glances toward Anna. I follow his gaze across to the DJ's area, and I see her look over at us and smile.

"I think I'll go do the chaperone thing. Make sure no one's getting into trouble."

"Yeah, you do that," I tease. It's like I can feel the sap in the air, between his giddy-lovey mood for Anna and his sense that he's sufficiently parented me for the night.

Gag.

I intentionally don't look in Dad and Anna's direction. But as I wave to Maya, who's still groovin' on the floor (man, can that girl move), I realize that Steffi is still nowhere to be seen.

Not. Good.

I can't imagine her missing out if she thought this was the cool place to be tonight, which—contrary to early indications on ticket sales—it obviously is. But as I hand out bottles of water and try to calculate change, I tell myself that I need to believe in Georg. To forget all about Steffi. Even if she's at the same party where he is—probably by sneaking her way in—it's not like anything's going to happen.

Not like it did with David.

I can't help it. The thought pops into my mind, probably because of the near-constant reminders I'm getting from Jules, Natalie, and Christie that I need to come clean.

At that moment, I realize that they're right. I can't wait any longer. I *have* to tell Georg about what happened over break in Virginia. Otherwise, I'm always going to worry that something could happen to our relationship.

And not because of Steffi. Because of me.

Because I know how I'd feel if I suspected Georg was hiding something from me . . . even if it were something like the (way short) time I spent with David. Time that didn't mean a thing. I'm going nuts just thinking about what he's doing tonight, and it's probably just some dumb thing for his parents. No different for him than Nat's parents' dinner party is for her.

Maybe, if I'm lucky, Georg will be home from his party when I get back to the palace.

If he is—and if I can convince him to come over—I'll tell him tonight. He might not take it well, and I know there'll be a lot of groveling on my part, but as much as it's going to rot, at least I'll know I've been honest with him.

The palace looks completely normal as we drive up. In other words, all the lights in the public areas are on, but the section that houses Prince Manfred and Princess Claudia's private apartments is pretty dark. Only one light is on that I can see.

I don't know what I was expecting, since it's nearly

midnight. Guess I was so fixated on my monumental decision to tell Georg about David that I blanked on the fact that he might not be available for a while.

"Doesn't look like they're home yet," Dad says as he turns the car into the courtyard and shows his employee ID to the bored-looking guy at the gate, who waves us through.

"Did Georg's parents go to the Oscar party, too?" I ask. "You never did tell me where it is."

Anna glances at Dad, then turns to look over her shoulder at me. "Prince Manfred and Princess Claudia had to go to Italy tonight. They're flying home in the morning.

"So . . . the same thing Georg went to?" He didn't mention Italy. Or being gone overnight.

"No. They're at an opera premiere," Dad says as he pulls into a covered area on the side of the palace close to where we live (the older, unrenovated, not-so-glamorous area) and cuts the engine. "Georg is here in Schwerinborg. I promised his parents I'd check in on him when we returned from the hotel."

"Um, wouldn't he have to sign in with security when he gets back? His parents would hear pretty fast if he didn't come home when he's supposed to." That's his usual routine, and he once told me that if he doesn't follow the proper safety measures, his parents give him a serious lecture (though I imagine it's done in a very restrained, royal-ish way).

"Of course," Dad replies. "But I think they like having a little extra assurance."

We get out of the car and start walking toward the palace. As we crunch across the gravel courtyard, heading for the door closest to our apartments, Dad reaches out and takes Anna's hand like it's an everyday thing.

I'm not sure I like it, but I'm finding I don't *dis*like it as much as when we were on the ski trip.

I must be mellowing. I mean, it's hitting me that I'm starting to think of her as Anna instead of The Fräulein—and not cursing myself out when it happens.

"Why don't you go check on him for me?" Dad asks, looking over his shoulder at me. "I'll see Anna to her car."

Since Anna lives in downtown Freital, I guess she must've left her car here after work. Probably so she'd have an excuse to ride with me and Dad to the dance, but whatever. I guess I should be happy that at least someone's relationship is working.

"I can take a hint," I say under my breath. Then louder, I say, "Sure. I doubt he's home yet, though."

"If he's not there, I'll meet you at our place. He'll know to call me when he gets in."

When I get to the doors in the fancy wing—where

Georg and his parents live—I go through the metal detector and fill out the guest form like I always do, though I have to wonder if Georg's around. And whether I'll be able to get the words out about David.

"How long will you be, Miss Winslow?" the guard asks.

"Um, I'm not sure. Is Prince Georg home?"

"Yes." He gives me an odd look and I realize he'd probably have sent me back home without the whole metal-detector inconvenience if Georg weren't around. Even though I'm here all the time, it's not like the security guys would let me wander around the family's private wing alone.

"Maybe an hour, then?" Could be five minutes, though—about the length of time it takes for me to spit out the David story and Georg to throw me out.

I suppose if Georg does tell me to take a hike (though I know he's too polite to use those exact words, my gut is telling me the sentiment could very well be there) I can always turn on the Oscars and e-mail the girls in Virginia with my comments on which actress has the ugliest gown.

Nothing beats an ugly feather dress—which the entertainment reporters are bound to note costs the equivalent of a year's college tuition—for getting guy frustration out of my system.

Of course, the thought of bad clothes reminds me that I

haven't looked in a mirror all night—not since before leaving for the dance. I looked decent when I left home, but Georg probably spent the evening around glamorous model types, so a checkup is definitely in order.

As I walk down the corridor, I rifle through my purse, manage to find my compact—which is a little dusty from disuse—and groan when I look in the tiny mirror. Sure enough, there are the telltale mascara marks from spending too long in a hot room. Ego crash number two on the night.

I run a finger under my eyes and fluff some powder on my face. Not great, but hopefully better than the demon-from-the-dark look I'd been sporting.

Georg opens the door on the first knock.

"Hey," he says. He's grinning ear to ear. And he's still in his tux. Maybe he just got home?

"Hey, yourself." Man, does he look good. Edible good. Like he could attend the real Oscars and not be dissed by the style gurus. And I tell him so.

"Thanks," he says. "Come on in. The preshow is just beginning."

"You're watching?"

He opens the door wider, pulling me inside. We walk through the formal rooms toward the more casual family room, where he and his parents hang out and watch the news in the evenings. The smell of popcorn hits me, and I take a deep breath. Then I hear voices and the words *Harry Winston necklace*. "You really are watching TV! And it's in English!"

As he opens the door and flips on the light, I swear, my heart almost stops.

The place is full of flowers. And I mean *full*. Like, every available space in the TV room has them. The coffee table is covered, and so is the side table near the sofa. Even the top of the television is a mass of roses and these gigantic, sweetly perfumed white lilies that Dad says are Princess Claudia's favorite. There are two champagne glasses and a bottle of non-alcoholic champagne sitting on the floor, right in front of the coffee table and the big pile of pillows where Georg sometimes crashes to do his homework.

And of course there's a huge bowl of fresh popcorn.

He sweeps a hand out to encompass the room, as if playing the role of maître d' at a five-star restaurant. "Valerie Winslow, welcome to your first official Schwerinborg Oscar party."

I can't even speak. I cover my mouth with my hands for a moment, trying to absorb it all.

"You like?"

Do I like? Is he freaking kidding me? This is infinitely better than the fantasy I had at the dance. "You planned all this?"

"There are some advantages to being a prince. I might not be able to go to public events with my girlfriend right now, but damned if I couldn't get dibs"—he pauses on the word "dibs"—"on the leftover flowers from last night's economic summit banquet to make up for it. To make it up to you. Took me a while to get them set up, but it was fun."

It's just now hitting the dim recesses of my brain. *This* was his Oscar party? "So you never went out tonight?"

"Nope."

"And my dad must've known—"

"Yep."

How could I have been such an idiot?

I glance back toward the formal part of his family's apartments. "And your parents are—"

"In Italy. At an opera. They asked me to go last week, right after we got back from the ski trip. When I told them about the dance and how disappointed you were when I said I couldn't come—and that it was your Oscar night—they agreed to let me skip the opera and take over the TV room. Of course, I didn't know you'd have to be there so late, but when Ulrike's father was at the palace last week, I asked your dad if he'd volunteer to chaperone so he could make sure you got home before the Oscars. And so he could make sure you came over here to see me instead of just going to sleep."

Okay—having my boyfriend enlist my own father's help in surprising me is strange. But I'm not going to gripe. Especially when he's wearing that tux.

"Come on," he says, leaning over to grab a glass. "Have some fake champagne and some popcorn."

"But of course!"

We sit on the floor and I watch him pour, even though I feel dorky being so casual when he's so dressed up. Who am I kidding? It *all* feels dorky. But I love it.

He takes the remote and clicks up the sound so I can hear the commentary as actresses walk up the red carpet, stopping to strike poses for cameras or to sign autographs for fans.

We toast the Oscars, then settle back against the pillows. Georg sits so that I can snuggle into his shoulder. We watch the screen for a few minutes as I try to savor the moment.

When the first commercial hits, I ask, "So did Dad tell you how late I could stay?"

"I think as long as the show's on," Georg says.

"I think that's, like, five a.m." A long time to keep my head happily cradled against Georg's shoulder, breathing in the wonderful way he smells, feeling his arm pulling me close to him. "Dad's being awfully trusting."

"I think he's going to be checking in. He told me he'd see Anna home first, but he made it pretty clear that we weren't supposed to be doing anything to corrupt each other up here, or, I believe his exact words were, 'I'll find out when I come to check in on you two, and you won't see my daughter again because this time I'll send her back to the States for good.'"

I pop a piece of popcorn—which is downright heavenly—and grin. Leave it to Dad to stand up for my honor.

I twist my neck so I can look up at Georg. I'm surprised to see a serious look on his face. "What?"

"You wouldn't rather be there, would you? Back in the States?"

I know he's thinking back to our conversation in the hallway at the guesthouse. I shake my head. "I miss my friends, but this is where I belong. Dad, too. I don't know how serious he is about Anna, but it seems to be going okay. So I guess that's even more incentive to stay."

And since I can't help but tease him, I tickle his stomach and say, "Plus, you provide me with popcorn. My friend Jules only has Ho Hos, and even then, she doesn't share."

He grabs my hand to stop the tickling, then pulls my fingers up to his mouth for a kiss.

Omigosh. Somebody cue the music, because I'm about to get emotional and girly. To keep myself from getting too sappy, I say, "You don't mind that I'm not dressed for the occasion, do you?" He did spring it on me.

"Nah. The tux was actually your dad's idea. I would've had to wear it to the opera, so I figured why not wear it for the Oscars? And I had no idea how you and your friends dressed for your Oscar parties."

"Not in formal wear." I pull at his lapel. "But this is still cool, even if it's my dad's idea of what a girl wants. Guess it worked."

"Guess so." He grabs a handful of popcorn, then glances sideways at me. "You know, I'm glad things with your dad and Anna are going okay. I think it's good that he's getting out and seeing someone."

I nod. "Yeah, that's what I'm telling myself. He told me tonight that they're not exclusive—that was his phrase—so I think he's trying to take it slow."

"Probably smart." He plays with my hair as he speaks, which makes me go gooey on the inside. "Even for adults, I think it's all about finding what you want."

Finding what you want. Exactly the phrase my mother used with me when I told her how guilty I felt for seeing David. She said I needed to know what I didn't want so I'd be better at finding what I did want.

"So," I say, grabbing my own handful of popcorn while he starts to munch on his. "You think it'd be cool if he ends up deciding to date around?"

He leaves the question unanswered as we both stare at

the screen—last year's Best Actress winner is on the red carpet, and she's wearing a dress that's totally cut to *there*. The kind you know will be flashed on the news during the recaps of who was wearing what.

"Wow," Georg says. "That's a ten."

"No kidding." "Wow" is an understatement. "I wonder how she's keeping her boobs in that thing. Gotta be tape."

Georg thinks I'm kidding, but I'm not. And it takes him a sec to figure that out. Once he does, he makes a very unroyal yakking noise and says, "There are some things guys are never meant to know."

He takes a long drink of his pseudo-champagne as the actress glides along the carpet, waving to the stands full of fans who showed up at four in the morning so they could stake out prime star-viewing territory. She turns to the side and I absolutely lose it, because I can tell Georg's staring at the cut of her dress, trying to figure out where she's got the tape.

"Cut it out," he says when he catches me watching him. "Because of you, now every time I go to any of my parents' formal events, I'm going to wonder what these women have holding up their dresses. And I really don't want to be having those kind of thoughts about them."

"I don't think they're going to be dressed quite like she is." Though I would if I had a bodacious bod like that and I regularly got invited to ritzy events like the Oscars, where nobody even blinks if you wear dresses so sexy they require tape.

As it is, it's going to be hard enough for me to find a dress I can wear to the prom when I'm a senior. Not without a ton of help from Dad *and* a really good push-up bra to hold up whatever creation he finds at the store. Tape alone wouldn't cut it for me. There's nothing to tape.

"Probably not," Georg concedes. "Most of the people who come to my parents' parties are older. I'm always relieved when they bring their kids. Gives me someone to talk to and hang out with."

And he never went out with any of them?

"Never met one I wanted to get serious with, though."

The guy is a freaking mind reader. "So does this mean you're not the type to, um, date around? See more than one person at once?"

"Depends on the situation." He plays with my hair again, which is kinda distracting. "If you're asking about your Dad, if he and Anna aren't all that serious about each other, then it's probably a healthy thing if they go out with other people."

The actress has stopped to talk to one of the entertainment reporters, but neither of us is listening anymore. I feel Georg press a kiss to the top of my head before he says,

"But if you're asking about us, Val . . . I have no desire to see anyone else right now. I'm happy like this. I meant it when I told you that I love you."

Hoo-boy. "I meant it too. I hope you know that."

I feel my fingers flinch in his. Damn. He felt it too, because he sits up so my head is no longer against his shoulder, then turns so his whole body is facing me. "What?"

Now or never. I try to picture Jules lacing up her combat boots, telling me to spit it out.

"Well," I say, trying to fight back the sick feeling in my stomach, "there's something I've wanted to tell you since I got back from Virginia, but I was never sure how. Or how you'd take it."

"You went out with someone else while you were home." He says it as a statement of fact, not even a question. Like he knew this was coming once I started asking him what he thought about Dad and Anna. I just nod.

"Was it serious?"

"No. Not at all." He doesn't look the least bit angry, so I take that as a good sign and barrel on, "It was this guy I've known since kindergarten. I had a huge crush on him, but he never even looked at me. When I went home for break, Christie set us up on a blind date without my knowledge. It was one of those things where I didn't feel like I could say no."

"So why do you seem so upset about it?"

Breathe in. Breathe out. "To be honest, at the time, I wasn't sure I wanted to say no." I can barely get the words out. I hate saying them, but I feel like I'd be hiding something important *not* saying them.

Georg obviously thinks so, too, because he looks troubled. "Was it . . ." He fiddles with a piece of popcorn, then tosses it back in the bowl, something Dad wouldn't approve of. "Was it because I'd told you I wanted to cool it?"

"That was part of it. And I'll admit, I *did* have a thing for him for, like, forever. So I was curious."

He's just quiet. The actress with the eye-popping gown is off the screen, and they've cut to a commercial—something in German for an orange drink that looks positively gross—and the weird music only seems to emphasize the awkward silence between us.

I do *not* want my relationship to go into a tailspin during an orange drink commercial. It just seems wrong.

"Georg, I know you're probably mad. But you should know it turned out great—"

"Great?"

"Yes. Great. Because I found out what I want." I'm as serious as I can be, trying to ignore the goofy cartoon, which is now showing exploding oranges.

I reach over and put my hand on top of his. "Even if you

had meant that you really wanted to cool it—as in break up with me—I figured out that what I really wanted all along was you."

He looks down to where my pale hand is resting on top of his. "So why didn't you think you could tell me?"

"'Cause I know how I would've felt if you told me you'd gone out with Steffi while I was gone." I gesture toward the screen. I can't help but laugh now, because the commercial is ridiculous. "I'd probably do like those nasty oranges. Kerblooey."

I should shut up. I mean, sheesh. Sometimes I say things that are just stupid. They leap out of my mouth before my brain can grab them back.

And worse—I laugh while I say them.

"I sincerely hope this guy wasn't as bad as Steffi."

I shake my head. "Nah. But he's not you."

"Then that's all I need to know."

"Seriously?" He's not going to grill me about whether or not I kissed David? Or whether I'm e-mailing him or if I'm dying to go back to Virginia to be with him? Because those are the questions most guys would ask.

Then again, Georg is not most guys.

"Seriously." His fingers tighten around mine. "So what made you think about Steffi, of all people?"

"Well, you know how she is."

"She wasn't at the dance bothering you tonight, was she? Making all her little comments?"

I love that he sees her for what she is. It boggles my mind that no one else catches on to her slick little compliments that really aren't.

Though, given Maya's comments at the dance, I'm beginning to wonder if she at least is starting to see the light.

"Nah. Steffi didn't make it to the dance for whatever reason. You know . . ." I make a face that's less than polite. "I actually thought she might be trying to find you."

"Hmmm. She might've been."

There's something about the way he says it that makes me do a double take.

"I did mention that I had an Oscar party, remember?" His smile is positively wicked. "When we were all at the lunch table."

"Oh, I remember." Steffi even looked at me and said it wasn't meant to be with me and Georg.

Ha. She can bite me.

"Well, yesterday I also made certain to mention an event I have to attend at the Freital Hilton. Didn't say *when* . . ."

I totally lose it. Totally. I can't believe he would even *think* to do that. "You're as evil as Steffi!"

"It was for a good cause. And maybe when she spends

an evening hunting me down for nothing, she'll realize how insane she's being."

Another celeb is on the red carpet, and I hear the entertainment reporter gushing about a green dress, but I can't look at the screen. I don't want to. I only want to look at Georg and think about how lucky I am.

How could I have stressed out over telling him about David? Especially when the girls were bugging me about it, and they've never steered me wrong.

I know—I didn't want to lose him—but I should have known him well enough to know how he'd take it. A-list opinion or not.

"I never told a girl I loved her before." Georg's voice is gentle compared to the gushing reporters on the television.

"Then I'd better not drink, 'cause I never told a girl I loved her before, either."

I. Must. Stop. Kidding. Around. When. I. Am. Nervous.

Must, must, must.

He just looks confused, so I explain, "Sorry. I Never. It's a drinking game Jules said she heard about once. Someone says, 'I never,' and then follows it up with a crazy statement. Something like, 'I never walked out of my house naked.' Everyone who can say truthfully 'I never' to the same statement says it, but everyone else has to take a drink." I roll my eyes. "It was just a bad joke."

What is it with me and my mouth?

He seems pretty fixated on the joke, though. "So everyone who actually has walked out of their house naked would end up drinking?"

"Apparently that's the game."

"I never played I Never."

"Me either, and I have no desire to play. Ever." Good thing, too. I got in enough trouble when people simply *thought* I was smoking. If anyone gets the impression I'm teaching Georg drinking games . . . geez, I am so dead.

He gets a funny look on his face, but before I can ask him what he's thinking—I know, I know, girls should never ask guys the what-are-you-thinking question, but I'm dying to know—he scoots a few inches closer to me, and either the light from the TV is reflecting in his eyes, or they're actually shining. "I bet I can change your mind. Say we play for kisses instead?"

Oooh, now that's got my interest. "All right. I never told a guy I loved him before. But I do love you."

He starts to lean in to kiss me, but stops with his mouth about an inch from mine. "Wait a minute," he says. "Do we kiss if it's an 'I never' or kiss if it's something we have done?"

"Does it matter?"

He doesn't answer. He just gives me what probably rates as the best kiss of my life. The kind that lets me know exactly what he's thinking.

To: Val@realmail.sg.com

From: CoolJule@viennawest.edu

Subject: THE PARTY!

Hey Val,

OMG. You missed a KILLER Oscar party at my house last night.

First, you know it's always a girl thing. Just the four of us. Well, not half an hour into the preshow, when Angelina Jolie's strutting along the red carpet showing off her numerous assets, Jeremy shows up. He has flowers in hand (no, really), and he tells Christie how sorry he is for bailing on her the last few weeks while he's been marathon training. She, of course, loves the whole sappy flowers-with-apology routine, so she invites him to stay. And they are beyond mushy now, lemme tell you. It's blinding to see it.

Jeremy comes up for air (from kissing Christie) long enough to ask if he can call David Anderson. Just 'cause we're all having so much fun watching the Oscars and it's Saturday night and all. So about fifteen minutes after Jeremy gets there, David shows up.

Then Natalie—being her late self—finally arrives. Her parents let her come, since she swore to them she wouldn't go anywhere else except straight to my house and back, yadda yadda yadda. Apparently, they had some dinner party with Dr. and Mrs. Petrie last night and Natalie actually behaved herself just so she could come. (I know, I know, I found it very hard to believe.)

Well—guess what? There was another reason she was on her best behavior for her parents.

SHE BROUGHT JOHN!!!

No warning. She didn't ask me beforehand or even give me a hint she might bring a guest. She just brought him. (Not that this was a problem . . . it was just a shock.)

And you know what? John's actually pretty cool. Very much a chilled-out type and not someone who'll take Nat's snarky comments seriously (which is key).

That's not even the best part of the night.

Sit down. This is huge.

Okay . . . you sitting?

After I get my fill of tuxedos and gowns, I go to the kitchen for more Diet Coke. I turn around to walk back to the family room and realize that David has followed me to the kitchen.

Get this: He was trying to get me alone because he wanted to know if maybe we could go out sometime.

I actually laughed in his face. I didn't mean to, I swear.

He's a nice enough guy and all But CAN YOU IMAGINE? After all these years of him going for the big-boob cheerleader types. Then him finally going after you (after waking up to the fact that you are COOL). Now he comes clawing at my door.

Needless to say, once I managed to stop laughing, I told him no.

He was really cool about it, though. (Surprise, surprise.) In fact, we hung out in the kitchen for a while, making fun of the two lovebird couples In the family room. (And man, were they lovey-dovey. I swear, I've never seen Christie or Nat so happy. Go figure.)

I'm sure you'll get the scoop from Christie and Nat once they wake up and can get on e-mail, but since they're going to be all gushy when they write and will probably go on and on with their whole I-had-this-GUY-thing-happen-to-me crap, I figured you ought to hear my totally unbiased perspective on it all. And I figured you'd want to know that all is right with the world.

Love,

Jules, single girl extraordinaire and proud of it

PS—So tell me about your night with Georg. Yeah, we knew all about it. How else do you think a total Oscar virgin like him would know how to find a network over there carrying the preshow in English? Or how you can't watch without popcorn? Or who might've tipped him off on how to ditch that Steffi chick you whined to us about when you were home for vacation?

PPS—Blame your dad. He gave Christie's e-mail address to Georg so he could get some coaching from those of us who love you best.

To: CoolJule@viennawest.edu
From: Val@realmail.sg.com
Subject: RE: THE PARTY!

Dear Coolest Jules,

Thanks for the inside scoop on the Oscar party. Of course you know I trust your version of events as the One True Story. (Ha. I'm SO gonna e-mail Christie . . .)

I'm very happy for Christie and for Nat. You're gonna love this, though: I literally fell out of my chair laughing reading about David, so your warning to sit down before I read about it didn't do much good. I was leaning back in the chair, tears running down my face, and somehow my chair fell over backward. I stuck out an arm to save myself, but still ended up whacking my head on the wall.

Even worse, Dad came running into my room to see what

happened and I was just sprawled on the floor, laughing so hard I thought I might actually throw up. Now he thinks I'm insane because I'm laughing-slash-crying while alone in my room.

Anyway—I'm about to head out with Dad to run errands. He's taking me to the Schwerinborg Walmart. No kidding . . . they have Walmart here. It's like they're going for world domination. (Even worse than McDonald's, which I will confess I am having total cravings for.) But as soon as I get home, I'll send a longer e-mail and tell you everything about my completely romantic, perfect night. (Though since apparently you guys were planning this with Georg ahead of time, you know a lot of it already. This is why you, Nat, and Christie are my absolute A-list and I will love you forever.)

In the meantime, I'll sum it up this way: I totally agree with you. I needed to tell Georg about David, so I did. And now all is right with the world. Well, other than the large purple lump that's bound to show up on my noggin, but since I have Georg to kiss it and make it all better, it's not a major concern. More info later, post-Walmart.

TTYS,

Val, not a single girl extraordinaire . . . but very much happy with that

About the Author

Niki Burnham is the RITA Award–winning author of several novels for teens, including *Sticky Fingers*, *Goddess Games*, and *Scary Beautiful*. She attended high school in Germany, but unlike her character Valerie Winslow, Niki never lived in a palace or met a prince.

After high school Niki received her BA from Colorado State University and both a law degree and a master's degree in political science from the University of Michigan. She currently lives in Boston, Massachusetts. You can visit her website, post to her message boards, or sign up for her e-newsletter at www.nikiburnham.com.

More to love! Check out:

A Funny Thing About Love

Erin Downing

Super Freak

Olivia Phillips's first-ever celebrity sighting was going all wrong.

She had just landed flat on her butt, her long legs splayed at awkward angles across a busy sidewalk in the middle of central London. She had a discarded cigarette butt stuck to her jeans, her face was splotchy, and her curly brown hair was stuck to her lip gloss. Though she didn't want to look, she was pretty sure the bottom of one leg of her jeans had crept up above the cuff of her athletic sock and gotten stuck there.

Liv—as her friends called her—couldn't remember a time in recent history she had looked *less* fabulous.

Tragically, it was at this very moment that Josh Cameron,

International Pop Star and *Celeb* magazine's Hottest Guy, was staring straight at her. *The* Josh Cameron, whom Liv had fantasized about a million and three times, was standing less than two feet away, casting a shadow from his perfect body onto Liv's disheveled figure on the sidewalk.

Why, Liv wondered, *do things like this always happen to me?* She had arrived in London from Ann Arbor, Michigan, less than two hours earlier . . . and she had already made a complete fool of herself in front of the world's biggest celebrity. *How is this even possible?!*

Because Liv was Liv. And she had a tendency to turn ordinary embarrassing moments into extraordinarily embarrassing ones—which meant this moment could get a whole lot worse. And it did.

Looking up at Josh Cameron, Liv was unable to stop a goofy, uncomfortable sort of smile from spreading across her face. She lifted her hand in a little wave and—very much against her will—blurted out, "Cheerio!"

Three hours earlier . . .

Gazing out the airplane window at London's sprawling suburbs miles below her, Liv couldn't believe she was actually here. In her sleep-deprived state, it still didn't feel real that she had been selected as one of Music Mix Europe's summer interns. But now that she was settled into a cramped window seat and minutes away from landing on the other side of the Atlantic, she finally let it sink in: She would be living in London!

Liv had spent every waking minute since she had gotten her acceptance letter daydreaming about days surrounded by rock stars and nights out tra-la-la-ing from club to club. Of course, deep down, she knew the Music Mix internship would be a lot of work, too. But she had somehow managed to avoid thinking about that part. Why not focus on the good stuff?

When the plane landed, Liv grabbed her black wheelie from baggage claim and followed airport signs to the Gatwick Express. Hustling through the terminal with her suitcase and overstuffed carry-on tote, Liv's excitement bubbled into giddiness. She heaved her stuff onto the train into the city, and a chirpy English voice wished her a good day and a pleasant journey. She just loved the British accent. It always sounded so civilized and kind.

The train began to roll toward downtown London as Liv flipped through the on-board magazine, reading about London's neighborhoods. Music Mix was setting her up with an apartment as part of the internship—she couldn't wait to find out where her roommates would be from, and where they would be living. Notting Hill, Chelsea, Greenwich . . . they all sounded fantastic.

Since she had never been anywhere more exotic than Ely, Minnesota, they all sounded a little intimidating and foreign, too. She had only lived away from home once before (Liv always gagged when she thought about that terrible summer her dad had decided to send her to an all-girls camp on Lake Michigan), so this was definitely going to be an adventure.

Paging through the magazine, Liv quickly studied British lingo and discovered that if she wanted to fit in, her roommates would actually be flatmates, the subway is the tube, and she absolutely must eat something called bangers and mash.

Eventually the train heaved out one final puff, and the doors sighed open to let Liv out into central London. She had arrived!

Making her way into Victoria train station, Liv scanned the signs overhead, looking for the London Underground. Dodging through the crowd, she found an open ticket booth and bought a monthly travel card. Studying the tube map in her guidebook, Liv found the route to Oxford Street, home of Music Mix Europe's central office. She had been told to "pop by" the studio to pick up keys to her flat.

Hustling through the corridor toward the tube, Liv eyed the advertisements pasted on the walls. Next to an ad for Cadbury chocolates (*Yum . . .* must *get some of that*), Liv spotted a poster of Josh Cameron. She slowed her walk slightly, scanning the advertisement for details.

JOSH CAMERON: SPECIAL APPEARANCE, LIVE IN LONDON! Liv stopped briefly—her eye had been drawn to a small detail in the lower corner of the ad: "Sponsored by Music Mix Europe." Liv wondered if she would get to help with the concert. . . . That certainly wouldn't be a bad way to spend the summer. She was just the tiniest bit obsessed with Josh Cameron, and would give pretty much anything to meet him in person. There weren't a lot of celebrities floating around Ann Arbor.

Liv could hear the subway train rolling into the station just ahead of her, and she hustled to catch it. She pulled her suitcase and carry-on clear of the doors just before they swooshed closed and the train roared out of the station. Two stops later the train's doors slid open and she stepped onto the platform as a freakishly polite mechanical voice reminded her to "mind the gap." Liv passed through one of the arches leading her away from the platform and rode the long escalator up and out onto the street. Red double-decker buses breezed past, stuffed with passengers out for a day of shopping. People packed the sidewalk, hustling past Liv, who stood rooted to her spot just outside the Underground exit.

The noise and speed of the crowd was overwhelming. The time difference had started to catch up with her, and Liv realized that it was the middle of the night back in Michigan. Hit with a wave of sleepiness, Liv glanced down Oxford Street and spotted the glowing Music Mix sign.

She applied a coat of gloss to her lips and hastily made her way toward the sign. She lifted her suitcase, slinging her carry-on tote over a shoulder, and pushed into the office's revolving entrance doors.

Liv's reflexes had slowed from lack of sleep, and she realized too late that she had forgotten to get out of the revolving door on the inside and was back out on Oxford Street. Blushing, she made another turn around in the door and stepped out into the large, open lobby, tucking a stray curl behind her ear. She looked around quickly to make sure no one had seen her mistake. Coast clear.

Liv smiled widely as she approached the security desk. "Excuse me . . . I'm one of Music Mix's summer interns. Can you tell me where should I go?"

The security guard looked up briefly, then returned to the tabloid he was reading. "Third floor, miss." Liv muttered a quick thanks, resisting the urge to curtsy, and took the escalator up. She stepped into a round, colorful sitting area whose walls were filled with floor-to-ceiling television screens playing a variety of music videos.

As Liv approached the circular desk in the center of the room, she could hear the receptionist chatting animatedly. Peeking up over the edge of the tall desk, Liv could see that the receptionist's dyed blond hair was formed into a dozen long thick dreadlocks and was pulled back from her face with a hot pink scarf. She was wearing a short strapless dress and an armful of silver bangles that set off her dark skin perfectly. She motioned to Liv to wait, and quickly finished up her conversation.

Looking up at Liv, she smiled. "Welcome to Music Mix. Here to check in?"

Liv grinned. "Yes, I am. My name is Olivia Phillips."

"It's lovely to meet you, Olivia. I'm Gloria. Here's the scoop: I give you keys to your flat, and you're on your own for today. Settle in, meet your flatmates, get some sleep. Just be back here at nine tomorrow morning. Simon Brown can be a bit testy in the morning, so don't be late—it's best to stay on his good side."

Liv recalled that her acceptance letter had come from a guy named Simon Brown—she now realized he must be the one in charge. What a fabulous job.

Gloria shuffled through a box on her desk and plucked out a small yellow envelope. She pulled out two keys and a card with an address printed on it. Scanning the card, Gloria passed it across the desk to Liv, along with the keys. She pulled a pocket-size London Underground map out of her desk drawer and circled one of the stops in hot pink marker.

"You're sharing a flat with two other girls," Gloria explained. "They have both checked in with me already, so they should be at the flat when you get there. Think you can find it?"

Liv nodded again and turned toward the escalator. "Thanks a lot. I'll see you tomorrow." Gloria smiled and pushed a button to answer the phone that had just started ringing.

Riding the escalator down, Liv could see that the Music Mix lobby had become much more crowded since she had arrived just a few minutes earlier. She scanned the faces and chic outfits as she passed, wishing she were dressed just a little cuter and didn't have her bulky wheelie and carry-on—she knew she looked like a tourist.

Liv glanced down to study the tube map as she made her way into the revolving door to leave the building. Distracted, she didn't notice someone step off Oxford Street and into the door as she exited.

Suddenly, Liv was jolted backward. As she lost her balance, both Liv and her wheelie toppled over onto the sidewalk. Though she had come out on the right side of the door this time, her bulky carry-on bag had not been so lucky. The strap of the bag was still attached securely to Liv's shoulder, but the bag itself was stuck on the other side of the glass in the compartment behind her. The revolving door had come to a complete standstill.

Liv pulled her arm out of the bag's strap to release it and craned her neck around, hoping no one was stuck in the door. Her face reddened as she realized that someone was definitely standing—trapped—in the other glass compartment. The person turned to face her, and Liv's mouth dropped open.

Staring at her from the other side of the glass, stuck in a revolving door between Oxford Street and the Music Mix lobby, was Josh Cameron.

Back to the Future . . .

It felt like hours had gone by. Josh Cameron had quickly freed himself and Liv's bag from the door and was now standing—staring—at Liv on the ground. And was it her imagination, or had she just shouted "cheerio" to the world's biggest pop star? Liv straightened her legs, but continued to sit on the sidewalk, stumped and horrified. *Nice first impression, Liv. Suave.*

Josh Cameron smiled as he held Liv's carry-on out to her. "I believe this is yours. . . ."

"Um, thanks." *Um, thanks? Really great response . . . very witty and charming.*

Josh Cameron tilted his head to the side just slightly and looked at Liv with concern. "Are you okay? That looked like a pretty bad fall." She scrambled to her feet and took her bag from him, groping for the right words.

Come on, supersexy girl within, Liv begged inwardly, *say something clever and alluring! Oh God, you're just staring. . . . Say something!* "Yeah, I'm fine. Just a little embarrassed. You don't think anyone saw that, do you? Hah hah hah!" Liv laughed too loudly at her own nonjoke, quickly straightening her hair and brushing the cigarette butt off her jeans.

"I'm Olivia, by the way. And I'm really sorry. It's just that, well, my friends always say this is the kind of thing that I do, uh, you know, when I guess I want to meet celebrities, or, um, make a winning first impression, or uh . . . hah hah hah," *Shut up, just SHUT UP! What are you talking about?!*

Josh Cameron was smiling at her, clearly amused. He patiently ran a hand through his gorgeous curls as Liv stuttered through her ridiculous monologue. By the time she finally had the self-control to shut up, he had begun to laugh.

"Well, Olivia, I better be off. It's been lovely meeting you. I really do hope you're not hurt." As he made his way back through the revolving door, Josh Cameron turned once more and looked at Liv. He smiled his famous smile, and walked into the lobby toward the waiting crowd.

Liv stared after him for a few seconds, then backed away from Music Mix's front doors. She was pleased to see that her white athletic sock was definitely poking up over the cuff of her jeans. *Really cute, Liv. Very chic.*

As her mind replayed the past five minutes over and over—coming up with about twelve significantly more glamorous ways she could have met the biggest pop star in the world—Liv made her way back to the tube and toward her new home. She had been in London less than three hours, and had already managed to fit in a lifetime's worth of humiliation. And, much as she hated to admit it, Liv suspected this wasn't the end of it.

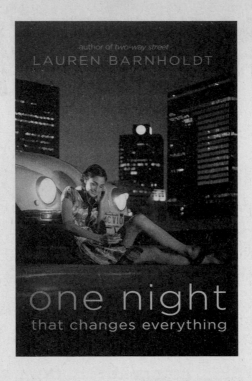

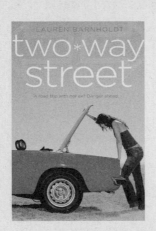